FREECURRENT
THE LEGACY

DEANNA J. COMPTON

Published by IGH Publishing

 IN GOD'S HANDS
PUBLISHING

ACKNOWLEDGEMENTS

Thanks to my family for their support during this process, especially my husband Jim who has always encouraged me to pursue this dream. My thanks also go to Heather UpChurch of Expert Subjects who did the graphic design for Freecurrent I, II and III. She did beautiful work and I love the results. Thanks to all of those who encouraged me. You know who you are. I urge my readers to give me feedback at my e-mail address "freecurrent@comcast.net". Please also post your reviews online. Reviews are extremely important to new authors like me. Most of all, thank you for reading my book. I hope you love it as much as I do.

e-mail Deanna Compton at: freecurrent@comcast.net
Visit my website: freecurrent.net

PRELUDE

old wet rain kissed his face as he rode at a fast gallop. Clinging to him was the woman he loved, Molly. They were being pursued by his father's guards and the well armed and brutal men were gaining ground. Candaz kicked the horse's sides with his boots and flicked the reins. "Come on! Come on! Faster you old nag!" he shouted.

The time had come for them to escape from under his father's thumb. The old man did not understand that they were young and in love, nor did he care. Ban had plans for his son and had no tolerance for the distraction of romantic love. Had he known that Molly was the focus of his son's attention, she would have been disposed of discretely and without mercy. It had been done before back when he was sixteen years old and showed an interest in a beautiful girl named Nell. The callousness Ban showed as he killed the girl in front of Candaz to make his point plain was profound and certainly unforgettable. He still saw her face in his nightmares as Ban's sword ran her through and the light left her eyes. She had her gaze locked on him when it happened and he was powerless to save her. That was four years ago now.

Burning hatred permeated his soul and he found that lashing out with cruelty of his own helped him deal with the pain. As he matured into a man Candaz learned to seize control and power at every opportunity regardless of the repercussions to anyone else. He was ruthless in his ventures, being both cunning and manipulative with a charm and viciousness that was natural.

When Molly came into his life and swept him off his feet with her intelligence, energy and her beautiful smile, he knew that his father could never know of their relationship. They planned their escape, setting a day and time when they could sneak away in the middle of the night without being caught, but that night would never come. Ban had found out their secret and Candaz was tipped off that the old man knew by a faithful servant. So they fled.

Behind him he could hear the shouts of the men chasing them. As he turned to look, the closest man loosed an arrow from his bow. Although Candaz swerved, he was too late. The shaft hit Molly directly between the shoulder blades and she slumped against him. Without making another sound she fell from the horse dead.

"No!" he screamed as he turned his horse and pulled his sword. His eyes fell on Molly for only a split second before he charged at the three men, gathering freecurrent energy as he went. Hurling the ball of magical electricity at them, he followed up with his sword and they died before they knew what hit them along with their mounts who did not escape Candaz's wrath. Blood splattered everywhere as he hacked their bodies apart being driven by the anger that submerged any good that was left in his soul.

His heart felt like it was being shredded to bits along with the bodies of his father's men. Returning to Molly, he sank to the ground and pulled her lifeless body into his arms. Something changed forever within him and his mind snapped. He took out his knife and taking Molly's delicate hand in his own he severed it from her wrist. The ring he had given her remained on the middle finger as he wrapped it in silk torn from her dress and placed in one of the many pockets of his long black cloak. Taking her body in his arms, he walked to the nearby cliff. Waves of the ocean crashed below in a constant powerful rhythm. The wind blew her hair into his face and his placed a kiss on her cold lips before tossing her into the surf below along with what remained of his sanity.

Chapter 1

THE TRUNK IN THE ATTIC

Rays of sunshine glanced through the second story window and soaked the bed in warmth, gently nudging Jessica Gates awake. Shaking off the last misty remnants of sleep, she began to plan her day. Almost indifferently she remembered that there was a party she was supposed to go to that night. Her friend Rhonda was wasting no time shirking off her parental chains while her parents were in Hawaii on vacation. It wasn't really Jesse's "thing," but a wise person once told her "relationships require sacrifice". She would make an appearance for her friend. Crinkling her brow, Jesse realized she would have to find something acceptable to wear. She could just throw a scarf on over her normal t-shirt and jeans. That would do it.

She stretched indulgently, wiped the sleepy sand out of her eyes, and rolled out of bed, her feet coming to rest on the soft carpet beside her very best friend. Felcore, her golden retriever, got to his feet, brushed languidly against Jesse's leg and immediately demanded attention. She reached down and scratched his head as he looked up at her with intelligent shining gold eyes. Kneeling on the floor, she hugged him to her, feeling the softness of his fur against her bare skin, "How's my big boy this morning?"

Felcore wagged his tail, rhythmically thumping the floor in response. Smiling affectionately at him, Jesse stood back up and donned her silk robe, beautifully decorated with colorful birds and flowers, and headed straight for the bathroom down the hall.

As she brushed her teeth, she critically examined her image in the vanity mirror. Although only seventeen, she could well pass for a more mature woman. Her milky complexion was clear and smooth. Jesse's auburn hair, having a hint of red in certain lighting, was thick and healthy, hanging well below her shoulders in delicate waves. She seldom had to fuss with it, just wash it in the evening and brush it out when she got up the next day. The eyes that gazed back at her in the mirror were coppery brown, surrounded by dark thick lashes and accented with perfect eyebrows. She washed her face quickly and dried it vigorously with a hand towel. Jesse's natural beauty required her to wear very little makeup so it only took her a couple of minutes to complete her morning routine. She hung up the towel and cleaned up the sink with a dirty one she got out of the hamper.

A knock on the bathroom door and a grumpy "hurry up" coming from her fourteen year old brother Jacob made Jesse smile with amusement. His disposition in the morning was always the same, as if he had slept all night upon a bed of nails and had nothing better to look forward to all day than a bitter cup of coffee for breakfast. Jesse loved to torment him by being exceedingly cheerful and always greeted him in the morning with a bright smile.

Opening the bathroom door, she smiled sweetly and chimed, "Good morning, Jake. Sleep well?"

Jacob brushed past her, murmured something about perkiness between clenched teeth and slammed the door shut behind him. He was a typical fourteen year old boy, trying to get beyond childhood into manhood.

Jesse entered the kitchen with Felcore on her heals and began to prepare breakfast. The Mr. Coffee was on an automatic timer and the pot was already full and hot, the rich aroma wafting in the air enticingly. Jesse poured herself a cup and added plenty of milk and sugar to dilute the strong brew. Her father liked his coffee black and potent. She decided to make sausages and blueberry waffles, her favorite. She got a frying pan out of the cupboard and started the sausages before going to Felcore's bowl, filling it to the rim with dog food and giving him fresh water. While the sausages were sizzling boisterously in the frying pan, Jesse's father walked up behind her and wrapped strong arms around her waist in a gentle hug. "Mmm . . . smells delicious. I'm hungry this morning. Waffles?"

After turning each sausage link with individual attention, Jesse turned to her father and rubbed at his unshaven chin with the back of her hand, "Yes, blueberry." She grinned, and standing on the tips of her toes gave her father a quick peck on the cheek. Jesse's father, William Jack Gates, was a large man, standing six foot three inches tall with strapping broad shoulders and a rugged athletic figure. His face was handsomely chiseled with defined cheekbones and ash gray eyes that complemented his dark gray speckled hair.

Sorrowfully, Jesse thought of how the sparkle had gone out of her father's gray eyes when her mother was killed in a car accident three years ago. Her parents had been more than just in love; they were the best of friends. Bill had never remarried.

He had dated a few times, finding single life difficult at best, but his heart still belonged wholly to Marguerite. Jesse hoped deep down that someday he would find another to love again so he would no longer be lonely. She sighed sadly.

Jesse's mother, Marguerite, had been a gorgeous woman with dark features suggesting the strong Latino influence in her bloodline. She had fallen in love with Bill when she was still in high school and married him when she was eighteen. Marguerite had her first child when she was nineteen, a healthy baby girl she and Bill christened Jessica Gabriel Gates. After Jesse was a year old, Marguerite started taking classes at New Mexico Institute of Mining and Technology in Socorro, New Mexico, and graduated four years later, and another baby later, with a bachelor's degree in geology. After a short hiatus, Marguerite was offered a job with the National Park Service.

The Gates family had spent many summers together camping, hiking and exploring in the southwestern United States. Jesse always enjoyed those trips immensely and was constantly asking her mother about the history of the landscape. She found her mother's knowledge of the land fascinating and could sit and listen to her talk for hours about how things came to be the way they were.

While Bill and Jacob enjoyed fishing, Jesse and her mom would go off and explore their surroundings. It was during one such expedition, near Mt. Charleston in Southern Nevada that they found a cave tucked away in the mountains. They had seen many caves before, but this one was particularly special to Jesse.

She and her mother had been hiking that afternoon when they noticed dark storm clouds blowing in fast from the west. They began to seek shelter. Large droplets of water were just beginning to hit the ground when a strong gust of wind came up, nearly knocking Jesse over, and blowing dust into the air.

Against the dark gray sky, the desert seemed especially brilliant with various shades of green, yellow, gold, brown, and black dotting the ground with diverse low-growing vegetation and in the naturally sculpted rock formations that surrounded them. Joshua trees, whose appendages were ornamented with dark green needles graduating to an almost mint green tone at the tips, stood rigidly against the onslaught of the wind. Ancient specimens that had long ago given up the fight for life drooped brown and withered branches to the desert floor. A dust devil swirled sand skyward in a feeble imitation of a tornado as it made its way across the desert floor. Jesse brought her hands up to protect her face from the blowing sand.

When the dust had settled, she noticed a cave entrance slightly higher up the hill they were climbing. She pointed it out to her mother. The dark hole was covered with brush, nearly blocking the entrance. They climbed cautiously up the rocky slope, reaching the spot where they had seen the cave as the rain began to fall in earnest. Marguerite entered first and encouraged Jesse in after her.

Jesse let her eyes adjust to the sudden dimness and then looked around. She saw a huge cavern with a flat floor and high domed ceiling. There was starlight streaming in through a jagged opening opposite Jesse that was shaped in a zigzag resembling the sharp edges of a bolt of lightning. She had a sudden feeling of déjà vu as she took a tentative step forward. The back of the cave seemed to draw her toward it. Time appeared to stop and the space between her ears felt hollow as she fought against the compulsion to go through it. Her feet moved of their own volition, walking toward the lightning bolt-shaped crack in the back of the cave.

A firm hand on her arm and her mother's voice broke the spell, "How about some lunch, Jess?"

Jesse paused and felt the urge pass without further thought. She answered, "Sure, mom."

Marguerite took off her backpack and suggested a picnic while they waited out the storm. They gathered up some sticks and started a small cooking fire at the cave entrance. Always prepared, she took out a small pot and, after pouring some water into it from her canteen, started hot water for tea. On a small table cloth she laid out half of a loaf of French bread, some colby and baby swiss cheese and two shiny red apples. She unwrapped some smoked turkey from the deli paper, took out her jackknife and cut everything into bite-sized pieces. After withdrawing two small tin cups from her pack, Marguerite prepared tea for herself and Jesse. They relaxed and enjoyed a leisurely meal while the rain continued to pour outside of their dry haven.

Jesse asked her mother to tell her more about her grandmother, Gabriel. She rarely spoke about her mother and Jesse wished to know everything about the mysterious woman. Marguerite told her how Gabriel had disappeared following her marriage to Bill, about eleven years ago. Gabriel had put all of her possessions into storage. Some still remained in the attic where they presently lived. She had made out a will, leaving her beautiful residence to her only son, Peter, and the rest of her wealth, including a fortune in jewels to Marguerite to be gifted immediately. Once all of her legal affairs were in order, Gabriel came to visit her one day as if nothing unusual was about to happen. Gabriel never even gave a clue that she was going to leave, but the next day she was gone. Marguerite had been hurt by her mother's disappearance, especially by the fact that Gabriel had never come back home to meet her grandchildren. After all of these years, she thought she would have heard something, but never did.

6

Marguerite indicated with a slight shrug that it was not unusual for her mother to disappear from time to time. Gabriel traveled extensively and was sometimes gone for months or more. But, she always returned home to her children, without fail, until the last time, when she was never heard from again.

They finished their picnic lunch, packed everything back into the pack, and set out to explore deeper into the cave. Even with the faint light streaming in through the back of the cave, there remained cracks and crevices well hidden in velvet blackness.

Jesse pulled her flashlight out and switched it on, shining the bright beam around into elusive corners. She wondered if they would find bones of some unfortunate explorer or a treasure chest left behind by marauding pirates. She giggled at her own sense of adventure and was about to include her mother in on her imagination when her light picked up a flash refracting off something shiny.

Jesse called her mother over and together they went to investigate. When they reached the rocky shelf, Jesse shined her light down upon a pendant on a sparkling gold chain. They had found a treasure after all. Her mother picked the trinket up and examined it closely. It was a gold pendant, approximately an inch in diameter, with the symbol of a lightning bolt engraved down the center. Marguerite's face took on a wistful look as she gazed at the pendant that rested in her palm. She noticed her mother's expression and asked her what was the matter. Marguerite shook her head and said that she guessed it was nothing. But, Jesse thought her mother looked like she had just seen a ghost.

Marguerite's hands trembled slightly as she opened the clasp and fastened the chain around Jesse's neck. She looked down at the pendant and touched the cold metal with her fingertips, her sensitive skin feeling the edge of the engraving. The metal seemed to spark at her touch. Her mother lifted Jesse's chin and looked into her eyes. Leaning forward, she kissed her daughter on the forehead and said, "Wear this for good luck, my sweet".

. .

. . . Jesse unconsciously fondled the pendant hanging around her neck. Her eyes were far away. "You are thinking about your mother," her father observed, taking hold of the pendant between his large forefinger and thumb.

Jesse looked up into his eyes and saw the pain there; feeling it mirrored in her own grieving soul, "I still miss her, dad. Will it always hurt this much?"

Bill turned away from Jesse to fill his coffee cup, leaving the question unanswered, floating in the air like a heavy black cloud, ready to burst open any minute and fill the room with sadness.

"What's for breakfast, Jess?" Jacob asked as he crossed the kitchen to the refrigerator and poured himself a glass of orange juice. "I'm starving!"

Jesse wiped a tear unobtrusively from her cheek and took a deep breath before answering, "You're always hungry, Jake. Give me a hand and we can eat in a few minutes. Here, put these in the toaster." She handed him a box of Egg'O waffles. "Then grab the butter and syrup from the refrigerator. The sausage is almost done."

When breakfast was finished Jesse loaded the dishwasher and then headed to her bedroom to get dressed. She threw on a pair of comfortable old blue jeans, a white pocket tee shirt, and her tennis shoes. On her cell phone she selected Rhonda's number and waited for her to answer.

"Hi, Jesse," Rhonda answered right away.

"I just wanted to know if you needed any help getting ready for tonight," Jesse said.

"Yeah, that would be great. Why don't you come over a couple of hours early and you can help me with the munchies. Hey, did you decide what you're gonna wear?"

Jesse cringed slightly and asked herself, does it really matter what I wear? She answered, "Not yet, but I think there are some old scarves and stuff of my grandmothers in the attic. Maybe I'll take a look. What time do you want me there?"

"I don't know. How about three?"

"I'll try," Jesse said. She really kind-of hated parties.

There was a pause before Rhonda said, "Hey, Jess. . . I hope you don't mind, but I invited Mat. If you want, I'll ask him not to come."

Jesse did mind, a lot, but what could she do? It wasn't her party. She said, "No, it's okay. I'm sure I can handle it. After all, I'll see him in school this fall anyway. I might as well face him now. I really don't see why you invited him, though. He's such a jerk. . . an arrogant, self-centered jerk."

"I know, Jess. But Gary wouldn't show up if I didn't invite Mat. I'll make sure he doesn't come anywhere near you," Rhonda said.

"Yeah, no problem. Well, I have things I've got to get done. Give me a call if you need anything," Jesse said, not wanting to discuss it further.

"See ya later, Jess."

She ended the call and headed up the stairs to the attic door. Upon opening it her nose was instantly assaulted with the scent of stale air, rich with mold and dust. She flipped on the light switch and the hanging bulb at the top of the stairs flared to life. Jesse took her time climbing to the top, making sure of her footing on the small steps. A loose board creaked as she reached the top step, and Jesse giggled with amusement. "Spooky," she commented quietly to herself. Glancing around at the dust covered boxes and old furniture, Jesse discovered what she was seeking tucked back in the corner behind an old red naugahyde rocking chair. Behind the chair, piled with various other junk was the trunk she sought.

It was an upright wardrobe trunk from times past that had stickers plastered on it from Greece, Venice, Nigeria, Moscow, Paris, Nepal and London, just to name a few of the foreign lands it boasted having been. Jesse wondered if her grandmother had personally visited all of those places or if it had belonged to some other adventurer before her. She thought with a certain amount of envy and wistful delight how exciting it would be to travel to foreign lands and meet people from all over the world.

Hefting the chair aside, and removing the stuff that throughout the years had been piled carelessly on top of it, Jesse brushed a thick layer of cobwebs off from it. With a little applied force, the latch clicked and the door to the trunk swung open. A sense of excitement washed over her.

The trunk was divided into a section for hanging clothes with three drawers underneath and a place for hats on top. There were dresses of various styles and lengths hanging from the bar. They were obviously expensive and well preserved. One dress was a beautiful beaded red gown, dangerously low cut in the front and back. Jesse immediately thought of the upcoming year's prom and wondered if it would fit her. She decided she would take it downstairs and try it on later, knowing realistically that her father would never let her wear something that daring. There was a basic black cocktail dress made of velvet with small rhinestones accentuating the "v" at the bust line. Jesse thought this dress was much more practical and she decided to take it downstairs and try it on as well. Another dress was made of exquisite white lace with hand sewn beads and a plunging back line. Jesse went on to examine the hats in the top section of the wardrobe. They were coordinated to go with the dresses, one red, one black, one white and a simple straw hat.

Opening the top drawer revealed some beautifully delicate lingerie in black, white, and red. She ran her fingers over the silky soft material. There were also gloves--short, long, black, white and red and several pairs of silk stockings. She opened the bottom drawer, finally coming across what she was looking for. The drawer contained several lace and silk scarves. Jesse took one out and ran it through her hands. It felt wonderful against her skin. She drew the silky cloth to her cheek, luxuriating in the smooth texture.

Her eye caught sight of a lace scarf that remained alone in the bottom of the drawer that had shiny golden strands woven in an intricate leaf pattern. That's exactly what she wanted. She put the other scarf aside and attempted to pull the lace one out of the drawer, but it was caught on the bottom. Being careful not to rip the delicate material, she bent over and lifted the scarf around the edges, trying to find out where it was caught. A small portion of it was wedged into the bottom corner of the drawer. She pulled carefully and upon closer examination, it became evident that there was a cleverly hidden false bottom.

Jesse's heart skipped a beat and she realized after a moment that she was holding her breath. She looked for some kind of latch or handle on the door to open the compartment, but found nothing. Running her finger along the edge of the drawer, Jesse came across a button. She pushed it. With a "pop" the compartment lid came smoothly open.

Inside the compartment there were several photographs scattered about. They were all old black and white portraits of people Jesse did not know. She turned a picture over and read the back of a family portrait, "Louis, Carmelita, Jose, and Gabriel Sanchez." Gabriel appeared to be approximately two years old in the picture. Jesse gazed with interest at the image of her great grandparents and Grandmother Gabriel a few moments longer and then continued sifting through the old photos until something beneath them caught her eye.

Buried under the photographs was a leather bound book. The tan leather of the cover was worn and extremely soft and pleasant to the touch. She felt her heart fluttering with anticipation. Jesse opened the cover and read the front page, "Personal Diary of Gabriel Carmelita Sanchez Thomas."

A quick look at her watch told Jesse she had spent the entire morning in the attic. She enfolded the diary carefully in the lace scarf and set it aside. Meticulously, she returned all of the other contents of the trunk to their original places, closed the drawers, and took one last look at the beautiful dresses before she shut the door. Picking up her bundle, she headed down the narrow stairway and shut off the light, closing the attic door behind her. Felcore welcomed her in the hallway with a quiet "woof."

"Hi, boy." Jesse reached down and patted his head. With Felcore at heel, she quickly made her way to her bedroom. Settling stomach-down on the bed and propped comfortably on pillows, Jesse took out the diary and began to read.

Chapter 2

A RELUCTANT FAREWELL

Personal Diary of Gabriel Carmelita Sanchez Thomas.

April 14, 1983. I am beginning this diary because I believe it necessary to record the events leading up to this day and henceforth. I cannot be sure what fate has in store for me, but I fear my life will never be the same again.

A few days ago I was approached in the market by a man. The man was not only dressed in a bizarre fashion, but his long hair and unusual style made him appear out of place in the small southwestern town where my family lives. He wore tan leggings with a brown tunic that hung to about mid-thigh and was belted at the waist, a hooded long black woolen cloak that came well below the top of his brown animal hide boots, and soft leather gloves. He approached me at the fruit stand as I sorted through a display of red Delicious apples, attempting to choose the best ones for my family. After he removed his hood and I scrutinized his handsome rugged face, noting beautiful green eyes that exhibited his serious intent and betrayed a measure of suffering. His long blonde hair was cinched in back with a leather tie.

He introduced himself as Theodore Jacob Wingmaster III and then proceeded to tell me a most fantastic tale. According to Mr. Wingmaster, he is heir to the throne of Brightening in a land called Risen. His people and land are being threatened by a faction of ruffians who rule a land to the north called Saberville. They have in their realm a sorcerer named of Candaz who is enlisting the powers of the corrupt forces to aid the Sabers in their war against the Brights. He is young at the age of forty, but very powerful. The Brights' sorceress has a debilitating sickness and is unable to continue the battle in her weakened condition. Mr. Wingmaster claims that all will be lost if they do not find a magic wielder to take her place. He states that I have been chosen to become the next sorceress of Brightening.

Despite the deadly serious look on the man's face, I laughed heartily at Mr. Wingmaster's story and thanked him for entertaining me. I asked him if my husband, John, had put him up to this rather strange practical joke. Mr. Wingmaster reacted with offense to my humor and I could see the beginning of anger touch his face as he furrowed his brow. He proceeded to withdraw from his cloak a scroll tied with a red ribbon, which he handed to me, requesting that I read it. Feeling particularly uncomfortable, my stomach tightening with tension, I untied the ribbon, broke the wax seal and unrolled the parchment. Before giving my attention to the document, I again contemplated Mr. Wingmaster's eyes, looking for a sign to suggest his purpose, finding to my trepidation only sincerity. The document read:

THE LEGACY

To Mrs. Gabriel Thomas

Earth, Galaxy XXIII:

You have been chosen to fill the position as head sorceress for the land of Brightening (Risen, Galaxy III) for such time as it takes to fulfill the responsibilities of said office, i.e. the destruction of the dark sorcerer, or upon training an apprentice to take your position and all of the responsibilities the office therein imposes, or upon your death. I have sent my son, Prince Theodore Jacob Wingmaster III, to guide you and protect you until such time as you can assume the responsibilities of sorceress. I urge you to begin your journey henceforth. My people are dying and need your help to repel the decay that is upon the land. I await your arrival with a sword in my hand and a prayer on my lips. I wish you safe journey.

Signed: King Cleotus Ivan Wingmaster IV.

I looked up from the note and gazed into Mr. Wingmaster's bright green eyes, searching again for any sign that he was playing me falsely. He held my gaze steadily, indicating his earnest intent and unwavering determination.

Even as my fear grew, my instincts determined the truth before my conscious was able, I asked him, "How can you possibly expect me to put any merit into this nonsense?"

He reached down and grasped the hilt of his sword. Until that moment it had remained well concealed beneath the folds of his cloak. Seemingly unconscious of the movement, he said, "I can prove that what I have told you is true, Mistress, if you take us to a place where we can talk in private." He looked around at the various people walking by, some of whom glanced curiously at the sword and the man, before hurriedly returning to their own business. Mr. Wingmaster let his cloak settle back in place around him, concealing the weapon once again.

I proceeded with caution, dubious of the little voice inside telling me that I could trust this man to be honorable. Escorting him out of the market, I proceeded down the sidewalk at a brisk pace, nodding to acquaintances along the way who acknowledged me with expressions of mild concern. The spring day was comfortably warm and dry. Turning the corner brought us into my neighborhood where children could be heard playing gleefully at some game an adult imagination would not indulge. My house was the third one down the street on the left, the yard enclosed with a white picket fence that needed painting. I swung open the gate and headed for the small barn just to the right of the small ranch house, both of which also were in need of new paint. I opened the double doors to the barn and entered to the familiar scent of hay and horses. Leaving the doors wide open, knowing that if I screamed the neighbors would be able to hear me and hopefully call the police, I turned to Mr. Wingmaster and immediately demanded the proof he had promised me earlier.

Mr. Wingmaster threw back his cloak without hesitation, reached to his side and drew forth the sword from an etched leather scabbard, making the blade sing boldly in response. I jumped back away from him automatically with my eyes locked on the weapon. The sword's hilt was gold and encrusted with sparkling green emeralds that reminded me of Mr. Wingmaster's eyes. The blade was smooth and glinted with captured light from the afternoon sun.

He examined the blade with fondness, caressing the golden hilt with the gentleness of a lover, "This sword was handed down to me from my grandfather. He was presented the blade by his wife, the sorceress, Shareen, on their wedding day. Legend says that the sword is enchanted, having magic enabling the wielder to seek out and destroy evil. However, the sword is cursed. You see, Shareen, the apprentice to the Saber's sorcerer, Ban, fell in love with my grandfather, Theodore II. She turned her back on the Sabers and her mentors in order to marry the man she loved. Ban took revenge upon Shareen and the King by placing a curse upon the sword to nullify its magic. The curse will only be released when the next true sorcerer or sorceress of the Brights lays his or her hand upon the blade."

Mr. Wingmaster knelt before me with his sword stretched out before him. He demanded boldly, "Mistress Gabriel, lift the curse from this sword."

I began to deny him, but hesitated, "I . . ."

He stood fast, his beautiful green eyes flashing with authority, "You must."

Slowly, the moment seemingly frozen in time, I extended my hand to the tip of the sword and touched it with my fingertip. The edge was sharp and I instinctively drew back and glanced down at the bright red blood swelling from a small painless slash in my skin. The gold pendant that hung around my neck, a family heirloom, burned suddenly against my chest. I glanced back at the sword and saw that the blade was afire with electric blue light that ran from the tip to the hilt and continued up around Mr. Wingmaster's hand. We both gaped at the sword in awe until the fire finally died out, leaving the blade etched with the sign of the lightning bolt down each side. The scent of electricity hung heavily in the air as if following a lightning storm. Mr. Wingmaster ran his hand down the blade, touching the pristine etching with delicate inspection before giving me his approval with a smile.

"Mistress Gabriel, you will accompany me to Brightening and help us defeat the corruptive forces that plague our land."

The statement smothered me like an untimely shroud. I wanted to explain to Mr. Wingmaster that I was the mother of two children and a wife with responsibilities and could not even consider leaving my home. The whole idea was ludicrous. It wasn't that I no longer disbelieved Mr. Wingmaster's story, bizarre as it was, or that I didn't want to help him out, I just couldn't up and leave my family. It was unthinkable.

"No. Not now. Not ever. I will stay right here and raise my family. You are welcome to spend the night in the barn, as long as you are on your way in the morning. Dinner will be served at six o'clock."

He took my hand and kissed it briefly and said, "Call me Theo. I would be honored to be your guest but you must reconsider your denial. We are desperate."

That evening while I slept, I dreamed of a dark man in long black robes with a sinister smile and villainous eyes. The man said to me, "Be warned, Gabriel. Do not attempt to cross the gateway into Risen." The scene widened and I could see two children sleeping soundly in their beds. Before my eyes the man in the black robes drew a knife across their necks and their life blood spilled from them onto their pillows. "This will be the fate of your own children should you dare oppose me."

Awaking with an impact, I cried out, "No. . .!" John pulled me into his arms and held me close, comforting me with soothing words and gentle caresses. The terror of the dream remained with me as I cuddled as close to John as I could, trying to find the security I had always known in his arms.

When I awoke the next morning I told Theo of my dream. He swore soundly, calling the man in the black robes, Candaz, many foul names. He then said to me, "Candaz has given you this vision to frighten you away. He knows if you do come to Risen his days are numbered."

He began pacing the room in agitation and said, "You have the power to keep Candaz away from your family. I can teach you a spell that will hide your family from him." Theo stopped before me and gripped my shoulders tightly. "But, I will not give you the spell unless you promise in return to go with me to Risen. I hope you understand how important this is to me and my people. Candaz will not give up as long as you remain a threat to him. I am sorry it has come to this but I don't see where either of us has any other choice."

I refused to go and Theo stayed one more night to try and convince me otherwise. That night screams came from the room where my children slept. John and I ran to them immediately and found them huddled together on the floor crying. After rendering what comfort I could, my son, Peter, the eldest, was able to tell me that he had seen a man dressed in black and carrying a long knife. The man had touched his sister, Marguerite, on the forehead and then turned to Peter and caressed the shining blade as if he intended to use it. Peter thought he was dreaming until the man approached his bed and touched his forehead also. He swore it was real.

John and I reluctantly returned to our own bed after seeing the children off to sleep. I had never seen my son so terrified of anything before. His small face had been white as a ghost. He had always been a brave child. His uncharacteristic behavior made me consider the implications of Theo's proposal more seriously.

Before the midnight hour another scream brought me out of my bed. With John in the lead, we made our way to the children's room again.

Peter cried out as John and I walked into the room, "Mom, he was here. . . that man! He tried to hurt Margie, but, I hit him and he stopped. He grabbed me and started to pull me away. . .

and. . . and, I screamed. I hit him as hard as I could. . . then.
. . then you came in and he let go." A suppressed sob shook
his body as I hugged him close. A stolen look at John, who sat
holding Marguerite on her bed, showed me his outrage. Peter
pulled away from me and looked around the room cautiously. "Is
he gone Mom? Will he come back?"

My own anger rose instantly, flooding my cheeks with heat
when I saw the red welt around Peter's upper arm where he had
been grabbed. Why would this sorcerer attack my children? His
plan to threaten me to keep me away was going to backfire.

I realized in that moment that my destiny was being decided
for me. No matter how hard I wanted to fight against it, I would
have to leave my husband and children and travel with a stranger to an unknown land. My determination to protect my family
far exceeded my fear of the unknown. "No, Peter," I answered
my son, "he won't be back." *Not if I can help it!*

My concern for my family's safety drove me to make the
move as quickly as possible. John and I spent the remainder of
the night discussing the situation and he reluctantly agreed that
I should make the journey without him. The next morning I
wrote to my youngest sister telling her I needed to be away from
home for an extended trip and asking that she come care for the
children in my absence. After dinner I packed my bag with as
little as I deemed necessary and put the children to bed. "I will
be back," I whispered quietly as I wiped my tears and closed the
door behind me.

Departure

Theo was waiting for me in the barn, leaning against the old ford
pick-up John seldom used and had offered for our trip. I frowned
at him a moment and demanded impatiently, "The spell please?"

He took me by the hand and led me to the sidewalk in front of my house where John joined us a moment later. Extracting a book from his cloak, Theo whispered softly, "Gabriel, this was Shareen's spell book. It is yours now." He opened the book to a page marked with a red ribbon. "This is the spell you will use to hide your family from Candaz. Repeat these words three times after drawing the symbol illustrated here. Use this drawing stick made of a chemical potion designed especially for this spell. It was mixed by a student of the art. I hope he did it correctly."

He took me by the hand and led me to the sidewalk in front of my house where John joined us a moment later. Extracting a book from his cloak, Theo whispered softly, "Gabriel, this was Shareen's spell book. It is yours now." He opened the book to a page marked with a red ribbon. "This is the spell you will use to hide your family from Candaz. Repeat these words three times after drawing the symbol illustrated here. Use this drawing stick made of a chemical potion designed especially for this spell. It was mixed by a student of the art. I hope he did it correctly."

"I do, too," I growled at him and took possession of the book and stick as I glanced at John for support. The illustration was simple and easy to draw. I stood before it and began to recite the oral portion of the spell, repeating the words three times. Upon speaking the last word I felt a rush of heat flow through me. I gasped at the surge of power. My gold pendant again burned against the skin of my chest. The air around the house glowed as if plunged into daylight for only a split second and then grew dark once again. "Oh my!" I said.

Theo smiled broadly and commented, "It seems to have worked."

Standing behind me, John placed his hands on my shoulders and spoke to Theo, "I hope you are right."

I looked back down at the opened book for a moment, realizing for the first time that the words I had just read were in some foreign language, formed with letters unfamiliar in the English language. I ran my finger down the page, touching the text gingerly, wondering at the fact that I could read them, pronounce them, and find their meaning clear. "Magic," I whispered quietly to myself.

"What?" Theo asked.

I looked up at him and managed to smile, ignoring the sickness in my belly. "I am ready," I said and we headed back to the barn. John and I said a private goodbye just outside the door as Theo waited.

Holding back a flood of tears and trying to be strong I smiled up at John as he whispered, "Good luck. I love you."

I climbed into the driver's seat and watched Theo seat himself as passenger with an uncomfortable and somewhat terrified expression on his face. "Are you all right?" I asked.

"What is this thing? How does it go? Is it magic?" Theo asked with an inquisitive scowl on his face.

"This is a truck," I replied. "It runs on gasoline. It's a machine. Let's just get going before I change my mind."

We headed north-northwest of El Paso taking back roads that were virtually deserted. When exhaustion started claiming the best of my eye sight we pulled over to sleep the rest of the night.

Today we drove from the first light of dawn until dusk when the sun set serenely over the darkly silhouetted mesa to our west. I was thankful to stand up and stretch after so long on the road. After a sparse dinner of cheese and dry French bread, Theo retired to his sleeping bag and went directly to sleep. My family is constantly in my thoughts and I pray continuously for their safety. I am very tired and although the ground is hard and I ache for my husband's warmth, the air is fresh and I think I will sleep well tonight.

April 15, 1983. We have been on the road now for two full days. John's old ford pickup was not made for speed and I have to refrain myself from pushing it too hard. The terrain streams by insignificantly.

I have spent the last couple of nights studying Shareen's spell book. The spells range from making chicken soup to changing a horse into a mouse. She calls it freecurrent magic. Last night I attempted to make chicken soup. On my first attempt I recited the words precisely as written in the book, but we ended up with chicken feathers snowing down upon us from the heavens instead of chicken soup in our pot. Theo thought it was very funny, and laughed until I threatened to turn his highness into a toad, which only made him laugh more. When he was finished with his outburst, he gave me encouragement by saying it would take practice to become proficient at the skill and to give myself time. I have to agree but I've never been patient.

I looked up from my diary to see the camp fire glowing warmly on Theo's face as he stared into its fiery depths wistfully. I was wondering what he was thinking when he spoke to me softly, "I am sorry I had to drag you away from your family and friends, Gabriel. It must have been hard. If only it wasn't necessary. . ."

I felt my throat constrict with emotion as I recalled the pain I was trying so much to suppress. "Is it really? Necessary, I mean?" Unrealistically, I wanted him to answer, *"No, I guess not. Why don't you go back home?"*

He gazed at me across the firelight that separated us, his green eyes glowing brightly. "You are the one, Gabriel. I do not question it. My family, my people need you to help them. There is no other. You show great honor."

I sighed heavily, feeling more of a fool than a savior. Not for the first time, I questioned what I was doing. Why did I come? Honor? I could have used Shareen's spell to protect my family and then headed right back into the house and into my husband's bed. Instead I left the people I love to travel in a rattling bolt-shy pickup with a man I barely know, heading for a world other than my own. Fool? Crazy was more like it! I could choke on the word "honor".

Theo interrupted my self-examination with his low meditative voice, saying, "My father, the king, is a wonderful man with a generous heart and an honorable soul. He raised me and my younger sister, Kristina, on his own after my mother died when I was young. Kris was two at the time, just a baby still. Although he could have left the raising of us to the servants, having plenty of fine people under him to rely upon, he did not. He did what he felt was right."

"Does your sister have the same admiration for your father that you seem to?" I asked.

Theo chuckled. "Kris. . . " his crooked grin belied his affection. "Kris is a free spirit, strong willed, temperamental, witty and beautiful. She loves father in her own special way and he loves her in return, giving her anything she can manipulate out of him. It is a game between them--Kris manipulates and father gives in, grumbling the whole time and loving every minute of it. God pity the man who takes her to be his wife."

"She sounds spoiled," I commented, trying to sound light.

"Oh, yes. . . and she knows it too. But, Kris isn't arrogant. . . snobbish as you might expect." Theo picked up a stick and began stirring in the fire.

When he said no more, I asked, "How old are you, Theo?"

"Twenty-seven."

"What about a girl? Friends?" I went closer to the fire and sat beside Theo on the ground.

I saw the sadness in his eyes before he vanquished it swiftly. "Being the Prince of Brightening and General of the King's troops leaves me little enough time for fun. There is Joshua, Alexander and Lan, whom I grew up with. They prevent me from taking myself too seriously. And, of course, there is B.F."

"But, what of a girl, Theo? Someone special?" I asked.

He blushed deeply before answering, "I do have a true love. Her name is Jessabelle." Theo's cheeks continued coloring a deeper rose. "Jessabelle's father has forbidden us to marry because of my race."

It took me a moment to realize that Theo's cheeks were red from anger and not from passion. "Your race?" I asked incredulously, thinking of the present racial issues in the United States. Theo fought to regain control of his emotions as he spoke deliberately, "Yes, my race. She is a kendrite."

When Theo saw the puzzled look on my face he explained, "Jessabelle is of a race that has the ability to alter their form called kendrites. They have a gift enabling them to change into eagles, wolves and even dolphins. Kendrites can instantly adapt to their environment should the need arise."

"Fascinating," I commented, trying to imagine what it would be like to change shape.

Theo's eyes sparkled and a smile touched his lips as he remembered the woman he loved. He said, "She is amazing. Jessabelle has a tall and powerful figure, a face that reflects her pride and passion, long red hair and flashing gold eyes. She is quick with a smile and slow to anger, but is a lethal opponent." Theo's smile faded. "Even though Jessabelle has sworn her love to me, she acquiesced to her father's wishes and declined to marry me."

He cleared his throat and threw the stick he had been holding into the fire. "I joined the elite cavalry and buried myself in my work after I lost Jessabelle, attaining the rank of General soon thereafter. We devised a plan to reorganize Brightening's troops into a more efficient fighting force. My father asked me to accept this quest just after we started implementation. I wanted to decline in order to continue the work I had begun, but my father can be very persuasive and in the end I agreed to make the journey."

As the coals begin to die and what lingering light remains slowly fades away, I find my eyelids tugging insistently urging me to find my bed. Tomorrow we will be another day closer to our goal. . . and another day further from my family.

April 17, 1983. We are camping tonight on the south side of Hoover Dam. This is the first long break we have taken in some time. I am exhausted and after dinner want nothing better than to crawl into my sleeping bag and find the luxury of sleep.

Chapter 3
THE DESERT CAVE

Las Vegas

April 18, 1983. As we crossed over Hoover Dam, Theo's eyes were wide and his mouth agape as he stared at this marvel of engineering. I explained to Theo that a hydroelectric dam such as this one provided electricity for the surrounding cities. Theo asked what electricity was and how it was used. I told him simplistically that electricity was like a bolt of lightning manufactured, stored and distributed in a manageable form.

It surprised me when he commented that it was similar to the way sorcerers used the energy around them to perform their magic, gathering it within themselves and using the freecurrent power to perform spells. The question of how the sorcerers accomplished collecting the energy intrigued me. I asked Theo if he knew the answer, but he shook his head negatively and said that sorcerers did not reveal their secrets. . . not even to their prince.

We arrived in Las Vegas early that evening, driving down into the valley while the lights of the city glowed brilliantly. After checking to see how much money we had left and finding about ninety dollars remained, we decided to head downtown and spend the night at a hotel. We drove down the Las Vegas Strip passing brightly lit casinos along the way. Theo's eyes were wide open in wonder as he gazed at the flashy casinos decked out in multi-colored neon. When he asked, "What kind of magic is this?" I answered "Las Vegas," and left it at that.

We pulled into the parking lot of the Golden Gate Hotel and Casino past a glittering gold neon sign and about a half an hour later we were checked into room 214 with two double beds and some very gaudy gold and white decor. Theo examined the television that sat upon the dresser with curiosity. He turned knobs and pulled on buttons until the set switched on. Letting out a gasp of surprise, he jumped back, all the while keeping his eyes glued to the picture.

My first priority was to reach John and find out how things were back home. I dialed John's number while my stomach tightened with anticipation and listened to his phone ring four times, then five, then six. After twelve rings I hung up, wiped escaping tears, and vowed to try again later.

I left Theo gaping at the television and went in to the bathroom to take my first hot bath since leaving home. After a luxurious amount of time soaking in hot fragrant bubbles, I reluctantly got out of the tub and dressed in my only clean clothes, a plain cotton shirt style dress, and called room service to have the rest of my clothes picked up and laundered. With the telephone still clutching in my hand, Theo walked up to me and asked what I was doing. After explaining to him that one person could talk to another over short or great distances by dialing a number, all he said was "Amazing."

I tried John again, hoping and silently praying that he would pick up this time but there was still no answer. I was upset, angry and scared. An urgency to leave and be alone became compelling enough for me to heed. Crossing the room, I grabbed some money from my purse and opened the door to the hallway, muttering to Theo, "I'll be back in a while."

Stairs at the end of the hall headed down into the casino and hotel lobby. The red carpet adorning the stairs matched the newer carpet in the hallway but was worn and tattered in several spots. The area was dimly lit. Upon reaching the first floor, the sound of talk and laughter, shouts of joy and groans of disappointed, as well as the jingle of money, constant and unrelenting surrounded me as I headed to the bar in the corner of the casino.

A dark-haired woman in a long silver dress was singing Patsy Cline's "Crazy" in the lounge, swaying seductively back and forth to the music. The crowd in the lounge was small, consisting mostly of elderly gentlemen who sipped their drinks in an indifferent manner. After choosing a dark corner table, I ordered a gin and tonic from the cocktail waitress whose outfit did little to hide her voluptuous figure. When my drink arrived, I paid her what I owed and added a respectable tip which earned me a quick smile.

Sipping on my drink, I thought about my situation. We would be arriving at the gate sometime in the next couple of days where a new world awaited me and I was terrified. They expected me to be some kind of miracle worker, a sorceress, a wielder of magic, but I could barely make chicken soup. I felt reasonably sure that I was missing something, some technique or method I had overlooked. The key had to be the ability to draw power from other sources and utilize it. "Freecurrent" Shareen had called it. The power was a part of me, but I didn't have the slightest idea how to call upon it. My thoughts were interrupted by the waitress bringing me another drink. "The gentleman at the bar sent this," she said and then walked keenly away.

I looked up as a strangely dressed man at the bar raised his glass to me in salute. He was an unrefined middle aged man with gray streaked hair, a choppy gray beard and a long-handled mustache that hung raggedly over an odious mouth. The man looked very out of place from his dirt-stained cloak to his high leather boots. Suddenly, I could feel power in the form of fear grip me like long icy fingers wrapped tightly around my soul. It seemed like an eternity before I could move, frozen in an awareness I did not understand. All I could do was stare at the man while he laughed, loud and cruel directly at me. Fighting my fear born paralysis, I reached for my drink and gulped it down. The alcohol burned my throat and my stomach, but it was quick to clear my head. When I looked back up to where the man had been sitting, the bar stool was empty.

Leaving the lounge as fast as I could, I headed directly for the stairs on the other side of the casino. I ran up them and headed toward our room thinking to warn Theo, but as I was about to insert the key into the lock, a calloused hand clamped over my mouth and an arm grabbed me tight around the waist. I kicked hard at my attacker's legs and bit into the hand. He only tightened his hold on me and began pulling me down the hallway away from my room. At the end of the hall he took his hand from around my waist and opened an unlocked door. While I struggled desperately, he dragged me in after him. Grabbing a cord from the dresser, he forced my arms behind my back and bound my wrists. I screamed as loud as I could and buried the heel of my shoe into his foot. With one swift movement he tossed me on the bed.

I took a deep breath in an attempt to regain control over my emotions, choking back unwanted tears and swallowing the wail that vied to be released. I was so angry. Moving was awkward with my hands tied behind my back and my skirt twisted around my legs, but I managed to position myself so I could see my captor. He was a short stocky man built on a wide frame that was not well muscled, giving him a sloppy and lazy look. In his right hand he held a dagger that he was using to clean underneath the fingernails of his left hand. The smile on his face camouflaged cruelty that showed in his eyes. There was a strange odor, like rotting flesh that hung on him.

"Where is the book, Gabriel?" his voice ground on my nerves like a child's persistent whining.

As in the bar, a sense of cold fear was present. Strength inside me became evident and I felt confident I could take control of the situation. I responded to his question with elaborate indignation, "I don't know what you are talking about. My name is Thelma. You have the wrong woman. Let me go!"

"Nice try, Gabriel," he sneered hideously. "You have the book of Shareen and I am going to get it from you one way or another." He approached the bed with the dagger extended before him. "Now where would a lady like you hide a book?"

"I told you I don't have any book. I don't know what you are talking about. Let me go!" I yelled at him with disgust as he continued to come closer to me, praying that he would not touch me.

"You're lying, Gabriel, and I am going to find it." He slapped me hard across the face.

As he brought his fist up to strike me again, I said, "I don't have the book with me. It is down in my truck. If you untie me, I'll get it for you. It's useless anyway. There are key words missing."

The man backed off and rubbed his chin thoughtfully. "Missing words you say? The master has been trying to get his hands on that book for years. He will not be happy about this. But, that is not my concern. Tell me where the book is."

"Untie me and I will take you to it," I said. The gold medallion burned hot against my chest as I tried to compel the man to do as I wished.

He sneered and said, "You will stay here while I retrieve the book. Now, where is it?!"

"It is in my truck. The keys are in my room," I said.

"What does this truck look like? Where will I find it?" He asked as he approached the bed again and pressed the tip of his dagger to my neck.

"It is old and gray and parked in the back lot," I said.

"I will be back," he said.

As he turned to go, the door to the room resounded with a heavy impact before being burst in, splintering shards of wood onto the red carpet floor. Theo stood in the threshold taking in every inch of the room with wary eyes. When his gaze rested on me, I felt once again the surge of power through me and my pendant become hot. The sword he held vibrated with power and glowed with blue light up and down the blade where the lightning bolt etching sparked with an electrical charge. His eyes flashed with anger as he approached my captor.

"It seems that Candaz has sent a fool to do his dirty work," Theo mocked. "How did you find us?"

"The master does not reveal his secrets to me," he returned. "I was only sent to retrieve the book and kill the woman. Now I'll have the pleasure of killing your highness as well."

With one swift move he plunged the dagger toward Theo's heart. Theo danced deftly out of the way and he missed his mark, the dagger slicing harmlessly through the air. The man's second plunge met with success as the blade cut through Theo's cloak, grazing his ribs and causing blood to seep down his left side. "Ha ha. I hope you have another hero to back up this one, Mistress. The prince will not be returning home to daddy's throne."

"You will be the one not returning home," I retorted. Still feeling the flow of warm energy, I concentrated hard on channeling all of my strength toward Theo.

He swung his sword, oblivious to his injury and skillfully knocked the dagger from the stranger's hand with minimal effort. A serious expression replaced the once cocky smirk across the man's face as he stepped back in surprise.

Pulling a shiny object from his cloak pocket, the man brought it up in front his face and whispered words in an unintelligible tone. Bright rays of light shot out of the object aimed directly at Theo's broad chest. Swiftly bringing up his sword Theo blocked the light, sending the bolt of energy hurling back at the object with awesome intensity. It exploded in the man's hand on impact, showering sparks all over the room.

Moving with startling speed, the man attacked, countering with a sharp blow of his fist to Theo's temple. The blow staggered Theo back against the bed and I saw more blood trickle down his cheek. His opponent reached behind his back and drew a sword from the scabbard hidden beneath his cloak. Trying to take advantage of the moment, the man pressed forward. Theo immediately regained his balance and attained a defensive stance. The distance closed between them.

The man spoke with an undertone of hate, "Your people will applaud the day Candaz takes control of Brightening for himself.

They will kiss the ground he walks on for taking the kingdom away from an old man whose heart is as soft as his bloated gut."

Theo responded with elegant grandeur, "Until that day comes I will fight for the honor of Brightening and her king with everything I have."

Bringing his sword up in challenge, Theo stood before the stranger eager for battle. As steel met steel, the stranger's defeat was swift as Theo moved with skillful grace and agility. Although the man fought ferociously, he died instantly when Theo's sword pierced him through the chest.

"Hurry, Theo, we must get out of here now. Cut me loose," I said with excitement pitching my voice. He unsheathed his blood stained sword from the man's chest and cut the cords binding my wrists. We rushed through the threshold where the now shattered door once hung. We hurried back to our room to retrieve our packs and my purse. In less than five minutes we were on the highway heading north.

"Theo, how did you find me?" I asked when my heart slowed down enough to allow me to talk.

"I sensed something was wrong. When I went downstairs to look for you, you were nowhere to be found. Back in our room I snatched my sword from where it lay on the bed. When I touched the hilt a subtle charge of electricity ran up my arm. I unsheathed the blade to make a closer inspection of the weapon and found that the lightning bolt etching had begun to glow with blue light up by the hilt. It led me to you. As I drew closer to where that cur held you hostage the blue light extended further down the blade until it reached the tip just outside the door to the room. It was amazing. I am grateful to you for restoring its magic, Mistress."

"Yes. . . well. . . you are welcome. I am grateful to you for saving my life," I said.

A shiver ran up and down my spine and I suddenly felt very weak. "Theo, I think it is time for your first driving lesson. I need to rest. But, first I'm going to stop here and call John. Wait in the truck," I said.

I stopped at a small bar located just outside of Las Vegas that seemed pretty isolated. As I entered the smoke filled room, I spotted a pay phone near the door. I went directly to the telephone.

With trembling fingers I inserted a dime and dialed "0", asking the operator to make the call collect. After two rings John answered and we spoke with synthetic casualness about each other's general well-being. I neglected to tell him the story about my recent kidnapping. He assured me that he and the children were fine and informed me that my sister, Carmen, had arrived safely. After an uncomfortable silence, with unexpressed emotions lodged thick in my throat, we said our goodbyes. Stifling insistent tears, I returned quickly to the truck.

I bound Theo's wounds with cloth torn from my cotton slip. The cuts were superficial and seemed to cause him little pain. Theo assumed the driver's seat and after a few ground gears and a couple of hair-raising moments, he was driving swiftly down the highway heading north. We turned left when we came to a sign that indicated Mt. Charleston and headed up into the mountains. After forty-five minutes more on the road, we pulled over to sleep for the night. I was thankful the awful day had finally come to an end. Curling up in the bed of the pickup with my diary and my sleeping bag wrapped warmly around me, I looked up at the stars and wondered where Risen lay among the multitudes that spanned the sky.

Tomorrow we will start out on foot into the mountains to find the gate.

35

Lightning Bolt Gate

April 19. I woke up this morning feeling very hungry. The first thing I did was start a small campfire. With a little concentration I was able to rub together my forefinger and thumb, causing a spark to light my kindling. Feeling more and more confident with this new power, I began preparing breakfast, taking small amounts of food from our badly depleted stores and expanding it until I had an ample breakfast prepared.

As we ate, Theo commented that I was learning very quickly. Once in Brightening, I could study the art under an experienced tutor. Until then, we needed to proceed with caution, considering our encounter with Candaz's man at the Golden Gate. Theo was concerned trouble would be waiting for us after we passed through the gate and he wanted to avoid any confrontation at this point because of my inexperience. We packed our meager provisions and started out on foot, cross-country.

We hiked next to one another, keeping a steady pace, making our way around the desert vegetation which grew plentiful on the dry and dusty desert surface. Along the way Theo spoke of the troubles between his people and the Sabers to the north. "The war between the Brights and the Sabers began a few generations ago. There was a time when the Sabers and the Brights enjoyed peace. They traded goods, ideas, and sons and daughters in marriage. The nations came together once a year for a huge week-long festival to celebrate their continued peace and prosperity. People bought and traded goods, ate glorious delicacies being sold at various booths throughout the festival grounds, the young men participated in tournaments of skill, and the young ladies paraded their new fashions and everyone shopped to their heart's content. The evenings were filled with grand feasts, abundant wine and ale, music and dancing. All of the different races of Risen participated in the festivities--humans, kendrites, bandergs, wisps and torgs ate, drank, bantered and danced together, sharing comradery and friendship. Prejudice was unknown throughout Risen." Theo's hand clenched the hilt of his sword as he spoke. We walked in silence for a short time while a dark cloud shaded Theo's expression.

The princely mask returned to his face as he continued, "A young sorcerer named Mercin, the predecessor of Ban, discovered an ancient book of magic and studied it obsessively until he had mastered the magic. He didn't know at the time that he was delving into corruption. Mercin sunk deeper and deeper into the pit of darkness and became more and more powerful. He devised an elaborate scheme to seize control of the nations of Saberville and Brightening by killing both the reigning kings and their royal families. As the evil web was woven, the five races were slowly split apart and turned against each other, learning to distrust their differences and unknowingly facilitating the hatred Mercin nurtured." Theo paused and shook his head in disgust.

The terrain was becoming increasingly treacherous as we climbed further into the mountains. We had to slow our pace to avoid losing our footing on the rocky slopes. After climbing in silence for about an hour we came across a small meadow and decided to break for lunch.

Theo picked up his story where he had left off, "Festival was held for the final time under a dark cloud of suspicion and distrust. Mercin took full advantage of the atmosphere he had created. Stirring his cauldron of hatred, trouble erupted during the tournament as the young men of Saberville and Brightening looked upon each other with a seriousness the competition had never before known. Using his power to stimulate irrational fear and hatred, Mercin was able to inject decay into the hearts of men left vulnerable by their dissolution. When sword met sword, blood was spilled on the tournament grounds and soon a fearsome battle was at hand. Seeing there was trouble, the two kings descended down to the arena and tried to put a stop to the barbarism. Sitting astride their mounts, they called to the men who fought all around them and ordered them to throw down their weapons and cease their butchery. It was too late however; the battle was at a full fever pitch. King Landtamer of the Sabers was struck down, run through with a sword and left dead upon the gaming field. History does not reveal who killed him. However, some say that Mercin was seen with King Landtamer's own sword dripping with the dead king's blood."

Theo concluded, "Mercin took control of Saberville that day, taking up residence at Castle Xandia. The men he had been able to corrupt invariably followed him and became his personal army. The Brights went back to their own homes and prepared for war. The rightful heirs to Xandia's throne disappeared. The nations have been split apart ever since. Mercin and his successors have brought the people of both nations into poverty and deprivation. A closed society does not sustain prosperity. Market places cannot buy and sell wares due to the lack of trade. The economy is virtually at a standstill. The Brights have fought hard and long to bring back freedom and equality to the people of Risen. They have been losing the battle mainly due to the hatred and prejudice that has prevailed over the land, unable to get past petty differences and join forces to defeat the common enemy. Free enterprise has been unable to prosper in the culturally isolated atmosphere, leaving the realms of all nations to fend for themselves. And, of course, Candaz keeps derision stirred up."

"It seems awfully hopeless," I commented to Theo as we began to pack up our lunch gear. "What can I possibly do to help that hasn't already been done?"

Theo looked up at me and gave me a winning smile. "There are small threads of hope remaining. Gabriel, you are the needle that is going to take those threads and weave them into a beautiful tapestry."

"I have never been much good at sewing," I replied without humor.

We continued hiking lost in our own thoughts until the sun began its sleepy descent over the mountains. Storm clouds started billowing in from the west and soon the wind was gusting and rain pelted the ground with hammering force. Theo grabbed my arm and drew me close. He shouted over the clamber of the storm, "The cave is up there." He pointed up the hill where a cluster of desert brush braced itself against the gusting wind. "We must proceed cautiously. If one of Candaz's men could find the gate, there could be others. Wait here while I make sure the cave is unoccupied."

Theo made his way slowly and quietly up the slope, pushing aside the brush at the entrance. He drew his sword and disappeared behind the thick foliage. A minute later he appeared again and motioned for me to come up.

The slope was rocky and slippery from the rain, so I proceeded with caution, making sure of my footing on the treacherous ground. Theo stood at the mouth of the cave, holding the brush aside for me to enter. The cave was dimly lit, with only a faint glow coming from the far end where a jagged slit cut deeply into the rock revealed another world beyond. The gate that Theo had spoken of stood before me, gaping with its intent unknown, mimicking the vision of a powerful lightning bolt. Without delay Theo attempted to start a fire. The dry kindling caught quickly and he fanned it into a blaze. Without looking at me he said, "We will go through to Risen when the Condor Constellation can be seen through the gate. If we are too early or too late we could end up in a different world altogether. We must be diligent. I'm not sure how long we have to wait."

After a dinner of thick, hot and hearty stew and some leftover bread from lunch, we retired to our sleeping bags for warmth and an attempt at sleep. My thoughts wandered once again to my family left behind. Their faces flashed through my mind and I longed to hold them in my arms and feel their warmth . . . their love. I thought about everything Theo had told me about his world and wondered what difference a housewife from Texas could possibly make in a place where war was a way of life. I must have dozed off because I awoke suddenly when Theo touched my face and said, "Gabriel, it is just about time. We must get ready to go. The gate will only be in the right phase for about five minutes. If we miss it tonight, we will have to wait several more days.

I glanced at the gate and saw the constellations change from one to another, revolving at consistent five minute intervals before my eyes.

"The Condor will be next." The excitement in Theo's voice was obvious now. He kicked at the fire until only smoldering embers remained. I rolled up my sleeping bag and stuffed it into my pack, trying to ignore the tension that clenched my belly.

"It looks like we are ready, Theo. I have to ask you a question before we go." I paused for a second while Theo gave me his full attention. "How did you know where to find me? How did you know it was me you sought?"

Theo gazed into my eyes for a moment, the sparkle of anticipation intense in his own before he looked at the gate. I followed his gaze. The night sky blurred for a second and then a constellation in the shape of a condor appeared. Theo spoke with urgency in his voice, "We must go now, Gabriel." He grabbed my arm and started walking toward the gate.

Stopping short of the threshold, I freed myself from Theo's grasp and demanded, "Wait. I must know now. Tell me how you knew it was me."

"The sword . . . the sword homed in on your medallion," he said.

Releasing Theo's arm, I moved my hand up to touch the gold medallion through the material of my dress. It felt cold between my breasts as I pressed it against my skin . . . and then I felt it began to turn hot! I quickly unbuttoned the top buttons of my dress and pulled the medallion out. The gold gleamed in the starlight. Turning it over in my hand I saw the lightning bolt engraving was ablaze with electric blue fire. "How . . . "

"There is not time. We must go now!" Theo said as he took me by the arm and pulled me up to the opening. A cool breeze brushed my face from the other side and a strange delicate musky scent mingled with the night air. Theo paused for only a second to look into my eyes before he grabbed my hand and pulled me through the gate.

Chapter 4

EAT, DRINK, AND BE MERRY

Jumping with one powerful leap onto the bed, Felcore startled Jesse with an insistent "rrowwf", followed by an affectionate nudge with his wet black nose against her cheek. Jesse reached up and scratched Felcore's ear idly as she thought about Gabriel's diary and its implications. She wondered why her mother had never mentioned anything about it to her, and then realized that perhaps Marguerite hadn't known about her mother's adventures; perhaps Gabriel had kept the truth from her daughter for reasons of her own. Still clutching the diary in her hand, Jesse thought about the description of the cave in Gabriel's diary, wondering if it was the same cave where she had found the pendant that now hung around her neck, the pendant with the lightning bolt symbol etched in fine detail upon the gold disk that she had worn since she was eleven. Her right hand came up and caught the disk between sensitive fingers, feeling the coolness of the metal and the texture of the etching, remembering her mother's expression when she had examined the pendant in the cave six years earlier, as if Marguerite had been looking upon the ghost of an image from her past. A chill ran down Jesse's spine as she thought of the coincidence . . . or more distinctly frightening, the purposeful design involved. She instinctively reached out for Felcore, drawing him close to her to bask for a moment in the familiar comfort of his warmth.

The digital alarm clock on her nightstand read 04:38 and Jesse realized she had been locked in her bedroom reading all afternoon and if she didn't hurry she would be late getting to Rhonda's party. Reluctantly letting go of Felcore, Jesse bounded off the bed and began to search through her closet for her clothes. She stripped down to her bra and panties before dressing quickly in her jeans and a light blue tank top. Grabbing her Grandmother's lace scarf from off the bed, Jesse turned toward the mirror and gazed at her reflection as she began to tie a knot, noting the glimmer of gold around her neck before abruptly setting aside all thoughts of the diary. She was picking up her hair brush when her cell phone rang. "Hey Rhonda."

"Jess, where are you? Get over here," Rhonda said with a somewhat winy tone she used when things were not going quite the way she planned.

"I have the keys in my hand right now. I was just heading out the door," Jesse lied, knowing Rhonda wouldn't be aware of whether she was there in ten minutes or twenty.

"Okay, see you in a few minutes," Rhonda said before ending the call.

Jesse brushed on a little eye shadow, freshened her mascara and dabbed on some lip-gloss. She selected her favorite shoes from the closet, moccasins made of soft deer hide that came to

just past her ankles, fringed around the top and decorated pret-
tily with colored beads. Her friend Scott had made them and
given them to Jesse on her sixteenth birthday and Jesse treasured
them. Her boots had a built-in sheath for the knife she carried
with her discretely hidden away.

Entering the living room after descending the stairs, Jesse
spotted her dad lounging on the couch in front of the TV watching baseball. She grabbed her jean jacket off from the back of
the gray La-Z-Boy where it had been draped since yesterday and
checked the pockets for her car keys. "See you later, Dad," she
chimed with the keys in her hand as she turned and strode toward the door, where she was met by an expectant Felcore.

Jesse knelt down and stroked Felcore's head, kissing him on
the nose and showing her love with a gentle hug as he gazed up
at her with soft gold eyes. "Sorry, you can't go this time boy."
Jesse patted him on the head in dismissal. Felcore moved with
determination, lying down in front of the door, intent on keeping Jesse from leaving. She grinned at his stubborn behavior.
"No, Felcore, not this time." He whimpered slightly, showing
his displeasure, but did not relinquish his position from in front
of the door. Jesse knelt down and stroked him kindly. "Go on
now, Felcore. I have to leave." The golden retriever remained
planted. "Move, boy!" Jesse pushed the one hundred pound dog
out of the way with great effort.

He "rrowffed" once, as if in remonstration, turned and padded quietly up the stairs. Jesse scratched the spot where her gold
pendant rested against her skin, slightly puzzled by his behavior
as she watched him go.

Jesse's dad's voice touched her ears causing a twinge of irritation as she turned the doorknob. "Jesse, don't stay out too late
. . . . You can always call me, you know. Be careful."

"I will Dad. Bye," she said and with a sigh Jesse headed for her car, a 1979 Buick Skylark her father had given to her for Christmas last year. It was blue and ran well, nothing fancy, but she loved it.

Rhonda didn't live far and Jesse only had to drive about five blocks before she arrived in front of the white two-story home, large and grand with four columns adorning the front entrance and precisely trimmed hedges lining the walkway. Walking through the front door was like walking into the pages of "Better Homes and Gardens", a decorator's dream. She parked in the street behind a brand new white Lexus, the car that Gena's parents had bought her for finally getting all "A"s on a report card.

Walking in through the front door without knocking, Jesse looked around until she finally saw Rhonda's little sister, Julie, heading for the kitchen with her arms laden with grocery bags. "Let me help you with those," Jesse said as she relieved Julie of some of her burden. They walked into the kitchen together and dropped their bags onto the center island. "Where's Rhonda and Gena? Are you helping out of the goodness of your heart or did Rhonda bribe you?" she teased the fourteen-year old girl.

"They're upstairs picking out what Rhonda's going to wear. You know Gena 'the fashionista' always knows what's best with what," Julie spoke with obvious sarcasm.

"Why do you dislike her?" Jesse asked, as she glanced at Julie who made a sour face in response. "Never mind. I should have brought Jacob with me to keep you company tonight. He thinks you're cute, ya know."

"Does he really? Not that I care really, he is too immature for me," Julie said with a healthy blush on her cheeks.

"Julie, he's fourteen, the same age as you. Do you want me to call him? He can walk over. It's not that far." Jesse asked Julie seriously while she started unpacking groceries onto the counter.

"No, that's okay," Julie said shyly and walked out of the kitchen without another word.

Jesse was just about done unpacking popcorn, chips, pizza, soda, and a variety of other party junk food when Rhonda and Gena came down the stairs into the kitchen. Rhonda was dressed in a black dress with spaghetti straps that clung to her like a second skin, black boots and large silver hoop earrings with a cross in the center of the one on her left earlobe. Gena had on a skirt outfit that was neon green and purple with a leather jacket and boots to match. Her blond hair was tied on top of her head in a ponytail with a ribbon, making her look like a Barbie doll. Jesse thought she looked ridiculous. The two teenagers entered the room with energetic excitement, their voices and laughter filling the large kitchen and setting Jesse's teeth to grind. She shouldn't have come she thought. This kind of thing wasn't within her comfort zone.

"Jesse, you made it," Rhonda began, "I thought you were never going to get here. We have a million things to do before everyone arrives." She walked over to the cupboard and started taking out bowls of all shapes and sizes. "Here, put something in these," she said as she started loading the refrigerator with pizzas and sodas.

People started arriving, mostly in groups of four or more, and soon the house was full, with crowds in the kitchen, living room, and up and down the stairs. Some of the kids brought booze and she was sure she smelled weed. Jesse wanted to leave. She had dabbled in the past with alcohol and drugs, but had put all of that behind her. With it came trouble and she wanted nothing to do with it.

Instead she chose to ignore it and enjoyed seeing her friends, some of whom she hadn't seen since school ended in June. Even though she wasn't excessively popular, Jesse radiated a sense of self-confidence that drew people to her.

She was nibbling on some chips and salsa and talking to a group of people when she felt a hand grip her shoulder. When she turned around to see who it was, her smile quickly faded and her persona grew icy as she came face to face with Mat. He casually sat a six pack of beer on the counter and popped one open.

Last year Jesse had agreed to go to the Christmas dance with Mat. They doubled with Rhonda and Brad that night and had a lot of fun. Mat and Jesse went out a couple more times, but nothing ever developed, which suited Jesse just fine. She just wanted to be friends.

At the end of the school year, they met at a classmate's pool party. Jesse accepted Mat's invitation for a ride home after Rhonda left the party early with Mat's friend, Brad. On the way home Mat took a detour to a spot on the edge of town. Jesse was uncomfortable and asked Mat to take her home. Mat assured her that he just wanted to talk for a while, so Jesse reluctantly agreed although her instincts warned her against it. They talked about school and teachers and mutual friends and she started to relax. Mat seemed to sense that she had let her guard down and suddenly changed moods, becoming aggressively physical. He grabbed her by the hair and pulled her down onto the seat. She immediately reached for her knife, which she didn't have on her. Instead, she punched him across the face and was able to escape out the door.

Rhonda and Brad had just pulled up next to them and witnessed her dramatic departure. They immediately intervened and took Jesse home. Mat apologized over and over again, saying to Rhonda and Brad that things had just gotten a little carried away and that Jesse was overreacting. On the ride home Brad convinced Jesse not to pursue the matter further, and even though it was against her better judgment, she agreed to keep the incident quiet.

She couldn't help but wonder if what had happened with Mat was in some respect her own fault, maybe she had led him on or had in some way encouraged his rough behavior, maybe she *had* overreacted. She let the matter go, but Jesse promised herself that she would never fall prey to another man again. Never again would she be foolish enough to end up in a situation that she couldn't control.

The sight of Mat standing before her now, looking the harmless clean-cut boy, solidified her conviction. He was so arrogant. His touch made her cringe inwardly and she looked at him with contempt as he smiled back charmingly. "Jesse, you look great. Do you want a lift home?" He laughed quietly, masking sadistic cruelty under his fraudulent decorum and started to turn away.

It didn't take but a split second for Jesse's anger to rise. She felt her cheeks burning with rage and she clenched her hands into tight fists. Her heart was beating rapidly in time with the blood throbbing in her ears. She bit off the curse that was on her lips. Instead she watched as he walked up to a girl who had transferred to their school district over the summer. She smiled politely and made conversation with Mat while he sipped on his beer. He tilted the can back to drink, swallowing deeply . . . more deeply than he intended. He began choking and beer spewed out of his mouth even though he continued pouring more liquid down his throat, clutching at the can as if it were attacking him. The girl he had been talking to stealthily moved away. After a minute, he quit choking, put the beer can down and looked around the room in embarrassment. Jesse smiled wickedly for a moment and then froze.

She realized that she had wished the entire scenario upon him and it had been played out before her eyes and before the eyes of all of her friends. She had wished for him to choke and he did. It seemed to Jesse as if a puppeteer had taken hold of Mat's strings and controlled his moves from above at her behest. Swallowing hard, she turned back around to face her friends, feeling the gold pendent that hung around her neck burn with a peculiar sensation.

Jesse felt like she had been dreaming; that she and Mat were the only two people in the room, and when she again heard the voices around her talking and laughing, she felt a little uncomfortable, like her thoughts had been as loud as the voices around her. Rhonda was standing in front of her saying, ". . . had a few too many. Maybe someone should take him home."

Rhonda looked at Jesse, noting instantly her distress and asked, "Are you okay, Jesse?"

"I'm not feeling good. I think I'm going to go." Jesse smiled at her and gave her a hug before heading for the door.

The patio was brightly lit and Jesse breathed in the cool fresh outside air with relief. Her moccasins made only whispered "swishing" noises on the cement walkway as she made her way out to where her blue Buick was parked on the street. A shadow moved from behind the hedge, and out of the dark stepped Mat. "Jesse," he began, "I'll give you another chance . . . but just one more. Do you want to go out tomorrow night, maybe catch a movie or something?" He stepped boldly forward and attempted to reach for her.

Jesse, noting the slur in his words proceeded with caution, getting a firm grip on her keys; she backed away from him toward her car. "No thanks."

Mat pushed toward her, his voice becoming vicious, "Come on, Jesse!"

She reached for the knife she kept in her boot and had it in her hand in a flash. She brandished in front of his face. "Stay away from me!" she ordered before she jumped in her car, locked the doors and started for home.

Anger hammered at her as she pulled into the driveway. All she wanted to do was go upstairs, take a long hot bath and get back to reading her Grandmother's diary. She felt a hint of depression setting in and a sense of fear that she couldn't identify. She thought fleetingly back on the evening and recalled the incident in the living room at Rhonda's house involving Mat and the beer. She touched the pendant that hung coldly around her neck, remembering how strangely warm it had felt. Her muscles tensed at the thought that it might have been magic that caused Mat to choke on his beer. How could it be freecurrent magic? Really?

Dismissing that line of thought, she wrote off the incident as coincidence only and her perceptions as imagination, finding it easier than coping with the prospect of possessing the ability to use magic.

The house was silent as she slipped in through the kitchen door. Her father had left the light on over the stove, as he always did, but everyone had already gone to bed. Jesse opened the refrigerator and gazed in for a moment, but found nothing of interest. She closed the door again, turned off the stove light and headed toward the stairs. Felcore met her at the bottom of the staircase with his tail wagging joyously and demanded attention. Jesse sat down on the bottom step and began to stroke, scratch and hug her dog, which Felcore reacted to with growing enthusiasm as he did his happy dance by turning in circles every couple of strokes and pushing his large wet nose against Jesse in an insistent manner.

She had received Felcore from Santa Claus for Christmas the year that her mother had died, about five years ago. She had fallen instantly in love with the roly-poly puppy with soft blond fur and large golden eyes. Felcore had immediately taken to Jesse and followed her around everywhere, sleeping with her at night and waking her up in the morning with soft wet puppy kisses on the face. Jesse named him "Felcore" after a character in the movie, "The Never Ending Story", a luck dragon who looked just like her puppy, only bigger. He was a source of great comfort for her during a very difficult time in her life and their friendship became forever cemented. He was the one friend Jesse could always count on, no matter what. Felcore grew his first year from a five pound puppy to a one-hundred pound dog. His coat was a shiny reddish gold, with light blond fur behind his shoulders and feathers, accented with thinner white belly fur. He was extremely soft and loving, with a playful and gentle demeanor. Jesse and he were constant companions, they did everything together and Jesse took him everywhere.

Sitting on the stair stroking Felcore calmed Jesse down. Watching him play happily without a single care always made her look at her problems a little less seriously. "Come on, boy, let's get you some dinner," Jesse said as she started up the stairs with Felcore taking them two at a time in front of her. He waited at the top, looking down at Jesse with glowing gold eyes as she ascended at a slower pace. When she reached the top, he headed for Jesse's bedroom and was sitting in front of his empty food dish when she entered. With a pat on his head, Jesse filled the dish that said "dog" on it and left him to devour his dinner and satisfy, for a short time, his very healthy appetite.

Jesse headed down the hallway to the bathroom and started hot water in the tub for her bath, putting in just enough bubble bath to enhance the relaxation mood she was trying to create with a gentle herbal scent. After a quick trip to her bedroom to strip her clothes off and get into a robe, Jesse locked the bathroom door behind her and slowly sank into the tub of hot sudsy water. With her neck resting on a folded towel propped on the edge of the tub, the hot water started to work on releasing the stress from Jesse's muscles. She sighed deeply and closed her eyes. As her mind began to wander, the incident with Mat came into her thoughts once again. Reaching up to grasp the pendent that hung loosely between her breasts, she thought of the words Theo had spoken to Gabriel. "The sword . . . the sword homed in on your medallion." Jesse pondered again the possibility if what she had witnessed had actually occurred as a result of some unknown power within herself brought into action by the magic of the pendant. She almost laughed out loud at the audacity of it. Experimentally, she looked down at the pendant and concentrated her will on making the lightning bolt glow blue. Nothing happened. This is ridiculous, she thought. Taking in a deep breath she relaxed deeper into the hot comfort of the water, closed her eyes and drifted off to sleep . . .

. . . Rain came down in torrents turning the already muddy field into a quagmire. Lightning flashed in the sky with bright intensity. Thunder rumbled and the pelting rain was loud, but not loud enough to drown out the sounds of men shouting and horse's hooves pounding all around her. Jesse scrambled on her feet in the thick mud, dodging horses and soldiers as they ran here and there to meet the enemy assault. Everything seemed unreal. She didn't know what she was doing in the midst of a battle, but seeing men dead and dying around her, she began to run in terror. The ground was slick with mud and spilled blood, making footing treacherous and she struggled for every inch of ground. She wondered what had become of Felcore.

The battle raged around her and Jesse began to fear that she was moving in the wrong direction when abruptly she tripped on something and sprawled face first in the mud. After regaining her senses, Jesse sat up and wiped the mud out of her eyes. A hand grabbed her arm and squeezed hard. She heard a voice behind her plead miserably,

"Help me." Turning to look, Jesse gazed upon a soldier clad in armor who was covered in blood. His arm looked nearly severed at the elbow and his other hand held her arm with a vice-like grip. His eyes were full of terror and pain. Stifling a sob, Jesse could not help herself as she turned from the man and emptied the contents of her stomach onto the ground. Regaining some of her composure, Jesse looked back at the man and began searching for something to bind his wounds. She realized with deadened surprise that she was attired in a dress with a long skirt with layers of slips underneath. She quickly began ripping the skirt into strips of cloth and administering first aid to the man, continuing on to another man, and another, as the night went on endlessly and the rain continued to pour down.

As dawn arrived in faint gray, blue, melting into orange light, as the sun peaked over the horizon, Jesse continued to work among the injured soldiers, finding more dead than alive after having their blood and their lives washed away with the rain throughout the long night. She was working on a soldier who couldn't be much older than seventeen, when she felt a hand on her shoulder and a strong but gentle voice speak to her in a familiar manner, "The medics are on the field now. Please come. You must get some rest before tonight. This battle is not yet over."

Without looking up, Jesse protested weakly, "No, I cannot leave this boy to die. Give me some more time."

"I am sorry. You can do nothing for him. Please, come with me now," the man said, with a hint of urgency in his voice.

Looking up for the first time from where she sat on the ground, hands and face covered with blood stains and mud, Jesse gazed into the eyes of a man who stood towering over her. For some reason she felt she should know him. The man was tall, well over six feet. He was dressed as a soldier and was covered from head to foot with brown and crimson stains. He extended his hand to Jesse, and upon her taking it, lifted her to her feet as if she were no more than a feather.

As she looked into his fiery gold eyes, she felt a deep aching within her heart and had to look away or risk being overcome. She noticed the helmet he held beneath his arm and gasped at the bold insignia . . . a golden lightning bolt on a field of black. Automatically Jesse reached up to touch her pendant. It was warm . . .

. . . A cold wet nose touched her left hand. "Felcore, you're okay, boy!" Jesse, overpowered with relief, reached out to hug the big dog and got him all wet with bath water. The bubbles on his nose made him sneeze making bubbles fly into Jesse's face as well. The dream haunted Jesse for only a moment until Felcore made her laugh by rubbing his nose with his paws, frantically trying to rid himself of the irritating soap. "Let me help," she said as she attempted to rub Felcore's nose with a towel, which he avoided by backing up just out of her reach. Getting out of the tub, she dried herself off, put on her robe and spent several minutes brushing her hair, remembering the beautiful gold eyes from her dream as she gazed unseeing at her own reflection in the mirror. She stopped brushing abruptly and looked at Felcore strangely for a moment, not understanding how he had gotten into the bathroom when she had closed and locked the door. Jesse scratched absently at the tingling sensation present where the pendant rested against her skin as she gazed questioningly into her dog's glowing eyes. Her puzzled expression remained as she said, "Come on, boy, I have some important reading to do," and they headed to the bedroom to settle in for the night. Jesse picked up her Grandmother's diary off from the dresser where she had left it earlier and opened it to the place marked with a red ribbon.

Chapter 5
WELCOME TO RISEN

A pril 20. The gate appeared a mirror image of the other side, including the cave which I could easily have mistaken for the exact cave we had just left, absent the smoldering fire. Looking back through the gate I could see that the constellation was no longer "The Condor", but something else. I didn't understand how I could be seeing stars when I knew for a fact there was a cave on the other side of the gate, not open sky. It mystified me. I was intrigued to find out more about the gate, being in complete awe of its design and in wonder of its magic. I was tempted to go back through, just to make sure I could and I started in that direction when I was stopped short by Theo tugging me in the opposite direction by my hand which he still clutched tightly in his own. We gazed at each other for a moment and then silently headed for the cave entrance from which a cool breeze softly emanated.

Maintaining our silence, Theo and I stood just inside the cave entrance and gazed out into the dark night. Instead of the desert landscape we had left behind, we were looking out into a thick forest of cedar and birch. Pleasant aromatic pine touched my senses and I breathed in deeply, enjoying the freshness of the air. The musky scent I had noticed earlier was more pronounced and I began to ask about its source when I was interrupted by a predatory roar that ripped through the velvet darkness and shook the ground with a slight tremor. Theo drew his sword in one smooth stroke and backed us up against the rocky wall inside the cave entrance, forcing me against the cold hard surface with a strong outstretched arm. I held my breath while we waited and listened to something enormous crash through the forest, coming toward us at an unbelievably rapid rate of speed. I swallowed hard trying to rid myself of the sour taste of fear in my mouth and wished fervently my heart would quit pounding in my ears so I could hear more efficiently.

Only seconds had passed before the creature was standing in the cave entrance. With wild menacing eyes and saliva dripping freely from its jowls, it sniffed the air, quickly picking up our scents. It growled deeply, curling its lips to display a savage array of teeth, its bear-like mouth brandishing a set of four-inch fangs. Deep set eyes surrounded by heavy brows considered us swiftly. Theo stood in front of me with his sword up, facing the animal, waiting and watching in anticipation, muscles taunt and ready. The animal made his move, charging at Theo with a mighty roar that filled the cave. Theo swung his sword at just the right moment in a graceful arc, slicing through the heavy fur and muscle on the animal's right shoulder, successfully robbing it of the use of its right arm. The bear-like body trembled with the magnitude of its rage. The animal swung his massive left arm, hitting Theo on his right side, causing his arm to bend at an awkward angle and knocking the sword from his hand.

The animal retreated for a moment and made a semi-circle before starting toward us again. I watched it approach, biting my lip in terror as Theo stood before me doubled over in pain and cradling his arm protectively. Desperately, I concentrated on trying to remember a spell, setting it into action by speaking the foreign words with a quaking voice as they came instantly to me. The beast took one more step before freecurrent transformed the hard rocky ground into a mud quagmire beneath its feet. As it plunged forward through the mud, it made amazing progress, even with a seriously injured limb and I knew it would only be delayed temporarily.

Wrapping my arms around Theo's waist, I shouted, "Let's go!" He took a moment to grab his sword before I half-dragged, half-carried him out of the cave. The beast's cries roared behind us. Turning back, I saw the animal had freed himself from my trap and was heading directly for us, bulldozing through everything that lay in its path. I held onto Theo and heard a cry escape my lips as I watched it advance.

The beast was nearly on top of us, so close that I could smell its stench and feel the heat of its breath on my skin. I thought frantically, trying to come up with a plan, any plan, when I saw a blur in front of my eyes. A giant winged creature swooped down out of the star-filled sky, grabbed the beast with its great talons and glided gracefully away with the animal struggling and screaming in its iron grip. The musky scent I had noticed earlier nearly knocked me over as the wind from the creature's wings engulfed us in a storm of dust and leaves.

"What was that?" I asked in amazement and relief as I watched Theo sink heavily to the ground.

"A ripgar, an animal with a keen hunger for humans," he said as I knelt before him. I took his arm gently in my hands and began administering first aid. He flinched in pain as I felt the position of the break with my fingers. Working quickly in order to minimize his discomfort, I ripped some cloth from my already tattered dress, found two relatively straight sticks, and fashioned a splint for his arm. I could almost feel Theo's pain as I set the break, although he barely groaned through his clenched teeth. When I was finished tending him, he stood up without a word and headed back to the cave to retrieve our packs.

I watched him go for a moment and then decided to head after him so I could at least carry the packs and ease his burden when I again heard the "whoosh" of wings. A breeze touched my face that carried with it a sweet musky scent, identifying the beast that had saved us earlier. My attention was drawn up to the sky where I saw a large silver dragon hovering between the cave and myself. Softly he landed before me.

The creature cooed softly as he folded his silver wings to his glistening body. He settled himself comfortably on the ground in front of me, dwarfing me. He had a sinuous tail on one end and a long thick neck on the other that held up his massive head. Nostrils the size of basketballs drew in deep breaths of air causing windy drafts around me. The scales that covered his body shown with silver brilliance in the faint star light as he observed me closely with large intelligent eyes that swirled hypnotically with a bright red radiance. I stood frozen in place while the creature looked me up and down, not making the slightest menacing move, just observing with cat-like awareness.

Theo emerged from the cave, walked briskly up beside the beast and patted him affectionately on the neck. He smiled at me and said, "Gabriel, I would like you to meet Balls of Fire, a dragon who has been my close friend and companion since both of us were hatchlings so many years ago. B.F., I would like you to meet Mistress Gabriel Thomas of Earth, Galaxy XXIII. She has agreed to be our new sorceress."

The dragon, B.F., sank his head down low in a semblance of a bow, as I heard a deep resonant voice in my head say, "*I am awfully glad to make your acquaintance, Mistress Gabriel.*"

Theo smiled at me, obviously amused by my startled expression, and said, "B.F. says, he's awfully glad to make your acquaintance, Mistress Gabriel."

"Yes, Theo, thank you. I heard him quite clearly." I curtsied before the dragon and said to him, "*Thank you very much for saving our lives, Balls of Fire, I am truly in your debt.*"

"*Please, call me B.F., Mistress.*"

"*You can call me Gabriel.*"

Theo's princely mask slipped and with a befuddled expression on his face, he looked back and forth from B.F. to myself and asked, "You heard him?"

"Yes," I replied slowly.

"Dragons communicate with mental telepathy. It is exceptionally rare for a person to have the gift of understanding them, unless, like with me and B.F., the dragon and human are bonded. I can converse freely with B.F., even at a distance, but I cannot communicate with other dragons at all. Let's see if this gift of yours works both ways. Gabriel, see if you can communicate an idea to B.F."

B.F. interrupted with his smooth base voice inside my head. "*She can,*" he said simply.

This dragon could devour me in one bite, but seemed as mild mannered as a summer breeze. B.F.'s eyes shone brightly back at me as I heard him 'say', "*I would be glad to accommodate if you two would like a ride home.*"

I would have dearly liked to have gone home, not what B.F. considered home, but my home in Texas. However, I knew it would be some time before that was possible.

The sun was just beginning to ascend over the horizon by the time we were mounted just behind B.F.'s neck. Theo had a difficult time getting into position with his broken arm hampering his movements, and I, of course, had never ridden dragon back before. Also impeding us was the absence of a saddle which was normally used for securing the rider to the dragon and providing some cushion between the rider's fleshy parts and the dragon's hard and slippery scales. Theo kept scolding B.F. about his lack of proper planning, until B.F. silenced him up by saying, *"I could have left you for ripgar bait and only saved Gabriel, who seems to appreciate me and doesn't nag."*

With B.F.'s help, we finally got settled into place between his shoulder blades and neck, and without further formalities, B.F. launched his huge body into the air, flapped his massive wings until he gained enough altitude to glide on the wind currents high above the forest and we cruised smoothly into the sunrise. The forest eventually turned into rolling green hills that were dotted sporadically with cabins and trees. We crossed over a winding river that sparkled in the star lit night. Several hours later a village came into view. Theo whispered in my ear that it was called, "Lakeside". The smell of smoke and baking bread reached my nose and lingered there enticingly making me realize how hungry I was. We landed, had some dinner and stretched our tired muscles, but were quickly back in the air.

The village dwindled away making room for farms and pastures as the sun rose. After a few hours of flying, another village became visible. Rising up from the hill before us was a magnificent castle. *"Castle Gentlebreeze."* I heard B.F. mentally, as he trumpeted audibly, announcing our arrival.

Constructed of white stone, the castle's architecture was beautiful and defendable. Four large towers stood at the corners of the square with smaller turrets on both sides of each tower. The center portion of the castle rose six stories in height with many windows running the entire span of the building, lending to the castle's grandeur. A massive rampart surrounded the entire castle and grounds inside of which a small market place had sprouted up. As we circled the grounds the people gazed up at us casually. We came around to the back of the castle where I could see stables and corals with horses running energetically within the confines of their fences. On the far side was a large arena complete with stands and box seats, now empty, save for a couple of men astride black horses who waved to us in greeting. Two white horses grazed indifferently in the center of the arena. B.F. descended gracefully and landed gently on the ground a few feet from where the men on the horses stood.

After B.F. was settled, the men dismounted their beautiful pure black mounts and came forward on foot. A ladder was propped against B.F.'s back and Theo descended before me to the ground. I stood by and watched as he was met amiably by the two young men. After I descended the ladder, Theo noticed me standing next to B.F. and came over to take me by the hand and guide me to his friends. He introduced them to me as Joshua and Alexander and they both smiled pleasantly and bowed as Theo introduced me as Mistress Gabriel.

The three of them started discussing the business of soldiering, so I wandered back over to B.F. and began idly scratching his nose ridges. B.F. cooed out loud to me, but berated Theo mentally, *"One would think a prince would be a much better host, going off to talk business while a young and beautiful lady is left to wait, dusty and exhausted with not so much as a bath or a proper meal. I would never treat you so rudely."*

Theo raised an eyebrow at the dragon, but he cut the conversation short, walked over and patted B.F. affectionately on the neck.

Joshua approached me, "It would be my honor if you accompany me to the castle. I brought extra horses for you and the prince."

As we neared the castle, I saw B.F. overhead and he shared with me images of his home, a large cave nestled in a rocky cliff of black stone that overlooked a warm sandy beach with sand as white as the cliff was black in contrast. Ice blue water lapped rhythmically on the shore. The feelings he sent me of warmth and security were so overwhelming it brought tears to my eyes.

"*Rest well, B.F.,*" I said.

Theo spoke as he rode next me, "Balls of Fire is leaving for his own cave to get some rest. He shows up here or wherever I need him or when he just wants some attention or wants to nag me to death."

I heard B.F.'s voice come back, "*I never nag you . . . It wouldn't be worth the trouble . . . you seldom defer to wisdom.*"

Although I couldn't hear his reply, Theo grinned good-naturedly.

We rode in through the open gate side by side and were greeted by waving hands and calls of welcome from the people on the street. When we arrived before two massive carved wooden doors, we dismounted, gave our horses to a couple of stable boys, and headed up a walkway trimmed with colorful pink, purple and yellow pansies. The heavy-looking door was opened for us from the inside and we were greeted by two men and a woman, who relieved us of our packs.

The room we entered into was a large foyer, furnished comfortably with large cushioned sofas and ornately carved tables with large vases of flowers upon them. There were double doorways to the left and the right and a beautiful oak winding staircase at the far end of the room. Large windows on either side of the staircase and the entry doors made the foyer very welcoming.

Theo introduced the servants to me as Roger, the doorman, or butler if I preferred; Han, his personal servant; and Loni, one of his sister's maids. Roger was an elderly gentleman with gray hair and a skeletal face, who held himself rigidly aloof. Han was very handsome in a simple manner and, if I guessed correctly, only slightly younger than Theo. Loni gave off a clean shine as she smiled at me with bright blue eyes. She was dressed in a simple white dress and had her black silky hair tied in a bun on top of her head.

They all turned as a tall young woman with long shiny blond hair, wearing a vibrant purple full-length dress came running down the stairs at top speed. She stopped short of Theo, examined him critically with bright green eyes, and exclaimed dramatically, "Oh my goodness, Theo, you are injured," before giving him a gentle hug and a kiss on the cheek.

"I'm fine, Kris, just a little sore." Theo hugged her back with his good arm before gently setting her aside. Glancing at me, he said, "Gabriel, I would like you to meet my little sister, Kristina. Kristina, this is Mistress Gabriel Thomas, our new sorceress."

Kristina smiled pleasantly, and after taking my hand in her own, she said, "Welcome. I hope your trip with my brother wasn't too tedious." She glanced at Theo tauntingly before returning her gaze to me. "You look tired. I am sure you would like to get cleaned up and rest after your long trip. I'll have Loni show you to the room we have prepared. She will be at your disposal during your stay with us, so if there is anything you need, please feel free to ask her."

I realized I must look frightful, with my dress dirty and torn and my hair disheveled. Feeling a little embarrassed, I smiled back at Kristina and replied, "Thank you for your generous hospitality, Kristina. A hot bath would be heavenly. I'm afraid I have a small problem, however. All of my clothes were lost during our trip and I'm afraid I have nothing clean to wear. Perhaps I could borrow something while I wash out my dress."

"Nonsense," Kristina said as she guided me toward the stairs. "I have plenty of clothes I never wear that I am sure would fit you. We are about the same size. Come with me, I'll find you something." Looking back at Theo she said, "Get that arm looked at immediately. I'll talk to you later . . . maybe even show you how to deal with a hungry ripgar." Turning to me with a mischievous smile, she added, "It can't be that much more difficult than dealing with a hot-tempered man." We giggled together as we headed up the stairs and I knew that Kristina and I were going to be good friends.

After going through Kristina's enormous closet and taking hand-me-downs that she "never wore", I had more dresses, lingerie, stockings and shoes than I had ever before owned in my life. Although I tried to refuse, she insisted and kept adding things until Loni and I had more than we could carry and she had to send another maid along to help us to the my room.

The guest room was much larger than I expected, with an enormous bed in the center of the room, canopied with soft white linen. A polished oak chest and closet stood on the far wall flanking a full length beveled mirror. Next to the bathroom door was a small writing desk, complete with stationery and writing implements.

A hot bath was awaiting me and I eagerly stripped off my dirty dress and sank into the fragrant hot bubbles, feeling that it truly was heavenly.

After my bath, I sank into the soft white bed with fresh smelling linens that Loni had turned down earlier, and I fell immediately into a deep, deep sleep.

I was awakened by the sound of pounding on my door. Wiping my eyes, I found that I must have slept the rest of the night and most of the next day away. The lamp on the bedside table was lit and radiated a soft yellow glow and a fire had been set in the white stone fireplace. Loni had laid a robe across the foot of my bed and a complete outfit was sitting on the chair next to the dresser. The pounding continued and I heard Theo's voice call, "Gabriel, wake up. I am going to come in there if you don't answer me. Wake up."

"Hold on, I am coming," I yelled back. I reluctantly climbed out of my warm bed and wrapped the delicate white robe around me, as I walked over to the door and opened it to let Theo in. "I'm sorry. I must have fallen asleep."

Theo's expression was one of bewilderment; his eyebrows were drawn in, tight and serious. "Father wishes to see you. I expected to introduce you at dinner, but I guess Loni decided to let you sleep through it. I'll tell her that you're up and to have a tray sent to your room."

"Thank you. I am rather starved," I said as my stomach growled loudly in confirmation.

"I'm sure you must be hungry," he said, smiling.

I stood up and walked to the dresser, picked up a silver brush and started running it through my hair, enjoying the clean feeling and the fragrant scent. "When am I supposed to see your father?" I asked.

"You have enough time to eat and dress. I'll come for you," Theo said as he turned to go.

Loni arrived shortly after Theo's departure, bringing a tray laden with roast turkey, potatoes, gravy, carrots, and spiced apples along with a carafe of hot coffee. The food was delicious and I was almost able to finish it all. I had no idea I was so hungry. Loni brushed out my hair and arranged it out of my face with cords that matched the midnight blue dress she had laid out for me earlier. Sparingly, I applied some of the foreign-looking make-up Kristina had sent me, enhancing my features subtly, before squeezing into my dress and throwing on some comfortable slippers.

Audience with the King

Theo and Kristina arrived together. Both of them were dressed beautifully, Theo in his General's dress uniform, black pants and overcoat with green trim and gold ornamentation, and Kristina in a boldly cut jade gown with black lace trim. I was a little nervous about meeting the king, and I told them so. They just laughed and, exchanging meaningful glances, said I had nothing to worry about, which worried me even more and I began to wonder what was in store for me.

I expected to see a throne room when we entered through the double doorway, but was surprised to walk into a massive library, with heavy wooden book cases covering the walls, and a roaring fire in the stone fireplace opposite me. The center of the room contained two large leather couches facing each other with a wooden coffee table in the middle, scattered all over with maps and books.

We walked toward the right side of the room where a man sat behind a bulky desk with his back to us gazing out the opened window. The night time breeze was cool as it filtered into the room, gently caressing the heavy draperies before mixing its freshness with the scent of pipe smoke, mingling with the comfortable smell of leather and wood. The desk was scattered all over with maps, books and papers, leaving only a small work space in the front center available. Turning his chair to face us, an elderly man sat his pipe down on the desk and nodded to me. "So this is our new sorceress," he stated as a fact, not in question to the validity of his claim.

As he looked me over, I returned his scrutiny, taking the opportunity to assess the man who had ordered me brought to this faraway land called Brightening. My first impression was that he looked much like the characterizations I had always seen of Santa Claus, but instead of jolly, this man was deadly serious. He had long white hair, a long white beard and mustache. He wore a simple gray tunic that did nothing to brighten his stern facade. Serious dark gray eyes gave away nothing of the man's intent or expectations.

Panicking, I remembered that I hadn't asked Theo what to do--how to act, should I bow, curtsy, fall to my knees, plant my forehead on the floor, or just say, "howdy". All three of us approached the desk as the man stood up.

The king stepped forward and taking my hand delicately kissed it, all the while looking deeply into my eyes. Without conscious effort, I did a slight curtsy. As he released me, I said, "Your Highness, I am pleased to meet you."

"Please, call me Cleo in the privacy of my suite. I am very glad you are here. I know it was difficult for you to leave your family behind in order to answer my summons. I assure you that I would not have sent for you had it not been necessary."

The king greeted his son and daughter with warm familiarity. Taking Kristina by the shoulders, he kissed her delicately on the nose, making her giggle slightly, and said, "Sweetheart, you look stunning. Whose heart are you planning to steal tonight?" Blushing appropriately, Kristina gave her father a kiss on the cheek and whispered something privately in his ear. Cleo smiled at her with a trace of the devil in his grin, but did not comment on whatever she had said.

Theo stepped up with his hand outstretched and offered it to his father. Cleo took it in his own before embracing his son with care taken not to jar his injured arm. "It is good to have you home, son."

"It's good to be home, father." Theo stepped back away from the king, took my hand and placed it on the crook of his arm somewhat possessively.

"Kris, will you fetch us something to drink, something to take the chill off?" Cleo asked while striding to the center of the room. "Come, let us sit down and get comfortable. We have much to discuss before the night is through."

"Perhaps some tea, father?" Kristina asked with a knowing smile on her face.

"Tea won't help take the chill off from these old bones, child. Bring us some nectar," Cleo said with impatience edging his voice. Kristina just laughed and left the room to do her father's bidding.

The three of us chose seats on the leather sofas, with Cleo sitting next to me and Theo on the opposite couch. Kristina brought a tray laden with four crystal goblets and a decanter containing some type of liquor I assumed. After she served us all, she took a seat on the couch next to Theo. The aroma of the liquor was strong and enticing. I tasted mine with a small sip and discovered it was some type of orange flavored brandy, similar to Grande Marnier, only a little more delicate in texture. The king took his time and sipped his drink, savoring the flavor, before he began, "I am sure that Theo must have filled you in on some of the events leading up to our decision to bring you here. The war has cost us many lives in our attempt to keep our people safe from the evil that has spread throughout the land.

In fact, at this very moment a number of people who were once under our protection are living in desperation under the tyranny of the corrupt sorcerer, Candaz, who bleeds them dry of their crops, food and money, and eventually their spirit." Cleo paused to take a sip of his nectar before he went on, "We cannot let him gain any more of his objectives. It is imperative that he be stopped. My people are suffering. It cannot go on!" Cleo spoke with anger and passion, banging his fist on the table and making the decanter rock dangerously back and forth.

Theo stepped in quickly, giving his father a chance to regain his composure. "Father, with the reorganization of the troops, the other Generals and I feel that we can easily protect any land that is now ours and repel any and all further attempts by Candaz's troops to seize more ground from us. I am confident that we will soon be in a position to begin regaining some of the terrain that has been lost. With Gabriel's help, we will attack at the heart of Candaz's force, his sorcery, tear it out from the roots and be rid of this plague once and for all."

Cleo considered me a moment before he addressed me without responding to his son, "It will be your job, first of all, to learn all you can about sorcery in order to utilize the powers you already possess. You will train under a master of the arts. If you are willing to begin at once, you can leave tomorrow. Anything you can do to expedite your training would be greatly appreciated. Once you have mastered your skills, you will work closely with Theo in order to enhance the troops' performance and repel any corrupt magic used against them. Finally, you will be responsible to do everything you can to bring back peace by personally confronting and defeating Candaz."

Feeling like a trapped wolf in a cage, I gulped some liquor, seeking courage at the bottom of my glass. I wanted to run back to my home and hide in the comfort of John's arms, to wake up and find that this had all been a nightmare, but I knew I couldn't. I had to see this through to keep my family safe.

Cleo leaned over and filled my goblet and then filled his own before he saying, "So, you will leave tomorrow?" His wise old eyes stared into mine, testing my mettle.

Kristina spoke for the first time since we had sat down, gaining her father's attention, "I will be going with Gabriel, father." Before Cleo could begin to protest, Kristina continued, "Do not argue with me. My mind is made up. I am sure Gabriel would enjoy having some company on the trip, wouldn't you?" she asked, as she gave me a bright smile and a wink.

Cleo scowled at Kristina and uttered cantankerously, "We will discuss this later, Kris." He put down his glass and stood up as if to end the conversation.

"Excuse me, Cleo, but I do have some questions," I boldly stopped the king from leaving. Cleo did not look pleased as he sank slowly back down into the soft leather couch.

I turned to him and met his eyes squarely. "What if I decide to just leave and go back home? I'm not sure about all of this."

Cleo looked thoughtful. "You can leave right now if you want to. I will not hold you prisoner here. You are free to do as you please. However, consider the condition of my people seriously before you decide to leave. It is my belief that you are their last hope. I beg you not to abandon them."

His eyes sparkled and he chuckled a little down deep in his belly. "I have a feeling, Gabriel, that even though you desire to return to your own world, you will not because you have great compassion and will not turn your back on those in need. You have already come this far. You must be at least a little curious to know more about this freecurrent magic you possess and how to use it."

I thought for a moment and then laughed also. "I can see that you are a very wise king, Cleo . . . and a very good judge of character. I must admit that I am curious about my abilities and about this place you call Risen, not to mention the eagerness I have to know more about the gate. But, I can't help but to also remind myself that curiosity killed the cat and honestly, my greatest desire is to return to my family."

A puzzled look washed across all three faces and Kristina asked, "What is a cat?"

I sighed heavily, resigning myself to my providence, "I'll explain later." I took another drink of the tasty liquor they called "nectar", letting it linger on my tongue before swallowing. "The gate that we came through from my world to yours also goes to other galaxies, does it not? How many worlds are there? Have you ever been to any? What are they like?"

Theo and Kristina both looked to their father for answers to my questions and I noted a hint of equally acute curiosity in their gazes. Cleo seemed to hedge away from the topic, looking contemplatively from Theo to Kristina and back again to me. He cleared his throat and said, "Well, actually, we haven't been to any of the other galaxies, except, of course, Theo, who went to yours. I have heard there are two thousand and something." He waved his hand in a feeble motion of dismissal.

I was surprised by his lack of enthusiasm in something so spectacular and gave him a bewildered glare. I couldn't help but ask, "How could you not explore . . . ? The possibilities are overwhelming."

The king's indolent tone told me that his interests clearly lay elsewhere. He said, "The gate has been kept a secret from everybody until just recently when its existence was revealed to us. Perhaps after the war is over we'll send a team to explore the different worlds. At this time we have enough problems here that need attention. Of course, you will get paid for your services. We will provide room and board, travel expenses, food, clothing, and funeral expenses, if required."

Looking at Cleo with a significant frown, I returned, "If funeral expenses happen to be required, I trust in your honor to deliver any accrued salary to my family."

Cleo smiled at me with respect and returned, "It will be taken care of, if deemed necessary. If there isn't anything else, I am very tired and would like to retire--and you have a long day ahead of you tomorrow--you will be travelling to Ornate to meet your tutor." Cleo stood up and offered me his hand. "Gabriel, it has been a pleasure meeting you."

I stood up and took his hand, but I wasn't quite finished. "If you don't mind, there is one last thing I am curious about."

Cleo sighed, "Mistress, you are beginning to remind me of my late wife." He smiled with an affectionate gleam in his eyes.

I smiled back with an initial understanding of Theo's tender feelings toward the king. "I was just curious about my pendant. How does it work? How did Theo use it to find me?"

Laughter resounded from the king in a joyous cascade of chuckles before he answered, "My dear, Gabriel, you will have to ask that of your tutor. I have no idea how such things work. I am, after all, just the king." He leaned over and kissed my hand.

"Of course, your majesty," I curtsied slightly. "I will do my best to serve you well. Will I see you again before I go?"

"I will see you tomorrow at breakfast," Cleo smiled. "Theo, will you show Gabriel back to her room? Kris and I have some things to discuss before we go to bed." He gave his daughter a meaningful glance, which she returned without flinching.

"Goodnight father," Theo rose and offered me his arm.

Kristina stood up, walked around the table and put her arm around her father's waist before catching my eye. "I'll bring you some traveling clothes in the morning, Gabriel."

"Thank you. You have been very kind," I said to her as I took Theo's arm.

We were silent, absorbed in our own thoughts as we headed back to my room. I was hoping that Kristina would be able to convince her father to let her go with me, purely for selfish reasons. I didn't want to go alone. Theo and I had been together since leaving home (was it only nine days ago?) and I was going to miss his companionship. My anxiety over meeting my tutor made me even more hopeful for Kristina's company. She apparently was already acquainted with the person. I wondered what kind of relationship they shared. I broke the silence with a question, "Who is going to be my tutor?"

"Do you remember me telling you the story about my grandfather and his wife Shareen? Shareen is my grandmother. She is the one who will teach you," he said as we stopped in front of my door.

I felt somehow betrayed and said angrily, "I don't understand. If Shareen is still alive, what do you need me for? Surely she has the power to help your people."

"Gabriel," Theo began, taking me gently by the shoulders, "my grandmother is very old and crippled, her legs no longer work efficiently and her hands are almost useless from the swelling in her joints. She is incapable of performing the responsibilities required of a sorceress at war. Grandmother has not left the Tower of Ornate in over ten years and I'm afraid she will remain there until she dies."

I said nothing more, not knowing whether to be angry or compassionate and feeling a measure of both. Theo smiled at me with his charming grin and said, "I am going to miss you Gabriel. You are a very special woman."

I couldn't help but smile back, being genuinely touched by his friendship. "Thank you. I will miss you as well," I said and standing on my tip toes, I kissed him quickly on the cheek.

He colored slightly and then became all business. "B.F. will be flying you and Kristina to Ornate tomorrow. I will be gone before sunrise, out with the troops, reviewing maneuvers, so I won't be able to see you and Kris off. When you are ready to leave, simply 'call' B.F. to come and get you. I'll inform the stable boy to saddle him when he gets here. Tell him to take you straight to Ornate. He knows where it is. The trip should take you half a day, so you will probably want to get a fairly early start. I'll come visit you when I get a chance. Good luck, Gabriel."

"Thank you. Goodnight," I said dismally, feeling unexpectedly lonely. After closing the door behind me, I got ready for bed. Not being inclined to sleep, I sat down to write in my diary.

Tomorrow should be a very interesting day.

Navigator Dragon

April 21. I awoke this morning with Loni gently shaking me by the shoulder. "Wake up, Mistress," she requested with a light and considerate voice.

She smiled down at me when I opened my eyes and I said, sleepily, "I sure did sleep well last night. Can I take this bed with me?"

"Only if B.F. agrees to carry it for you," she said, laughing. "Kristina brought these for you earlier this morning." She held up a pair of dark green woolen trousers, a flouncy white blouse, a pair of tan high-calf boots, made of soft leather, and a hooded cape that matched the boots. You will need these as well," she said as she placed a pair of leather riding gloves on top of the cape.

Together we packed about half of my belongings into saddle bags designed especially to fit over a dragon's back. Loni sent for two young men to take my bags downstairs, where I joined Kristina and Cleo in the dining room for a light breakfast. I discovered that Kristina was dressed similarly to me, only her trousers were light brown as opposed to my green. I was very glad she was going and not at all surprised that she had persuaded her father. I had a feeling that she got her way most of the time.

After breakfast, Kristina and I headed to the kitchen to pack a picnic basket for lunch. Then we headed to the library to say goodbye to Cleo. He was involved in reading a document when we arrived, but welcomed us with a warm smile. He hugged us both, kissed Kristina on the cheek, wished us both luck and warned us to be careful. I told him not to worry, that I would watch over Kristina, and Kristina told him not to worry, she would watch over me.

As we started to head toward the front door, where we had two horses waiting to take us to the arena, I remembered I hadn't summoned B.F. yet, so I concentrated my thoughts, attempting to project them to B.F., "*B.F. are you listening?*"

Nothing . . . nothing . . .

I tried again, "*B.F., it's me Gabriel, I need you to come and get me.*"

I listened hard, trying to keep my mind clear and open, anticipating a response. When B.F.'s booming voice sounded in my head it startled me into dropping my riding gloves. He sounded sluggish, "*Sorry . . . I was sleeping . . .just give me a chance . . .AARGH . . .to wake up . . .AARGH . . . Is that you Gabriel? Did you say something?*"

I smiled in amusement as I reached down to retrieve my gloves from the floor and said, "Yes, B.F. *Kristina and I need a ride. Are you willing to convey us?*"

"*I'll be right there,*" he replied.

Kristina and I mounted our horses, two beautiful snow white mounts that awaited us in front of the castle and headed for the arena at the back of the grounds. As we passed through the gate, the guard in the tower saluted us with his sword and Kristina acknowledged the tall, dark haired soldier with a kiss blown off from her gloved fingertips. Just outside the gate, we had to move cautiously through a throng of people who stood about on the roadway. "What are all of these people doing milling around the gate? I would think they would have better things to do this time of day," I asked Kristina.

She gently nudged her horse to avoid a woman in the street who was artistically seeking handouts with her only remaining hand. Kristina leaned over to press a coin into the woman's outstretched palm, as she did with many others as we passed. "Most of these people are waiting to see father. The king makes himself available to the general public for two turns every morning. With the oppression over the land, the economy suffers and so do the people. Some of them are citizens with legitimate grievances over land or property rights and come to seek the advice of their lord, some arrive looking for employment or for handouts, some to join the army and fight in the war. Still others come as couriers with messages or information, being otherwise unable to get in through official channels. Usually such people are spies willing to sell what they know for an inflated price. We have our own couriers and informants who can enter the grounds at any time of the day or night, but sometimes buying information from outside sources can prove useful. No one is turned away from Castle Gentlebreeze, in any case."

It was an enormous task to see such multitudes in only two turns, which equaled about two hours. A "turn" from Risen phraseology comes from the amount of time it takes the stationary gnomon on a rotating dial to travel from one marking to the next. Actually the dial doesn't rotate at all but remains stationery along with the gnomon in its center, moving with the cycle of the day, very much like a sundial. The Bright's term is purely illusion. Two turns was not enough time for the king to handle all these peoples' problems. The magnitude of the throng we had just ridden through was colossal. "How does King Cleo see even half of these people in just two hours . . . two turns?" I asked.

Kristina laughed as if I had said something foolish. "He won't *personally* see all of these people. A special staff is in charge of interviewing people before they are allowed to see the king. The people are channeled to various department heads who handle the hiring, legal disputes, intelligence and recruiting. The king personally sees anyone with a problem his staff may be either unable or unwilling to handle. The system works very well, but it is necessary that the staff members be completely trustworthy and loyal to King Wingmaster or corruption would surely follow. My father is very selective when it comes to his staff and his judgment of character has not proven wrong yet."

We discontinued our conversation as the crowd ended and we headed toward the arena at a full gallop. B.F. was already waiting when we arrived and he greeted me with his usual charm, "*Good Day, Mistress Gabriel, you are looking very beautiful today. Please convey my best wishes to Princess Kristina. Where are we going? A picnic, perhaps?*" he asked. His deep mental voice betrayed his excitement as his red eyes swirled with good humor.

The luggage, packed in two large saddle bags, had already been secured on B.F.'s back behind the two leather saddles that sat between his neck and shoulder blades. A ladder was propped against B.F.'s sides as he awaited his passengers. "We're flying to the Tower of Ornate today, B.F. A picnic would be lovely if we can find a nice spot along the way. Are you ready to go?" I recited out loud as well as mentally so Kristina would be privy to our conversation.

"*Oh, Yes!*" B.F. wiggled and squirmed with excitement, knocking the ladder to the ground and causing wisps of smoke to curl out of his nostrils and dust to fly into the air. "*Oops, sorry,*" he said as he settled down again and let the ladder be reestablished.

After Kristina and I were strapped into our saddles and we secured the ladder into place at B.F.'s side, the massive silver dragon launched his sizable form into the warm morning air and flapped his wings until we were at an altitude high above the tree tops. The saddle was comfortable and as soon as B.F. reached his cruising altitude, the ride was smooth and enjoyable. When I was able to catch glimpses of the land below the colors of spring leapt up in a vibrant array. Bright green grasses covered the ground below between patches of yellow, pink, violet and crimson. Trees displayed fresh buds in a variety of shapes, colors and textures. Recently plowed earth stood out dark black in contrast to the bright colors as it sat upturned, ready for planting.

Kristina, who sat behind me, pointed out various landmarks along the way, farms, ranches and some wealthier estates. She gossiped incessantly about this farmer's son or that nobleman's daughter. Her bright and chatty demeanor began to irritate B.F. after a couple of hours and he started making rude comments for my ears only, about maidens making excellent appetizers. About three hours into the trip, with sore muscles and tired ears, I was ready for a break myself and started looking for a good place to have a picnic. I spotted a sparkling stream meandering along the landscape down below. *"B.F., do you see that stream down there?"* I asked.

"Of course, my dear," B.F. returned.

"Could you look for a nice clearing on the sunny side of the stream where we can stop for a bite?"

"There is a lovely spot just up ahead where we can stop. Where, exactly, would you like me to bite you, sweet lady?"

"Do try to behave yourself!" I reprimanded my new big friend lightly while I scratched the back of his neck.

"Gabriel, I am a dragon and I always behave as such," B.F. said with unfeigned pride and dignity as he began his descent toward a beautiful open grassy section on the creek's eastern shore, where the water wound its way restfully in a large s-curve.

We ate a peaceful lunch sitting next to the creek that playfully trickled over rocks. B.F. drank his fill of water and enjoyed some fresh fish for lunch (who just happened to be swimming in his drinking water). We stretched out and relaxed in the sun for a good part of the afternoon. Much too soon, however, we mounted B.F. and were back in the air heading toward our destination.

After a short time, I started feeling anxiety tugging insistently at my nerves. The sun began to set over the horizon in a golden liquefaction of light as I gave in to my impatience and asked B.F. how much further we had to go.

His soft base voice spoke inside my head, *"By comparing the y-axis and the x-axis in correlation to the landmarks within my superior dragon sight with the destination's known axes points, add two, multiply by 30, take the square root of that sum and divide the product by the natural plane distortion factor, and there you have it."*

"Have what, B.F.?" I asked incredulously, and a little too irritably, thinking afterwards that it might not be a good idea to be short-tempered with a dragon.

"*Never mind, human,*" B.F. returned condescendingly. "*It will be a while yet.*"

Not more than thirty minutes went by when B.F. started to descend and announced, "*I'm afraid we are going to have to make a little detour.*"

Startled at this sudden turn of events and more than a little worried, I demanded, "*Where are you taking us?*"

B.F.'s calm demeanor did little to assuage my fear, "*There is something important that we need to do . . . it is necessary.*"

Chapter 6

TO ASSAULT AND PERISH

Interrupted by a knock on the door, Jesse marked her page with a red ribbon and placed the diary next to the clock radio on the nightstand beside her bed. Rubbing her weary eyes, she sat up wondering why someone would bother her at this late hour. A glance at the clock told her it wasn't late after all, but early in the morning, past time to get up and start breakfast. With a sense of incredulity, Jesse realized she had been reading throughout the entire night. She felt a little dizzy, but not at all tired. A knock on the door once again, and the sound of her dad's voice brought Jesse up off from the bed. "Jess, wake up. The coffee is hot and breakfast is almost ready."

"Be right there, Dad," Jesse called back. Her eyes navigated toward the closed diary sitting beside the clock radio. She wanted to pick it up and continue reading, but could not just ignore the rumbling in her belly or her need for a cup of coffee. With reluctance, she turned away from the book, brushed her hair, and dressed quickly. She threw on a pair of comfortable blue jeans, a tank top and her favorite yellow cotton sweater that fastened down the front with pearly white buttons. Bending down, Jesse scratched the still sleeping Felcore behind his ears until he opened his eyes and looked up at her, started thumping his tail on the floor and tried to reach far enough to lick her face. Jesse avoided the moist tongue by less than inches as she pulled back. "Come on, boy, it is breakfast time," she said and stood up as Felcore leapt to his feet and followed her downstairs to the kitchen.

The smell of bacon cooking caressed Jesse's appetite before she reached the kitchen. Her mouth was watering as she walked through the divider and she paused to observe the activity. Her father was busy at the counter cooking pancakes on an electric skillet as he whistled cheerfully to himself, flipping the golden discs with experienced ease. Jacob was pouring milk into three glasses that sat on the table, which was already set with plates, silverware, napkins, butter and syrup, and individual bowls of freshly sliced bananas. Jesse realized suddenly how ravenous she was as she took a mug out of the cupboard and poured herself a cup of coffee, generously adding flavored cream. Peering over her father's shoulder as he worked, Jesse needled, "I guess you two don't need me anymore to take care of you. You seem to fend for yourselves just fine."

"No way, Jess," Jacob's eyes widened in feigned horror. "You can't expect me to eat Dad's cooking all the time--I might die a slow, terrible and painful death," Jacob said. He grabbed his throat, making disgusting sounds like he was gagging, rolled his eyes and fell on the floor writhing in an extravagant dramatization.

Jesse couldn't resist the opportunity to kneel beside her brother and begin to torture his most ticklish spots, which she knew from years of experience. Jacob screamed shrilly and began fighting back immediately. Soon the two siblings were wrestling noisily on the blue tile floor and Felcore started barking, joining in on the tussle.

Bill put an end to it all with a mighty, "Okay, enough!"

Jesse was glad to get up off the floor and end the game with her brother without having to concede victory to him. She out-sized Jacob, but he fought much more aggressively, like a cornered tiger, and Jesse found that the older he became, the harder it was to subdue him. Jesse knew that one day soon he would be physically superior to her, and even though she liked Jacob as a brother, she didn't want him to gain the upper hand in the family's power structure, which he would likely do if he found he could master her so easily. No way!

After breakfast, Jesse and her father relaxed at the table and enjoyed their last cup of coffee. Jesse asked inquisitively, "Dad, what do you know about Grandmother Gabriel?"

Bill's eyebrows pressed together and he twisted the gold wedding band that he still wore on his left hand. He looked at Jesse with memories crowding the space between them. "Well, Jess, I really didn't know her very well. She disappeared soon after your mother and I were married. I only met her a couple of times, one of which was on our wedding day.

"The first time I met Gabriel, she had invited me over for dinner at the request of your mother. I guess it was time for her to check out the guy her daughter was dating to see if I was good enough for her little girl. Marguerite and I were sitting in the study sipping wine when Gabriel walked into the room. She was gorgeous, in a black velvet cocktail dress with a figure that would turn the head of any man. She looked better than most women do half her age. Her long dark hair was pulled back and bundled at the nape of her neck, exhibiting clearly her warm brown eyes. After she placed a kiss on Marguerite's cheek, Gabriel appraised me shrewdly with a magnetic focus. Smiling disarmingly, your Grandmother sat next to me on the couch and, taking my hands in her own, gazed deeply into my eyes, giving me the sensation that she was seeing directly into my soul. Speaking to me for the first time, she smiled and said, 'You will love my daughter well and bring her much happiness throughout her life.' A shadow of sadness swept across her face for barely a moment and then was gone. It was weird, like she was foreseeing the future. Maybe it was just my imagination."

He paused a long time, sipping his coffee, alone with his thoughts. Jesse didn't speak, giving her father the time he required to sort things out. Bill's jaw muscles twitched spasmodically as he attempted to take a firm hold on his emotions. Jesse observed silently, knowing his inner turmoil, waiting for the inevitable relaxation of tense muscles that would indicate when the battle was won. She waited, knowing from experience that when he was ready he would continue the conversation.

"Dinner was ready soon afterwards and we adjourned to the dining room to enjoy a wonderful meal that Gabriel had cooked herself. Even though she could have afforded a four star chef, she preferred to do all of her own cooking. I can understand why. The meal was exquisite." Jesse smiled as she pictured Gabriel in her big gourmet kitchen zapping meals into existence without anyone being the wiser. Her father continued on without noticing Jesse's amusement, "Gabriel had a personality that sparkled with life. It seemed to me as though she possessed some type of special power and people around her reacted to her automatically with respect and reverence. She was a very worldly woman, having travelled extensively after her husband died and she was fluent in several different languages. She was the kind of person who is easy to like.

"Your mother was very hurt when Gabriel disappeared. I recommended that we hire a private investigator to find her, but your mother wasn't interested. She seemed to think that if Gabriel had wanted to be found she would be. Marguerite wanted to concentrate on her own family and their happiness, not to dwell on the pain her mother had caused; pain that she felt powerless to do anything about. I thought she was being irrational about the whole thing, so I hired a private investigator myself, without your mother's knowledge. The investigator I hired found no trace of your grandmother after a long and expensive search. I eventually took your mother's lead and gave up."

Bill considered his daughter with questioning eyes and asked, "Why the sudden interest in your Grandmother, Jess?"

She weighed whether or not to tell her father about Gabriel's diary. A little voice in the back of her mind told her to keep it quiet. Jesse didn't like keeping things from her father, not after everything they had gone through together. But, for some reason she felt she would be betraying Gabriel by telling her father about the diary. She decided to keep it a secret, for now anyway. With her decision made, she answered his question, "I ran across some of grandmother's things in the attic yesterday. Naturally, my curiosity was aroused. Did you know that there is a large trunk up there belonging to Gabriel, filled with clothes and pictures and stuff?"

"Sure, I knew it was up there; has been for years, ever since your Grandmother's disappearance. Your mother said it was just a bunch of old clothes, and in fact, was going to give it to charity, but never got around to it." Bill got up from the table and walked over to the coffee pot and upon finding it empty, rinsed his cup out and sat it in the dishwasher. "I suppose I should go through the attic and get rid of all that old junk," he said looking stressed at the thought.

"No!" Jesse almost shouted, making Felcore, who had been lying quietly at her feet sit up in an attentive stance. Jesse patted him on the head to soothe him. "Please, Dad, there are some things in that trunk I would like saved. The clothes in there are beautiful and obviously expensive, probably antiques," she told him.

"Well . . . maybe," Bill said skeptically.

"Don't get rid of it without my permission . . . promise me," Jesse begged with urgency.

"Okay. Don't panic. I won't. You and Jacob can clean out the attic next weekend," Bill said smiling as Jesse groaned. He walked across the kitchen to give her a quick hug and Felcore a pat on the head before leaving the kitchen.

Jesse felt the need to get away, get some fresh air and exercise to clear her head. She decided to go to the park to do some hiking. She could bring along a picnic lunch and relax in the sun while she read the diary. After a shower, she dressed in the same clothes she had on earlier, pulled on her moccasins and headed out the door after packing a small lunch. The diary rested securely in the pocket of her jean jacket and Felcore galloped happily by her side. Jesse felt a sense of relief already, an attitude of freedom that made her feel good to be alive.

Before they reached the car, Felcore spotted a rabbit grazing on the violets in the garden and took off after it at full speed, chasing it across the vacant field next door. Jesse watched him go, marveling at his speed and magnificent beauty as he dashed through the tall grass after his prey. His head was held high and his tail stood straight up displaying flowing white feathers as he ran. Jesse called to him a couple times, but soon gave up, deciding he had found his own diversion for the day. She didn't mean to be disloyal to Felcore, but she did hope that the rabbit would get away.

She drove to a secluded area of the nearby park where she used to go with her mom. She hiked through the trails the rest of the morning before returning to the car for lunch. Taking a red plaid blanket out of the trunk, Jesse spread it on the ground and began eating her turkey sandwich hungrily, quenching her thirst with tepid water from her water bottle. Stretching out on her back in the warm afternoon sun, she soon drifted off to sleep . . .

. . . "Jesse . . . Jesse . . ."

Jesse could hear her name being called, but when she attempted to answer the words were whipped from her mouth by the strength of the wind in her face. She felt as if she was being suffocated in a dream. A realization gripped her with sudden terror that she was traveling at an extreme rate of speed through the air. She groped frantically about, trying to stop herself, but found nothing above her to gainsay her descent. Movement under her told Jesse that she was not falling at all. She clutched onto the leather straps she found in front of her and tried to breathe normally. Through watering eyes, Jesse's blurred vision revealed to her that she was flying just above tree-top level on what appeared to be a dragon. The saddle into which she was strapped was attached to a large shiny-scaled creature that had its massive wings spread and was descending rapidly toward a large stadium with a grass field. "Where are we going?" she wondered, now more curious as she got control over her fear.

A reply inside Jesse's head made her bite her tongue with surprise. "I am taking you home. I am afraid the prince has been wounded in battle. You must attend to him immediately."

Fear made Jesse's stomach turn and the fast descent was making her head spin. "Who are you? What are you? Where am I?" she asked.

"*Really, this is no time to play games. Maybe you are going into shock. Do try to relax. I am sure everything will be all right,*" said the voice in her head.

The dragon settled on the ground amidst a cloud of dust. Jesse coughed and closed her eyes tight until the dust settled down around them. She could hear the heavy breathing of the dragon as air rushed in and out of her monstrous nostrils. Between her thighs, Jesse could feel the vibration of the mighty animal's lungs expanding and contracting with each intake of breath. A heavy scent of musk lingered in the air around them, which Jesse found strangely comforting. She watched as two men approached on horseback, heavily clad in black and gold armor that jingled in musical tones in a haphazard melody. They were leading a splendid looking horse of the purest white that reminded Jesse of the Lipizzaner stallions she had seen perform as a child. One of the men spoke to her urgently, "*Please come quickly.*"

Jesse appraised them a moment before unbuckling the straps that secured her to the dragon. She swung her leg over and found a ladder waiting.

She mounted the white horse and was ushered by the two soldiers out of the field and toward the castle walls. The gate to the castle stood closed and surrounded by numerous soldiers who milled about killing time, awaiting orders. Jesse could feel the tension in the air as if it were a tangible physical presence. The soldiers watched her advance, bowing their heads in respectful acknowledgement as she rode by. When they arrived at the front door to the castle, Jesse was assisted off of her horse by the soldier who had spoken to her so briefly in the arena. The walkway to the front door was lined with flower gardens displaying a wide array of colors. The soldier escorted her to the front door, which he opened courteously for her. Jesse stepped into a large sunny room, open and airy with floor to ceiling windows and a polished oak winding staircase at the far end. The room was sparsely, but tastefully furnished, with bright bouquets of flowers displayed in *both porcelain and crystal vases. She looked curiously around, wondering what to do.*

A woman in a plain white dress ran to her after descending the stairs. She curtsied slightly and tried unsuccessfully to catch her breath before managing, "Please, you must come immediately. I'm afraid it doesn't look good. The wound is very deep and the prince has lost a lot of blood."

Without hesitation, the woman grabbed Jesse by the hand, pulled her toward the staircase and ascended it without further word or explanation. Jesse followed quietly. Three well lit hallways branched off from the top of the staircase. Jesse's moccasins swished quietly against the highly polished floors as she walked, following as the woman led her down the middle hall to the fifth room on the right where a set of double doors stood closed. The woman in the white dress smiled nervously as she opened wide the double doors for her to enter. She glanced at the woman briefly before invading the dimly lit room. The doors closed behind her and she felt instantly trapped. The sound of her heart thumped loudly in her ears as she beheld a magnificent bedroom decorated in burgundy and gold. Jesse crossed the sitting area that was furnished for comfort with a couch, two high back leather chairs, and a coffee table that was laden with books, writing utensils and stationery. A half-finished letter lay abandoned next to an old fashioned ink well and pen. She resisted the temptation to read it.

The only source of light in the room came from a raised platform that was set apart from the sitting area. A large poster bed sat upon the platform, draped with sheer gold draperies that were pulled back casually. As Jesse approached the bed she heard a man groaning weakly and pleading softly, calling her name, "Jesse . . . Jesse." She held her breath and continued to move toward him, placing one foot in front of the other, making as little noise as possible while blood pounded in her ears.

Again he called to her, "Jesse . . . "

Jesse hesitated, feeling anxiety, excitement and fear. Her mouth was dry and she licked her lips in an attempt to assuage her thirst. She didn't understand what was happening. How did the injured man know her? Why was there no one around tending to his needs?

Another groan from the man propelled Jesse forward until she stood beside the bed. The man who lay upon it was tossing and turning in his delirious condition. His eyes were closed, but his alluring lips mouthed words silently as he rolled his head from side to side. Tan skin glistened with perspiration as it stretched taunt over muscles that convulsed with exertion as he fought against some unknown foe. Tentatively, Jesse reached out her hand to touch his arm. Sighing, she pressed the back of her hand to the man's forehead and diagnosed a fever. She noticed the wound on his ribs was bleeding crimson stains through fresh white bandages and the white sheets underneath were blood stained as well. Why didn't they stitch it? She looked around, trying to find some extra gauze, and was about to go for help when the man reached up and grabbed her arm with his left hand as he opened his eyes. "Jesse, my love, you are finally here," he stated with raw emotion as he gazed up at her with bright gold eyes . . .

. . . Jesse was awakened harshly out of her dream with a painful slap across the face. She opened her eyes and was petrified to see Mat grinning sickly down at her. "Mat! . . . What are you doing . . .? Get your foot off me!"

She tried to sit up, but was being held forcefully against the ground with Mat's tennis shoe planted squarely in the middle of her chest. Struggling to get away, Jesse pounded her fists against his leg. Unaffected, Mat increased the pressure on her chest until it seemed her heart would burst. "Let me go! I can't breathe!" Jesse cried, feeling panic erupt. She shoved ineffectively against him.

"You're not going to get away from me this time, honey," Mat sneered.

"Mat, you don't want to do this!" Jesse said as her fear escalated. The look in Mat's eyes was crazy. She knew he was anything but rational. Jesse choked back a scream that implored to be released and tried desperately to come up with a plan. How was she going to get out of this? She never should have come here alone. She had to get away from him . . . somehow. Her knife was in her boot, but she couldn't reach it. If she could just get out from under him, she would have a chance. "Let me go!" she said.

Mat snatched a hunting knife from behind his back and sat down on top of her, putting the blade to her throat while she thrashed underneath him. "Don't move or I'll kill you," he threatened as he began tearing one button at a time off her sweater, leisurely enjoying his torture. Jesse continued fighting against him with no success. He leaned over and kissed her roughly on the lips.

She screamed. He slapped her hard across the mouth and laughed, sickening Jesse with the pleasure he showed in hurting her. "Go ahead and scream. Nobody's going to hear you," he said.

"No! . . . Mat, stop! Why are you doing this to me? Oh God!" Jesse choked, feeling the knife cut into her throat with every word she uttered. Tears coursed down her temples and into her ears as she labored to get out from under his weight.

"Shut up!" His hand slammed across her face once again. Before she could get her breath his mouth came down hard upon her own savagely. The taste of blood was strong as she tried to catch her breath. She began to choke.

With a sob, she thought of Felcore and wished with all of her heart that he was with her. He would have protected her. She shouldn't have come here alone. Again she tried to twist from underneath the weight on top of her.

Mat grabbed Jesse's hair and pulled hard, careless of the knife that cut dangerously into her throat. "You should have been nice to me when you had the chance," he said. When he released her hair, Jesse screamed again, the sound reverberating off of the surrounding hills in a terrifying chorus of echoes.

Mat slapped her repeatedly until Jesse quit screaming. He began tearing at her clothes with his right hand, still holding the knife tightly against her neck with his left. Jesse was losing her strength, but still fought with all of her will, fed by the terror that enveloped her. Her throat seemed to burn where the metal of the knife touched her skin.

Mat froze suddenly and stared with wide eyes over her head.

A vicious snarl filled Jesse's ears. She cut off a sob that escaped her lips and tried again to push the boy off from her.

He back handed her hard across the face. The knife flashed in his hand as he brought it up and down again plunging toward her heart.

A blur of white crossed Jesse's vision and suddenly she could breathe again. With one mighty leap, Felcore had launched himself into the air and knocked Mat from her. She sat up and watched in horror.

One minute Felcore was on top and the next Mat. Over and over they rolled. The knife glimmered in Mat's hand as it reflected off the late afternoon sun. He plunged for the dog's stomach again and again and missed. Felcore tried to latch on to the wild boy's arm with his teeth. A desperate attempt by Mat brought the knife within a hair of Felcore's exposed stomach, but the boy lost his balance at the last second. Taking advantage of his opponent's awkward position, Felcore lunged, sinking his powerful jaws into Mat's throat until he lay motionless.

Jesse felt dizzy and nauseous as she slowly pulled herself up off the ground. Felcore trotted over to her with his tail wagging and pushed his cold wet nose into her neck. Leaning heavily on Felcore for support, Jesse walked over to where Mat's body lay and examined him for any sign of life. His knife lay harmlessly in the grass. Jesse examined her dog closely and was relieved to find no serious cuts. With Felcore's help, she managed to make it to her car and retrieve the first aid kit from the trunk. After administering to Felcore's cuts, she sat in the driver's seat and applied a bandage to the cut on her neck, touching with her finger tips tenderly the bruises that were already forming as swollen red welts on her face. Glancing back at Mat's body where it lay sprawled upon the ground, Jesse felt hysteria rise and her stomach twist tightly.

"Oh my God! What am I going to do?" Jesse cried in a heaving voice. "Oh my God! He's dead. Felcore killed Mat. Mat is dead . . . I have to call the police." She reached for her cell phone, but just held on to it. Jesse's emotions all worked against her to cause more hysteria. "Felcore killed Mat. They'll take him from me. They'll put him to sleep. Mat's parents won't let you live. No . . . No . . . No . . . " Jesse held Felcore close and cried frantically into his fur until she was gasping for breath.

The sun was starting to sink lower in the sky, elongating shadows in the park. The warm summer evening held no comfort for Jesse. She glanced again at Mat's still form and wiped her tears. "I won't let them have you, Felcore. This was all his fault. Oh God! We'll have to leave; run away." Jesse looked down at the diary that was sticking out of the pocket of her jean jacket and said to Felcore, "I think I know where to go."

She drove back home and was pulling into the driveway as dusk was settling over their quiet suburban neighborhood. Expertly avoiding her father and Jacob, Jesse snuck into the house and packed clothes, food and cooking essentials into her backpack along with Felcore's food dish and her MP-3 player.

Intentionally, she left her cell phone on her dresser. She desperately wanted to take a bath, but that wasn't possible. She had to get out of the house without being seen. From the camping gear which was stored in the garage she took the small tent, a sleeping bag, the oil lantern and an extra canteen of water. Luck had it that a full forty pound bag of dog food had been recently purchased and sat just inside the garage door. She packed all of these items into the trunk of her car and got into the driver's seat next to Felcore. Looking at the house, she thought of the warm loving home she was leaving. She reconsidered. Tears brimmed in her eyes as she thought of Mat lying on the ground, dead, cold and alone. Hysteria threatened to take over. With her body shaking and teeth chattering, Jesse started the car and headed down the road toward the highway.

After driving for several miles on a mostly deserted highway, Jesse spotted a small motel and pulled over for the night. She was physically and emotionally exhausted. Although the desk clerk looked at her strangely, the woman was too busy on her cell phone to take any action to try and help the beat up girl who stood in front of her. Jesse was given a key to Room 114 and was soon settled into a hot bath. The heat felt good on her bruised and sore muscles and she scrubbed off the grime and dried blood that clung to her skin. Her face and various parts of her body were extremely tender to the touch, so Jesse took extra care in gently cleaning the injuries. Several times during her bath Jesse broke down crying, grieving for the cruel boy that was now dead and grieving for the life she felt forced to leave behind.

Felcore wouldn't leave her alone, staying alert and attentive in a highly protective manner. Jesse couldn't relax either. She was still shaking when she dried herself off and sank into bed. She decided to read for a while to take her mind off from the events of the day. Taking Gabriel's diary from her jacket, Jesse lay back on her pillow, wiped away her tears and opened it to the red ribbon.

Chapter 7

MIDNIGHT MEETING

B.F. descended rapidly, making my stomach feel as if it was going downhill on a rollercoaster. As we approached tree top level, a clearing came into view. Kristina asked me what was going on and all I could do was shrug my shoulders, not knowing myself what to expect.

The forest around the clearing was thick with tall dark trees, giving the feeling of ancient stoicism. The history of the forest was well hidden beneath layers of deteriorating leaves that had long ago fallen from their days of glory in the breeze to stillness on the ground. A new crop of leaves whispered their secrets to any who might listen with some urging by the wind, at times gentle and other times fierce. The clearing was perfectly round. Short cropped grass covered the area, glowing softly iridescent in the moonlight. A pleasant earthy scent was present in the air, not strong but subtle in its intensity.

FREECURRENT

B.F. landed in the center of the clearing, settling lightly on the ground without so much as a bump. Immediately, a figure came forward through the woods cautiously, with slow fluid movements and stopped just within the shadows, waiting and watching. The hood of the individual's cloak was pulled down low hiding the face within.

"B.F., what is this all about?" I pleaded silently with him to tell me something about what we were getting into.

"I do not know, Gabriel. I only know it is necessary that we be here. I guess we will find out soon enough." As he spoke, the person in the long dark cloak emerged from the shadows and walked gracefully forward with a dagger clasped tightly in hand.

A woman's voice, bold and harmonious, spoke to us in a demanding tone, "I recognize this dragon as Balls of Fire, the prince's companion. State your business."

I answered, trying to keep the apprehension out of my voice. "I am Gabriel Thomas. This is Princess Kristina Wingmaster, the prince's sister, and you obviously already know Balls of Fire. We are on our way to the Tower of Ornate. Who are you?"

The woman looked distressed as she sheathed the dagger inside her tall black boot. Under her cloak, I could see she was dressed in riding clothes similar to what Kristina and I wore, only black. We dismounted B.F. and approached her, my question still hanging unanswered in the air. Reaching up, she pulled back the hood of her cloak, revealing long shiny red hair. Her gold eyes flashed in the moonlight as she introduced herself with an unusual, almost musical lilt to her voice. "I am Jessabelle. Your company is well met. Theo has sung your praises to me, Kristina."

Before I could reply, Kristina stepped forward and slapped Jessabelle soundly across the face. "You broke Theo's heart. I don't know how you can stand to live with yourself, you . . .

you kendrite whore." The ugly words were spit out of Kristina's mouth distastefully like sour milk.

After overcoming my shock at Kristina's behavior, I tried to intervene, knowing how Theo felt about Jessabelle. He had confessed his love for her to me and I knew that Kristina was out of line. I said, "Please, Kristina, I am sure Jessabelle never intended to hurt Theo. Why don't we let her explain?"

"I won't listen to anything that beast has to say," Kristina declared, lifting her chin in defiance as she stubbornly turned on her heel and stomped away, walking to the far side of B.F., who observed the whole incident without comment.

Jessabelle and I both watched Kristina storm away and then looked at one another in dismay. Jessabelle sighed heavily and said, "How the girl feels, I guess I can understand. But my intentions toward Theo were never harmful. That man I love wholly and completely."

She went on, "A fine day such as today it was the day we met. Theo was riding Balls of Fire and I was gliding through the sky in eagle form. Theo spotted me and came in for a closer peek. He told me later he had never seen a bird such as me, with a head and tail feathered white. Indeed there is no other such as me when I fly." Jessabelle's eyes sparkled brilliantly as she spoke and she smiled in remembrance.

Gabriel wondered what it would be like to fly, not like they did on B.F., strapped into a saddle, but to soar free. "Where I come from you would have been called a bald eagle. The bald eagle is an honored symbol in my country. Of all the birds it is the most honored."

Jessabelle grinned crookedly and said, "Your country's choice in birds, I respect, but the word 'bald'?" She touched her lush hair in demonstration, amusement flashing in her eyes.

I laughed, feeling very comfortable with Jessabelle and enjoying her good nature.

She continued her story as I leaned casually against B.F.'s side. "Not long did it take us to find love. We became instant friends and soon found that we couldn't bear to be apart. Happiness was ours for the taking. Only a formality, marriage would be. Bound we were already . . . mind, body and soul."

Suddenly Jessabelle's gold eyes sparked angrily. "My father, King Shane, ended it. He refused to listen to my pleas, calling Theo foul names . . . and all because the man I love is a human. It would have mattered little enough to me what my father thought and I told Shane that he had seen the last of me, that I was going to marry Theo Wingmaster with or without his consent. When I turned to leave my father's chambers in Colordale that evening, Shane laid down his threat, spewing forth his venom to my back. He promised that if I defied his wishes, he would hunt Theo down and kill him. Challenge him I did, but he would not back down. My honor I was forced to sacrifice and also our love in order to keep my Theo safe. No business did that old fool have meddling in my affairs. I hope he chokes," Jessabelle said defiantly through her tears.

Kristina came slowly around from behind B.F., looking down and then back up at us again as if unsure of herself. She had tears rolling down her cheeks that she kept dabbing away with a silk handkerchief. When she got close enough, Kristina reached out and put her hand gently on Jessabelle's shoulder. After taking a deep breath, she said with a shaky voice, "I'm sorry Jessabelle. I didn't know. Please forgive me." Kristina handed Jessabelle the handkerchief as an offering of peace. Jessabelle took the hanky and gave Kristina a gentle hug before stepping back and drying her own tears.

B.F.'s deep voice commented to me silently, "*This is all very sweet, but just what is this girl doing out here in the middle of nowhere alone at night. It seems very odd, Gabriel . . . very odd indeed. I don't believe it was she who summoned me.*"

I replied silently to him, "*I think it is time we found out what is going on here.*"

"Jessabelle," I began while I studied her expression closely. "Can we give you a lift somewhere? I imagine that you must be tired and hungry, perhaps you could spend the night at the Tower of Ornate with us." She looked confused at my question and then looked up at the sky, analyzing the position of certain stars to ascertain the time. When she looked back at me, her eyes held mine, boring into my soul as she attempted to judge my character.

A beautiful smile crossed her face and she said, "Somehow I don't think that our meeting was the reason I was persuaded to be here tonight. 'There is more,' the wind whispers. Listen to the leaves. Can you hear it?"

Kristina and I both cocked our heads and listened intently to the soft breeze rippling through the leaves. Simultaneously we gave each other questioning glances before turning to Jessabelle.

Her smile broadened. "We are friends, newly met. I will take you into my confidence. The leaves whisper of magic in the air. Something is meant to happen here tonight. We could very well witness the beginning to the end of the darkness. About one week ago a wisp, a small, cheerful fellow named Rew, landed on the window sill outside of my bedroom in Colordale. After persuading me to let him in, he told me it was urgent that I be here by the high-night turn. A meeting was to take place and information to be revealed regarding a way to bring an end to the present day intolerance on Risen. Of course, with my father as deeply afflicted as he is, I figured that some positive action against the hatred might cause him to reconsider his position and permit my marriage to Theo. So, what I can do? I am here to find out. Perhaps you are meant to be here as well. Wait with me, will you?"

Kristina nodded her head affirmatively when I looked to her for an opinion. Turning to Jessabelle, I answered, "Yes, we will wait with you. B.F. said it was important that he land here. Perhaps this meeting is the reason for our detour."

The darkness in the clearing was cool and echoed of anticipation as the three of us waited with B.F. sleeping noisily nearby. Long before midnight, guests invited to this night's exclusive party began arriving individually and uniquely.

The forest around us hushed for a brief moment, hinting of an intruder. B.F. came fully awake and lifted his head, scenting the air with his massive nostrils. I watched alertly, knowing something was about to happen, observing B.F. intently for any sign of danger. Without any warning, the tone of wings vibrating the air sped past my right ear and then past my left ear, humming like a large winged insect in flight. I swept my gaze around, trying to catch a glimpse of the creature that was presently doing his own reconnaissance of my friends and me. B.F. seemed to particularly draw his attention. The dragon only mildly returned his curiosity with his eyelids halfway open in a lazy half-hearted examination of the tiny creature. Only a blur crossed my vision before the fleet person was standing before me with a semi-sweet, somewhat devilish grin on his face. The scant attire he wore consisted of a G-string pant that covered only his genitals and a pair of leather sandals.

He nodded to Jessabelle, acknowledging her with a brief wink, before letting his gaze rest first on Kristina and then on myself. The curly blond hair on the top of his head stirred softly in the breeze. He was quite humanoid in appearance, except he stood only about a foot and a half tall, had pointed ears with tufts of soft gold fur on the tips, and four beautiful iridescent wings growing out of the center of his back. His wings reminded me of those on the dragonflies I used to see frequently flying across Miller's pond where my husband and I used to fish when visiting John's parents back in Michigan. The cherub quality of the face before me contradicted the mischievous look in the bright blue eyes that gazed back into mine.

The cheerful highlight of his voice made me smile with delight. "My name is Rew. You must be Gabriel. Shareen told me you were coming to the meeting." He turned to Kristina and bowed at the waist, "Your Highness." Fluttering his four long wings, Rew lifted into the air, cruising with ease over to B.F., where he landed atop the dragon's nose ridge and started chatting excitedly.

Moments later I heard B.F.'s resonant voice state calmly, "Another has arrived."

Jessabelle peered into the woods and sniffed the air. "A banderg it is, travelling alone," she announced quietly.

"What is a banderg?" I asked curiously.

Kristina answered, "The banderg race is a hard-working people. They are robust in body and spirit. Their society is closely knit, which makes them an extremely loyal people to their family and friends. Naturally fun loving as well as hardworking, they love to drink ale, feast, sing songs and tell stories. Inherent miners, they dwell in the Skyview Range which is the natural barrier between Brightening and Saberville. These facts I know from my childhood teachings. I've never met one."

Everyone watched warily, waiting a few more minutes before the banderg appeared, striding in from the northeast. Short and stocky, standing about chest high to myself, the banderg wore a thick black beard that hung down to the middle of his round belly. His robe was made of an intricately woven fabric in patterns of blue and green, synched at the waist with a tooled leather belt. The soft leather boots he wore matched the bandana wrapped tightly around his head. A heavy pack was slung over his shoulder, bulging with curious lumps and bumps, but the banderg seemed oblivious to his burden. As he crossed the clearing and headed toward us, his dark blue eyes assessed each of us in turn. Shaggy black eyebrows that moved up and down in contemplation gave him a menacing, sinister appearance. Keeping the long dagger he carried casually in his right hand, he hailed us by proclaiming, "I am Linkjimbodanderfrymanherheart. I was told to be here and I am." He stood before us patiently and waited for a response.

While I made introductions, Rew flew up and down and all around the banderg in an extremely agitated and excited state. He pulled on the bandergs beard, touched his eyebrows, tugged on his sleeves, and lifted his robe to peer underneath, all in a less than a breath's time.

Linkjimbodanderfrymanherheart attempted to skewer the pesky little wisp with his dagger, trying unsuccessfully to rid himself of the annoyance.

If it weren't for the seriously deadly look in the banderg's eyes, I would have found the entire incident exceedingly amusing. Swallowing the laughter instead of giving in to it, I stepped closer and demanded, "Stop it, Mr. Linkjimbodand . . . stop it, you'll hurt him. Rew leave him alone!"

Rew took one more tug on Linkjimbodanderfrymanherheart's beard before flying over next to B.F., where he sat with his eyes glued on the banderg.

The banderg grumbled loudly and examined himself briefly to make sure everything was still where it should be. He sheathed his long dagger in the custom-made sheath attached to his pack.

Kristina commented, "I have never seen a wisp so excited before. I wonder what that was all about."

Linkjimbodanderfrymanherheart eyed her for a prolonged moment before responding. "He's probably never seen a banderg before. For generations we have kept to ourselves, not venturing far from Skyview."

"Yes . . . that must be it." Kristina looked over to where Rew was sitting and gave him a speculative glance.

"Say, is that your dragon over there?" Linkjimbodanderfrymanherheart asked Kristina. "You wouldn't happen to have any ale or food in those packs, would you? I sure could go for a mug of ale right now." The banderg tugged expectantly on his beard with a gleam in his eyes.

I answered him with a chuckle and a genuinely cordial smile. "Mr. Linkjimbo . . . Linkjimbo . . ."

He smiled back at me and said, "You can call me Link."

"Very well, Link. I think Kristina and I can dig up something to eat and drink. I'm pretty hungry myself, now that you mention it. Do you like dark ale or pale ale?"

"Any ale, as long as it is wet and brings warmth to my cheeks would be thankfully consumed, Gabriel. My thanks."

Kristina and I unpacked the extra food we had brought, which I expanded into enough for a feast with my limited skills. Ale was something I had some practice with and I managed to come up with a pretty good keg, a hardy red ale that was smooth and tasty. Judged by banderg standards, it was "suitable", according to Link.

Link started a bonfire in the center of the clearing which lit up the entire area, making the surrounding woods seem suddenly very dark and forbidding. We ate and drank, gathered around the cozy fire while Link regaled us with tales about his people, his home and his wife and daughter, Berry and Fibilinkberrymyheart.

"A banderg's name," he explained to us, "identifies lineage, marital status, and occupation. My name for instance begins with 'Link', which is my parental given name. 'Jimbo' was my father's parental given name. 'Dander' was my mother's parental given name. 'Fryman' indicates my occupation."

"Which is cook," Kristina interrupted with a supercilious smile.

"Yes," he answered, while I refilled his mug with ale. "Actually, I'm chief fryman in all of Skyview. Which means I have to coordinate meals, order supplies, inventory the stock and meet once a week with the council to go over everything with them . . . and, 'OHH!', the paperwork involved. I am going to be so far behind when I get back." Link started tugging at his beard aggressively. "My apprentice has only been training under me for ten years. I sure hope he doesn't mess everything up."

I attempted to assuage his worry by being supportive, "Ten years is a very long time. Surely your assistant will manage. I'm sure your years of tutoring have made him a very competent fryman."

Link grunted loudly, drank a long pull from his mug, and looked at me with his eyebrows twitching nervously. He said, "I hope you are right. He is only a mere fifty years old, still awfully young to be taking on that kind of responsibility . . . anyway, where was I? Oh, yes, my name, the last part 'herheart' means that my heart belongs to my mate, Berry. You'll notice my daughter's name Fibilinkberrymyheart doesn't yet indicate an occupation because she is only about twenty-five, still enjoying her childhood and 'myheart' identifies her as not yet mated." He grumbled unintelligibly to himself, before saying defensively, "She is just not ready for boys yet. She is far too young, no matter what Berry thinks."

I thought it funny that he seemed just like a typical American father, protective, jealous and irrational when it comes to fathers dealing with their daughters' interest in boys.

Loud crashing sounds moving through the woods brought all of our attention to the western edge of the clearing. B.F. was oblivious and was at the moment engaged in snoring loudly. The air around the clearing seemed to intensify while we watched with sharp apprehension as something big approached. The trees parted as if of their own volition, making way for the advancing monster. The wind stilled. Appearing was an awesome creature, breaking tree branches and trampling saplings as he guided the animal he was astride into the clearing.

The massive horse-like animal had long shaggy gray hair dangling from its broad shoulders, running the length of its back to the huge hind quarters where it melded into black down through the tail. More than twice the size of a Clydesdale, it lifted its substantial head and sniffed the air, indecisive as to whether or not it should approach. It came forward with some gentle urging by its rider, a mountain in the guise of a living breathing being who nudged the mount with his knees.

He dismounted, jarring the ground and waking up B.F. in the process, who mumbled something about torgs being inconsiderate to sleeping dragons. The torg strode slowly up to the group gathered around the fire with wary green eyes darting back and forth, taking note of everything. His twelve foot tall frame was richly endowed with rock hard muscles that bulged in his legs and arms when he sat his bulk cross-legged on the ground. Rusty red locks hung down to his shoulders in an unruly manner. I noticed my friends watched the torg with great interest.

"Bring me ale!" he ordered nobody in particular with a deep demanding voice. We all stared at him for a moment and then looked at each other waiting for someone to get up and comply with the hulk's request.

"Bring me ale!" he demanded again.

Kristina and I were both on our feet at the same instant and we headed to the keg together while I grabbed an empty mug. Whispering softly, I asked Kristina her opinion about our newest arrival. "Do you think he's at all dangerous?"

Kristina began filling the mug with the rich brown ale and leaned over close and whispered, "Torgs are mainly peaceful creatures when they are not provoked, or so I have heard. I have never met one before."

"Don't you ever get out of the house?" I asked, nudging her teasingly.

She smiled and gave me a wink and said, "Let's find out what we can about him." Kristina turned and headed back toward the fire with the full mug of ale slopping over the rim and onto her hands as she tried to steady it.

She approached the torg with a casual arrogance while his green eyes observed her every move. He accepted the mug from her and took a long hard pull on the cold brew. The smooth tan skin that stretched across his bulging muscles glistened in the firelight and a hint of a smile stole across his lips. "Thank you," he said deep in his throat in what could almost be called a growl as he lifted the mug once again to his mouth and drank deeply of the rich liquid.

He observed Kristina as she stood before him, just out of arms reach and began making introductions, "My name is Kristina Wingmaster. This is Gabriel, Jessabelle, Rew, Link and the dragon is B.F." She glanced at each of us in turn and then back at the torg.

When he finally spoke it was in a low, sad voice that almost persuaded me to tears. The torg looked at each one of us individually with his penetrating eyes and told his story. He began, "I am known as Kaltog Vengar by my people who dwell in the Farreach Mountains on the western coast of this continent. For many generations we have dwelled there, hunting, fishing and growing crops in peace. Having no neighbors of any other race nearby for hundreds of miles, we have prospered and enjoyed our solitude. Recently, however, things have changed. A group of humans on horseback arrived in our land and began demanding goods and services from my people. They ordered that we pay homage to their leader, Candaz, in return for his 'protection'. Of course, we refused their demands and told them we had no need of 'protection', but if they wanted to trade with us on an equal basis, we would be honored by their new friendship."

Kaltog bowed his head for a moment and then shook it slowly back and forth. Draining his mug, he sat it beside him on the ground and began to speak again, "They laughed in our faces and threatened to take everything from us if we did not willingly do their bidding. My people are not a violent race, but neither are we blades of grass. Our leader, Rocnor, my father, told them to leave immediately and never return or we would show them what an angry torg could do to a human's tiny body. That is when they used their evil magic against us. They began to chant, casting some type of spell. The air grew thick and I could not breathe, my stomach twisted violently and my head felt swollen, as if ready to explode and buzzed like a beehive. One of the men told me to stand on one foot and I did. Although I fought hard against doing as he said, my body was under his complete control. They enslaved all of my people in this manner and they remain to this day puppets of Candaz and his men." He mocked the name with hatred sharpening the edge.

"Last week as I worked in the field clearing rocks and trees, a cold gust of wind slapped me hard in the face and I was myself once again. It was like waking from a terrible nightmare. My head cleared and my body was once again my own to control. Anger boiled in my soul. I wanted to go after and capture the humans who had done this to my people and grind them slowly into the ground. Freedom cried to be won for my people. Insanely, I ran to the few who were working with me in the field and tried to get through to them. I screamed, I stomped, I shouted, I even slapped their faces, but they did not wake up, only continued to work on as if they didn't even know I existed. Desperately, I began to run in the direction of the village, hoping to find this Candaz skunk and squish him under my thumb like a bug, when the one you call Rew appeared before me. He told me that if I wanted to help my people I would need to show up here at this meeting tonight. It took a lot of convincing on his part, but I am here." He looked about him at our serious faces and smiled wanly, picked up his mug, and said to Kristina, "Bring me ale."

After everybody's mugs were refilled we all sat around the fire and quietly deliberated about why were we there. It was nearing midnight and the full moon was a bright white ball in the sky almost straight above us. The second larger moon was showing a sliver of soft white light just over the horizon to the east. The breeze that whispered through the leaves was cool, but not cold enough to cause a chill. Link had added more wood to the fire and the flames hungrily licked the new fuel causing a warm glow all around. I looked to where B.F. lay just at the edge of the clearing and noticed he was snoring loudly and rhythmically once again, occasionally using his hind leg to brush away a pesky insect.

The feeling that we were being watched had been with me all night and I began to scan the shadows for glowing eyes or any other sign of life. When I spotted two eyes shining in the distance, I blinked and rubbed my eyes, not quite believing what I was seeing. Looking again, I spotted the eyes looking back at me and then movement as whoever those eyes belonged to began coming toward us. "Jessabelle," I whispered. I leaned close to her, but kept my eyes upon the stranger who advanced through the woods. "There is someone coming . . . look." I gestured toward the movement in the trees.

Jessabelle put a comforting hand on my shoulder. "He has been there all night watching us. In fact, he was there before you and Kristina arrived. He is male, human. I can tell from his scent." She inhaled deeply. "Wounded he is and bleeding."

I stared at her in wonder and asked, "How can you tell all of that with just your nose? I can't even smell you and you are sitting right next to me. I can, however, smell Kristina's perfume from across the clearing."

Jessabelle smiled at me and laughed. She said, "Kendrite I am. My gift to transform into a wolf or an eagle or a dolphin that swims the ocean allows me enhanced abilities in human form as well. Personally I prefer being a wolf. My instincts are more in tune to that of a wolf. Eagles are much too serious and dolphins are much too playful, although I truly enjoy the freedoms both forms offer. Anyway, wolves have a very sensitive sense of smell and I retain a measure of that aptitude, as well as others, when I am in my human form." Her gold eyes sparkled with enthusiasm as she spoke about her race. I thought she was marvelous.

A man walked into the firelight with his hand resting on the hilt of his sword. Dark hair that grew long down his back was gathered in a pony-tail at his neck. He had dark, almost black eyes and a strong handsome face with highly defined cheek bones. Standing over six feet tall, he was dressed in dark dusty trousers, a voluminous shirt that had once been white, a long black coat and black leather boots that went to the top of his knees. Two daggers were sticking out from sheaths in his boots, one on both sides, and a long sword hung visibly through his coat on which he rested his hand.

Suspicion filled his eyes even though he walked confidently forward. "I am Serek." His demeanor indicated that he expected a reaction from the mention of his name. He seemed somewhat disappointed when no reaction was forthcoming. "I come to you as a traitor to my own people, the Sabers. Seeing what I have seen has turned me away from my master . . . ex-master, Candaz." 'Candaz' came out of his mouth in a hiss of disgust. His voice took on a challenging note as he glared at each of us in turn. "I was told to be here tonight if I wanted the opportunity to thwart his cause and right some of the wrongs I have done in his name." Serek stood rigidly before us awaiting an argument or an assault.

I didn't know what to make of this man, Serek. He seemed confused and hostile. I didn't trust him. The thought occurred to me that instead of being a traitor, he could have been sent by Candaz as a spy. Of course, it wouldn't be fair to Serek not to take his story at face value, at least until it was otherwise refuted. In any case, he would certainly need to be watched very closely.

I walked up to Serek and asked, "Would you like something to drink? We have some cold ale available, or maybe you would like something to eat?"

My hospitality seemed to take him by surprise. "Yes . . . I . . . Serek swayed and then slumped to his knees as if his body weight had suddenly become too heavy to bear. For the first time I noticed the pain chiseled into his expression as he grabbed his sword arm just above the elbow. Blood ran down through his fingertips and dripped on the ground below forming a small dark puddle.

Before I could react, Kristina was beside him. She said nothing but gazed into his eyes for a moment before turning her attention to his arm. She examined the damage closely and sent me to get bandages from B.F.'s packs. When I returned with the supplies, she had cleaned and dressed the wound as well as any professional doctor could. Serek and Kristina responded to each other immediately. There was striking electricity between them and they seemed to recognize it as well. A serious warning would be necessary as soon as I could talk to Kristina alone. I just hoped that her being attracted to Serek would not cause her to become blind or careless, but I had seen it happen too many times before to be reassured. This attraction was going to be a problem.

After we brought Serek some food and ale, we all settled down to wait for the unknown to happen. Time seemed to cease as midnight drew near. I felt strangely intense and my awareness heightened considerably. Kristina, Jessabelle, and I spoke quietly amongst ourselves, as did Link and Kaltog. Rew sat next to B.F., who appeared to be asleep, and Serek sat alone staring into the fire with a woebegone expression on his face.

Sorceress Possessed

A strange feeling suddenly washed over me, making me feel disjoined from my body. I heard a voice inside my head that was not B.F.'s say, *"Gabriel, do not fear. Let me in. I need to speak through you. I won't hurt you."* I could feel the essence of the woman known as Shareen. My skin felt wrinkled with age, my body tired, the joints in my hands felt like they were made of rusted metal and my legs screamed with a constant aching throb. I doubled over and gasped for a breath of air and my face contorted with the pain.

"Help," I tried to scream, but the sound only came out a garbled groan. Kristina and Jessabelle gaped at me and reached out to help, but did not know what to do. As suddenly as the pain began it stopped and I felt my body stand up and walk to the center of the circle. My consciousness remained subdued, observant and serene.

I watched the expressions on the faces of those who observed with curiosity. Kristina and Jessabelle both looked concerned and whispered to each other in earnest. Link tugged on his beard fiercely as he watched my body take its position. Kaltog and Serek both wore puzzled faces, while Rew watched with enthusiasm. B.F. continued to sleep. Those gathered watched and listened with interest as Shareen's voice, my own, only slightly accented, addressed the group, "Thank you all for coming tonight. I know that many of you have travelled far and through many dangers to be here at my request. Yes, it was I who invited you all here tonight. I am Shareen, Sorceress of Brightening. Do not be frightened. I could not be there personally tonight so I speak to you through my new apprentice, Gabriel. Please do not be alarmed, Kristina . . . everyone. Gabriel is quite safe. It is necessary for you to hear me out. What I have to say could very well have a far reaching influence on the future of Risen. My time is short, so please do not interrupt.

"I have studied long and hard the manuscripts left by our forefathers and ancient scrolls containing the histories of people now long dead trying to find ways to help our current situation. Secrets have been revealed to me that I dare not speak aloud. The time has come, however, when one such secret must be revealed. I place the burden of keeping this secret upon all of you here tonight. DO NOT BETRAY ME! About one year ago I began reading a scroll written in the Second Rotation, an accounting of trade goods and such. I came across some text written in the old language, which translates as follows:

Break the chains that bind us all with hate,
Swords are drawn in war; blood spilled, souls released,
In an endless play for power.
A table in round renders all races equal.
The end of intolerance is at hand.

"The passage haunted me day and night. I only found one more reference to this passage, a footnote that mentioned another scroll that was much older from which the passage had been copied. A quest was undertaken by some very courageous individuals to find the scroll and return it to me. It was discovered that the scroll lay in the possession of Candaz in his stronghold's library. Two men risked their lives in order to bring me the scroll which did, indeed, contain vital information that I will share with you now.

"Not long after our forefathers came to Risen and had built settlements and begun working the land, all the races came together in the city of New Chance and constructed a table made with loving care and the finest craftsmanship and materials available. You see, they had fled a land where prejudice and hatred were the way of life and they wanted such folly eradicated from their own new homeland. Their intention was to have this table as a symbol of their solidarity and commitment to work together for the good of all. The high sorcerer at that time, whose name was Queu, obtained as a gift from the dragons the inner core for the table capable of magically eliminating hatred between the races. When the table was finished, the people celebrated the day with feasting, song and dance. A dedication ceremony took place with a high born representative of each race present. Queu placed the magical core, which looked like a large crystal sphere, in the center of the table and everybody gathered around the table's perimeter. The core began to shine bright colors as the souls of the people emanated their good will. The illuminated core sank down into the center of the white marble surface to remain there, forever promoting peace and friendship among the nations of those races who stood before it.

"The table remains intact to this day within the public library building in the ruins of the ancient city of New Chance. Evidence shows that the table has been corrupted, probably by Mercin himself, and is now controlled by the forces of corruption. The core is rotting away from the inside in the same manner that our present society is rotting away with hatred and bigotry. However, it is my belief that the corruption can be lifted from the table and the core replaced which in turn will return peace between our races and further us in our goal to defeat Candaz and his corrupt forces.

"Princess Jessabelle the White; Prince Rew of the Wisps; Kaltog Venger, heir to the throne of Farreach Mountains; Linkjimbodanderfrymanherheart, High Councilman of Skyview; Prince Serek Landtamer; and Princess Kristina Wingmaster--it is you I have chosen for this quest. Together you must go to the ruins of New Chance and find the library where the table was once housed. Once the table is located, you must put all hatred aside, assemble around it. Purge your souls of all darkness and let goodness prevail. Recite the words as your forefathers did. The corrupted core must be destroyed and replaced. Your task will not be easy. Your journey is long and once you arrive at your destination, finding the table could prove difficult in the rubble that once was the magnificent city of New Chance. I wish you luck and I will be with you in spirit."

A wind brought about by the wings of a dragon wafted in their faces and before them stood a magnificent beast. He was silver in color and he held his head high and proud. In the dragons mouth was a glass sphere. Gently he placed it on the ground before them and immediately took back to the sky, acknowledging his fellow, B.F. with a mighty trumpeting bellow.

The parties of the newly formed company whispered to each other in disbelief.

"The dragon mage, Skymaster, has set before you a new core forged by dragon fire from the dragon Temple of Neeg on the Island of Zedra. It is precious. Before I leave you there is more I wish to say. Kristina, I will notify your father that you will be away from home for an extended period of time. Do not concern yourself with him. Kaltog, Gabriel and I will be working on some way to free your people. I am sorry you cannot help, but you must go to New Chance with the others. Be strong and follow your hearts. As I have said before, all of our futures depend on your success. I must leave you now for I am weakening and must rest. Good luck to you all."

I felt a rush of energy leave my body just before I blacked out.

A Company of Strangers

Kristina and Jessabelle were leaning over me and Rew was hovering a foot above my face when I awakened with a start. Feeling like I had drunk a whole bottle of wine, I sat up and watched the world spin crazily. The cold compress that was pressed against my forehead felt good and I lay back down for a moment to stop the world from twirling so fast. I silently thanked whoever had placed it there. B.F.'s voice intruded on my suffering, *"Gabriel, are you all right?"*

"Yes, I think so."

"She had no right taking your body like that without asking you first. How undignified." B.F. roared mentally and out loud, causing me to wince. *"Maybe I should set fire to her tower. That would teach her a lesson or two."*

"Please, B.F., not so loud. Look, I'm fine." I sat up ignoring the spinning to show B.F. that I could. When the world seemed to stabilize, I got to my feet and walked over to the dying fire. I glanced around at the persons Shareen had named to go on the quest. Serek avoided my gaze by staring at his feet. Kaltog and Rew both met my eyes squarely with their own confident gazes.

Addressing them all at the same time, I asked the question that was on everyone's mind, "Who is going to accept this challenge? Who among you will go on the quest Shareen has assigned to you?"

Jessabelle answered first, her chin held honorably high and her eyes shining beautifully, "Go, I will. It is my obligation to act if I can do something to change things for the better. Our future depends on it."

Rew flew over to where Jessabelle stood and said in his spirited voice, "You can count me in."

"Me too," Link stood tall and proud. "I am, however, concerned about my apprentice. I sure hope he doesn't starve my people to death while I'm away, or forget to do the inventory or attend the committee meetings . . . Oh, dear." He moaned miserably as he sank back down onto the boulder and began pulling on his beard.

"Link, I'm sure everything will be fine," I tried to reassure him. "If you would like I can have a note delivered to your wife, Berry, asking her to keep an eye on things for you."

"Yes," he paused and drew his shaggy eyebrows together, "that might help . . . maybe. Thank you, I would appreciate it if you would do just that."

Kaltog groaned and we all looked in his direction as he lifted his head from where it had been cradled in his hands. "My people need me. How can I abandon them and leave them slaves of Candaz? How can I go off on a quest?" he asked as his bright green eyes filled with tears. He looked beseechingly in my direction.

"Kaltog, you heard what Shareen said, and I give you my word of honor that I will do everything possible to expedite winning the release of your people. I cannot make this decision for you, but you have my word that your people will be my first priority if you decide to go." I looked into his sad eyes, meaning every word I said.

"I never thought a human could be my friend . . . I was wrong. Thank you. I accept," Kaltog said and walked over to me in one massive stride and bent down to hug me close until I thought my ribs would be crushed. He then proceeded to pick up the core and place it gently in his leather pack.

"Serek?" I addressed him questioningly, observing that his head was bowed in thought.

When he looked up at me the inner turmoil was obvious in his eyes and on his face. He said, "What did she mean by calling me, "Prince Serek Landtamer?" I am not a prince, just an unrecognized servant of the 'corrupt sorcerer' . . . I mean I was . . . Anyway, now I'm just a traitor, a nobody. Does she really think we can put an end to a spell that was cast by the master himself? It's preposterous!" He snickered cynically, causing a chill to run down the base of my spine. "Surely, we will all be killed . . . "

Kristina interrupted, glaring at Serek with anger. She declared, "I will go. Anything that has to be done to defeat Candaz must be done, even if it means losing my life." The fire in her eyes challenged Serek to show some valor.

Serek scowled at Kristina, although his eyes shown with fire tantamount to her own. "It seems to me this quest is doomed. However, I will accompany you."

The sun was just peaking over the horizon when we said our goodbyes. I wished them all the best of luck, but my heart felt heavy as we parted. Intuition told me there would be tough times ahead for their little company. As they started out on foot toward the east, I climbed up to my saddle on B.F.'s back. I watched them go for a moment, quietly wishing them all well. A sudden breeze rustled the leaves of the forest, but whether the words whispered were of hope or despair I could not discern.

Candaz's Rise

Five years had passed for Candaz since the death of his beloved Molly. He was twenty-five. He had not gone back to Castle Xandia as his father Ban would have wanted. Instead he ventured out on his own to discover what fate belonged to him and him alone. He had power; great abilities to wield freecurrent magic and a gifted tongue that gave him the power of persuasion. A lust for authority was born as he won the trust of men and his charm kept them enthralled and following him blindly. Those who did defy him paid a high price as it gave him an opportunity to exercise his cruelty. His hate allowed the wounds of his past to inflame the anger and bitterness that motivated him. Spending his days perfecting his skills as a sorcerer and his nights in pleasures to ease his demented mind, he was beginning to clarify in his thinking the path in front of him.

With his small army Candaz rode north to lay siege to Castle Xandia. They arrived late at night and quickly massacred the unprepared guards. The slaughter continued as they strode boldly through the castle, engaging any who came to defend Ban's regime and dispatching anybody who simply got in their way. Candaz showed no mercy. He wanted to possess Castle Xandia and he was willing to wipe it clean in order to get it. Women and children he encountered were shown no more clemency than the men. As he marched through the hallway towards Ban's quarters, a woman he had once known got down on her knees and begged him to spare her young son's life. He killed her and her frightened child too without hesitation or compassion and cleaned his bloody blade on the skirts of her dress. Nothing was going to stop him from fulfilling his destiny.

Alone he approached his father's bedroom and opened the door. He was hit immediately with a surge of freecurrent energy. Ducking in avoidance, the majority of it glanced off his raised sword and refracted back into the room. He countered with his own sphere of electricity. The air sizzled with scattered voltage as he and his adoptive father battled back and forth with magic.

"Candaz," the old man called from where he crouched beside his bed.

"What is it Ban? You know you are finished," he said.

"Why are you doing this? You are my heir. There is no need for this," Ban said.

"I will not live under your control. Today is the day I inherit Saberville. Castle Xandia is mine. Your life is forfeited," Candaz said. From his fingertips emanated great currents of freecurrent energy, blazing the air between them.

The floor beneath Candaz's feet began to shake. He approached the old man who was focused on drawing runes on the floor and pointed his sword at his chest. "Stop," he said.

Ban did stop, but his fingers were on fire with energy and he grabbed Candaz's leg causing him to scream in pain as the burn ran up to his thigh. The sword was thrust automatically through the other man's heart and Ban's dying gasp echoed in Candaz's ears.

His father was dead and he was king. It was a victory that left him feeling hollow, alone and lonely. His lust for power was not satisfied. The pursuit of it would not cease. Candaz was far from over with his quest for domination. He had just begun.

Chapter 8

JUST A GIRL AND HER DOG

Waking the next morning, Jesse felt very stiff and sore as she climbed out of bed. The vision she saw when she looked in the bathroom mirror made her groan with despair and her spirits sink lower. The deformity of her face went from swollen, cut lips to ugly discolored welts on both cheeks, up to her eyes that were black, puffy, and red from spilled tears. The knife cut on her neck had stopped bleeding and looked like it would heal well, perhaps even without scarring. Once again Jesse felt the sick feeling in the pit of her stomach when she thought of what Mat had done to her and his subsequent death.

She took a hot shower that did little to ease her discomfort. Makeup did not even begin to hide the damage that Mat had wrought to her face. She decided to buy a wide pair of dark sunglasses and a hat at her first possible opportunity to try and

FREECURRENT

hide her bruises. She would also need a road map so she could plan her route and locate camping areas along the way.

Jesse fed Felcore after lovingly scratching his head and ears. She pealed and ate an orange for her own breakfast. Felcore finished eating and went to the door and wagged his tail, looking at Jesse, requesting to be let out. Taking his leash off of the dresser, Jesse clipped it on his collar and walked him out to the grassy area behind the motel. Feeling very lonely, she watched the traffic on the freeway pass by while she waited for Felcore to finish his business. "Good Boy." She praised him when he was finished, an old habit from when he was a puppy, before they headed back to the motel room so she could finish packing.

Jesse decided to call her father and explain her situation to him. She had left her cell phone on her dresser at home. Tracing a cell phone was easy business and she didn't want to be found. She missed her phone already though. Hesitantly, Jesse picked up the motel phone and dialed her home phone number along with a zero, asking the operator to make it collect. After her father agreed to accept the call, the operator put her through.

Shaking and trying hard not to cry, Jesse swallowed the lump in her throat. "Hi Dad. I'm afraid I've gotten myself into a mess."

"Where have you been all night? I've been worried sick. Why haven't you answered your cell? Get home immediately or do you want me to come and get you?" Bill said, his tone sounding angry and desperate.

"Look, Dad, it's not that easy. Something really terrible has happened."

"I don't care what has happened. Come home," he demanded.

"I'm sorry, Dad. Mat's . . . dead. Felcore killed him yesterday." Felcore's ears perked up and his tail began to wag when he heard his name. He walked over next to Jesse and nuzzled her

126

hand. As Jesse experienced the warm soft moistness of Felcore's nose against her skin and the innocent look in his gold eyes, her heart tightened. She felt the tears filling her eyes before they began to flow freely. "Felcore saved my life, Dad. Mat attacked me. He beat me up. He would have . . . well . . . I can't come home. They'll blame me for Mat's death. They'll take Felcore from me." Jesse suppressed the hysterics that threatened and wiped uncontrollable tears that streamed down her face with the back of her hand.

After a moment's silence her father's calm voice came back on the line, "Jesse, where is Mat? I've got to call the police and let them know what happened. You come home right now. I promise you we'll work this out. Do you hear me, Jess?"

"No, Dad, I can't. Please try to understand . . . I can't go through it . . . not now. I won't let them take Felcore away from me . . . ever! Do you remember where we used to go hiking? That's where he is. Call the police. Do whatever you have to do. I'm sorry, Dad . . . it's just too much to deal with right now. Please understand. I've got to go," she said.

"No, Jesse . . ." he said desperately.

"I love you, Dad," Jesse whispered and then hung up the phone, feeling as if her world had just ended.

Turning to Felcore for comfort, Jesse hugged and stroked her big dog while the tears rolled unheeded down her cheeks. Felcore sat patiently next to his mistress, letting her pour out all of the anguish, anger and frustration of the last twenty-four hours. She was so thankful to have such a faithful friend. Her resolve to keep Felcore safe, no matter what the cost, strengthened. A new force drove Jesse to move forward. The lead blanket that had been resting on Jesse's soul slowly lifted, freeing her to resume the struggle one step at a time away from the past and toward the future. Jesse dried the tears off her bruised and swollen face before heading to the car. Felcore loped easily at her side, ready to begin their journey.

Her first stop was the gas station on the corner to fill up the gas tank. She picked up a map of the United States, some provisions, a pair of big sunglasses that hid much of her face, and a black baseball cap that said "New Mexico" in bold gold lettering. When she checked out with all of her items, the elderly woman clerk scrutinized her. She rung up the items on the small digital cash register before asking Jesse if she needed help of some kind. The woman suggested that she could call the police if Jesse required assistance. Jesse declined her help, smiled politely, and left the convenience store feeling uncomfortable. In the back of her mind was the itching feeling that the clerk would call the police despite Jesse's objection. She got into the car and left, wanting nothing more than to put miles between herself and the New Mexico state line.

She drove only about six hours the first day, feeling somewhat tired by the physical and emotional ordeal she had been through. The miles slipped away without notice, the landscape only a blur. Following a mark on the map, a small triangle that indicated a campground, she pulled off the expressway until she found it. Finding a nice secluded site, Jesse set up her tent and went hiking in search of firewood so she could enjoy a hot meal before retiring for the evening. The campground was empty, save for one couple and their black lab who had set up on the opposite end of the camp from Jesse's site. They waved to her as she walked by and she returned the greeting with a friendly smile. Felcore and the black lab, both off their leashes, examined each other with interest, smelling and maneuvering around each other in the ritual doggy greeting until their respective masters called them apart. The campground appeared to be seldom used because fire wood was in abundant supply and Jesse soon had several bundles sitting next to the roughly stoned-in fire pit at her site.

Working with the kindling first, Jesse lit a small fire, adding larger pieces of wood to it until it was a good sized cooking fire. She took the small coffee pot out of her backpack, filled it with water from her canteen and sat it on a flat rock just inside the fire pit. Jesse opened a can of chili with the can opener she had brought and sat the can next to the coffee pot to heat. She complied to Felcore's insistent nudging by getting out his dog dish and filling it with dry brown morsels of dog food. He downed the entire bowl of food hungrily and washed it down with water, slurping noisily, before settling down next to her. The quiet of the park was relaxing and Jesse sat back and munched on an apple while she enjoyed the chirping of the birds and the rustling of the leaves as the breeze stirred them gently.

When the chili was hot she devoured it with an appetite that had been absent for some time, enjoying the smoky flavor the campfire added to the bland canned food. She felt fully satisfied after her third cup of hot coffee and lounged on a blanket in front of the warm fire. Felcore remained cuddled securely beside her. As the sun settled in hot colors of pink and orange in the western sky, her eyelids slowly began to drop and she fell into the world of dreams . . .

. . . *The cave walls were illuminated by flickering light from the campfire that burned near the center of the floor. Jesse knew immediately that it was the same cave from her grandmother's diary and the one she had visited with her mother as a little girl. Jesse couldn't discern how she knew this, she just did. Although she was completely aware, she felt somehow translucent. Remnants of food and utensils were scattered about as if someone's dinner preparation had been suddenly interrupted. Jesse glanced curiously about the cave, looking for that someone, but found no one. She walked cautiously up to the fire* and examined the evidence left on the ground, finding the food fresh and concluding that the fire itself couldn't be more than a half hour old. Again, Jesse glanced around the cave looking for someone. A shadow moved across the background where the gate entrance stood and Jesse moved quickly and quietly toward it, wishing all the while that Felcore was at her side and wondering where he was. "Hey! You there! Stop! I won't hurt you. Come on out and talk to me," Jesse persuaded the shadow as she continued her watchful exploration of the small cave.

"Squeeeeee!" A scream startled Jesse. She looked down to find that she had stepped on the tail of a very large rat who was struggling madly to get away from under foot.

"Eeehhhhhh!" Jesse screamed. She jumped off the rodent's tail, turned to make a beeline for the cave entrance, but was stopped short by what she saw. A woman sat next to the fire calmly cutting vegetables with a small knife and putting them into the pan next to her. She didn't seem to notice Jesse standing there at all and continued to work quietly and efficiently. Jesse took a step forward and then stopped again, looking more closely at the woman, who had long dark hair and clothes that were somehow oddly familiar. She took another step forward. The woman looked up, directly at Jesse, and a confused expression spread across her face. Jesse nearly stumbled, close to fainting, as she gazed into the face of a woman she had not seen in many years.

"Mom?" Jesse stared into the questioning eyes of her dead mother. She began to shiver uncontrollably at the site of Marguerite.

Standing up with a smile lighting her face, Marguerite greeted her daughter warmly, "Hi, Jesse. Dinner is almost ready. Are you hungry?"

Jesse choked down her sobs and moved forward to engulf her mother in her arms. Marguerite felt as fragile as a fine crystal wine glass and Jesse instinctively relaxed her hold slightly, afraid of breaking the frail body. She remembered the scent of her mother's perfume and drank in the aroma, savoring the memory of good feelings it brought with it.

After a short time Marguerite pushed Jesse gently away. Her eyes reflected sadness as she wiped her daughter's tears with cold finger tips. Turning from her daughter, Marguerite quietly resumed her cooking, as if the last minute was forgotten.

Jesse was more than a little confused and upset as she sat down beside her mother and watched her work. Marguerite looked as young as she had the year she had died, except thinner. In fact, the clothes she wore now, a blue cotton dress with white polka dots, was the same dress she had on that night . . . the night of the car accident . . . the night she had died. Jesse squeezed her eyes shut and then opened them again, thinking that maybe she was seeing an apparition, but the image remained clear. Jesse wondered if she was dreaming, but everything seemed so real. She could even feel the heat radiating from the fire upon her skin.

"Mom, why are you here?" Jesse asked her mother, who continued working, ignoring the question or having not heard it. "Mom, why don't you come home with me? We can leave right now and be home in a few days. Dad will be so happy to see you." Jesse reached out to take her mother's hand, but Marguerite pulled it away, out of reach.

"Jesse, I can't leave with you. This is my home now," Marguerite said, as she put the pan on the fire and began slowly stirring the contents. Almost as an afterthought she said, "You can stay here if you want."

Frustrated and confused, Jesse begged, "Mom, please come home. I know Dad wants to see you. Please . . ."

A rumbling growl brought Jesse's attention toward the cave entrance behind her. She felt her pulse race as she stared into the glowing eyes of a wolf. The wolf stood just inside the cave entrance in a statuesque pose, ready to pounce with its teeth bared in greedy anticipation. *Reacting instinctively, Jesse grabbed a burning brand from the fire and turned it toward the wolf, while she moved slowly toward where her mother sat. Marguerite seemed oblivious to their danger and continued stirring the contents of the pot diligently.*

Jesse reached down and grabbed her mother under the arm and propelled her backwards, moving slowly with the brand outstretched toward the wolf. The gate was behind them and it became her clear destination. Keeping her eyes on the wolf, Jesse grabbed her mother's cold hand. She turned and made a leap through the gate as she heard the wolf make its move behind them. Jesse's sigh of relief ended in panic when she saw that her mother hadn't come through the gate with her. The brand still burned hot in her hand but her mother was nowhere to be seen. Stomach muscles cramped in fear as Jesse thought of her mother being attacked by the wolf. She couldn't face losing her again.

Desperately, Jesse turned to go back through the gate when a hand was placed on her shoulder from behind. Swinging around, ready to fight whoever was holding her back from going to her mother, Jesse almost didn't recognize the face of her father staring down at her. "Dad?!"

"*Jesse, you have got to come home immediately,*" *Bill commanded with authority in his voice. His eyes were strangely vacant of emotion as he looked at her, making Jesse feel cold with fear.*

"*Dad, wait. Mom's in trouble. I have to go back. Come on, hurry,*" *Jesse pleaded as she pulled on her father's arm trying to get him to move toward the gate.*

Bill didn't move, but stood rock solid, holding Jesse firmly in place. "*Jesse, your mother is dead. Come home now. Jacob and I need you. We love you.*"

"NO!" *she screamed at him.* "*Mom is over there. I have got to help her. Let me go!*" *She yanked her arm from his grasp and ran* to the gate. "I'm sorry." Jesse could hear Bill behind her calling her name as she vaulted through to the other side.

"I'm sorry, dad," she called behind her again. The cave Jesse entered was dark, with no sign of life. Jesse held back a sob that was lodged in a big lump in her throat. When her eyes finally adjusted to the dark she could see that the cave was clean and empty. The entrance was in front of her and she could smell a strange scent brought softly in with the breeze. Curiously, it reminded her of her mother's perfume. Looking outside proved to Jesse what she most feared. She was lost . . . lost through the gate.

The sound of horses made Jesse duck back inside the cave entrance out of sight. She could hear voices shouting and the jangle of harnesses as they approached the cave entrance rapidly. Jesse looked around trying to find a place to hide. She felt suffocated in panic. Spinning this way and that, she could find nowhere to go. Backing against the stone wall, she heard someone dismount directly outside. A tall man entered the cave and looked around, squinting as his eyes adjusted to the dim light. Standing still and trying not to breathe or make a sound, Jesse watched quietly as the man made his way toward her.

"Jesse," he said, "there you are. I have been looking all over for you. You must come home immediately. You can ride with me." The man took her hand and led her to his horse.

She followed hesitantly and then pulled her hand away. "Wait! I'm not going anywhere." Jesse looked up into his face and asked, "Who are you?"

His sparkling golden eyes shone brightly as he laughed and answered with an amused tone. "Surely madam, if you don't recognize your husband or your prince, you recognize the man who shared your bed last night. Perhaps a kiss will refresh your memory. He leaned over and kissed her lips with such tenderness and passion that Jesse felt her heart melt . . .

. . . Jesse, her body still quivering with longing, was awakened suddenly when Felcore jumped up and growled, staring in the direction of the road. The sun was just breaking over the horizon washing away the dark blue of predawn with sleepy slowness. A morning chill lay across the ground, making Jesse shiver slightly and pull the blanket up around her neck. Ignoring the hungry ache that her dream had instilled, she looked in the direction that Felcore was facing and tried to penetrate the dimness with her vision, seeing nothing in the stillness. Felcore continued to growl deep in his throat and moved back and forth in agitation, but made no move to run after whatever it was he felt threatened them. Jesse looked harder, but still could not see anything. She called Felcore to her and petted him soothingly on the head, speaking quiet words of reassurance in order to get him to calm down. He lay down on the ground with a heavy sigh and placed his head upon his paws, watching the road attentively. Jesse turned her attention to starting a fire for cooking breakfast. She soon had a small blaze crackling and sat the kettle on a flat rock inside the fire ring to heat water for coffee.

After finishing two cups of coffee, Jesse packed her few possessions and tore down the tent she hadn't slept in, taking only a minute to fold it neatly and put it in the trunk. The campground's water source was near the bathrooms by the entrance to campground, so she decided to stop there on the way out and refill the canteens.

Jesse parked the car in front of the hand-pumped well and got immediately to work drawing water up from the ground. After filling both canteens, she filled Felcore's water dish and poured some dog food into a separate bowl. When he was finished eating, Jesse walked over to the outhouse. She let Felcore run free, his earlier caution forgotten as he zoomed from site to site, down the road and back again with his ears and tail held high, running with the simple pride of being a dog.

Eagerly, Jesse exited the outhouse and breathed in the fresh outdoor air, calling for Felcore to come. He was immediately at her side, breathing heavily with tongue lolling as he fell into easy stride next to his mistress. The path back to the pump was well traveled, the dirt below their feet ground to fine dust, making their footfalls soundless in the early morning stillness. Before they came in sight of the car, Felcore stopped dead in his tracks and growled with his lips curling up to expose shiny white fangs. Jesse's stomach dropped with fear as she proceeded cautiously. She placed her hand on Felcore's back to quiet him.

Her blue Skylark came into sight as they rounded a corner and so did the threat. A squad car sat with flashers blaring blue and red across the gravel road from where her car was parked. A policeman in a dark blue uniform was walking around Jesse's car inspecting it. Stopping in back, he jotted down the license plate number on a small pad of paper that he held in his hand. Jesse watched, concealed behind some brush along the path. The man returned to his squad car and talked into his police radio.

She thought desperately, trying to come up with a plan, thinking her limited options through. The policeman stepped out of his car and looked around. He spotted Jesse and Felcore almost immediately as Jesse tried to sink further into the shadows. He walked toward them and unsnapped his holster, preparing himself for any threat that might be forthcoming. Jesse hesitated. The sight of his gun forestalled her urge to run.

"Jessica Gates?" the man asked. She waited, not knowing what to do. When Jesse didn't answer him, he said in a strong and controlled voice, "Miss Gates, we have been looking for you. You will have to come with me."

Overwhelmed by anxiety, Jesse's only thought was she couldn't let this man take her. "No, I can't," she said and headed toward the car at a run, dodging at the last minute to stay out of the officer's reach.

Regardless, he managed to grab her by the shoulders and stop her. Jesse was quick to react and squirmed out of his grasp. She ran for her car, reaching the door in seconds and pulled it open.

The policeman shouted, "Stop! I can help you."

She stepped aside and yelled, "Come on, Felcore!" The golden retriever leaped inside the car and took the passenger seat. Jesse sprang in, locked the doors and started the engine. She whipped the transmission into drive and raced out of the campground raising dust into the air behind her.

Expecting pursuit, Jesse kept checking the rear view mirror for signs of the squad car behind her as she headed down the road. No one seemed to be following. She kept to the back roads and avoided the highway where she would surely be spotted. She would have to avoid campgrounds from then on.

Jesse drove all day until just before sundown. She succeeded in staying away from the police. Taking a two track she spotted outside of a small town, she located a secluded place to make camp for the night. Jesse didn't set up her tent, deciding to sleep in her car. After building a small blaze in a hole that she had dug in the dirt, she put water on to heat and opened up a can of chicken soup for dinner.

Stirring the fire with a long stick, Jesse thought about how close she had come to getting picked up that morning. It scared her. She knew that she had made the right decision in leaving home with Felcore and she didn't want to go back.

After feeding Felcore and eating her own dinner, Jesse cuddled into her sleeping bag with Felcore at her side, opened up Gabriel's diary and began to read.

Chapter 9
SORCERESS & SUCCESSOR

Candaz's Respite

Candaz rolled over in bed. The woman he had been with cringed away from his touch and anger instantly infused him. He pushed her roughly away and climbed out of bed. "Get out!" he said. She complied as quickly as she could, grabbing her things as she went. He paced the floor of his big bedroom at Castle Xandia feeling anxious and not knowing what to do about it. Being only twenty-eight, he had still not settled into his role as corrupt sorcerer, but his ambition to rule all of Risen was beginning to burn hot within him.

Tedium was setting in after three years. Ruling a land was dealing with one problem after another. He needed a break, a respite from the constant demands being put on him. Throwing his black cloak on over his clothes, he descended the stairs and went directly to the stables. He chose his favorite horse and headed east toward the northern forest.

Over the last few years since he had taken control of Saberville, Candaz was putting together a small laboratory on the outskirts of his land. It was a place that he could go to and experiment with potions and dabble in chemistry. He had many experiments going and wanted to check on them. It was about a day's ride and he enjoyed the solitude. Without the constant pressure from his staff he could actually think. Plans were in the works to build his army so they could invade Brightening. He had his top sorcerers working on recruiting men to fill his ranks. Once they were drafted they had to be trained. It all took time.

He was becoming increasingly restless. Brightening was just waiting for him to take over leadership from their pathetic king. Already he had sources in the area that would help further his cause. Skyview would have to fall first. The bandergs would be no match for his army. It was important that he find a way to ensnare a dragon. As of yet, he wasn't sure how to achieve that. He also had plans for the west coast of Risen, including something special for the great torg nation. As he thought of everything that needed to be done his anxiety built.

Tethering his horse, he removed the saddle and gave him some food. Walking a short distance to a door that was well hidden, he drew an intricate rune on the surface that glowed with freecurrent and unlocked the entrance to his laboratory. He took a moment before entering to examine the small apple tree just outside the entrance. It was growing beautifully and was healthy and strong. The buds on it would produce excellent fruit by the end of summer. Placing his hand upon the trunk, he checked to make sure the enchantment remained intact. It was still entrenched and in fact had become part of the life force of the tree. Good.

The small laboratory he entered was an underground tunnel that he had built himself. He had fused the walls with freecurrent making them sleek and smooth. A long work table ran down the center of the space which currently held only two barrels and a huge copper pot that he had left to simmer since his last visit. The walls were lined with shelves that had bottles of different types of concoctions and ingredients that he had spent a lifetime collecting. In the back of the laboratory was his desk where he kept important records and notes.

There were a couple of things he was working on that had great potential for being very useful. He walked to the back of the laboratory and rested his eyes on a glass jar that contained a small pile of shiny black stones. The stones had come from the vault at Castle Xandia. At first Candaz thought that they held some monetary value, but closer examination proved that they had a much greater value. He gathered together a ball of freecurrent energy, rolling it in his hands before opening the jar and placing the sizzling ball inside. Instantly the stones absorbed the energy. He reached inside and picked up one of the shiny pebbles between his fingers. Immediately he felt as if all of his energy, every ounce of his magic was sucked from him, absorbed by the stone. It was fascinating. Instead of returning the stone to the jar, he placed it into one of his pockets. The stone could prove to be very valuable indeed.

Turning to the small cage in the corner, Candaz checked on the mice he had left under an enslavement enchantment. He had set them to task moving beans from one end of the cage to the other and then back again to test the level of hold the enchantment had over the subject. The results were evident. There were four mice when he began the experiment. One of them had died with a bean clutched in its tiny paws. Three remained but they were weak from not eating or drinking as they remained on task, moving slowly, but determined to relocate the beans even to the death. Leaving them to their demise, he smiled with delight. The experiment was a success. The torgs would be under his control soon enough.

After taking a few moments to write down some notes, Candaz walked over to the copper pot. Taking a dropper full, he went to another cage, selected a mouse and put the dropper in its mouth, giving it a small portion of the stuff. At first the mouse seemed unaffected, but after a moment it convulsed and died. "Damn!" he swore. He had worked on the preparation of the mixture for months and it was worthless. After making some more notes, he disposed of the liquid and started afresh. Maybe this time he would get the mix right. Maybe.

Gabriel

May 11. It has been some time since I have written because Shareen has kept me hard at work day and night, meditating, practicing spells and studying mounds upon mounds of books and scrolls. My exhaustion has been complete and I have been fast asleep upon hitting my pillow every night. Shareen's own energy is unbelievable considering her physical condition. Even though crippled by arthritis and unable to walk unassisted, she works as hard as or harder than I do. I have gotten up early in the morning and found her still up and studying some ancient scroll or chart, sitting in the same place where I had left her the night before. She is a hard woman, unyielding in her convictions, and yet I find myself growing quite fond of her.

Tower of Ornate

After leaving the clearing in the forest, B.F. flew me to the Tower of Ornate. We arrived as the early morning mist was just beginning to dissipate off from the grassy plain. The white mist upon the golden expanse of long grass made me feel like I was still up in the clouds, even as we landed. Blue Lake sparkled like a jewel in the background while the Blue River snaked its way south from Blue Lake, a silver streak, as the calm water refracted the light of the sun. The tower stood alone on the western shore of the lake with the field of grass sweeping uninterrupted to the front entrance. It was a mystical place.

Expecting the tower to be a gray and dreary stone structure, I was delighted to see it was actually quite beautiful. Six stories high, it gave the deception of being built out of one solid cylinder of black marble. It reminded me of the rook in the black onyx chess set my husband had bought in Mexico several years ago. The shiny black surface reflected brightly the morning sun, the swaying grass and the sparkling blue lake with the efficiency of a mirror. A vine clung to the round surface, bright green contrasting against the dark black. The vine had blooms of delicate and aromatic purple flowers scattered along it, making a colorful and cheerful welcome to the sorceress' tower.

B.F. landed on the grass in front of Ornate. As I dismounted from the saddle, he told me that he would have to leave right away in order to answer a summons from Theo. I unstrapped my luggage, letting it fall unceremoniously to the ground and scratched B.F.'s itchy spots as requested. He wished me luck and I kissed him goodbye. I watched the grand looking dragon as he rose gracefully into the sky and flew away, feeling suddenly very tired and alone.

B.F.'s voice entered my head unexpectedly, *"Call any time you need me Mistress Gabriel."*

"Thank you, my friend. I will." I smiled in spite of myself.

I hefted my bags and walked slowly and awkwardly toward the double doors. I knocked five times and waited. Some time passed before a little old man with a bald head and a prominent paunch opened the door and demanded to know what I wanted. Explaining my situation to him seemed to do no good at all. I had to assume that he was hard of hearing because all the while I talked he just looked at me with a puzzled look in his eyes. "What do you want, woman?" he demanded to know again when I had finished.

A plump old woman came up behind him, took him by the arm and led him away. Looking back at me, she said, "I'll be right back, dear. You wait right here." She returned promptly, her large body bouncing gently as she walked toward me and her bright blue eyes gleamed good naturedly. "You must be Gabriel," she said, taking my hand in her own. "I'm very pleased to meet you, dear. My name is Nina and you have already met my husband, Hue. I'm afraid he's a little deaf. We have been taking care of Mistress Shareen for many years. Come on in. I'll show you around and introduce you to the Mistress."

The vestibule to the tower was stately, decorated in red and gold with tapestries covering the walls. Two high-back leather chairs sat in front of the black marble fire place with a plush white animal hide floor covering. Everything looked pristine. I had a suspicion that the room was seldom used.

Nina grabbed my bags and carried them as if they weighed nothing at all, leading me down a barren corridor and up a winding staircase to the second floor. The walls were bare, save for brass sconces that held tall wax candles. Going to the first room on the left, Nina opened a door that led to a small bedroom and dropped my bags on the floor in front of the bed. Furnished with only a bed, a dresser and a writing desk, the room was still quite crowded, leaving little room to walk. A door in the wall at the end of the bed led to the room's own private bathroom, complete with a roomy tub where one could sink down chin deep into bubbles, a wash basin with running water and an actual flush toilet. Everything was immaculately clean. "This is your room, dear. We'll unpack later."

Road to Knowledge

We left my room and Nina led me up another flight of stairs to the third floor. She knocked on the first door to the right and shouted, "Mistress Shareen, Mistress Gabriel is here." After waiting a minute and not hearing a reply Nina opened the door and stood back to let me in.

I hesitated a moment, feeling anticipation of my future and fear of the unknown, somehow knowing intuitively that once I walked through that door there would be no turning back. Taking a deep breath, I strode forward. The room I entered was a library with books stacked everywhere. Scrolls leaned against the walls in the corners and hung over the edges from cluttered shelves. In the center of the room was a large wooden table hidden under its burden of texts, some open, some closed. Seated behind the table was a small elderly woman who was busy studying a very large book. Her hair was silver, tied up on top of her head in a bun and held in place with a purple ribbon. As I took a step forward she said to me without looking up from her book, "Did you know that there are two thousand eighteen individual universes interconnected by the gate? Imagine the possibilities . . . the opportunities for gaining knowledge . . . Oh! How I would love to explore them."

She looked up at me, her bright gray intelligent eyes appraising me shrewdly before she said, "We have a lot of work to do, Gabriel, so let us not waste any time." Shareen raised her gnarled hand in the air and made a slight motion toward the bookshelf to her right where a book immediately dislodged itself from the bottom of a pile and flew through the air and into my hands. I grabbed it, feeling the rough leather binding with a sense of disbelief.

"You will start by studying the histories of past masters. It is necessary to build a foundation on which you can base your power and knowledge builds the sturdiest foundation of all. Learn as much as you can, Gabriel. Study hard. Do not worry too much about function and fanfare." She waived her hands in the air dramatically. "That will come later when you are ready. We do not have as much time as we need, but Gabriel we are going to do this right. I will not have you going out into this world with only mediocre skills. You will be a master or you will not be a sorceress. Now to work . . . to work." She immediately went back to her reading indicating the end of our conversation.

I looked around and found a chair in the corner piled with books. After freeing it of the same, I sat down at the table, cleared myself a spot, and began reading history. Although I didn't realize it then, that room was to become as familiar to me as the sound of my mother's voice.

The next few days were filled by the study of Risen history. Books, upon books, containing everything from the first landing to events as recent as the Battle of Fire, a battle in which Theo and a handful of warriors repelled 10,000 enemy invaders by riding their dragons and using dragon's fire against them; an unprecedented use of dragons in warfare.

Shareen continued to study the same manuscript that she had been reading the first day I had met her. My curiosity finally got the best of me and I asked her about it.

"Hmmmm." A smile stretched across her pale wrinkled face before she answered, "This book was given to me by the dragon high mage Skymaster after I saved his life by removing a very poisonous thorn from his . . . his . . . well, shall we say . . . backside and extricating the poison from his system." She giggled. "Needless to say, Skymaster has kept his distance from bloodspur bushes since that day. Anyway, Skymaster offered me a reward for my services and I didn't hesitate to take him up on his offer. I asked him for knowledge. It is well known that dragons possess almost unlimited knowledge, knowledge handed down from their ancestors and I wanted a taste of it. Skymaster agreed. The book was located in the ancient dragon Temple of Neeg on the Island of Zedra, located off the coast of the Farreach Mountains. We found it after weeks of searching in a hidden room where the dragons keep their most precious treasures. Skymaster brought me back here to study it at my leisure while he went off to the dragon mating grounds to continue pursuing his own interests. I wasn't sorry to see him go. He was becoming quite unbearable. Dragons can be very zealous during mating season, and therefore extremely insufferable, even more so than usual. Skymaster is the only dragon I have ever been able to talk with. It is unfortunate because dragons are very interesting creatures, very interesting indeed." She sneezed suddenly and wiped her nose on her sleeve.

"Come over here Gabriel. Let me show you something," she said. Shareen motioned with her crooked hand for me to walk over to her side of the table. "This," she pointed at the page, "is a rune. You drew one when you used the spell of protection from my old spell book. Remember? This entire book is written in a very ancient language. Runes can be very powerful magical tools when used correctly. I have been working on interpreting these runes to a language that I can understand, a most tedious task, since rune lore has never been my line of expertise. However, I have made significant progress and, in fact, have discovered the key to reading this language. What we have here, Gabriel, is the instruction manual to the gate."

Thus began my lessons in rune lore which were added to my curriculum on top of my study of history. The study of runes fascinates me and I am lapping up the knowledge as a kitten would lap up a bowl of milk. Structures so very intricate in detail could only have been invented by a soul of art personified. Combining the structures in different arrangements causes the meanings to change accordingly, just like our alphabet. Shareen tells me that magical runes use their arrangements to influence the flow of energy and thus create physical reactions when the energy is channeled through them. I plan on studying everything I can lay my hands on concerning this phenomenon.

A Glimpse Into the Past

May 25. Today started out normally with Nina serving Shareen and I breakfast in the library, where we continued reading while eating our food. The book I was reading was written by an apprentice sorcerer to the Master Mercin covering the period of time during Mercin's rise to power. The apprentice expounded on the everyday tedium of life at the Castle Xandia, serving his master, going on and on about such things as what was served for dinner, the guest list, what time they went to bed, etc. The thought of spending all day reading such dry text made me restless and annoyed, so I began fidgeting like a school girl and skimming through paragraphs in boredom, wondering what good this type of knowledge could possibly do me.

It wasn't until after Mercin had killed the King of Saberville and took over the throne that I finally found some juicy stuff. Mercin had a frequent dinner guest by the name of Grebar, his wife Lenasha and their daughter Riva. Apparently Riva had shown a certain flair for sorcery and her parents, using their wealth as incentive, where trying to persuade Mercin to take the girl in and teach her as an apprentice. Attracted to the young Riva, Mercin agreed to teach her for a minimal fee not mentioned. Mercin took the young maiden under his wing and began her training, personally showing her the fundamentals of the art. Riva, a beautiful girl of seventeen years, was in awe of her master and put him on a tall pedestal, giving him and his instructions her full attention and admiration. Without much effort, Mercin seduced young Riva and together they conceived a child.

As the months went by and Riva's belly grew, Mercin turned away from her to find his pleasures elsewhere, leaving Riva heart broken and alone. She was eight months into her pregnancy when she learned of Mercin's plot to take the baby from her and inform her parents that she had died in child birth. He planned to raise the child to be his heir if it was a son she bore him. If it turned out to be a daughter, the child would be put to death along with Riva.

The terrified girl enlisted the aid of the author apprentice whose sympathy she had gained. The apprentice helped Riva escape the confines of the castle and took her to a safe place to hide where she could have the baby and raise it without Mercin's influence. The baby girl was born a healthy seven pounds ten ounces. The child remained in safety with her mother in a place where Mercin would never find them. On the day of her birth, the child was given by Mercin's apprentice a gold medallion bearing the mark of a lightning bolt, enchanted with a spell of accumulation. The book did not mention the baby's name or where Riva had been taken, nor did it mention the name of the apprentice who authored the book.

"Shareen, excuse me, but I have some questions," I interrupted her studying and waited patiently for her to look up and acknowledge my presence. The gold medallion hung heavily around my neck, the weight suddenly palpable. "This book speaks of a child born to Mercin and a young girl named Riva. Can you tell me more about this?" I asked.

Her eyes focused for a moment on the medallion where it rested upon my chest before she replied, "I am familiar with the history. Riva had a baby girl named Sonia, Mercin's daughter, his only daughter to be born alive. Mercin fathered several sons from different women, but he denied himself a daughter. He was afraid of the power she might one day use against him. I think it was Mercin's fear of losing his power to a daughter that drove him to murder any woman who carried his female child. You see, Gabriel, a prophecy had been written years earlier concerning a corrupt sorcerer's downfall at the hands of a female descendant. Mercin believed this sorcerer to be himself and was obsessed with destroying any female descended from his blood. Riva had escaped him and he found no trace of her anywhere, even though he searched for her until his death many decades later."

"The pendant the child was given, is it the same as mine?" I asked.

"Yes. The pendant you wear is one in the same. It has the ability to gather freecurrent energy for use in magic."

"An amplifier?" I asked.

Shareen shrugged her shoulders and replied, "If that is what you wish."

I reached up and touched the medallion, feeling its accustomed chill against my skin. "Where was Riva hiding that Mercin was unable to find her?"

Shareen looked at me, her dark gray eyes penetrating the space between us, her soul seeming to reach down into the core of my being. "Can't you guess?" she asked lightly. I did not respond. "Very well," she waived a negligent hand in the air between us. "I will tell you what I know."

"The apprentice took Riva, heavy with a child, out of Risen and into Universe XXIII to a world called Earth. Riva raised Sonia alone in poverty, because Riva had no useful skills other than sorcery, but they were happy and Sonia grew up loved. When Sonia became old enough she married the man she had fallen in love with and they had children, a girl and a boy, Carmelita and Emelio."

I gasped in disbelief. It didn't seem possible.

Shareen smiled, knowingly. "Yes, your mother, Carmelita and your uncle, Emelio. Sonia was your Grandmother. Mercin was your Great-Grandfather and the apprentice who helped your Great-Grandmother, Riva, was my Grandfather, Ivan. He was secretly in love with Riva and felt a special attachment to Sonia, so he kept an eye on the family throughout his lifetime, even though he still served Mercin.

"Ivan had learned about the gate by reading a scroll that Mercin kept in his private collection. The location of the gate was descriptive, but it said nothing of where one would end up after going through or a word concerning the constellations and their meaning. Ivan and Riva ended up on Earth strictly by chance and Ivan made it back home to Risen strictly by luck. He gave the medallion to little Sonia in hopes that she would someday return to Risen. She never did. It was passed down as a family heirloom and now it belongs to you, Gabriel."

Not knowing quite how to feel about being the descendant of an evil sorcerer such as Mercin, I decided I needed some more information concerning my family tree. Looking up at Shareen, I noticed her watching me closely and awaiting my reaction. "What relation is Candaz to me?" I asked.

"Candaz is the grandson of Mercin through his son Trent; that would make him your second or third cousin . . . something like that. Having never married, Mercin had nine sons born of different mistresses over a period of thirty years. Trent was Mercin's seventh son. Greatly ignored by his father, he grew up hiding behind his mother's skirts. He was a spoiled little brat who grew up to be a spoiled bigger brat.

"Although still a very powerful sorcerer, Mercin was growing old and had made provisions for his top apprentice, Ban, to take control of his realm. At about that time Trent was in his late teens. Ban despised Mercin's offspring because he envied their blood ties to his master and feared their interference with his succession. After he gained control of Saberville through Mercin's death, he became obsessive about having Mercin's sons acknowledge him as the rightful heir to the throne; making them, on bent knee, swear allegiance to their new king or find their fate at the end of a sword.

"Trent, being at the age of twenty-two then was notorious for indulging himself shamelessly in wine and various liaisons. When a summons from the king was delivered to an intoxicated Trent, the young man decided to make an appearance simply for his own amusement. Trent knelt before Ban and in a mocking and disrespectful manner swore his allegiance to the new king. The enraged Ban did not hesitate to act out his hostility. The master sorcerer said a few jumbled words and a cloud of green smoke appeared around Trent which dissipated quickly and left nothing but a small drunken lizard in its wake.

The lizard scurried away to do whatever it is that spoiled little brat lizards do.

"I arrived at the fortress a short time later to serve as apprentice to Ban, and learned through the grapevine that a woman was pregnant with Trent's child. A boy was born several months later that showed potential early signs of being gifted. Unknown to Ban that the child was Trent's issue, the king took the boy to be raised as his own and brought up Candaz with an iron fisted rule and cold steel love. When Candaz was twenty, he rebelled against his strict adoptive father and set out on his own to practice his sorcery and look for adventure. He soon found out that the power he possessed over people was significant and he took great delight in inflicting pain and horror upon any who would not pledge their loyalty to him.

"Candaz soon became bored playing games with the common folk and organized an army intending to attack Ban's fortress and take it for himself. Many lives were lost fighting his personal war, but in the end it came down to sorcerer against sorcerer, father against son, master against master, and Candaz was victorious. The display of corrupt power that day was stupendous, the largest ever seen in Risen, and hopefully the likes of which will never be seen again."

A Glimpse of the Future

Tears misted Shareen's eyes and I wondered what the cause of her pain was. She surprisingly looked very vulnerable. I approached her slowly and reached out to take her hand in mine, to make a small gesture by reaching out to a human in need. Her skin was cold to the touch as she clenched my hand with a grip I would not think possible for a hand so badly swollen with arthritis. She looked at me with her fiery gray eyes and said in a voice that caused my blood to run cold, "You are the person named in the prophecy, Gabriel. It must be you." She looked away, distracted. "Let me see if I can find the text. It must be around here somewhere." Shareen started searching through scrolls and books, piling and unpiling them as she went through the library like a whirlwind.

"Ah, here we are," she said and walked over to the table with a very worn and yellowed scroll in her hand. Sitting down at the table, she pushed aside the opened book before her to make room for the scroll. With fumbling fingers, Shareen began to undo the gold cord that was tied about the center of the ancient parchment.

"Here let me help you with that," I offered my assistance and reached out my hand.

"No, I can do it," she growled defensively and glared at me in challenge. I stood back and waited patiently while Shareen continued to work at untying the cord. After succeeding at the task, she carefully flattened out the brittle parchment on the table and anchored the corners with paper weights. She took several minutes to examine the scroll, mumbling to herself something I couldn't understand.

"Come here, Gabriel. Take a look," she said without looking up.

I stood beside her and gazed down at the aged parchment beautifully adorned with a graceful handwritten script. A summary of the text I set forth below:

A vision has been sent to me, for what reason, I know not. The feeling and fear and sadness assaulted me in the beginning of this vision. A fear so terrible I felt the weight would crush me or drive my soul itself from my living flesh. When I was finally able to open my eyes I saw a darkness fall over the land, not as night would fall, but as if the sun, the stars, and the moons suddenly ceased to exist. I began to run, not knowing where I was going, but feeling as though I must flee for my life. The Castle Xandia came into view as I crested a hill, the only light in the darkness. Relief briefly brought an end to my anxiety and I started toward my home. As I drew closer, however, I noticed that the castle, once familiar, had changed. It was the same, but different too. I began to wonder if it was really my home. Instead of town's people traversing the grounds on business or pleasure, there were troops of armed men patrolling the perimeter.

Without moving my feet, I found myself inside the castle walls looking upon a large room with a throne which was occupied by only a few people. A man who was unfamiliar to me stood before a glass window. He seemed to carry himself with great arrogance. He was richly dressed in black and red. I knew at that moment that he was the cause of the pall that lay over the once bright and shining land. Standing before the man was a young woman wearing a gold medallion with her companion. Two others were there also; a man and a woman. They spoke to each other passionately before the woman attacked the arrogant man, making him suddenly no more. It didn't take long. He was there and then he was gone and she was left alone with the other two. She seemed very sad.

I found myself once again upon the hill, looking over the land as the darkness faded and the moons illuminated the clear and star covered sky.

I read the passage and then reread it again, not quite wanting to believe that this prophecy was mine to fulfill. Time would tell.

June 14. My training is progressing quite well. In addition to studying books and scrolls in the library for hours on end, Shareen has been teaching me the physical aspects of freecurrent magic, which takes a lot of practice and patience to learn. The technique I am learning relies upon the flow of energy. The trick is to bend the flow of energy in a manner necessary for a specific use. One of my exercises is designed to strengthen my concentration on and my awareness of the energy flow surrounding me.

It is something like meditation. I sit cross-legged on the grass in front of the tower and relax every muscle in my body, intake long deep breaths and clear my mind of distracting thoughts while I concentrate on the energy being expelled on every level of my natural surroundings. All things give off excess energy in one way or another. The goal of a sorceress using this technique is to recognize the energy and to be able to persuade the flow in the desired direction. It is a matter of becoming one with the natural world, learning not to limit one's self to his or her physical domain, but to let the spirit soar on a new plane of reality.

It took me a while to learn how to completely relax, to purge my mind of worries and thoughts and not be touched by those pesky stray tangents that a mind has a tendency to pursue. After many frustrating sessions, however, I finally succeeded and was able to actually see the energy flow free on the air currents, subject only to the touch of the wind. My first experience with this beautiful new plane ended abruptly, however. Excited with my accomplishment, I lost my concentration and returned to the burden of my physical presence before I could recover control. With much practice the task has become easier and more like an automatic response or a reflex reaction, taking minimal effort to get my mind to do as I intend.

Sitting on the grass, I watched the beautiful colors drift softly and sometimes fiercely, eddy and swirl in a myriad of brilliant shades, textures and designs. Experimentally, I touched the flow with my mind easing my way into it until I could feel the motion. For many hours I drifted along with the tide and enjoyed an enormous feeling of freedom. I had become one in the same with the world. The trees, the rocks, the grass, the soil, the water, the air and everything else were part of me and me a part of them. I am a function of God's creation and everything that is was created by His awesome power. The first step of my training has been accomplished.

The Power of Sight

July 24. A knock on my door this morning brought me out of my warm comfortable bed earlier than usual. I padded in bare feet across the cold stone floor to the door. Nina stood outside looking worried as she announced that Mistress Shareen required my presence. I wrapped my robe around my night gown and followed Nina up four flights of stairs, where they ended abruptly at a wall with only one door in the center. The door stood closed and I could feel my anxiety build as I turned the door knob. Shareen was sitting at a small round table in the center of an otherwise unfurnished room when I entered. Shear black stone ran from floor to ceiling, glowing dully from the candle light of a single column of wax perched upon the only sconce which was attached on the wall to my left.

"Please come in, Gabriel and close the door behind you," Shareen beckoned to me in a voice that seemed to exude authority. I did so without hesitation and took the chair opposite her. The table appeared not to be a table after all, but a basin filled to the rim with a dark liquid, the surface of which was so smooth it appeared solid like glass.

When Shareen spoke again, she sounded older than I had ever known her to sound. "What you see before you is sight water, a tool used for communication over the centuries by sorcerers and sorceresses like yourself. I used the sight the night I came to you in the forest and spoke through you to the company. Today we are going to attempt to make contact with the company who are on their way to find the table of alliance. I want to know how they are progressing and it is a good time to give you a lesson in the use of the sight."

"We will attempt to contact the wisp Rew. I have sighted with him before on several occasions. He is easily accessible because he does not have barriers set up at every turn and has a wonderfully open mind. Rew has given me permission to sight through him and his assent to help train you," she said.

"I do not want you to speak with him, Gabriel, only to see through his eyes. Wisps have very delicate brain structures and only an expert at this process should ever attempt to communicate with one directly. You must very gently enter his mind and see through his eyes, hear what he hears, listen to his thoughts. Your experience melding with the natural world has prepared you for this new task. It is similar in ways . . . only different in that you will not become one with Rew. You function as an observer only. I warn you again, Gabriel, do not attempt to speak with Rew. You could do irreparable damage to our small friend."

Shareen paused a moment to catch her breath and I suddenly noticed how weak and feeble she looked, even though her eyes shined brightly with her life force. Her hands trembled uncontrollably as they rested on the edge of the basin and she clenched her teeth tightly together to maintain control. Pain was clearly draining her resources and causing her distress.

"Are you okay, Mistress?" I asked with concern. "Perhaps we could do this later."

"No. We will do it now!" Shareen retorted brusquely with strength that was not evident by her physical condition.

"Are you ready?" she asked as she gazed at me intently and waited for my acquiescence.

I shifted to a more comfortable position in my chair, wishing I had taken the time to put on a pair of slippers and then answered her affirmatively, "Yes. What do I do?"

"Just relax. Clear your mind. Think of only Rew, his face, his eyes, and his voice. Picture him in your mind." She extended a crooked finger and drew a rune on the surface of the water. The symbol glowed bright green, reflecting on Shareen's face to make her look ghost-like. "This rune activates the sight water. Remember it. Now, take your right hand and gently make contact with the water using your fingertips. Think of Rew and the water will search him out. It shouldn't take long now. Remember all I have told you. When you wish to break the contact, do it ever so gently. Lift your hand from the water and the encounter will end. I'll be right here with you."

The touch of the cold water on my fingertips acted like a tranquilizer on my mind and I relaxed my taunt muscles. I pictured Rew in my mind and before long his bright blue eyes appeared in the water gazing up at me. In less than a second his cheerful face and curly blond hair completed his image. Not knowing exactly how I was to proceed, I waited, watched and listened. Link's voice could be heard in the far distance. A strange sensation came over me, a feeling of warmth and security, like being at home in front of a glowing fire while a raging snow storm buries everything under a thick blanket of white. Comfort. Completely relaxing my body and my mind, I watched as Rew looked impatiently at Link while the banderg talked about his wife and daughter . . .

Chapter 10
KIDNAPPED!

". . . Fibi has the most beautiful eyes I have ever seen in such a young girl and they sparkle with intelligence and good humor, just like her mother's," Link continued talking even though Rew had lost interest and was gazing about at his surroundings ignoring the talkative banderg. The rented boat they were in was cramped with the whole company on board and wreaked with the smell of wood permeated by fish oils. But, he didn't mind. He was too excited about being in an actual boat. Rew had always flown everywhere he went, but was extremely fond of new experiences, and therefore very much looking forward to seeing the lake from a new perspective. He liked the sound the water made as it flowed smoothly past the boat and enjoyed the feel of the spray in his face when Kaltog rowed fast enough to get some real speed going.

With Kaltog's bulk powering the boat, they were actually cruising along remarkably fast. The grassy slope of the shoreline raced by and Rew could see Kaltog's massive mount running along the eastern shore, his tail and mane flying out behind him as he raced to keep an even pace with the boat. Every so often the mighty horse could be seen cocking his head to the left to check on his master. Rew wondered what it would be like to ride the big animal. Probably bumpy on the bottom . . . but fun!

Houses appeared sporadically along the banks of Blue Lake, each with its own small dock. Boating was the major means of transportation in the area. Rew wondered why none of the docks had any boats tied to them as they passed one empty dock after another. *Maybe there is a fair in town today. That's where everybody went. A fair would be fun. Fairs always have lots of good food to eat and plenty of ale to drink.* Rew's mouth watered as his imagination generated pictures of succulent delicacies.

His thoughts were interrupted as Kristina, Jessabelle and Serek became increasingly loud in their discussion about racism. *More fighting.* Rew's forehead wrinkled in irritation. *Won't they ever learn?*

Kristina contended angrily that it was only natural for humans to be in control, stating that natural leadership qualities and good common sense made them the best candidates to hold definitive power. She was of the further opinion that if the other races were ruled over by an absolute government, peace would eventually reign.

Serek, on the other hand, said that the population had changed so terribly over the last few generations that an all-out extermination would result if the human race attempted to take control over the other races. He believed that the traditions and principals were so drastically different in each individual racial background that a union would be impossible. Serek thought that a better solution would be to form a council made up with representatives from the various nations to make laws and rule over the land.

Jessabelle held the position that each of the nations already had good quality leaders who ruled over their own people. Each of the various cultures held to diverse traditions that might not be understood by outsiders. It would be impossible and dangerous to try and usurp the present leadership. A more practical solution would be to let each race continue their self-rule and perhaps reestablish the yearly festival where the leaders of the different nations could come together and discuss national laws of conduct and make decisions regarding issues that concerned everyone.

The three of them scowled at each other's ideas, discarding each other's recommendations without serious thought or consideration. *If only they could hear themselves bicker. If the three of them cannot learn to listen to each other, how can we expect entire nations to make peace with one another?* Rew felt anxiety, not a good feeling at all. *They have good souls. But, they have a lot to learn.*

The population along the shore thickened. The small town of Lakeside came into view. Boats of various shapes and sizes were tied to the crowded wooden docks. On the shore, warehouses and taverns lined the streets, displaying bright signs advertising their wares and enticing consumers to spend money in various establishments. However, the run-down appearance of the buildings spoke of unprosperous times. People were bustling about, loading and unloading freight from a variety of boats moored to the dock. Rew licked his lips as he spotted a crate of plump red apples. *I wonder what there is to eat. I'm hungry.* A crowd was gathered around a speaking platform a short distance off shore. The people in the crowd were shouting angrily. *This doesn't feel right.* Rew looked around at the company to see if anyone else felt anxious. Everyone looked preoccupied, except Link, whose face grew sterner as they drew closer to the nearest dock.

Kaltog barely avoided hitting the other boats as they squeezed their little fishing craft in between two large cargo vessels. The boat made a grinding thud as it came up against the wooden dock, drawing the attention of the people within earshot. They were scrutinized rudely as word passed up and down the streets throughout the water front area that strangers were coming ashore. Shouts of violence rang in Rew's ears as he saw a mob start toward them. It became quickly evident that they were not welcome travelers in Lakeside.

Kristina and Jessabelle were the first on the dock, followed immediately by Serek, who kept his hand on the hilt of his sword, finally cognizant of their danger. Rew extended his wings and floated gently up and hovered there while he watched Link and Kaltog move awkwardly as they disembarked the small fishing craft. The horde was closing in on them.

The man in the lead yelled to them in a haughty voice, "We do not welcome filthy animals into our village. If you leave now we will not have to kill you." Rew recognized the man as the one he saw speaking on the platform a short time ago. He was tall and handsome and carried himself with a self-assured attitude, but his eyes were cold and merciless. The sword he carried was richly adorned with gold and jewels.

The man's eyes came to rest on Kristina and confusion contoured his face and then anger. "What is the meaning of this?" he asked. "Princess Kristina?"

Kristina stepped forward and said, "Gerod . . ."

Before Kristina had a chance to speak, the man lunged at Serek with his sword flashing. Serek parried his blows well, avoiding hitting Kristina as she attempted to intercede. The mob was on top of them in moments.

Rew watched from above as his companions defended their ground. Serek fought like a man possessed, fighting off people left and right, with his sword manipulated brilliantly in his expert hand. Link covered Serek's back with his long dagger drawn as he fended off blows coming from all directions. Jessabelle, with dagger upraised, danced effectively out of the way of her attackers while she quickly and agilely inflicted wounds on the enemy with her sharp blade. Rew caught sight of Kristina as she was apprehended by the man with the fancy sword. She screamed and struggled in his iron grasp, pleading for him to let her go so she could go to the aid of her companions. Ignoring her pleas, he started dragging her away from the mob toward his awaiting carriage. She tried to fight him off, but he was much stronger and overpowered her. Rew rushed to the rescue, but was knocked roughly to the ground by an unseen assailant. He gained his feet just as the carriage drove away and headed south.

Rew flew back to the fighting and found the giant torg keeping people at bay with minimal effort. "Kaltog!" Rew yelled, landed on the giant's shoulder and shouted, "Kristina's been taken!"

"I'll get us out of here!" Kaltog roared furiously and started knocking people down, throwing some of them from the dock and into the waters of Blue Lake, clearing a path through the throng. The rest of the company followed in Kaltog's wake as they moved through the center of town.

Serek ran up ahead and shouted to them as he rounded a corner, "This way!"

They caught up with him on the next street and Link grabbed Serek's arm and spun him around. "We've got to go after Kristina," he managed to rasp out through his huffing and puffing.

"Later!" Serek bellowed. "We've got to get out of here, now. Follow me."

Link and Rew exchanged looks of exasperation before starting out after Serek.

By the time they reached the outskirts of town, Kaltog had discouraged any followers and they left Lakeside unescorted. The tired company continued walking until they came across a large grassy plain. Walking through the area was like walking through a ghost town, with an eerie feeling lingering like the dead disapproved of their slumber being disturbed. They moved slowly and explored the grounds, sometimes stopping to pick up some odd discarded relic of a time gone by.

"This must be the old festival grounds," Jessabelle commented as she examined a dusty, but beautifully handcrafted piece of jewelry before throwing it back onto the ground.

Link stopped in his tracks and looked up with a horrified expression on his face. "I've heard that the old festival grounds are haunted," he said as he pulled on his beard anxiously and glared at Serek.

"You are welcome to go back into town, banderg. The villagers might kill you for fouling their precious garbage heap of a town, but at least you won't get eaten by ghosts," Serek snapped as he turned his back on the company.

"Humpf!" Link snorted loudly with his eyes boring into Serek's back.

Jessabelle sat down on the ground and drew her knees up under her chin. She gazed thoughtfully at Rew and Kaltog, who stood the closest to her. "We have to go back and find Kristina," she said.

Serek turned on her angrily. "Are you crazy? That mob nearly killed all of us. Besides, she apparently knew that man. They're probably old *friends* . . . or *something*," he said. Rew could read the jealously in Serek's eyes as easily as he could see the sun in the sky. Serek turned his back on them.

"You are wrong, Serek," Jessabelle hissed his name. "Defending us she was. The girl fought hard to get away. Kidnapped she was. We will help her!" She slapped her knee stubbornly, defending her point.

Kaltog's booming voice rang out over the empty plain, rousing anything that may have otherwise missed their passing. "The kendrite is right," he said. "I will go. Mount!" He called into the dry air, followed moments later with the thunder of large hooves discernibly coming toward them.

Link watched as the dust plume came closer, pulled anxiously on his beard, and stated his opinion, "I agree that we must rescue the princess. But, we don't know where that man has taken her. We cannot just go back into town and start asking questions." Link pulled on his beard a little more and then his eyes brightened with an idea. He continued, "Although, there must be a tavern in town with plenty of ale and conversation to be had. Perhaps I could go there in disguise and find out the information we seek."

"You bandergs always think with your stomachs and not your shrunken brains," Serek sneered.

"What do you know of bandergs? You no good stinking . . ." Link began.

"You all stay here," Rew interrupted in a cheerful voice that didn't reveal his irritation with them. "I will go scout the area and locate Kristina by myself. It will be easy. If she needs your help, I will come back to guide you." He examined their expressions without seeming to study them at all. *They quit arguing, anyway, that must be a good sign.* When he didn't receive disagreement from anyone in the company, Rew fluttered his wings and gracefully sped away toward Lakeside. *Maybe I can find some food. I'm hungry.*

Rew covered the ground it had taken the company two hours to cross in only minutes. Dusk was beginning to settle as he landed on top of a roof to scope things out. The orange sky reflected off from the roof tops of buildings, giving the town an eerie glow. The streets were almost empty and Lakeside was quiet. Rew flew a little further into the center of town and came across a drinking establishment called "The Festival Inn". Rounding the corner and flying part way down a narrow alley between buildings, Rew found a window that was opened a crack. He made sure the alley was clear of any traffic before pressing his nose to the dirty glass. He could see humans sitting at a long bar in a small room and more people occupying tables that crowded the floor. A waitress dressed in a threadbare uniform was busy running mugs of ale to tables and serving the patrons at the bar. Rew inched the window open a little further until he could see and hear clearly the nearest table. Seated at the table were three burly men who slurped large mugs of ale, ate from lavishly piled platters of food, and bragged about their part in the day's foray.

The biggest of the men, who was facing the window, took a long pull on his mug and bragged to the others, "I got a hand on that kendrite girl, but she slid right out of my grasp. I think maybe she's part eel." He and his friends laughed at the absurd joke and emptied their mugs, banging them on the table until the waitress brought some fresh ones.

The man to Rew's right squinted as he watched the waitress clean a table near the bar. "Gerod wasted no time at all clamping on to the princess and high tailing it off to Wayfair Manor. I heard that he had been courting the girl all last summer at Castle Gentlebreeze, but she had firmly rejected all of his offers of marriage. Doesn't surprise me. That Gerod is a mean son of a bitch. Can't think of any wench who would gladly take on that scoundrel, except maybe Maggie here." He winked at the waitress as she passed by with a heavy tray of mugs and slapped her on the rear. She scowled at him.

As the man laughed, Rew quickly grabbed some food off from the platter on the table without being noticed. With the skill of a talented magician, Rew swiped a mug of ale from the man on his left and drank it down thirstily before replacing the empty mug back on the table. Swiftly, he flew south to find Wayfair Manor. In the distance behind him he heard a man shout, "Hey! Who drank my ale?"

Rew looked for the largest house on the shoreline, thinking that anybody who could court a princess would have to be fairly well-to-do. A brightly lit stone mansion came into view and Rew was there within moments, being sure to avoid the guards who stood like toy soldiers at the wooden gate. He flew around the entire mansion peeking in through windows until he finally found the one he sought. *Kristina!*

The large window Rew hovered in front of looked into a finely furnished dining room. Gerod sat at one end of the banquet sized table and Kristina sat at the other, sipping wine and enjoying a splendid spread of food. *Wow! That food looks really good. It looks to me like everything is okay. I think I'll knock and see if they'll invite me to join them. I can almost taste it!*

Rew knocked on the window with a smile on his face and hunger in his belly. Kristina and Gerod looked up at the same time, but their expressions were as different as night is from day. Gerod rose instantly to his feet, disrupting his wine glass in the process and creating a dark red splotch on the fine white tablecloth. Rew stood transfixed by the look on Gerod's face, an expression of shear malice. He saw Kristina stand up, the napkin on her lap sliding down her blue satin dress to the ground. She motioned for him to flee. He turned from the window, finally understanding her urgency, but it was too late. *Uh! Oh!* Two burly guards grabbed him by both arms and dragged him toward the kitchen door.

The marvelous aroma of roasted turkey assaulted Rew's senses as the guards carried him into the massive kitchen. *Mmmm . . . that smells delicious.* Gerod walked through the door to the dining room followed closely by Kristina. Rew noticed that Gerod had Kristina's arm grasped tightly in his right hand. She winced visibly as he propelled her forward.

"Please, Gerod let him go. He is no threat to you. I am the one you want. Don't do this," Kristina pleaded with calm dignity.

Gerod squeezed Kristina's arm tighter and said, "He is a spy. Is this the kind of scum you traded my company for? Guards, take him to the cellar and lock him up."

"No!" Kristina screamed and tried to pull away from him without success.

"Wait," Rew said, smiled warmly and tried to sound unconcerned. "I just wanted something to eat. It smells so good and I am so hungry. Please kind sir, if you haven't enough, I quite understand and I will take my leave of you and the lady straight away. I apologize for my intrusion." Rew fluttered his wings in an attempt to fly away, but the guards had him firmly by the arms. With unnecessary roughness, they took him away from the awesome flavors of the kitchen, down a flight of stairs, to a dark and musty basement. "Wait!" he called. *Wait!*

Rew could hear Kristina in the background, clearly upset, pleading with Gerod to let Rew go. A shackle was secured around his neck and the guards left him alone in the dark without so much as a turkey wing to appease his rumbling stomach.

This is a fine mess you've gotten yourself into, Rew thought to himself. *Here I am, locked up in this smelly old basement without a proper dinner. And now Kristina is no closer to being rescued . . . than I am. Poor Kristina . . . poor me. I've got to do something. But, what? Break out. But, how? This chain is as thick as my arm. I could use my magic . . . no, I can't, it would be cheating. Stupid wisp rules! I know . . . I'll wait until the guard comes down to check on me and I'll knock him over the head and take the key. Yeah! But, what if he's bringing me dinner? I know . . . I'll eat first and then I'll clobber him over the head and take the key . . .*

Rew sat awake all night long in the dark and dreary base-ment and considered his options. He had several alternate plans by the time the cellar door finally creaked open and someone descended the stairs. Rich perfume tugged on his nose. *Kristina.* "Thank God. You've brought me dinner," he said.

"I brought you some breakfast, but I can't stay long. Some-how I'll get us out of here. Wait until the time is right," she said as she gazed into Rew's eyes with anger blazing in her own. She touched his hand gently and left.

Rew nibbled at his food tastelessly, having lost his appetite. *Poor girl. I have to do something to get us out of here.* The shackle around his neck was heavy and uncomfortable. He pulled use-lessly on the chain that was attached to a ring imbedded in the stone floor. Another similar set up was lying on the floor about two feet away. The pair of shackles had to have been made to go around a man's wrists. He wondered why someone would keep something like that in his basement. A small streak of sunlight filtered through a tiny crack in the window to his left, giving Rew the opportunity to view his surroundings. The cellar was crammed with nondescript crates and little else. The writing on the crates had been blacked out with paint, but Rew thought he could make out the words "Xandia" and "Exporting". *Could Gerod be one of Candaz's men?*

Rew again pulled on the chain, testing it for any sign of weakness, but found none. Feeling frustrated, he sat back down on the ground and finished his breakfast. When he was through eating, he noticed that the other shackle appeared to be coming loose where it was anchored to the floor. The stone surrounding it was chipped and cracked. He worked his way over to it, stretching the chain attached to his neck to its full extent. Immediately he began digging at the loose and crumbling stone with his fork until the iron ring could be wiggled from side to side. Pulling on it and working it back and forth persistently made it finally give way. Swinging it experimentally to test its possible effectiveness as a weapon, Rew found it to be heavy, but usable. When the first opportunity arose, he planned to use the heavy iron to hit the guard on the head, knock him out, and relieve him of his keys.

The cold floor chilled him to the bone as he sat and quietly waited. Time crawled at a rate even a starfish would find tedious.

Finally, his wait ended as the cellar door creaked open and footsteps could be heard descending the stairs. Rew stood up, tested his grip on the iron ring clasped firmly behind his back and steadied himself for the attack.

He could not see the face of the man who approached him in the dark, but he could hear his heavy breathing. Tension filled the stale air. The man approached. Rew's hands sweated on the cold iron chain, threatening his grip. He waited until he was close enough and then began to swing the iron shackle, its weight giving momentum to the motion as it arched to strike.

"I have the guard's keys. We've got to find Kristina quickly and get out of here," Serek spoke urgently as he produced a ring of keys from his cloak. Rew had just enough time to pull back on his swing, the chain biting painfully into his fingers as it wrapped around his hands instead of smashing into Serek's skull.

"Where are the others?" Rew asked as he let the chain drop. The tall dark man unlocked the shackle from around Rew's neck and placed it noiselessly on the floor. "They're keeping the guards busy. We've got to hurry."

Rew rubbed his sore neck and fluttered his wings, feeling the pleasure of freedom again. He followed as Serek led him out of the cellar and into the kitchen. With his sword drawn, Serek made ready to search for their companion. Rew put a restraining hand on his shoulder. "Wait," he whispered. The little wisp sniffed the air and his tufted ears twitched as he listened.

"This way," Rew took the lead and began guiding Serek cautiously through the manor. They came to a locked door at the end of a hall and Rew motioned silently to him. Serek took the ring of keys from his cloak, being careful not to jangle them and began trying them one by one in the lock. A click brought the door open and they entered a luxurious bedroom suite that appeared to be empty.

Serek turned on Rew, showing his displeasure. "Stupid little imp. She's not here. You took us to the wrong place. I should have left you locked up in that cellar to rot. I will find her myself," Serek whispered, turned on his heel and headed for the door.

"Wait," Rew also whispered. "Listen."

Serek stopped walking and furrowed his brow. "What? I don't hear anyth . . . "

A small sound could be heard coming from behind a closed door at the far end of the room. Rew and Serek headed to the door to investigate together. Inside they found Kristina weeping softly with her knees hugged tightly to her chest and her long blonde hair hiding her face. "Kristina?" Serek said softly. The concern in his tone made Rew smile inwardly. *He is in love.*

Kristina looked up and wiped tear-streaked cheeks with her hand. She seemed to melt, the tension washed away from her shoulders and a smile instantly touched her lips. Rew thought she might start to cry again, but she didn't. Instead she jumped up and hugged and kissed her two rescuers joyously. Rew fell in love with the dazzling smile that crossed her face when she let them go and stood gazing at Serek with a look that turned Rew's heart to butter. Color highlighted Serek's cheeks as he lost himself in Kristina's vibrant green eyes.

They all turned their attention to the door as Gerod strode into the room with a sword in his right hand and the stench of hate oozing from his pores. "You are not going to leave here alive," he proclaimed as a death sentence for them all.

Serek proceeded forward with his sword raised, itching for a fight. "Stand aside. She is coming with us," he said.

Rew reached up and clasped Kristina's hand in his own while they watched Gerod and Serek begin clashing blades. The two seemed evenly matched as the contest went on and metal met metal. They circled around the room, knocking over furniture as they parried. Serek attacked and retreated in a sporadic pattern, keeping Gerod on the defensive. His superior skill became evident and he soon began inflicting biting wounds on Gerod's arms and upper body.

"She is rightfully mine," Gerod gasped through clenched teeth as he kept attacking. "She'll learn to love me eventually." He glanced briefly at Kristina who stood firmly fixed, holding Rew's hand with rage contorting the fine lines of her face.

"That could never happen. I don't love you and could never love you. Let us go!" Kristina demanded with royal authority.

"I won't let you go. You will be mine or you will be dead," Gerod roared as he plunged his sword madly at Serek.

Rew held Kristina's hand tighter and closed his eyes. A heavy groan and a thud on the floor announced Gerod's defeat. Kristina started forward and Rew opened his eyes to see their kidnapper's body lying dead on the floor with a sword protruding from his chest. Serek wrenched loose his weapon and watched warily as Kristina approached Gerod's dead form. She knelt beside him and gently closed his eyes with her finger-tips. Standing up, she looked directly at Serek, who returned her gaze defiantly. Surprise altered his expression as she went to him and kissed him lightly on the lips before saying, "Thank you for coming after me. You have no idea what a monster he was."

Serek was rendered speechless.

They could hear a commotion down the hall and were not surprised when the rest of their company clamored into the room, with the exception of Kaltog, who was too large to fit through the manor's doors. Jessabelle headed straight for Kristina and took the princess into her arms. The two young women spoke in low tones and Kristina brushed away several tears before Jessabelle again hugged her close. Link glanced at the dead body of Gerod briefly before heading over to Rew and clapping him roughly on the back. "That's the last time we send a wisp to do a banderg's job," he said.

"Let's get out of here," Serek spoke with annoyance once again grating his voice.

They all followed Serek, who moved rapidly down the hall, back through the mansion and out through the kitchen door. Kaltog stood just outside with the bodies of several guards strewn on the ground around him. The reunited company left the manor grounds and made their way past the village without being seen. Serek led them along a narrow path until they reached the outskirts of the old festival grounds, where they set up camp for the night.

As Rew gazed into the glowing campfire and nibbled on road rations of jerked black deer meat and long cakes (so named for their extensive shelf life, not because of the shape, which is short rather than long), he discreetly assessed the individuals of the company as they quietly went about their business. Serek sat apart from the group, cleaning and honing his sword. Occasionally he would glance over at Kristina who was sitting on her bedroll brushing out her long blond hair and from time to time would discreetly look toward the shadow of Serek where he sat in the darkness. *Those two are obviously attracted to one another, but what will come of it? Their backgrounds are so very different. Their personalities clash. Can love sprout in such a harsh climate? Of course it can. But, will it? Serek will have to shed some of that emotional armor he wears like a second skin in order to let someone close enough to love him. Kristina will have to be able to sacrifice some of her "royal pride" if they are to have any chance at all of becoming friends.*

Kaltog was brushing the shaggy coat of his mount with long strokes as he spoke to him soothingly. The animal stood still and tolerated the giant's ministrations with admirable patience. *I wonder what's going on in that torg's mind. I'll have to try to get to know him better. He seems so lonely. I'll bet he could use a friend.* Rew decided he would make it a priority to befriend Kaltog as soon as the opportunity arose.

Jessabelle was on watch at the moment and therefore absent from the camp. Rew remembered the horrorstruck look that came across Kristina's face when Jessabelle transformed her human form into that of a snow white wolf before taking the watch. Rew thought the transformation was a beautiful process and was enchanted to have witnessed it. *Kristina will just have to get used to the ways of the kendrite. She embraces Jessabelle as her friend, but is unwilling to let go of her prejudice against the race, like a child unwilling to give up a favorite blanket it has outgrown. Jessabelle will have to be patient with Kristina and show her the beauty of her essence.*

Link began singing softly an old banderg lullaby as the fire burned low down to coals. Rew felt his eyes becoming heavy as he listened to the gentle tenor voice of his friend. Somewhere in the distance a wolf howled welcoming the rising of the second moon. *Jessabelle?* A gentle breeze stirred the air bringing with it the sweet scent of jasmine. The stars twinkled brightly in the wide open sky. Rew watched them for only moments after laying back on his bedroll before drifting off to a deep sleep . . .

Chapter 11

WOLF'S SONG

Candaz the Corrupt Sorcerer

By the time Candaz was in his late thirties, he was determined to not only rule all of Risen, but to control everyone and everything within his realm. He had mastered the use of freecurrent magic. It was only a matter of time before he could confront Shareen and be done with that thorn in his side. His army was trained and ready. The enslavement enchantment had been tested and perfected. With a few small steps he would have the nations under his direct command.

He still coveted a dragon. His greatest wish other than to rule the world was to have his own dragon. The dragons, however, had sworn their fidelity to his opposition. As of yet, he was unable to come up with a solution to that problem either magically or chemically. He was consumed by it.

It was rumored that eating the meat of a dragon would imbue a person with the knowledge of the dragons. He doubted the validity of that claim, but was willing to give it try anyway. The knowledge of the dragons would be extremely powerful. He sent for his top men.

"Sir?" his top sorcerer asked as he poked his head in the door.

"Come in, Thalag. All of you come in," Candaz said.

They filed into the room and stood before their king.

"I want you to go to the dragon egg laying grounds and get me a dragon," he said.

They all exchanged looks without saying anything.

"Did you hear me?" Candaz asked.

"That would be highly dangerous, sir," one man said.

The sound of a sword rang through the air. Candaz sliced through the man's throat, killing him instantly. "A dragon egg I said I want," he repeated.

"We can try, sir," another man said.

Candaz approached him with cold and dangerous eyes as he pushed his sword tip into the man's soft throat tissue. "It will be done," he said as he slowly put pressure on the sharp blade until it cut into the man's skin.

"It will be done, sir," he said.

"That's better. Bring it to me alive. Do you understand me? Alive," Candaz said.

"Yes, sir," Thalag said. "Will that be all?"

"Yes. Dismissed. Take him with you," Candaz said and watched them go, carrying the dead man out with them.

Out of the pocket of his cloak he took a small bundle. It was wrapped in silk that was stained and tattered. Slowly he unwrapped the item and gazed at it. He gently touched the gold ring that remained on the mummified hand. Bringing it to his lips, he kissed it before wrapping it back up and placing it once again in his pocket.

Gabriel

July 26. My body tingled slightly as I gently lifted my fingers from the surface of the water, breaking the contact with Rew's mind. The experience left me exhausted and I wanted only to find my pillow and sleep. Shareen sat across from me with her eyes closed and the fingers of her right hand touching the surface of the water. She withdrew her hand and suddenly looked up at me with an insightful gaze. "You did well. Come here and help me up. Nature is urgently calling," she said.

I realized that I was feeling the urgent call of nature myself, but when I rose from the chair I found that my muscles were extremely stiff and reluctant to do my bidding. Clasping the back of the chair to steady myself, I stretched my legs in an attempt to restore the flow of blood, and after a few moments was able to move again. My head seemed to be swimming and the floor threatened to slide out from under me. Nina peaked through the door at that moment and came to stand by my side. "Oh, you're finally finished. Two days have passed since either of you have moved. I was beginning to worry terribly. I just hate these sessions, Mistress. The first order of business is a good hot meal with plenty of cool water to drink and then off to bed for both of you," she fussed.

"No," I said as I touched her arm in an attempt to blunt the cutting edge in my voice. "The first order of business, Nina, is the bathroom and in a hurry."

"Oh dear. Of course," she said. The cheeks on Nina's plump face reddened slightly. "Do you need help, Gabriel? You don't look very steady." Nina grabbed my arm with strong supportive hands.

I was still slightly dizzy, but my circulation had returned. "I'm fine. Help Shareen."

Nina's strong arms lifted Shareen's withered body with practiced ease and I followed them down the stairs. When we were all seated at the kitchen table a short time later eating ravenously the sausages, sweet cakes and sliced apples that Nina piled onto our plates, I asked Shareen, "Were you right there with us the whole time?"

Shareen drank down some water before she answered, "Of course, dear. Did you think I would let you solo your first time with the sight?"

"Well, yes. Why didn't I sense your presence?" I asked.

"Because, Gabriel, I observed only, just as you were doing. Rew didn't know that either of us was there with him when he was locked up in that dreadful cellar or that we shared the warm feeling he experienced when Link slapped him on the back in friendship," she said. Shareen took a bite of a sausage and wiped the juices daintily from her lips with a lace napkin. "I think things are progressing quite well with the group, don't you?"

I was a little surprised. "It seems to me that Rew is the only one out of the group who is not clinging to old intolerances. I'm also quite concerned about this attraction between Kristina and Serek. I don't trust him," I told her.

Shareen laughed, an unusual reaction for her, and looked at me for the first time with what appeared to be affection. "You are right and wrong at the same time, Gabriel. Rew's race has never been likely to court hate for other beings, having an enormous curiosity and possessing generous souls. Rew's only problem is that he thinks others lack the ability to overcome their paltry differences, which is of its own accord a subtle injustice. He doesn't have faith that love will eventually win over hate because he feels that the other races are unable to overcome their pettiness. I am afraid he has seen too much evil and it leaves him with very little hope to cling to. However, Rew is a wisp, an open minded and absolutely optimistic race. He will learn that the others in the company also possess the principals that he puts so much value in. It is the differences between the races in our little company that will make them stronger in the end, if they learn to work together. My hope is that they will all overcome their hate and fear of each other and learn to depend on one another for their actual survival. They already have to a point. Look how much they've already accomplished. As far as Serek is concerned, I understand your mistrust, and it has some validity. He has some important choices to make. Good or bad, it is for him to decide. We can only hope, Gabriel . . . hope. I believe Kristina's influence will help to inspire him. We shall see. Let's get some sleep. We have much to do once we are refreshed."

Nina helped Shareen to her room and I followed up the stairs to my own, feeling the exhaustion wash over me as I sat down upon my bed. My mind is racing, however, so I am taking the time to write this entry in my diary. Sleep will come soon enough. I pray that God will give me the strength to help me promote what is good.

July 27. I awoke this morning still feeling sluggish from the two day session with the sight. My grooming was a simple thing and quickly managed. I dressed in a beautiful green gown with a high collar and long sleeves, conservative by comparison with some of Kristina's other hand-me-downs, but, it suited me well. Placing the gold medallion in plain view outside of the dress, I felt an electrical tingle as the gold reacted to the touch of my fingers. The knowledge I have gained through my studies and the experience I have earned through practice has given me an awareness of, or sensitivity to freecurrent. Shareen says the magic is in my blood. After such a short time together, she has given me the title of "Master". I wonder if she might be too hasty. It is true that I do feel the magic as I never did before. But, I am not sure of myself. I feel I have so much yet to learn. And, yes, I am afraid.

Shareen was already in the study when I entered and Nina was just beginning to serve breakfast at the cluttered table. Shareen gave me a smile and nodded, indicating for me to sit down. "I am looking for references to 'enslavement' or 'slavery' or 'freedom'. You can start on this pile," She said and put her hand on top of a huge stack of books.

"Ahh . . . Kaltog's people. We are finally going to take some kind of action. Tell me, how did Kaltog gain his freedom?" I asked as I sat down at the table and began examining the books, sorting them from first to last, according to my own whim in the order I wished to start.

Shareen took a sip of tea before she answered, "It was Rew's magic that freed Kaltog. Wisp magic. I sent Rew to bring Kaltog to the meeting without knowing the torg nation had been enslaved by Candaz. Rew did the freeing on his own. I'm afraid wisp magic is beyond my comprehension." She chuckled with a faraway look in her eyes, before picking up the book she was reading and continuing her study.

"Rew is quite extraordinary," I commented under my breath as I picked up my first book and began reading while I ate my breakfast.

I wondered about the knowledge Shareen possessed that she did not share with me. With an enormous degree of curiosity, I wished I could read her history as plainly as I could read the book that lay open in front of me. General knowledge about her life, I already knew. She was Ban's apprentice in Xandia for a few years before she met and fell in love with the King of Brightening, Theo II, the present King's father. Her reign as Queen and sorceress of Brightening lasted many, many years until Theo II died and her son Cleo took the throne. Shareen retired to the Tower of Ornate, where she remains to this day as sorceress of Brightening. But, personally, she has only revealed herself to me in short glimpses. She has never discussed her past with me at all. I can see in her eyes that she has endured terrible pain but also tremendous joy. At times the cloud of memories almost seems to take shape in her dark gray eyes. But, she has never let me see the woman within. She keeps me locked out and remains aloof.

After Shareen and I had gone through about half of the books, skimming through them for any pertinent information and finding none, we finally came across a reference. It was contained in the diary of a librarian who kept records in New Chance after the original migration. The transcript was tedious. I would have missed the reference altogether had it not been for a clumsy mistake on my part. The tea I was sipping slipped and spilled onto the diary. When I was cleaning it up, I noticed the text.

Before the exodus was made to Risen, many of the founding fathers worked as slaves. Part of the reason they left their original homeland was because they were escaping oppressive living conditions. In order to gain their freedom so they could leave their home and come to Risen, the sorcerer, Queu, enchanted the slave masters into setting their vassals free. It is a short reference, mentioned only because the librarian was in charge of erecting a statue to honor Queu for his part in gaining the slaves their freedom. *How did Queu free the slaves?*

We were still hard at work when Nina brought us our dinners and we took a welcome break from our studies. There was a question I had wanted to ask Shareen, so I took the opportunity to bring it up. "You know, I was wondering, would it be possible for me to use the sight to check on my family?" I asked. My voice caught in my throat unexpectedly as I thought of how much I missed them. A sick nagging in the pit of my stomach made me want to wretch. I pushed my dinner plate aside, having suddenly lost my appetite. I missed them so much!

Shareen examined me for a moment with a gaze so intense I had to divert my eyes. With a controlled voice she answered simply, "No."

Not being the least bit satisfied with her answer, I pursued the subject, pushing her for an explanation, "Why not? Have you ever tried to contact someone outside of Risen?"

"Gabriel, you are the only person I know from outside of Risen," she said.

"Then, how do you know it cannot be done?" I asked.

Weariness came into her voice, "I did not say it could not be done. It could be dangerous. I forbid you to try it."

The tone in her voice made me pause. Was it fear? I still was not satisfied with her answer, but let the subject lie, discomfited by Shareen's demeanor. We went back to the books and were rewarded for our tedious task by finally finding the information we sought. It was recorded that the magical silver harp used to free the slaves was given in friendship to Prince Devon of the kendrites by Queu around the time when the table of alliance ceremony took place. Assuming that Prince Devon returned to Colordale with the harp, it could also be assumed that the harp could be found there still.

"I think I'll summon Skymaster and see if he knows anything about this silver harp. Perhaps he would do us a favor and transport us to Colordale," Shareen said with a gleam of excitement in her eyes.

She was silent for some time as she communicated with Skymaster with mental telepathy. I waited impatiently until she finally spoke. "Skymaster tells me that a silver harp was indeed used to free the slaves prior to their exodus to Risen. The last known origin of the silver harp was Colordale, where it probably remains unnoticed in King Shane's vast royal treasury. Skymaster warns us that if we intend to use the harp to free the torg nation we should be very careful. The harp takes emotions from its player and translates those emotions into notes and melodies. If the player of the harp is angry or hateful, those emotions are reflected in the music, and according to Skymaster, this can be very, very destructive. This is not going to be a simple task. Let's get some sleep, Gabriel. We have a job to do and may not get another chance for a while."

I looked at the old woman and wondered where she would get the strength to make this journey. Shareen seemed more at ease than I had ever known her to be and not the least bit worried about making the long trip on dragon back. She seemed so old and frail, but, I knew on the inside was a power house, charged and ready to detonate. Finally, I resigned myself to the fact that I had little choice but to go along with her. "I'll inform Nina that we'll be leaving and ask her to pack some provisions. How long do you think we'll be gone?" I asked.

"It will probably be no more than a few weeks. We should be able to retrieve the harp and be on our way north in a couple of days if everything goes smoothly. But, there is no sure way of telling how long it will take to free the torgs. A few weeks will probably be more than sufficient," Shareen spoke with such self-assuredness, who was I to argue?

Colordale

July 28. We arose early and waited in front of the tower for Skymaster to arrive. The summer morning was warm and dry, with stuffiness in the breeze that promised uncomfortably intense heat by noon. Nina fussed over Shareen until Shareen finally tired of her ministrations and sent the other woman away. She stood on her own two feet with amazing strength. I could feel the flow of energy in the air and knew she was using magic to enhance herself physically. Dressed in a light blue gown, with her hair tied back tight in a bun with a matching blue ribbon, she looked like she could be anybody's grandmother. The jaw muscles in Shareen's face spasmed as she clenched and unclenched her teeth while enduring the pain in her arthritic joints. But, I knew not to underestimate her. Power lurked within her. . . incredible, colossal power. I could feel the residual freecurrent energy in the air.

"Here he comes, now." I pointed to a speck in the sky to the west of us. The dragon came in fast and landed on the ground before us with a gentle "woosh" of wings. His silver scales shown bright gold in the early morning light.

Shareen made introductions out loud, "Thank you for coming Skymaster. This is Mistress Gabriel, my student and upon my retirement, the next Master Sorceress of Brightening. Gabriel, this is Dragon High Mage Skymaster."

"*Good morning Mistress Gabriel. B.F. did not do justice to your exquisite beauty. It will indeed be a pleasure to have you on my back.*" Skymaster's thunderous voice rumbled smoothly through my head. The tone was very much like B.F.'s deep resonance.

"*I'm enchanted to meet you High Mage Skymaster. Are all dragons as blessed with a silver tongue as you, sir, and my friend Balls of Fire?*"

Skymaster's eyes swirled red, reflecting slightly crimson on the silver scales that lined his eye ridges. He laughed, making the grass lie flat in front of his enormous jaws that were adorned with long white sharply-pointed fangs. *"Gabriel, I think I am going to enjoy your company. I am entirely silver, after all!"*

Shareen stood stiffly with a stern expression on her face. She looked at me strangely and I realized she had probably only heard Skymaster's remarks and not my own. Her appearance had altered into a very old, crippled woman, her power hidden deep behind the wrinkles of her skin. The pain I felt for her overshadowed the fear I presently had about my own mortality. I smiled with a loving heart and gently took her fragile hand. "Shall we go, Mistress?" Silently, I appointed myself Shareen's full time caretaker and helped her onto Skymaster's back.

I watched the small tower disappear as I sat saddled behind Shareen on the great monster's back. Skymaster was silent and I found myself enjoying the view on the ground as it skimmed rapidly past. The grassy plain slowly transferred from gold to green as we flew southwest. The tall blades moved in artistic formations as they swayed to the dictates of the breeze. The beginning of a forest came into view at about the same time I was beginning to wish for a more comfortable saddle. I adjusted my seat a little and eased back, knowing we had some miles to go yet. The trees grew denser and slipped silently underneath us. It grew cooler and the scent of pine freshened the air as we approached the foothills that lay along the coast.

The salty scent of the sea alerted my senses before Skymaster began to descend and I gazed north at the panoramic view of the Farreach Mountains' snow-covered peaks majestically looming over a fringe of deep green forest. Mist was thrust high into the air as waves from the deep blue ocean continually fought to devour the rocky coast. The scene was glorious. My soul seemed to soar along with Skymaster as I drank in the beauty of the land. Nature, ferocious and vital, roared in its exquisite glory down below. I could feel the rhythm of the land's life force alive with freecurrent energy with pure and powerful intensity and I rejoiced in the awareness.

Skymaster's voice dampened my joy with stinging sadness. *"The torg nation is suffering under Candaz's control. Farreach cries out to be free once again. I could feel the actual stone of the mountains aching as far south as the dragon breeding grounds when I was there last night. Nature fights against its corruption to no avail."*

As I took one last look out over the expansive mountain range of Farreach, I felt anger at the corruption that could cause pain for the sake of profit and outrage at the use of moral creatures to accomplish that end.

After circling the area to find a clear patch in the forest, Skymaster headed directly toward a beautifully built wooden structure. Its tall towers and colorful stained glass windows complemented its natural surroundings perfectly. The ground came up to meet us fast and I found myself closing my eyes in an attempt to keep my stomach in place. Once on the ground, I noticed nearby the large number of dwellings tucked away in the forest, camouflaged so well one had to look hard in order to see them. Roads were not to be found in Colordale. Only a slight traffic pattern indicated the existence of paths to and from each building.

The village seemed deserted, with no kendrites to be found as we dismounted Skymaster with a feeling of uneasiness. Shareen and I left the ancient dragon mage, still saddled, and headed for the large dwelling that stood before us. Shareen amazed me with her physical endurance, walking unassisted up to the double wooden doors and knocking the large brass door knocker with her swollen hand. I took a deep breath to ease my taunt nerves while we waited together for a response at the door.

Slowly, the door swung open and a man in a plain white hooded robe appeared. His lips were pulled back threateningly like a snarling wolf. "What do you want?" He demanded as he leered at us with hungry eyes.

Shareen looked him directly in the eye and stated succinctly, "We are here to see King Shane of the kendrites. You will allow us an audience, now."

The menacing look on his face turned into one of confusion and then compliance. "Yes, of course, Mistress." He opened the door wide and led us into the elegant manor. Wooden furniture, expertly crafted, smelling sweet and well oiled, sat in front of the stone fireplace and along the walls. Large stained glass windows cascaded bright colors onto the interior floor, walls, and wood furnishings as the sun filtered through various scenes of eagles in flight, dolphins playing in the ocean waves, and wolves running through the forest. We were taken down a hall and directly to a room furnished with a large conference table and chairs, where we were instructed to wait. Shareen sat at one end of the table and I paced while we waited what seemed like a very long time. Halting my redundant march, I listened as footsteps approached from down the hallway. The door swung open and a young man with long red hair appeared, richly dressed in silver and blue fabric. His handsome face, with finely etched cheekbones and bright gold eyes, displayed a frown. He was alone and unarmed. With arrogance he assessed Shareen and me before stepping forward and introducing himself.

"Prince Jacoby I am, son of Shane. What can I do for you?" Although he spoke cordially, his tone was such that ice sickles could have dripped from his teeth. The lilt in his voice was more pronounced than Jessabelle's accent.

"You are Jessabelle's brother," I stated without question.

"Yes. What do you know of her?" Jacoby asked, taking a threatening step toward me with and his gold eyes blazing.

"She is well," Shareen spoke from where she sat. "Jessabelle has been assigned by me to go on a very important journey. She accepted her responsibility with honor and pride."

"Who are you, old woman?" he asked. The tone of his voice made me look at Shareen in expectation of her reaction.

She cackled slightly and gazed deeply into the prince's eyes. Jacoby stepped back until he came up against the door as he stood spellbound by Shareen's stare. "For a young princeling, you are not very well informed, Jacoby. Has your father kept you so well hidden from the world, young man, unable to see beyond the edge of your tiny nest, that you cannot recognize an enemy from an ally? Is Shane in hiding as well? Not very smart to stay hidden from the world . . . sooner or later it all catches up . . . and then, where will Colordale be?"

Terror seemed to fill his eyes as he stared at Shareen and he stumbled on his words, "I'm not. . . hiding, we are not, just being cautious as to whom we befriend. Obviously, you are not aware of the evil that stalks the land, or perhaps one of *them* . . . you are."

"Foolish boy!" Shareen's biting voice was vicious. "I do not have time for this. Go tell your father Mistress Shareen Wingmaster, Master Sorceress and Queen Mother to all Brightening is here to see him. *Now!*"

The prince glanced in my direction, seeking support he did not receive, and turned on his heel to leave, closing the door behind him with a loud bang that echoed down the hall.

Again, we waited in the conference room as Shareen muttered to herself phrases that a lady should not repeat. The prince returned shortly and asked us to follow him. He escorted us down a long hallway and then through corridors that twisted and turned in an unending maze. The thought of trying to retrace my steps if the need arose to escape was not a comfortable one. I should have brought bread crumbs.

Prince Jacoby stopped in front of a large set of double doors and turned to us. "Father has not been well. Please do not overburden him. Watching, I will be and will not let him become disturbed. Do you understand?" His eyes rested on Shareen.

Shareen's only response was an audible "humpf", but I smiled at the young prince and his stiff expression seemed to soften somewhat.

Jacoby opened the doors and led us into a very large, but mostly empty room. It took a moment for my eyes to adjust to the dim lighting. At the far end of the room a very old man sat upon a throne that was decorated in gold, delicately sculptured with natural scenes featuring eagles, wolves, and dolphins. The king's head was bowed so his chin rested on the plain brown robe he wore. I thought for a moment he was asleep. As the three of us approached the throne, Shane's head came up and he sniffed the air, catching our scents. "Who are you and what do you want?" he growled his demand.

Jacoby strode forward and stood next to his father. "These are the guests I told you about father," he said politely. "May I introduce Mistress Shareen Wingmaster and . . . "

The old man's pitch was threatening and savage. "Shareen, you old witch. A long time it has been, but not long enough. I am surprised you are still alive. Another human there is with you. Who is she?" King Shane continued to scent the air, while he squinted his eyes in our direction.

I stepped forward and introduced myself, "I am Mistress Gabriel Thomas, your highness."

He addressed Shareen, "Business, I do not conduct with humans, witch. If you have come for my help with your petty war, disappointed you will leave. You humans started this mess, your responsibility it is to clean it up. I will not allow my people to be dragged into it. Leave me now." Shane gestured his hand in a sweeping dismissal.

Jacoby started toward us, but Shareen held up her hand and he halted. She stepped closer to the throne and I stayed by her side. "King Shane, as you know, the decay throughout the land is spreading. You cannot ignore it forever. Even now, Candaz holds control of the Farreach Mountains just to the north of your village. Do not be foolish enough to think that you are immune to the dark plague that fouls the very air we breathe."

Shane bellowed angrily, "My problem it is not!"

Shareen's voice filled with venomous honey, "Gabriel and I have not come to ask your assistance in the war . . . not directly. This is a very important matter and we ask that you hear us out."

The king sighed heavily and lowered his head before responding, "Very well, I will listen to what you have to say. But, I do warn you, Shareen, should I not like your words, you may pay for it with your life. The wolf in me has not hunted for a long, long time and hot in my veins does blood lust burn." His gold gray eyes glowed slightly in the dim light and I pictured him with a wolf's face and salivating jowls, not knowing for sure if it was just my imagination.

Shareen gritted her teeth against the pain she was enduring from standing so long. I wondered if she was going to be able to withstand much more. She looked very weak and ready to collapse. But, the power in her was strong and she wasn't going to let Shane see her weakness. Stepping even closer to the throne, she said, "I appeal to the goodness that is in your heart, King Shane of the kendrites. The torgs of Farreach Mountains have been enslaved by Candaz and his minions. They are being cruelly used to tend the crops that will feed his armies. Gabriel and I intend to set the torgs free. Upon investigation, it has become known to us that a silver harp exists with magical properties that will set the slaves free. Our intention is to play the harp for Candaz and force him to end slavery for the torgs. That harp was given in friendship to the kendrites decades ago. We believe that it is in your royal treasury. Gabriel and I would appreciate it if we could borrow it."

The king started laughing. Jacoby looked at him strangely as if he thought the old king had lost his mind and then glared at us with anger clouding his features. Getting control again, the king managed to speak, "The harp, you just want to 'borrow' from the royal treasury . . . just like that. Senility I think has taken hold of your senses, witch."

"You do still have it, don't you?" she asked. Shareen's irritation with the old man was beginning to show.

"Yes, have it I still do. 'Borrow' it you cannot. However, because you have amused me, my dinner you will not become; not tonight, anyway. Be gone." He waved his hand in the air as if that would make us disappear. Jacoby came forward and grabbed each of us roughly by the upper arm and began escorting us to the door.

"Wait!" I pulled my arm free and returned to the throne. "How about a trade, your highness?"

"A trade? The harp is very valuable and a woman of means you do not resemble," the king said tolerantly.

"Your highness is very perceptive. However, as you can see I wear gold around my neck and have magic at my fingertips." I brushed my fingers together to cause a dramatic spark in the dim throne room.

"Gold? Come closer, woman, so I can see you," he said squinting and moving his head as far forward as he could while remaining seated.

I moved forward slowly, noting King Shane's inability to see me clearly even as I neared the throne. His eyes were clouded over with cataracts.

"Let me see it. The gold let me see," he said.

Scooping the chain delicately off my chest, I held the pendant up for the king's perusal. "Would you like to see again, your highness?"

"Bah! A trinket is what that is. Gold. Hah!" King Shane sank back into the throne, slouching miserably.

I repeated my question, "Would you like your vision restored, your highness?"

"I can see," he grumbled.

"You are nearly blind . . . sir," I asserted.

"Enough! Jacoby call the guards!" Shane wailed.

"Wait your highness. If you are willing to trade for the harp, I will restore your eyesight," I said.

"Woman, I want no tricks. Can you really do this?" he asked. King Shane's voice lost its threatening edge. He was curious to know if it was possible.

"No tricks, your highness. If you would give me a moment to consult with Shareen, we will restore your vision. Is it a deal, your highness?" I asked.

"If what you say is true and you can restore my sight, I will be eternally grateful to you. Indeed, it is a deal! In many years I have not been able to hunt. Impossible, flying has been. Heaven, it would be to fly again, worth every single bauble in the royal treasury." His excitement was so complete, it caught me by surprise when he threatened me once again, "however, Gabriel, if for a fool you play me, you will not leave Colordale with your life."

"I assure you, your highness, I can help," I affirmed.

I took Shareen aside and together we discussed the procedure to clear the cataracts from Shane's eyes. When we returned to him, I covered his eyes with my hand and Shareen drew a rune on the back of my hand while I held it in place and said a silent prayer. She spoke quietly and heat coursed through my hand. When I removed it from Shane's face, he opened his eyes slowly. I held my breath.

Shane smiled. Jumping off the throne, he ran across the room and flung open a pair of heavy draperies that covered a large window, drenching the room in late afternoon sunshine. "See again, I can!" He jumped up and down and ran back across the room, coming to stand before Jacoby. Reaching out his hand, he touched his son's hair and face with complete tenderness as he examined the prince visually. "See you, I can!" He engulfed Jacoby in his arms and began dancing and laughing with his reticent son. Spinning around he pointed at me and at Shareen. "See you, I can and see you, I can. Hee! Hah!" At a run, King Shane swept me into a bear hug and spun me around and released me before doing the same to a very startled Shareen. "Jacoby, from the locked storage room fetch the harp and return it to me here," he ordered.

"Marvelous!" the king exclaimed when Jacoby quickly returned with the tarnished silver harp under his arm. He handed the instrument to his father, who looked at it with displeasure.

"This is hardly worthy of the gift you have given me. Perhaps you would prefer something else; something prettier . . . some jewels, perhaps?" He looked at us questioningly, with a happy smile on his face.

Shareen shifted on her feet uncomfortably and said, "No, Shane, just the harp. We thank you very much. We'll take it and leave you alone now."

King Shane stood up, still holding the tarnished silver harp in his hand. "Please, ladies, stay for dinner. This instrument I will have cleaned and polished for you while you enjoy some good food and drink," he said.

Shareen started to decline, but I interrupted, "That would be very kind, your highness. We would be happy to accept your invitation. Wouldn't we, Shareen?"

She shuffled slightly before answering between clenched teeth, "Sure."

"Wonderful!" Shane exclaimed as he strode toward us and escorted us out of the room. "Jacoby and I will join you for dinner, and son tonight hunting together we will go!"

Abominations

July 29. We traveled hard and fast, only stopping when necessity required us to do so. Although Shareen carried herself with strength and determination, her health was declining rapidly and many times I noticed tears streaming unheeded down her ashen face. I tried to persuade her to go back to the Tower of Ornate and let me finish the job, but she refused to listen to my pleas. I finally had to give up trying to convince her and put all of my energies into trying to assist her.

The first moon was high in the sky and the second moon was rising when we were finally settled in front of a small cooking fire with a hearty pot of stew bubbling gently over it. Skymaster had gone off to hunt for his own dinner an hour earlier after making sure the area was safe enough to spend the night. Shareen and I sipped on mugs of nectar. The warmth of the liquor spread through me and I felt my tired limbs relax, the tension releasing its hold, leaving me with a feeling of contentment.

We were camped on the southern bank of the Standing River in a small clearing that was surrounded by large gray boulders. Shareen told me the Standing River was so named by the founding fathers because the river freezes solid during the coldest part of winter. I always thought it was impossible for a river to freeze solid. Maybe it just appeared that way to them. Shareen and I discussed the possibility for several minutes before her face took on a somber expression and she walked over and took a seat next to me on the ground. She rested her hand on mine and looked deeply into my eyes as her own gray eyes misted with emotion. I felt slightly uncomfortable at her rare display of sentimentality, but resisted the urge to pull away. Instead, I smiled and brought my other hand to rest on top of hers.

She sighed and then smiled warmly. "Gabriel, you have grown very special to me over the short period of time I have known you. I am confident that you will serve Brightening as their sorceress with distinction. Your heart is good and love drives you rather than the darker emotions that inevitably lead to corruption. Always remember to strive for what is right . . . deep down you will know the truth," she said.

"We will be confronting Candaz, the corrupt master, tomorrow. Fifteen years the Sabers have suffered under his rule. He is truly corrupt, Gabriel . . . do not be imprudent enough to think otherwise. Be on your guard at all times. He is likely to send troops to waylay us, possibly even the torgs he has under his control. With Skymaster's assistance, however, we will easily pass through any lines of defense. Our goal is to locate Candaz first. He could be out in the field with his men or he could be walled up inside Castle Xandia. Once we find him, I think a little musical entertainment would be appropriate. . . something free and lighthearted for this special occasion. You will play, Gabriel, while I make sure Candaz listens. Skymaster gave us instructions on how the harp functions, but it may not work. The harp is untested. We do not know for sure . . . and will not know until we see a torg with or without his free will restored."

"Excuse me, Shareen, but I don't know how to play a harp," I said.

"Don't worry, child. The harp will teach you. Make a connection through the freecurrent . . . feel the power flow through you," Shareen instructed.

"I will do my best. I just pray that it will be enough."

Later in the evening when the fire had all but died out, the coals glowing softly under black ash, I sat awake pondering my present situation. I looked over to where Shareen slept uneasily on her bedroll near the fire. Although these people had taken me away from my home and family, I had come to care for them deeply. The obligation that had been thrust upon me had been completely unwanted and only accepted to protect my family at the time. But, my motivation has changed. I find myself wanting to help and embracing the responsibility to do so with an ardent passion. I have decided to find out from Shareen after this torg matter has been brought to a conclusion whether it would be possible to relocate my family here at some time in the near future so I can raise my children, be with John and still serve Brightening as their sorceress. The idea has given me hope.

July 30. The morning sun rose behind gray clouds illuminating but not brightening the land. The scent of rain hung in the air. Shareen and I rose from our bedrolls and grudgingly began our morning duties of cooking breakfast and breaking camp. I kept a close eye on her, knowing that her physical anguish must be incredible after a night of sleeping on the cold hard ground. She moved slowly, but did not curtail her activities, although she deferred most of the cooking and clean up to me. We spoke little, consumed in our own mental preparations for the day's encounter.

Skymaster flew in fast from the north, landing in a plume of dust. *"Warning . . . Warning! Warwolves are approaching from the north! We must go now, ladies! Mount up! Let's fly!"*

Shareen grabbed her bags and headed for Skymaster. I doused the fire and joined her. "WARwolf?" I asked.

The fear in Shareen's eyes made me cold inside. She said, "Warwolves are tools of Candaz. They were once wolves. They have been corrupted by his magic, making them fierce and unmerciful killers of any living thing that may lie in their path. No longer do they hunt for food for the sake of hunger, but are driven by the lust for killing alone."

I hefted my bags and began to work on securing them to Skymaster's saddle, feeling the coolness of his silver scales and the softness of the well-worn leather saddle against my skin, I thought about the degree of cruelty Candaz had shown and I wondered if the land would ever fully recover from his reign. Pity for the poor creatures he had defiled sat in my stomach like a meal gone sour. I sincerely hoped it was possible to return the warwolves back to what they once had been instead of having to kill them.

The sound of padded paws slapping the ground and rapidly approaching our position became increasingly audible. Instinct told me to mount Skymaster behind where Shareen was already saddled and get out of there fast. My hands, however, were not listening to reason and I felt a sense of being disjoined from the body as I began unstrapping the leather pouch that contained the silver harp from where it was secured to the saddle.

Shareen looked down at me anxiously. "What are you doing, Gabriel? There is no time. Mount this dragon immediately! The warwolves will be here soon," she said.

"I have to try something. I can't just leave them . . . the poor creatures. I'll be okay," I said, although I was deeply concerned I would become an early morning snack for the pack of warwolves who were just then crossing the river a short distance away. They numbered around fifty in all and were led by an enormous black and gray monster with sizable teeth exposed by lips that curled back in a hideous grimace.

"*Skymaster, get Shareen out of here!*" I ordered. With trembling fingers I began unpacking the harp. Once released from the leather pouch, the wind brushed against the strings making a haunting tune. I looked about me for a place that offered some protection and quickly appraised the large maple that was near our campsite. I ran to the tree and leapt for the lowest branch, hoisting myself up and over. The harp made the climb awkward and the rough bark tore at my clothes and scraped against my legs and arms. Shifting the harp several times, I eventually gained the next set of low branches.

"*Gabriel,*" Skymaster's voice interrupted my racing thoughts, "*do not do this. Let me come and get you. This is wrong.*"

"*Skymaster, take flight now!*" I ordered again.

"*Very well, Mistress,*" Skymaster said in uncharacteristic subservience as he took to the sky, billowing dust clouds into the air with his massive silver wings. "*I will not go far.*"

The first of the pack arrived when I was only about six feet off the ground. They took their time sniffing around the campsite and the place that Skymaster had recently vacated before the large black and gray animal took notice of me in my precarious perch in the tree. With fear-born haste, I continued to climb higher into the branches of the tall old maple. When I was about seven feet up, I found a suitable roost and made myself as secure as possible. Only then did I look down upon the pack of warwolves who circled the tree below me.

They snarled and growled and snapped their vicious teeth threateningly as they continued their march around my tree. The leader jumped and sunk his claws into the trunk leaving deep scars in the thick bark as he slid back down. His fur was long and tangled, with mud and sticks clinging to it in various places. His muzzle was coated with blood stains from previous kills. Yellow foam edged his lips and drooled from the corners of his jaw. Instead of a normal wolf-shaped head, his was grotesquely deformed with a deep valley between his ears and large bony growths behind his pointed ears that extended into three inch long horns.

The animals attacked each other as they fought for a position closer to the tree. They growled and spat viciously. Jumping and clawing their way up the trunk, a few warwolves reached the lower branches and began an awkward climb, closing the gap between myself and their snapping jaws. The tree shook violently as other warwolves jumped at the trunk. Fear gripped my soul.

The snarling became increasingly aggressive as I lifted the harp and began to play. The music merged with my feelings in a magical composition. I felt the magic of the harp grab hold of my sickening pity for the creatures and control my fingers as they stroked the strings. The melody I played was sad and tormenting, bringing to life the anger I felt for Candaz and the indignity I felt for these once proud animals.

Hysteria erupted in the pack and the animals turned on each other in their frenzy. Fur and flesh flew as teeth flashed and the warwolves attacked one another without mercy in their madness. They yelped piteously in their torment. The warwolves in the tree clawed crazily at the bark, trying to reach me. In a final desperate effort, they jumped. One almost snatched my foot with his teeth, but fell at the last minute and joined the rest of the warwolves on the ground.

I watched in horror as they fought each other to the death, spilling and spraying blood all over the campsite. My fingers continued to play although I tried desperately to end the torturous tune. When the harp finally ended its mournful song, not one warwolf was left standing. All that remained was a mass of bloody fur scattered on the ground below me. "No . . . !" I cried, with tears streaming down my cheeks and hysteria threatening to erupt. How long I sat choking and sobbing, I do not know. It was horrible and my emotions were spent. Looking with blurred vision into the sky, I saw Skymaster circling overhead.

Although it had saved my life, I grasped the harp tightly, revolted by its touch. My eyes were still tearing and my heart was beating fast and heavy as I began my decent. Keeping my eyes on the branches, I avoided for the time being the terrible view that awaited me when I reached the ground. My riding clothes were torn and my legs and arms were scraped and bleeding by the time I was down.

Hysteria again threatened as I looked at the dreadful scene of dead bodies, some ripped apart until unrecognizable as the wolf creatures they had been. Blood was everywhere and I made my way cautiously through the stretch of torn and twisted bodies. My only goal was to leave the horror behind me. Skymaster was descending toward where he had landed earlier that day. *"What have I done?"* I screamed mentally at him on the edge of madness. The stench made me gag and I bent over to release my breakfast onto the ground. As I wiped my mouth with my sleeve, I heard a growl behind me.

Turning slowly, I was confronted with the big black and gray warwolf. His eyes were glued on me as he stood with fangs brandished, warning me of my imminent doom. I froze.

"*Don't move, Gabriel!*" Skymaster's voice boomed in my head. The warwolf bent his legs slightly, getting ready to spring. I held my breath. It leaped. A shadow moved overhead and I felt the sting of heat on my shoulder and neck. Dust flew with the wind current blinding me temporarily. When I opened my eyes I watched in equal measures of horror and relief as the large warwolf was engulfed by dragon flames. My overburdened senses brought me down to the ground and into a merciful blackness.

When I recovered from my faint, Shareen was bent over me washing my cuts with water from the river. She smiled down at me as I opened my eyes. Clinging to her for comfort, I cried, letting my mixed emotions be released through tears. She held me for a long time before we mounted Skymaster and headed north.

Shortly after crossing the Standing River, we came into territory that had recently been burned severely. I spotted armed troops marching toward the southeast. A low chant was barely discernible at our altitude. The ominous cadence brought dread to my heart. Without warning, a large gray tower came into view on the cloudy gray horizon. The scent of salt water played lightly on the breeze. The stone structure rose high into the sky, almost touching the low clouds that hung heavy with rain. Moist green vegetation covered the area with large boulders jutting up from the ground in the uneven landscape. Although the ocean was in plain view, the gray water against the gray clouds made it immaterial in the monotone scene.

Shareen turned around and grasped my hand, looking into my eyes with her enchanting gaze. She smiled and squeezed my hand and I felt a flow of energy, strong and insistent, touch my soul. I realized in an instant that Shareen was revealing her essence to me. A shower of feelings and images assaulted my mind. My first reaction was to push away in self-defense, but Shareen gripped my hand gently and I found myself relaxing and absorbing her essence with breath-taking wonder.

The images she projected were not in the chronological order of her life. Some of what I saw and felt I can describe, but most was too much for mere words to express. Her son Cleo and her husband Theodore brought forth emotions ranging from exquisite love and happiness to rage, fear and gut-wrenching grief. Shareen showed me images of her childhood which were clouded with fear but also filled with a love and devotion to the man who was her father and a special warmth for a sweet woman who was her grandmother. The sadness of not having known her mother meshed together with the loneliness she felt after the loss of her husband. The delicate love of a grandmother for her grandchildren was accompanied by beautiful images of Theo and Kristina as infants, toddlers, teenagers and finally adults, which brought a heart bursting pride and explosive love. Dedication and strong will brought forth scenes of accomplishments made in her work, which graduated into anger for the man named Candaz, who had usurped her efforts to achieve good works for the people of the land she loved dearly. Skymaster's image was surrounded by love and good humor and a measure of awe. She showed me the love and pride she felt for me, making joy bloom in my own heart. At last a sense of loneliness for the loved ones who were now gone and a longing for the days when laughter, love and good health were present in her life brought about a serenity and peace that I could not quite understand. I watched my tears collecting on Skymaster's silver scales in small puddles, much as rain water would on a well waxed automobile and felt somehow tranquil in my spirit.

We began our descent toward the castle just as rain began to fall from the darkening gray sky. Shareen had accomplished lifting my despair, leaving me mentally prepared to face the confrontation soon to come. She had shown me that the pity and anger I felt as I played my last song for the warwolves had brought about the disastrous killing frenzy. I knew I must concentrate on good things, love, friendship and freedom to compose the melody effectively, draw forth from the joy that was in my heart from the love of my friends and family. I felt ready . . . afraid, but ready. The ground came up fast and I held tightly to the soft leather saddle until we landed gently outside of the castle walls.

Candaz's Time

In the middle of the night Candaz awoke screaming. Everything was starting to come together for him. Tomorrow was his fortieth birthday and he was going to start sending his troops south to Skyview. It was the beginning of the end for the Brights. The torgs were already under his control. The enslavement enchantment was working wonderfully. He also had word that his men had finally captured a live dragon. Why was he having nightmares? He kept seeing Molly's face, but it wasn't the Molly he had known but a horrendous mutilated Molly accusing him with her rotting horrible mouth.

He got out of bed and walked to the large mirror that hung on the wall. Taking a long time to examine his image, he was pleased by what he saw. His body retained the characteristics of youth with well-defined muscles and a trim waist. The face that looked back at him was mature and authoritative. His eyes were filled with power. Down his leg was a burn scar from when Ban had touched him just before Candaz had killed him. It was his only visible scar, but it bothered him often and caused him to limp sometimes. He hated it.

Soon everything was going to be within his grasp. Everything would be his to have, to command, to kill, to take, to do with whatever he wanted. Excitement coursed through his body. He would kill Cleo and his son and take his daughter to use as he pleased. That old witch Shareen would not be a match for his power. The races would all serve him. Maybe even the dragons would learn to bow to his authority.

Only one thing would remain once he had everything else he wanted. He desired an heir; a son who would be more powerful than even him; someone to carry on his dynasty.

Chapter 12
APPREHENDED

Jesse awoke the next morning with a warm wet tongue licking her face. She pushed Felcore away and wiped her face on the soft flannel lining of her sleeping bag before rolling over and rubbing her eyes with two closed fists. Felcore lay on his belly with his head on his front paws looking up at her with liquid gold eyes, brows moving up and down in a questioning manner. Jesse reached for him and pulled him close to her, stroking his velvet face with her fingers and then working her way down to his white belly, which she scratched vigorously.

The sun was just peeking over the horizon sending golden rays dancing through the leaves on the trees. The day promised to be sunny and warm. Jesse stretched the stiffness from her muscles before getting up to relieve herself nearby. She quickly gathered up her gear and loaded it in the trunk of her car, not wanting to delay this morning for any reason, not even for a hot cup of coffee. While Felcore ate the breakfast Jesse had served him in his bowl labeled "dog," Jesse ran a brush through her long hair and washed her face with some plain cold water.

"You ready to go, boy?" she asked when Felcore walked away from his dish, leaving it empty. She poured a little water in the same dish and Felcore lapped it up with very little concern for spillage. Jesse patted his side lovingly, picked up the dish and stowed it away with the rest of her gear. Taking some clean clothes out of her backpack, Jesse stripped down to nothing and changed into clean blue jeans and a soft cotton shirt of light violet. She watched Felcore for a moment as he ran here and there poking his nose into particular places before calling him to her. They both got into the car and watchfully returned to the road.

Jesse switched on the radio and listened to the end of a classic rock song before the DJ began reading a summary of the headline news. She switched off the radio and drove in silence for a while. It felt good to be on the road with nobody to answer to, no one to look after but herself . . . independent, but she had to admit a little lonely. She looked at Felcore dozing quietly in the seat next to her, head on tail, and smiled, glad to have the company of at least one friend.

By late morning Jesse was beginning to get sweaty and cramped. She decided to pull over at the next gas station to fill up her tank and grab a snack and a soda. After several miles, she spotted a Texaco sign up ahead. The small town she entered boasted a population of 1502, which was large enough to slow down to the twenty-five miles an hour posted on the sign. The gas station was just off the road and Jesse pulled up to one of the two pumps in front. A man in the garage looked up from under the hood of a car that was up on the rack for a moment before resuming his work. Jesse got out of the car and stretched leisurely before heading into the station. Felcore found himself a small weedy area beside the station and lifted his leg to several different places, enjoying his chance to roam free.

The inside of the gas station was small and cluttered. A cash register claimed most of the counter space, while the shelves adorning two walls contained items ranging from potato chips to motor oil, band-aids to licorice sticks, chewing gum to pencils. Jesse selected a couple Hershey bars with almonds and a carton of Pringles potato chips. From the cooler she grabbed a Dr. Pepper, before heading to the garage through an opened door to look for the attendant. "Excuse me," she said to the man in grease stained cover-alls who was still bent over the car. He straightened up and wiped his dirty hands on his clothes as he evidently did often. The name stitched to his coveralls was "Butch." Jesse showed him her groceries. "Excuse me, sir, but could you ring this up for me?" she asked as she handed him a twenty dollar bill. "I'll take whatever is left in gas."

Butch eyed her dubiously before taking the money to the cash register. He came back with a receipt. "That's five seventy-nine for the groceries with fourteen twenty-one left for gas, Miss. Do you want me to check the oil for you?" he asked.

"Yeah, sure. Thanks," she replied with a smile. Although Jesse felt a queer sensation of danger, she didn't want to raise Butch's suspicions.

Felcore came up beside her and together they walked back to the car. She pulled the hood release next to the parking brake and Butch swung the hood open and secured it with the metal rod. While he checked the oil, Jesse pumped the gas. The hood slammed shut and the man shuffled over to her. "Your oil's okay, but you should check it again the next time you stop for gas." With a gleam of concern in his eyes, Butch said, "I don't mean to butt-in, miss, but you look like you've been pretty messed up. Do you need some help?"

Jesse's heart fell with a thud into her stomach. She had forgotten all about the bruises that covered her face. "No, thank you. I was in a car accident last week," she lied, trying to make her voice sound steady with only marginal success.

"Okay, miss, if you say so," Butch scowled.

Jesse replaced the nozzle on the gas pump hurriedly and opened the car door. "Get in Felcore," she ordered as he simultaneously jumped in and resumed his passenger status. "Thank you," she said to Butch. A forced smile stretched across her face as she got in the car and left Butch staring after her as she drove swiftly away.

"Dang, that was weird, Felcore. Do you think he'll call the cops? We had better get off this road and find a different route." She pulled over a little ways down the road and took the map out of the glove compartment. After studying it for several minutes, she jotted down on a post-it note the turns she would have to make and stuck the note to the column of her steering wheel where she could read it easily. She folded the map back up, but did not return it to the glove compartment, instead keeping it handy on the seat beside her. She pulled back out onto the road and started putting miles between her and Butch.

After making two of the turn-offs she had planned on, Jesse began to relax a little. She leaned over and caressed Felcore's head before opening up her potato chips and Dr. Pepper. The radio station she had found was playing oldies and she sang along with the songs she knew while munching her chips, every once in a while tossing one to Felcore, who caught it and crunched the treat noisily and happily. The route Jesse had chosen forced them to take the expressway for about twenty miles before resuming the trip on preferred back roads. She had been on the expressway for about fifteen minutes before spotting two state police cars.

Holding her breath, she instinctively checked her speedometer, noted the seventy miles an hour, checked in her rear-view mirror and felt her mouth go dry when she saw both squad cars pull off of the center median and come up behind her. The helplessness she felt brought tears of frustration to her eyes that she brushed angrily away. The knot in her stomach tightened when she looked once again in her mirror and saw their lights flash on. Jesse bit her bottom lip and kept driving, reaching out a hand to touch Felcore for comfort. Sirens wailed as they closed in behind her. One of the squad cars pulled up next to her and a serious looking man in a blue uniform motioned for her to pull over.

"Crap!" Jesse thought fast, but could find no other option than to comply. She eased the car over and slowed to a stop. Her body was shaking uncontrollably and she once again reached for Felcore, who moved over and pressed his body protectively against hers. The patrol man approached her car cautiously with wary eyes. Felcore growled deeply and Jesse held him close. She rolled down her window a crack and locked the door before the officer reached the car. Felcore continued to growl.

The officer spoke in a heavy monotone, "Miss, may I see your driver's license and car registration?"

"It's in my purse," Jesse stumbled over the words. She reached down and grabbed her purse from the floor in front of the passenger seat, took out her driver's license and car registration, and handed them to the officer's outstretched hand. He continued to look around at the interior of the car before he glanced down at the paperwork.

"Miss, do you have a leash for the dog?" he asked.

"No . . . Yes . . . it's in the trunk," Jesse choked, trying very hard not to cry, her panic manifesting itself in a physical attack against her composure.

"Okay, I am going to have to ask you to step out of the car, Miss Gates. Tell your dog to stay where he is," he ordered. The patrol man stood back away from the car door and waited.

Jesse leaned over and whispered to Felcore, "I'm sorry, boy. I love you." Felcore licked Jesse's face as if to say everything was all right and that he understood. She unlocked the car door and opened it slowly. "Felcore, stay," she ordered through the large lump in her throat, making the command sound more like a plea.

"Put your hands up on the roof," the patrol man ordered while he pushed on her back, forcing her into the position.

"Please, don't hurt my dog!" Jesse cried.

He ran both hands firmly over her entire body before grabbing her wrists one at a time and clamping on cold steel hand cuffs. He showed her the knife he had taken out of her boot and then put it in his pocket. "Miss Gates, you are under arrest. You have the right to remain silent. Anything you say can and will be used against you in a court of law. You have the right to an attorney. If you cannot afford an attorney . . . "

Jesse didn't hear the rest of his speech. Blood pounded so loudly in her ears that she didn't even hear herself cry out with fear. Wet tears streamed down her face as she watched Felcore sitting in the car calmly watching the proceedings, his figure growing more and more blurred. "What about my dog?" she asked before the man was finished reading her rights.

When he finished she heard him say, "Your dog will be taken to the county humane society. Miss Gates, please cooperate. You will be taken into custody and either charged or released into the custody of your legal guardian."

"My dog . . . my dog's name is Felcore. Please don't hurt him."

The officer stated distinctly, "No harm will come to your dog. He will be taken to the humane society for now."

"Wait. Just wait," Jesse pleaded, trying to pull away from the officer with a twist of her body. His hand tightened securely on her arm and she forced herself to calm down. "My diary is in my backpack in the trunk. Can you please get it for me?" She looked up into the officer's severe eyes and saw a faint glimmer of compassion.

"Very well. Russ, can you unlock the trunk and retrieve this girl's diary from her pack? Get the dog's leash as well." He maintained his iron handed grip on Jesse's arm while they watched the other officer sift through her belongings in the trunk. Felcore watched out through the back window with acceptance evident in his relaxed features. The officer produced Gabriel's diary from Jesse's bag and held the leash loosely in his hand.

The humane society's van arrived a moment later. The diary was given to the patrol man who had Jesse by the arm and the other officer said, "Go ahead and take her in. I'll finish up here."

Jesse was put in the back seat of the squad car. The radio spit out dispatches and information in a garbled female's monotone voice. The officer said something into the radio and drove away. Jesse watched her car as long as she could; watching for Felcore. She saw men in beige uniforms lead him toward their van on a leash. Jesse noticed with a sense of relief that he was also complying with the authorities. The most important thing to Jesse was that Felcore not get hurt. Tears streamed down her cheeks in an unending stream. She gulped air, trying to force the panic away.

Once at the police station in the semi-small Arizona town, Jesse was led to a locked interrogation room and the cuffs were removed from her wrists. She rubbed the sore skin gratefully. They left her alone for what seemed a very long time in the sterile room which was furnished with only a plain gray table and two padded metal chairs. A good looking young policeman came in and seated himself across the table from her. She felt like all life had left her body. She found it hard to catch her breath, and when she looked at the man, tears brimmed on the edge of her eyes, threatening to be shed once again. Taking a deep breath to calm herself, Jesse reached up to her chest and grasped the gold pendant in her hand, immediately feeling the cold metal warm in her hand.

"That's a nice necklace you have there," the policeman said conversationally.

Jesse felt her whole body relax. Her tears dried up, and a renewed sense of courage overwhelmed her; a strength of will, fierce and determined. She suddenly knew somehow that every-thing was going to be okay. She was done with crying. She was done being a victim. It was time to take control of things. "It was my Grandmother's," she told the officer and smiled.

The young policeman smiled back. "Jesse . . . May I call you Jesse?" he asked. She nodded her permission and he went on. "You can call me Doug. We have looked into your situation and found some very disturbing information. You were reported missing by a Mr. William Gates several days ago in Socorro. He is your father?" Jesse nodded affirmatively. "We are attempting to contact him at this time. You are being sought in the State of New Mexico for questioning in a murder investigation. Judging from the condition of your face, I would hazard a guess that you have been recently physically assaulted." He paused to assess Jesse's reaction. Her face remained calm and unreadable. The officer went on. "Jesse, I would speculate that you are ultimate-ly a victim in this matter but, that is of course for the court to decide. You will be held in the juvenile center pending arrangements to transfer you back to Socorro. In the meantime, we will attempt to reach your father and coordinate with the other authorities in the State of New Mexico. Do you wish to make a statement at this time?"

Jesse gave him a clever glare and replied, "I think I'll wait until my attorney is present. I would like to make a phone call now."

"Very well," the policeman said as he got up from his chair and headed toward the door.

Jesse stopped him. "Oh, and just one more thing, I expect that my dog will be well cared for while he is in your custody. If anything happens to him, you will see a lawsuit against the responsible parties, I assure you," she said.

A glimmer of respect touched the young officer's expression before he opened the door to leave. Looking behind him, he said, "I'll have somebody come for you so you can make your phone call in a moment."

A matronly woman escorted Jesse to a phone booth in the hall and handed her a quarter. "Make it short," she said with her grimace still intact.

Jesse dialed her father's office number and asked the operator to make it collect from Jesse. His secretary picked up on the first ring. "Yes, I'll accept the charges. Jesse, are you okay? Where are you? Your father is worried sick." Martha's voice was an octave higher than usual in her excitement.

"I'm fine, Martha. Is my father there?" she asked.

"He just walked out the door a minute ago. Let me see if I can catch him. Hold on." Jesse heard the phone clunk on the surface of the desk and Martha shouting her father's name. She glanced at the policewoman who stood next to her and the woman looked impatiently at her watch.

"Jesse . . . " her father's winded voice came on the line. "I just spoke to the police in Arizona. Are you all right?"

"I'm fine, Dad. I'm worried sick about Felcore, though. I want you to see what you can do to get him out of the humane society as soon as possible. I don't trust them to treat him right. Can you do that for me, Dad?" she asked.

There was a long pause . . . too long. "I'm going to have you transferred back home, Jess, as soon as possible. My attorney and I are scheduled to meet within the hour. I'm not sure at this point what all the legalities are, but, don't worry I'll have you home soon. I'm afraid there could be a problem where Felcore is concerned. The police here are of the opinion that Felcore is responsible for Mat's death. Mat's parents are pushing for . . . well, they want Felcore euthanized. We'll fight it with everything we can, honey. But, the fact is that Felcore took the life of a human being. Even though it was in defense, I don't know if there is much we can do. I'm sorry, Jess."

"I won't let them do it, Dad! It's as simple as that. I appreciate your help, and I love you. Call me when you know something," she said.

"I'll call you, Jesse. I love you, too, and I'll have you home soon."

"Bye," Jesse gently placed the handset back in the cradle and took a deep breath. In the past she could always rely on her father to make everything better. She suppressed her disappointment for the time being. She didn't even want to consider the actuality of something happening to Felcore. She couldn't let that happen.

The woman with the sour face led her to a room to be finger printed and photographed. A degrading strip search followed and she was given a baggy pair of blue jeans and a white t-shirt that said Navajo County Juvenile Detention Center on it.

A squad car took her to a plain looking one story building that was surrounded by a tall wire fence. The girls and boys who were out in the yard raking the lawn glanced up curiously when the squad car pulled up to the front door. Jesse was escorted to a reception desk just inside the entryway.

A pleasant looking woman with dark hair and a warm smile greeted her and accepted the paperwork from the officer. After signing the appropriate forms, the policeman left and the dark haired woman showed Jesse to a room that had two twin beds, one of which was piled with personal belongings, including stuffed animals and school books. The woman indicated to her that the other bed was Jesse's and proceeded to show her the closet, bathroom, cafeteria and common area before returning Jesse to the bedroom. Her backpack was sitting on the bed when she got back. Jesse looked through it, finding her knife missing and her bottle of Advil gone.

A girl about the age of fifteen walked into the room and plopped down on the other bed. She had short blond hair, light blue eyes and wore clothing similar to Jesse's. She stared at Jesse appraisingly and then introduced herself, "Hi, I'm Maryanne. I guess we're going to be roomies for a while. Do you smoke?"

Jesse was surprised by the question, but said, "No, sorry. I quit. But, you go ahead."

"I just asked because I thought maybe I could bum one from you. I wasn't asking your permission." She grunted, lay down on her bed, picked up a book and began to read.

Jesse lay down on her own bed and took out Gabriel's diary. She opened it up and glanced for a moment at Maryanne, who was turning the pages of her text book looking at the pictures. Jesse sighed, settled back on her pillow and began to read.

Chapter 13

LET FREEDOM REIGN

Xandia

Shareen had lived in Castle Xandia many years ago when she was an apprentice sorceress, so she knew the layout well. She had Skymaster land on the western side of the castle, which was overgrown with tall grass. The experienced sorceress knew of an entrance that was well hidden from view that she and her friends had discovered and used for covert comings and goings. We unloaded our gear from Skymaster's back and freed him of the saddles. After a request from Shareen to update Theo on our situation through B.F., Skymaster said his goodbyes. Shareen and he shared a special private moment together. I saw her scratch Skymaster's eye ridges and kiss him delicately on the rim of his nose as a tear rolled down her cheek. Skymaster cooed softly to her for a moment, before he turned to me and said, *"Good luck, Gabriel. Take care."*

"Thank you, Skymaster . . . for everything."

He launched his massive body into the sky and was soon unseen to the naked eye. The ancient dragon's silver colored scales made him invisible against the rainy gray sky, and I hoped that our arrival at Xandia may have gone unnoticed. Shareen and I made our way through the waist high grass until we reached the stone wall of the castle. We turned right and walked along it until Shareen came to the place that she remembered as being the location of the hidden passage. She tapped at the center of the stone and then put her ear up next to it and listened. Shareen looked at me and smiled, saying, "Watch closely what I do, girl. You never know when you might need a back door." With her finger she drew a rune. Where her fingertip made contact with the stone, it began to glow neon blue. Pressing her finger to her lips indicating silence, Shareen took my hand and led me through what appeared to be solid stone.

The room we entered was a pantry. Pungent smelling herbs hung from racks in the process of drying. Sacks of potatoes, onions and some type of grain sat on a low shelf just above the stone floor. Many barrels were stacked against the far wall. We had entered from the back of the room where strings of garlic cloves hung from wooden pegs stuck into the wall. The slight scent of garlic mixed with the other scents in the room making a chef's potpourri. Shareen led me to the pantry door and peered out cautiously, checking both directions.

The kitchen we entered was a beehive of activity. There were men and women everywhere performing different phases of food preparation. A big man stood over a large pot in the middle of the room adding handful after handful of chopped vegetables and cubed meat. A large woman who looked amazingly like the man was dumping one jug at a time of liquid into the pot. Bread was being kneaded on one counter. Another worker put fresh loaves into and pulled baked loaves out of the brick ovens. Chickens were being basted as they turned on a spit in the opposite corner of the kitchen. My mouth watered with the tantalizing aromas in the air. Nobody took notice of Shareen and me as we walked through the industrious production. Once across the room, we went through a doorway that brought us into a large common dining area in the process of being set up for dinner. Torg women were at work placing dishes, silverware, mugs and pitchers on the long tables. A few looked up at Shareen and me for a moment, but immediately returned to their work, unconscious of our importance to their future.

Shareen led us down a couple winding hallways and then into a large high ceiling auditorium that was filled with people. Blazing torches lined the walls shining down on the boorish looking crowd. A man dressed in black and red stood on a dais at the end of the room. He was a tall man with a well-groomed dark beard and long black hair. His eyes were a rich brown, almost ebony, making the irises hard to differentiate from the pupils. Were it not for the severity of his demeanor, I would have thought him to be handsome. There seemed to be no source for the bright light that illuminated his presence on the stage. I knew instantly that he was Candaz. We stood unnoticed in the back of the room and watched the proceedings from deep in the shadows.

Candaz was speaking with poised arrogance to the audience, "We continue striving to bring a good living to all. Sabers will once again rule our great continent by bringing the people of Brightening to their knees before us. We have completed the first stage of our plan by gaining complete domination over the mighty torg nation to our southwest. As you know, this race was easily enslaved and now serves us by working the fields to grow us food, mining precious metals to build our weapons, and cutting lumber in their own once sacred forest to build our war machines. It will not end there, however. Soon you men will be training the greatest army ever assembled. Torgs will be incorporated into our already strong force, being utilized on the front lines in an effort to cut down on our own casualties. With the torgs as our shield, we will be unbeatable."

Cheers rang out from the crowd, while Candaz stood by patiently on the dais looking down patronizingly at his top commanders. He finally waived them to silence and continued, "I have arranged a little demonstration for you. Pain is coordinated with harassment and mind control in order to get the desired results." A torg was brought out to stand before the audience. A uniformed guard accompanied him, holding a leather whip and a broadsword. The torg stood before the crowd, ragged and dirty. He had many cuts and bruises. The expression on the torg's face showed no emotion at all, not pain, not anger, not humiliation, not even resignation. The guard drew the broadsword from its sheath and pressed the tip of the weapon to the kneecap of the torg, who winced but did not move. The guard then ordered the torg to take the weapon. Absently, he did so, towering over the man in blue by at least six feet in height. The young torg held the sword without regard, as an infant might hold a toy rattle while being engrossed in some more interesting distraction.

"He's just a boy," Shareen whispered to me.

I was outraged at the display of cruelty. I felt the anger rise bitterly in my throat. Fighting for control, I remembered Shareen's words about love and compassion and the need for me to concentrate on positive instead of negative emotions. Swallowing the hate and the anger, I quashed my outrage for Candaz and keyed on my compassion for the young torg. Trying to find love and warmth, I looked upon the giant as a mother would look upon her child. I was mentally prepared for this situation. The medallion that hung upon my chest was growing hot with the flow of freecurrent as I clutched the still encased harp to my breast in anticipation.

The guard began stinging the torg with his whip and hurling insults at the top of his lungs. The crowd jeered and enticed the young torg to lift up the sword and fight the guard. Instead the torg just let it hang uselessly from his hand. All the while the guard continued his harassment and the crowd laughed and screamed for more. Candaz stood back and watched the display with a fierce expression on his face and madness flashing in his eyes. My heart cried out to the torg and my intention to gain his freedom made my fingers burn expectantly.

Shareen took my hand, squeezed it tightly and said, "Stay here, Gabriel. Get ready to play, but wait until I am ready. Remember, be true to your soul . . . always." Before I could reply, Shareen was heading toward the dais, pushing surprised men out of her way with awesome bravery and determination. As she neared the front of the crowd, the audience turned to look at what was causing all the fuss and instantly cleared a path for the prodigious sorceress. When she reached the abusive guard she stopped and lifted her arms high over her head. The guard stood in his tracks and stared as if in a trance, the leather whip hung loosely from the hand at his side. The young torg male stood still with a blank stare on his face and his huge shoulders drooping into a slouch. The leather whip began to squirm and wiggle in the bully's hand as it turned into a writhing cobra. It lifted its head menacingly and hissed its outrage at the crowd. Shareen laughed as the guard dropped the snake and backed away in terror from the leather that had once again become a whip.

Candaz had been watching the scene from his place on the dais. He strode forward a step with a malevolent grin on his face and said, "Well Shareen, the traitor witch. You are a fool for having come here. What is your purpose?"

Shareen faced him defiantly with her hands on her hips and her head held high. She spoke loud enough so that all in the crowd could hear. "You are the fool, Candaz, for having tried my patience this far. This atrocity will end here and now. The torg people will go free. No longer will they be pawns of your cruelty." The people in the audience closest to Shareen pushed to move further back.

Candaz laughed, loud and sadistic. The crowd laughed with their leader as if on cue, although their nervous giggles were distinctly cautious and reserved. I could sense the fear in the air. He stopped his laughing and glared at the gathering, causing a tension filled silence to drop. "You have no power over me, old woman. Now be gone or I will have to kill you."

"We'll just have to see about that, boy," Shareen said as she began weaving her spell, using her arms and hands to gracefully draw elegant patterns in the air before her. A chant low in her throat filled the auditorium with anticipation of magic. Her body radiated brightly lit energy. The radiance reached out and engulfed Candaz. His face took on an expression of horror and his mouth worked wordlessly up and down. His hands came up and he struggled unsuccessfully to break free.

I drew out the harp and touched the strings experimentally with the tips of my fingers, making them hum softly in response. My emotions soared as I felt the strings on my fingers and I began to compose music of love, compassion and freedom. The song was sweet to the ears and healing to the soul. The melody wound its way through the hall touching the hearts of men and women. Some of them attempted to cover their ears to escape from the sound; others fell to their knees and began to cry. Candaz fought harder and harder to escape Shareen's magical cage, he scratched and punched at the light, but his efforts were futile.

The young torg was released from his mental hold and fell to the stone floor. He gazed around mystified, as if awaking from a surreal dream. He looked at Shareen for a moment before turning his eyes straight toward me. The torg bent and picked up the broadsword, rose to his feet and made his way unmolested through the horde to where I stood in the back of the hall.

An explosion tore through the air and I looked away from the torg in time to see Candaz break free from Shareen's hold. He hurled the bright energy back at her and she immediately burst into bright blue and green flames. I stood frozen, horrified, as she was swiftly engulfed, her long life snuffed out in the amount of time it took me to release a painful moan.

I heard myself crying her name and felt the harp drop from my hands and onto the stone floor, making a hideous wail on impact. My feet propelled me toward the stage, but I was held back by firm but gentle hands. "No, madam, we must go now. You can do her no good. She is gone," the torg's voice was deep and insistent.

I turned to look up into his eyes, to try and deny that I could leave Shareen, but I found that the words would not come. Tears streamed down my cheeks as I nodded my agreement. I knelt to retrieve the harp and heard shouts of anger rising behind me as fighting started to break out in the hall. Candaz, still on the dais, spotted me, pointed, and yelled for his men to stop me. Several tried, but huge torgs coming from Castle Xandia's halls fought against them and would not let them pass.

The young torg grabbed me by the arm and propelled me out of the auditorium and through the castle. Other torgs joined us in our hasty retreat and soon I was surrounded by members of the tremendous race, men, women and children alike. In the midst of the crowd two strong hands reached down and picked me up. I was carried like a child by a torg woman, who smiled shyly down at me from time to time as we made our way through the castle and out of Xandia through the front gate.

We continued our march until late into the night when we finally paused to rest. Fires were lit and a small group of torgs volunteered to cook for the rest of us. I sat and spoke quietly with the young male from the auditorium and the woman who saved me from being trampled (and seemed to have adopted me). His name is Brandig and hers is Lindi. They told me that they really had very little recollection of what went on during their captivity. Most of what they remembered was frustration over feeling strong emotions, such as anger, and being unable to act upon them. As far as actions and specific events or duties were concerned, neither could tell me any details of what they were forced to do, only vague ideas and emotions remained.

They both expressed to me the sense of joy they felt when they heard the harp play. Brandig described the captivity spell as feeling like his head was filled with a million bees, all trying to get out, so loud that he couldn't think. When he heard the music, the bees went away. Lindi agreed. She reached out with her hand, which was about double the size of my own, and touched my cheek ever so gently. She said, "Bless you girl for saving us and lifting the blackness from our hearts."

I hung my head, thinking of Shareen and the sacrifice she had made to free the torg nation. I couldn't believe she was dead. I kept feeling as though I would see her walking toward me at any moment. Looking up, I noticed that Brandig and Lindi were watching me closely with concern evident on their faces. I thought I should explain, "I was just thinking of Mistress Shareen. I did not know her a very long time, but we had become close in the short time that we were together. She knew she was going to die on this quest. I know that now, looking back on the things she said." My tears began to flow. "She shared her essence with me this morning. She was so strong and beautiful . . . and she was at peace with dying, maybe even embraced it. I will miss her." A crowd had gathered while I was talking and they sat quietly and listened to me pour out my heart.

One elderly torg male from the back of the group spoke with emotion infusing his voice. "We will not forget her, Mistress Gabriel. She will live forever in our legends as one of the two women who brought freedom to the torg nation. We will never forget her sacrifice." The others voiced their agreement in unison.

"There is another you must remember," I said. "Kaltog of your people has been assigned a task by Shareen. He accepted this assignment unwillingly because he did not want to leave his people in bonds. Kaltog would have refused to go if Shareen and I had not made a promise to him that we would continue his mission to free his people. Our promise to Kaltog is fulfilled."

Brandig responded with a hint of distress, "Kaltog is the son of our leader, Racnor Vengar. Your mission may not yet be finished. I am afraid of what we will find when we return to our homes. Racnor, along with a great deal many others of the torg nation remained at the Farreach Mountains, while the torgs you see before you were taken to the Castle Xandia to serve Candaz personally, and to eventually serve in his army. I don't know how your magic works, Gabriel, but do you think my people who remained home were also freed when the rest of us were?" Murmurs circulated throughout the torgs present as they voiced concerns about their loved ones back home.

Although I myself did not know how the magic of the harp worked, I thought it necessary to give the torgs before me some reason to hope. "I do not know if your people remain enslaved.

We shall have to wait and see. However, if they are, I assure you, they will not be for long. Freedom awaits them as soon as we arrive. Right now I need to sleep." I smiled up at the group of torgs, feeling extremely comfortable and safe in their presence. I found myself a spot on the ground in front of one of the fires and tried to get comfortable on the ground, feeling fatigue weighing heavily on my eyelids. The torg people had enraptured me with their gentleness, honesty and warmth. I marveled at their kindness as I drifted into a dreamless sleep.

Farreach

July 31. Morning came quickly, giving me the feeling that I had just lay down a few minutes earlier, although my body was stiff and sore from laying on the hard ground. The sun was peaking brightly over the horizon when I pried my eyes open and looked around. Many of the torgs were already up and were preparing breakfast at a nearby fire. Lindi approached me, "Good morning Gabriel. Breakfast is waiting. I hope you are hungry."

I greeted her with a sleepy, "Good morning."

Lodi smiled warmly and said, "Come. Let's join the others." We all sat down to breakfast together, about one hundred torgs and one human, before heading out on foot toward the Farreach Mountains.

August 3. It took us four days to finally reach the home territory of the torgs. Spirits have been high and talk over the miles has been of home and reuniting with family and friends. The torg people continually impress me with their down to earth values. I was very thankful for the opportunity I have been given to become acquainted with this wonderful race.

The afternoon was on the decline as we crossed a freshly harvested corn field within the boundaries of torg territory. It was a strange feeling to cross a field that had been planted by torgs for the benefit of their own people, knowing that it had been harvested by the same torgs enslaved for the sole profit of Candaz. Voices were quiet as we made our way through the rows of chopped off stalks. Cautiously we entered the mountain pass that served as the passageway into the great torg nation. A massive rock archway functioned as the natural entrance to Farreach. Two human guards were posted just inside. One male torg approached them slowly with the prowess of a skilled hunter. Before either had a chance to raise his weapon, the torg crushed both of their skulls with his two huge fists, clanking both of them on the head simultaneously. The two humans crumbled to the ground like wet rags.

Brandig led the way through the pass and we came out onto a cliff that overlooked a beautifully wooded valley. A large lake stood placidly at the center of tall pines and colorful birch, landscape nothing less than breathtakingly glorious. A sweet scent filled the air and birds sang cheerfully, while tree squirrels danced from tree top to tree top, rustling the leaves as they raced through the forest. We walked single file along the ledge of the cliff on a well-worn path that continued on around the mountain until we came to a fork. One way I was told headed down into the valley and then intersected with the main walkway into the village. The other path, which is the one we took, led directly to the back door of Farreach, straight into the kitchen.

The back door was locked and Brandig was just about to knock on it before I stopped him and shooed him aside. I didn't want to announce our arrival too boldly. Taking from my memory of the night we used the back door into Castle Xandia, I mentally watched Shareen draw a rune with her fingertip at the center of the secret passage. Imitating her drawing, I made my own rune at the center of this door. To my surprise and delight it began to glow bright neon blue. I prepared the harp by positioning it comfortably in my hands, experimentally touching the strings, sending ripples of soft sounds into the air. Mentally, I prepared myself with positive thoughts. I walked through the closed door first, followed closely by my giant torg friends.

The room was full of torgs busy cleaning up pots and pans and dishes with robot-like efficiency. A loud roar of laughter emanated from a door to our left. We headed in that direction and walked into the common dining room. Humans were sitting around at the oversized tables, eating and drinking in an excessive manner. I began to play, touching the strings of the harp tenderly, infusing into the instrument the gentleness, hominess, friendship, and love the torgs had shown me during the time we had spent together. I let the harp do its magic.

Torgs who had been serving their human masters dropped filled trays, spilling mugs of ale and serving platters full of food onto the floor. Their expressions became confused and then blissful and they were joined by the torgs that had traveled from Castle Xandia with hugs and kisses and more hugs until there were torgs dancing in the aisles. I kept playing the liberating melody as I spotted the stage in the corner of the room and ascended the stairs.

I looked down on the table lined with men and women, not sure of what to do and spoke loudly from the podium, "You humans will leave Farreach now. Go back to your homes. You no longer have power over this race."

There was a murmur throughout the assembly as a man approached the stage. He was richly dressed in a forest green cloak and tall leather boots that came up over matching leggings. His costume reminded me of Robin Hood. Valliant, however, he was not. His fat cheeks were unshaven and his hair was unkempt. An image of the man who had abducted me in Las Vegas came to mind. The slight stagger in his walk told me that his state was one of drunkenness. He stood arrogantly before me and expounded, "I don't know what kind of magic this is and we will leave, but I warn you that it will not end here. My name is Reid. Don't forget it. I promise you, we will meet again." Laughing loudly he turned to walk away.

I said, "I am Gabriel, Sorceress of Brightening. Candaz's reign is drawing to a close. Follow him and your demise is inevitable. Go now before revenge is sought by those you have wronged."

Reid continued to laugh as he grabbed his things from the bench on which he had been dining and strode from the room. The other men and women at the tables followed his lead, and soon the dining room was left with only remnants of the enforced servitude. A group of male torgs escorted the humans out beyond the mountain pass and watched as they made their way through the corn field and out of sight.

Brandig helped me from the stage and together we began searching for Rocnor Vengar through tunnels and passageways. Farreach was built into the mountain. Community areas seemed, on the most part, to be massive underground facilities, including the kitchen and dining hall. Each family had their own residence. Some residences were beneath the mountain and some were built above ground around the valley and near the lake. Brandig says that he prefers his cabin in the woods to living under the mountain because he likes his solitude. But, he understands why some might enjoy living amongst the populace in the mainstream of Farreach. It's a lifestyle choice.

As we searched for Rocnor Vengar, we asked several torgs that we passed if they had seen him, but they hadn't. Torgs were searching for loved ones throughout the village so the atmosphere was celebratory and chaotic. Some, who had already found each other, were standing about hugging and kissing and there were a lot of joyful tears being shed. Brandig and I headed for the leader's quarters first. We found that it must have been used as the headquarters for the humans. Many personal items had been abandoned in their hasty retreat. We did not find Rocnor, however.

Our search finally brought us to the forge, where we heard Rocnor had been assigned to work. But the forge stood cold and vacant. We headed for the village square where several hundred torgs were gathered. Many were looking for lost friends and relatives and thankfully most were finding their loved ones happy and healthy. Someone hailed us from across the crowded village square. Brandig and I made our way toward him as he approached us. We met in the middle, although it took him longer because he stopped to greet someone every two or three steps.

Brandig met him with a hug and turned to me and said, "This is Rocnor Vengar, our leader. Rocnor, this is Gabriel, the woman who freed the torg nation, and a friend." A wide smile stretched across his face.

Rocnor went on his knees, which brought us eye to eye. He said, "I am forever in your debt, Mistress Gabriel. You are a heroine to our whole nation and your name will not be forgotten."

I was embarrassed by his praise. After all, I was only doing my job. Shareen had sacrificed her life. "Sir, please do not give me all of the credit. There are many involved in this emancipation, including your son, Kaltog, and my very dear mentor, Shareen."

"You will have to tell me all about it," he said. To everyone who was gathered in the square, he announced, "Tonight we will celebrate. Let's put together the largest festival in torg history. Every year on this day from today forward we will celebrate our freedom." Cheers rang throughout the crowded square. I was left on my own as my friends were whisked away by members of their families or lost friends, newly found. With delight I sat back and watched the torg people rejoice in their recaptured freedom. It was a great day!

August 7. The festival lasted not only for one night, but consecutively for four days and nights. It was a joyful time seeing the torgs reunited with their family and friends. We sang and danced, hugged and kissed, ate and drank, slept, and then got up and started all over again. I was introduced to everyone in the village, from the youngest child to the oldest senior. I told my story to them, everything after the gate, especially about Shareen's part in their liberation. They set up a memorial for her in the village square where people left fresh purple flowers every day. The friendships I made during the time I spent with the torgs are very special to me and I feel they will always fill my heart with joy when I remember their faces. My time with the torgs was close to the happiest in my life. I was sad to have to leave. However, I needed to get back to the Tower of Ornate to check in on Rew and the company.

I sent out a mental message for either B.F. or Skymaster to acknowledge me and I received an answer from them both. B.F.'s response was first, "How's my beautiful young sorceress today?"

"Fine, B.F., except I have some bad news."

"Yes, we have heard the news about Mistress Shareen. We all mourn her loss. Her sacrifice for the torgs will not be forgotten. Indeed, the freedom of the torg nation is wonderful news . . . Theo sends you his warmest regards," B.F. said.

"Tell Theo I am sorry about his Grandmother and that hopefully I will see him soon. First, however, I must stop at the Tower of Ornate to take care of some business. How about a lift, B.F.?" I asked.

There was a slight delay while he conferred with Theo. "Sorry, Mistress, Theo says I am needed here with him. We are working with the troops in northern Brightening. He assures me that there will be some action in this ridiculous war eventually. I tire of it myself. I would much rather have your gorgeous behind gracing my back than Theo's big butt . . . Ouch. Stop that, Theo."

Skymaster cut in, "Well, B.F., I guess I get the lady again. I'll be right there, Gabriel. Right now I'm just to the south of you. See you soon."

"Thank you . . . both," I said, projecting the warm feelings I felt for both of the great big beautiful dragons.

Skymaster arrived not too long thereafter and I said my goodbyes to the people of the torg nation. Not a dry eye remained as Skymaster lifted us into the sky and headed east toward the Tower of Ornate. Skymaster and I spoke of our memories of Shareen on the trip, sharing our grief over the woman we both loved and missed.

We arrived at the tower late that night, with the full first moon shining brightly over Blue Lake and reflecting on Skymaster's scales, making them take on an iridescent blue glow. I kissed Skymaster lightly on the ridge of his nose and said goodbye. He answered, "Anytime you need me, Gabriel, call me. You are my friend."

"Thank you, Skymaster, and thank you for your friendship. I am honored," I said as I watched him lift into the sky with long powerful strokes of his wings and disappear into the moon lit night.

Nina and Hue met me at the door. Nina wrapped me in her plump arms and welcomed me home. We talked for a short time over tea before she sent me up to bed. She had also heard about Shareen through the grapevine a few days earlier. "I just had a feeling I would never see her again," she commented to me. We shed a few tears together and then said goodnight.

August 8. I got up this morning two hours before dawn and dressed quickly. My plan was to use the sight to find out the status of the company. A nagging thought in the back of my mind urged me to use the sight to check on my family back home. With a conscious effort, I quelled the desire, remembering that Shareen had forbidden me to do so. I went down and ate a sparse breakfast, saying good morning to Hue and Nina, who were sitting at the kitchen table talking over cups of tea. I instructed Nina to check on me regularly during my session, but not to disturb or interrupt me in any way.

I was a little nervous as I climbed the stairs to the room on the sixth floor. Anxiously, I opened the door and took a seat at the basin that contained the sight water. The surface was smooth and dark. Butterflies attacked my stomach with vivacity. I peered into the darkness and then over at the empty chair where Shareen had sat during our last session. Swallowing the lump in my throat, I reached out my hand and let my fingertips break the surface of the water, drawing the rune as Shareen had shown me to activate the water. I did my mental exercises to completely relax my body and mind, natural to me now after so much practice. Shutting out all the other stresses and thoughts, I concentrated. Rew's face and voice and laughter touched my memories and then I saw him in the water. He looked weary . . . he felt listless . . .

Chapter 14

DRAGON STEW

. . . Seeing in the dark of night was not a problem for the little wisp. Rew's problem was that he was bored. He didn't mind taking his turn at watch; he just wished something interesting would happen. Rew felt his head nod and shook himself to ward off the drowsy feeling that draped him like a soft blanket. Kaltog's snoring was beginning to lull him to sleep. *Watch . . . watch . . . watch . . . nothing to watch. I'm bored. Maybe there's something to eat.* He flew a short distance over to where the packs lay on the ground and began to scrounge for a snack. *Hmm, some jerked black deer meat, long cakes . . . boring . . . some berries and nuts.* Rew munched on some red berries and pine nuts while he continued looking through the packs for something better.

The sharp point of a sword in the small of his back made Rew cease his search and slowly straighten up. *Uh! Oh! I shouldn't have let my guard down . . . now what's going to happen?*

"Snooping around in other people's stuff is a good way to get yourself killed, peewee," Serek's grating voice challenged Rew. "Just what is it you're looking for, runt?"

Rew inched slowly away from the sharp tip of the sword and then leapt agilely into the air, gaining an altitude out of Serek's reach in a split millisecond. As quick as he was he barely missed Serek's fast swing as the sword came up in a wide arch. "I was just looking for something to eat, Serek. I didn't disturb anything. Don't be so paranoid," he defended himself.

"You lying little imp. You were looking for something all right . . . what was it? I know you are cleverer than you appear to be. Come down from there, or do I have to chop off your wings?" Serek said, jabbing and swinging his sword uselessly at Rew, who danced swiftly and easily out of the way as he teased the angry man. By then the whole camp was awakened by the commotion.

Kaltog came up behind Serek and took the sword with one rapid grab of his large right hand. "That's enough, Serek," Kaltog bellowed deeply as he buried the blade deep into the ground at Serek's feet.

"What do you think you are doing?" Serek protested, facing the twelve foot torg with foolish bravado. "The little sneak was going through our things. He has no right to be snooping around like that. I wasn't going to hurt him, just teach him a lesson."

Kaltog came forward a step and growled deeply, making Serek take two steps back, although he continued to look the torg in the eye challengingly.

"I was just looking for something to eat," Rew argued. "I was hungry . . . that's all."

"Enough, both of you," Kaltog roared. "We might as well start out the day now that we are all wide awake. Serek and Rew, get the fire started. Link, come with me . . . we'll find something to cook for breakfast. Ladies, pack up the bedrolls and the gear. We won't be long."

Serek and Rew did as they were told, although they both grumbled about it the whole time. Once Kaltog was out of earshot, Rew conspiratorially asked Serek, "Who suddenly made him the boss?"

Serek replied, "I don't know, but he sure is big, ugly and grumpy first thing in the morning."

Rew shot Serek an amused glance and said, "Huh! You're one to talk. You tried to skewer me this morning."

"Well I didn't, did I, twerp?" Serek sniggered. "I just don't like my privacy invaded. Got it?"

Rew added small branches to the already blazing pile of kindling. "Yeah, sure, ripgar bait. I apologize profusely for my lack of regard for your privacy." Rew rolled his eyes and grinned at Serek. He wasn't sure, but he thought he caught a hint of a smile on Serek's face and the man's eyes flash momentarily with good humor. *Maybe he has a sense of humor after all. Maybe.*

Serek added some larger logs to their fire and then sat back against a nearby tree trunk with his legs crossed out in front of him. "I guess our job is done," he said, yawning.

Rew sat down next to Serek and watched Kristina and Jessabelle packing up bedrolls and miscellaneous gear. Serek plucked a piece of grass from the ground and started twirling it through his fingers while he gazed over at the women.

"You're falling in love with her, aren't you?" Rew asked.

Serek looked down at the blade of grass in his hands, tore it in two, threw it away and then grabbed another one and began twisting it around his fingers. He looked up at Kristina with pain etched across his face. "She is the Princess of Brightening. It could never work out. She would never fall in love with someone like me. Besides she is a stubborn and opinionated woman. I don't think . . ."

He's definitely in love with her. This may be stupid, but . . . "Don't be so sure, Serek. I've seen the way she looks at you. She is interested. Don't sell yourself short. Sure, she's a princess, but didn't Shareen say something about you being the next heir to the throne of Saberville? 'Prince Serek Landtamer,' I believe she said. Could there be some merit to her claim?"

Serek sounded angry again, "I don't know what the witch was talking about." He took a deep breath and calmed his voice. "My mother and father were farmers in southern Saberville. They were killed when I was very young, leaving me an orphan. I can't even remember what they looked like. Anyway, I was raised in the orphanage at Castle Xandia until I was sixteen when I joined the army and learned the skills I needed to become a warrior. Candaz recruited me to serve him personally after I proved myself worthy. As time went by I became more and more aware of the cruelty the man was capable of and attempted to put a stop to it by turning his own men against him. It wasn't long before Candaz learned of my betrayal and ordered my execution. Luckily I escaped before his guards came to arrest me."

"Don't you see, Serek?" Rew spoke with excitement. "You said yourself you didn't even know your parents. How do you know that one of them wasn't the rightful heir to Saberville's throne? The true prince disappeared after his father's death at the hand of Mercin. I believe he was only two or three years old at the time that Mercin took control of Saberville. Nobody has ever been able to trace the whereabouts of the royal family since then. It very well could be that Mistress Shareen was correct in naming you Prince Serek Landtamer. I've never known her to be wrong about anything."

Serek looked questioningly at Rew. "I can hardly believe that . . . I suppose it could be possible . . . but, . . .How would she know?"

Shouting came from Jessabelle and Kristina interrupting their discussion. The two women's voices grew loud in the midst of a heated argument. They confronted each other over half rolled bedding and a disarray of equipment.

Jessabelle instinctively put her hand on the dagger sheathed in her boot as she asserted, " . . . in love with each other we are, Kristina. Can't you understand that? Theo has opened his mind to my ability to shape change. Can you not? We're not so different from humans, you know."

"That's just the point. Of course you are different," Kristina said, stomping her foot on the grassy ground, displaying her frustration. "Theo is to be the King of Brightening. Do you really think the people will accept a half-breed as his heir?"

Jessabelle's anger escalated, making her golden eyes flash ferally. "What do you mean half-breeds? Kendrites are everything humans are, only better. Humans and kendrites have joined before to have children, and the resulting off-spring either had the ability to shape change or they didn't. No monstrosities were created by such joinings. I think the real reason you still object to me and Theo's marriage is that you don't think I'm good enough for your brother. You believe humans are the superior race. It's as simple as that, girl. Prejudiced you are," she concluded.

Kristina sucked in her breath in disbelief and said, "How could you accuse me of being prejudiced? What do you think I'm doing here, away from home, in the middle of nowhere? What is this mission all about if it isn't to end such intolerance?"

Jessabelle sighed and looked sharply at Kristina for a moment before she said quietly, "Maybe you should take some time to think about that. Look inside yourself and be truthful about what you find there."

Kristina said nothing in reply, but turned and stalked away from Jessabelle toward the fire. "Can you believe she called me prejudiced?" she asked when she reached Rew and Serek, who looked at each other but did not reply, wisely keeping their opinions to themselves.

Kristina sighed and sat down next to Rew on the ground with her head resting on her hands. Jessabelle continued packing up the gear. Nobody said anything.

They were just on the western edge of the Skyview mountain range, where a small keyhole pass edged between the river and the rising peaks to the east. Their plan was to intercept the northern road through the forest and the swamp that would lead them to New Chance. It was a pass that was all but unknown to most. Serek had used it before travelling from the north to the south without being seen. Bypassing Skyview didn't sit well with Link, but they all concluded that anonymity was their best bet.

They all turned as he came running up to them, gasping for breath. Jumping to their feet, the party confronted Link, who was having a very hard time breathing, let alone talking.

"Troops coming . . . this way . . . Must hurry . . . Kaltog . . . keeping . . . an eye . . . on them." Link bent over, put his hands on his knees and sucked air into his lungs.

Serek took charge automatically, giving orders like a man born to lead. "Everybody grab your packs. I'll get Kaltog's mount. Jessabelle, you are on reconnaissance. Report back to me as soon as possible," he ordered.

Jessabelle instantly shape-changed into an eagle and flew in the direction from which Link had just come. *I wonder what happens to her clothes and gear when she does that?* Rew questioned, once again in awe of the magnificent process. *I guess she has her own kind of magic.*

With his boots, Serek kicked dirt on the fire until it was out. "Kristina, do you know how to use a sword?" he asked.

Kristina replied as she secured the pack on her shoulder, "Sure I do, but I prefer a lighter weapon." She eyed the daggers that were sheathed in Serek's boots. He reached down and drew one, tossing it to her. She caught it deftly and turned the dagger this way and that, experimenting with the grip. She commented, "A very good weapon, Serek. For a farm boy you have done well for yourself." She gazed at him appraisingly.

"These were my grandfather's weapons," he replied. Serek touched his sword affectionately, before turning away from the princess.

With Link in the lead, they headed toward a clump of trees northeast from where they had camped that night. Rew walked along with the others with a sense of unease. He felt something was terribly wrong, like a sin against nature had been committed. The strong scent of human, leather and horses hung heavily on the breeze. Somewhat familiar, but not quite distinctive enough to identify individually, was the musky scent of dragon. *A dragon? With the Sabers? That doesn't make any sense at all. The entire race of dragons has made it very clear that their favor belongs to the Brights, and until Saberville is returned to the rightful heir, they will not assist the Saber's cause.* Rew sniffed the air more aggressively. *This is indeed a dragon I've never met.*

When they reached Kaltog he was crouched down low to the ground watching a vast army progress slowly east through the valley below. While they observed, the troops called a halt directly to the north of their position. Although still a great distance away, the army could clearly be seen and heard due to its enormous size. The Saber's bright color red stood out on the troops' uniforms and on flapping banners displayed atop long poles in their midst. Dust billowed clouds of silt into the air in their wake.

With spectacular beauty and grace, a bald eagle glided into the woods and landed beside Rew. Jessabelle shimmered and took the form of a human before their eyes. Rew felt his heart flutter at the sight of her. The serious look on her face, however, made him concerned. He still had a feeling that something was very wrong. They all crouched down in a circle and awaited Jessabelle's assessment of the situation.

"Approximately one thousand men in all the outfit numbers. Of those, about two hundred are mounted and the others are afoot. Armed with lances and long swords they are. Traveling at the front of the army are two sorcerers, caped and hooded in black. Only one general rides with them, followed closely by several supply wagons, heavily loaded. In amongst the supply wagons, is a flatbed wagon to which is chained a baby dragon. Surrounded by guards, he is, and shackled around his neck and tail. His back and front legs are chained as well. The poor thing looks miserable," she reported. Jessabelle made the outrage she felt for such vile mistreatment of a baby dragon evident.

"We've got to help him," Kristina voiced what everybody was feeling.

Serek grunted and said, "But, how? Our small mismatched company up against one thousand well-armed and professionally trained men." He laughed without humor. "The odds are somewhat against us."

Reflecting calm and clear thinking, Kaltog voiced his own opinion, "We would not be able to take them by force, obviously. But it might be possible to sneak in and out without being noticed. An army of that size would naturally be overconfident in their security and probably likely to overlook noises or movement that might otherwise raise an alarm. We will have to follow them until they stop to make camp. During their dinner hour, while the troops are distracted with their hungry stomachs, we will attempt to rescue the dragon. Jessabelle and Rew, you will be especially needed for your flying skills."

"Just tell me what I have to do," Jessabelle spoke with eagerness.

Rew bit his lip and looked at the members of his company one at a time, letting his gaze rest at last on Serek. "That baby dragon needs our help," he said. "I can hear him calling, ever so quietly." Rew saw Serek furrow his eyebrows in concentration and tilt his head slightly to the left. Rew's gaze fell back on the torg. "What's the plan, Kaltog?"

"Jessabelle, you will assume eagle form and the two of you will fly into the camp where the baby dragon is being held. Rew, since you can communicate with the dragon, I want you to do everything you can to keep the baby calm while you check his restraints. I am assuming that the chains are paddle locked and will require a key to open them. If this is the case we can also assume that the guard will have the key on him. Once you obtain the key with whatever means you deem appropriate, free the dragon and the three of you take to the sky as fast as you can. Once you have gained enough altitude you should be safe from the troops. We will stand ready if you need us to intercede on the ground." Kaltog paused and looked thoughtful before he continued, "They probably have archers. Watch out for them most of all. If something goes wrong, get out of there and leave the dragon behind. We'll regroup and try something else." Kaltog sat back on his heels as his mount walked up and nudged him affectionately. He automatically reached up and started scratching the harry creature's nose.

Link continued staring at the ground. He started shaking his head and pulling on his beard uneasily, completely lost in his own thoughts. Jessabelle watched the banderg fret for a moment and then said, "I think we can do it." She turned her attention to Rew, "Rew?"

"I'm willing to try." *If we can avoid being killed, it's a great plan.*

Serek stood up and stretched his lean frame before he turned to the company and said, "You overlooked one thing, though, Kaltog."

"What's that?" Kaltog also stood up, towering over the tall human by twice his height.

"I am going too," he said.

Kristina put her hand out and grabbed Serek's arm, "Serek, don't be foolish. They can fly in and out of there. You can't."

"You don't understand. I have to. Call it destiny, call it fate . . . call it whatever you want, but his need for me to be there is overwhelming, more powerful than . . . " He stared into her eyes for a moment and then turned away, searching for the right words, fists clenched in frustration. "The young dragon calls to me . . . " Serek paused and listened for a moment. He almost whispered as he looked pleadingly back into Kristina's eyes, "His name is Breezerunner and he is very sad and very lonely."

Kristina captivated his gaze. She said quietly, "He has bonded with you, Serek. Do you know what that means?"

Serek looked wistfully at her without answering. *They are both beginning to understand.* Rew felt a ripple of hope across his soul.

Kristina smiled with a twinkle in her eyes. She asked, "Can he tell you how he is being held? Perhaps who holds the key that would free him?"

Spontaneously, Serek reached for her hand and held on to it tightly. A faraway look washed across his face for a short time as

THE LEGACY

he communicated with the dragon. "Breezerunner says there is nothing that he knows of called a 'key'. He says there are twisted wires that hold the shackles together but he cannot reach them to attempt to bite through them. His right wing is very sore, injured when they captured him. They are taking him to meet up with Candaz. When they reach their destination, they plan on killing him and making him into dragon stew. Apparently the sorcerers believe that anyone who eats dragon meat automatically acquires ancestral dragon knowledge."

"That's ludicrous!" Rew exclaimed in outrage.

Serek brushed away the tears that rolled uncontrollably down his cheeks in response to the overwhelming emotions the small dragon imparted upon him. When he looked down at Kristina, who still held his hand firmly and saw the compassion in her face he pulled away, once again building a defensive wall between them. Kristina stepped back in surprise. After clearing his throat, Serek said to Kaltog, "You'll have to go too. Breezerunner will need someone strong to assist him since he can't fly."

Link stood up and confronted Serek, "This is crazy. You expect us to just walk into the midst of one thousand men, two sorcerers and a general and not be noticed."

Distinctly Kaltog said, "We will do what we must."

"I have an idea," Kristina smiled confidently at Link who was again tugging viciously at his beard. "What we need is a diversion so that Jessabelle, Rew, Serek and Kaltog can get to the dragon and free him before anybody catches on to what we are doing. Link, that leaves you and me to create something to distract their attention." With a mischievous grin she asked, "Have you ever been a slave master before?"

Link scowled with disgust and replied, "Of course not!"

247

"Well, you are going to get your chance now. Here's what we'll do . . . " Kristina bent down and started explaining her plan to Link, who groaned and humpfed audibly several times during their conference.

Keeping their distance, the company followed the army of Sabers throughout the day. The higher peaks of the Skyview Mountains were drawing closer as the followed the army through the day. Link felt a pang of homesickness and mentioned to Rew how much he missed his family, even the incompetent apprentice who was probably destroying everything he had worked so hard to accomplish as head chef.

As the sun sank low over the mountains, the army called a halt and began making camp in a small valley. Rew and his friends stood on a ridge to the south of the encampment overlooking the valley which was now dotted with several campfires shining brightly in the descending darkness. The troops had positioned the supply wagons, including the one upon which Breezerunner was chained, on the very eastern edge of the camp to the small company's advantage. A large fire burned toward the center of the site.

Within the cover of the trees, they worked their way around the encampment until they were east of them, close to the wagons. The cloud cover kept the first moon hidden completely from view, making the night all that much darker. Stillness had settled upon the land, making nerves tense and senses alert. Rew watched with a good measure of concern as Kristina and Link walked together down the slope toward the army. Kristina had put together an outfit from her and Jessabelle's wardrobes that both concealed and revealed parts of her body until she was satisfied with the ensemble. As she descended the hill, her lean thighs flashed in and out of the slits in her skirt. She wore Jessabelle's dagger in its usual sheath inside the well-worn boots she had also borrowed from her. Link carried in his hand a wooden flute that he had retrieved from his pack. The long dagger he normally carried had been traded temporarily with Serek for a shorter more concealable weapon.

Jessabelle and Rew waited for Kristina and Link to get to the outskirts of the camp before she transformed into a handsome bald eagle and the two of them took to the air and descended toward where the dragon was locked up. Serek and Kaltog remained behind, waiting for the planned distraction. Rew watched Jessabelle glide gracefully on the air currents, her feathers rippling gently and her eyes focused sharply on their target. *She is so beautiful . . . so elegant . . . so regal. Theo is a lucky man to have such a gorgeous creature love him. I hope after this is all over, I can go back home and find a pretty young wisp to love me. There are a lot of females I know who would make wonderful mates. If I make it home again.* The wagons came into view and Rew could see the baby dragon lying motionless upon the flatbed. His iridescent blue scales reflected dully the light shining from the not-too-distant camp fires.

Jessabelle landed atop the roof of the wagon that was parked in front of Breezerunner's flatbed. Her perceptive eagle eyes watched as Rew descended all the way to the flatbed itself and landed as quietly as possible next to the dragon's head, which was at least twice the size of Rew. Breezerunner's eyes were closed when Rew put his small hand gently on the dragon's nose and rubbed the soft blue scales until Breezerunner's eyes peeked open, revealing fiery red pupils. "*You have come to help me?*" he asked.

"Yes," Rew responded mentally. "*Be very still and very quiet. My friends and I will get you out of here. My name is Rew.*" The dragon began to strain against the chains that held him fast. "*Stay calm, Breezerunner; relax and try not to move.*" Rew waited until he saw Breezerunner's muscles release their tension while he stroked and scratched the dragon's beautiful scaly face.

"*Where is Serek?*" Breezerunner asked.

"*He will be here soon. I promise,*" Rew said. A guard strode by the wagon without even looking toward it, oblivious to their silent communication. *Very sloppy guard work. . . . sloppy, indeed.* A commotion toward the center of camp drew Rew's attention as well as the guard's. The big man's head turned in that general direction, as he bobbed up and down on his toes, trying to catch a glimpse of what was going on. Roaring laughter and loud jeers reached Rew's sensitive ears and he thought of Kristina and Link. *I hope they know what they are doing.*

From out of the brush came Serek, silent and unseen in the darkness. With the skill of a ninja, he came up behind the distracted guard and clubbed him once on the head with the hilt of his sword. Uttering a shallow groan, the guard sank into Serek's waiting arms unconscious. He dragged the body into the nearby woods and then returned to the flatbed wagon where he immediately started examining the chains that secured the shackles around Breezerunner's head, tail and limbs.

Breezerunner cooed softly, "*You are my Serek.*"

Rew did his best to hush the dragon. "*He has come to free you. We must remain silent.*"

Shouts and laughter continued to sound loudly from the center of the camp where Rew could see a large congregation of soldiers had gathered around the bonfire. Rew wondered what type of performance was being staged by Link and Kristina. *They are playing for a dangerous audience.* "Hurry, Serek!" Rew pleaded, feeling anxiety creep up his spine.

"*I am your Breezerunner,*" the dragon said to Serek.

Jessabelle flew down from her perch and landed on the flatbed next to Rew. She trilled twice, indicating that someone was coming. Serek didn't hesitate a moment longer. He swung his sword high over his head and brought it down on the loop that secured Breezerunner's neck chain. The blade sliced through the metal like it was butter. Rew got busy clearing the chain from around Breezerunner's neck while Serek swung at the other links, severing them all with one stroke each. Once all of the chains were removed, Breezerunner lifted his head weakly and attempted to stand up on shaky legs. His diminished strength pulled him back down onto the surface of the flatbed where he lay disheartened.

"It's okay, Breezerunner. Rest easy. Our friend, Kaltog, will carry you," Rew reassured the baby dragon.

On cue, Kaltog came toward them from his hiding place in the brush and bent down to pick up the baby dragon, who probably weighed at least five hundred pounds. Breezerunner wiggled in his grasp but the torg held on tight.

Rew's ears registered the pounding feet. Two soldiers were coming toward them at a fast trot. As they neared they drew their swords. Serek yelled at Kaltog, "Get him out of here! We'll catch up."

Kaltog was gone before the soldiers arrived. Seeing the flatbed empty, the two men began sounding the alarm, "The dragon has been stolen!" They both raised their swords and challenged Serek, unaware of Jessabelle and Rew, who looked on from the shadows. Serek lifted his own sword in defense, swinging the blade expertly, clashing with first one then the other soldier's blades. The two men separated and came at him from opposite directions, dividing Serek's attention. He spun, ducked and jabbed left and right. The soldiers were unrelenting and Serek's attention was being spread too thin. One hazardous swing and his shoulder was bleeding with a deep cut. Serek backed away slowly and then rushed to attack again, ignoring the injury and the odds.

A crowd gathered to watch the contest. They yelled jibes at their fellow soldiers and insults at Serek, cheering for more action. Kristina and Link made their way through the riotous horde. They stopped and observed without taking immediate action. Serek was losing ground. His wounded shoulder sagged and he was beginning to stagger slightly. Every ounce of energy went to raising his sword in defense as they two guards pounded their blades at him. A swift twist sent Serek's sword flying from his hand, up and over Rew's head. The tallest soldier drew back his blade for a fatal plunge. Link and Kristina readied their hidden daggers, gripping them firmly in their hands as they sprang forward and defended their friend.

Jessabelle leapt impulsively into the air. With talons extended fully, the bald eagle sped toward the soldier as he began his thrust at Serek. She sunk her talons into the man's eyes and tore the delicate flesh. He screamed in agony as he flayed blindly with the sword to fend off his attacker. The blade missed. As Jessabelle dodged, the hilt of the sword struck her on the head and she fell to the ground. She lay in the dust motionless at Serek's feet.

Jessabelle!

"No!" Kristina screamed and ran forward. The blinded soldier kicked at Jessabelle's delicate body with a heavy boot. Enraged, Kristina attacked. Spinning, she lifted her leg and landed a swift kick to the man's head, followed with a backhand and a punch. She was agile and swift in her actions and her moves were like flowing silk. Following through, she plunged her dagger into the soldier's chest with a quick flick of the wrist. He slid to the ground dead.

Kristina knelt down beside the unconscious bird and carefully lifted Jessabelle's body into her arms, stroking the white head softly while she spoke to the bird in quiet tones.

Rew hefted Serek's sword off from the ground and laboriously delivered the blade to his wounded comrade. It didn't take long for the soldiers to respond. In mass, they descended upon the company. Link and Serek stood over Kristina and Jessabelle, facing the soldiers with only a sword and a knife. Their blades flashed back and forth with phenomenal speed, but the odds were overwhelming. It seemed hopeless.

Rew stood beside Kristina and whispered in her ear, "Is she going to be all right?"

The princess replied, "I don't . . . "

Thunder sounded in the woods behind them. They both turned their heads and watched as trees turned to splinters. Kaltog, astride his mount, raced into the clearing with a mighty war cry. The soldiers looked up in shock before terror crossed their faces.

Serek grabbed Kristina by the upper arm and propelled her down the path newly made by the heavy hooves of the monstrous horse. Link followed behind them. Taking their one chance to escape, they ran into the darkness.

At the same time several dragons swooped down from up above. The soldiers scattered as the dragons gave chase.

Kaltog immediately spun his mount around and headed after the rest of the company, leaving the soldiers far behind.

When Rew caught up, they were huddled around a tree examining Jessabelle tenderly. Kaltog dismounted and Rew flew lightly over to the party. "Is she going to be all right?" he asked, flying to each person in turn, trying to get someone's attention. Link swatted at him in annoyance. "Link, is she going to be all right?" he asked again.

Link curled the tip of his beard around stubby fingers as he gazed at the injured eagle, but did not answer.

Kristina, who was still cradling the injured bird in her arms, looked up at Rew and said, "I don't know, Rew. She won't wake up."

"Let me take a look," Rew said as he examined her. He tried his magic, but her wound was beyond his abilities.

Crashing through the woods made them all go for their weapons.

Serek laughed, shaking off the tension. "Relax, it's only Breezerunner." A few seconds later the baby dragon walked awkwardly into the clearing. He advanced toward them on very unsteady legs. His left wing was askew where it had been broken during his abduction. Kaltog and Serek began administering first aid to Breezerunner right away. They fashioned a splint and after rebreaking the askew bone, they wrapped it tightly in hope that it would heal correctly. Rew performed a little magic on the suffering dragon and made him fall into a deep sleep so they could perform the painful procedure.

"We had better get going," Serek said over his shoulder as he loaded the packs onto Kaltog's mount. After a lot of coaxing, Kaltog convinced his mount to carry the sleeping dragon as well and he and Serek secured the heavy baby to the back of the hairy creature with the utmost care.

Kristina leaned over to where Rew sat beside her on the ground and said, "We have to get some help for Jessabelle somewhere."

"Aren't we close to your home, Link?" Rew asked the banderg, as he stroked Jessabelle's soft feathers.

Link pulled on his beard with dirty hands as he paused in thought. "We're about fifty miles northeast of Skyview. It would take us at least a couple of days walking to get there, and with an injured dragon and an injured kendrite, probably longer. I don't think Jessabelle has that long to wait." He thought for a few more minutes, pursing his lips and furrowing his brow in serious deliberation. Link's hand shot up in the air with his first finger extended as an idea struck home. "However, there is a hunter I know who lives east of Skyview. If I can get my bearings straight, I should be able to find her. She is knowledgeable about animals including birds. If anyone can help Jessabelle, Anna can."

Rew felt hope rise in his heart. "Lead the way!" he said.

Serek helped Kristina off the ground as she tended to her burden, lifting her easily despite his recent injury. "She's going to be all right," he assured her.

Kristina looked up at Serek seeking confirmation of his words in his eyes. "I was wrong about her. It doesn't matter if she is a kendrite. She's my friend," she said.

Serek gazed compassionately at her and reached out to stroke her hair. She tilted her head toward his hand in response to his touch. His voice was gentle as he said, "I'm sure she'll be fine. Would you like me to carry her?"

"No. She is my responsibility . . . she is practically family," she said.

Serek stepped away from her, puzzled, but Rew understood what Kristina was feeling, and he smiled. *Please let Jessabelle be okay.*

"Just let me know if you want me to carry her, Kristina. She is my friend too," Serek said with a smile.

"Thanks," she said, smiling back.

The battered and tired company followed Link throughout the rest of the night. By dawn Kristina was leaning heavily against Serek for support, although she would not relinquish her burden. He kept his arm firmly around her waist. Breezerunner remained in quiet repose upon Kaltog's mount. They trudged quietly on.

The foothills of the Skyview Mountains provided neither easy walking nor simple navigation. Rocky terrain with uneven black volcanic rock tripped them up constantly. The forest was not thick, but trees grew where the flattest ground existed, so the path tended to go around trees and over the roughest ground. Darkness engulfed their way as the night lingered on. Bandergs were naturally at home in the mountains and Link was no exception. The steady pace he set was grueling on the already tired company. Only Kaltog, who also grew up in the mountains, had no problem keeping up with the banderg.

Rew flew for a time, but his wings became tired maintaining the slow pace required to stay with the company, so he decided to walk to give his wings a break. But, after walking for about a mile, Rew's feet became sore and he started to lag far behind. Kaltog spotted him and waited down the path for Rew to catch up. The torg eyed him speculatively and asked, "Why don't you fly?"

Rew leaned his head back and looked up at the giant. "I'm tired, my feet hurt, my wings hurt and I'm hungry." *I shouldn't have mentioned that. Now I am really hungry. Just don't think about it . . . don't think about food . . . or eating . . . or ale . . . oh no . . . don't think about ale.*

"Those are an awful lot of complaints for such a little creature. Why don't you fly up to my shoulder and have a seat. I will carry you the rest of the way. Okay?" Kaltog offered.

Rew lifted his head and answered brightly, "Yeah, that will be great. Thanks!" He fluttered his wings and came to rest lightly upon Kaltog's right shoulder. Kaltog might as well have been carrying a feather as much as Rew weighed, so the wisp was hardly a burden to the torg. Together, with Kaltog leading his mount, they set off after the others and quickly caught up to the exhausted company.

From his view on top of Kaltog's shoulder, Rew watched Link examine the path they had just intersected. The banderg turned around to face the rest of the company with a big smile on his face. "This is it," Link stated proudly. "This is the path. Follow me. We'll be there shortly."

Rew was excited to the point that he was bouncing up and down on Kaltog's shoulder. *I sure hope this hunter lady has something good to eat. Maybe she's a good baker. I would love some sweet pastries . . . and some potatoes with cream and ham bits . . . some cold milk . . . oooh! and maybe some ale . . .*

As they came around a sharp bend in the path, Link turned left and led them into a patch of woods that was flat and absent the rocky terrain they had been hiking through. Only a short distance into the woods they came across a modest clearing. Golden rays of early morning sun drenched a small stone cabin that sat serenely opposite them in the light of dawn. Smoke rose in delicate wisps from the chimney. White rocks lined a pathway that led up to the cabin's wooden porch. Flowers of many colors adorned the edge of the rock pathway, making a cheerful welcome to the homey cottage. Wood was stacked neatly upon the porch for easy access. The company approached the cabin quietly. Kaltog lifted Rew off from his shoulder and let him make his own way up the garden path.

The front door opened and a banderg woman appeared dressed in a bright pink robe that hung loosely on her trim figure. Rew could see that she was much older than Link, but still had strong muscles and held herself agilely. The silver hair on her head was long and luxurious. She looked up at the company and measured them with bright copper colored eyes. After spotting Link, she came forward to greet them, accompanied on the left and right by two beautiful golden retrievers. She took Link's hand and then hugged him enthusiastically. "Link, you old fool, what are you doing here? I just sent a shipment to your kitchens last week. Is your apprentice out of black deer meat already?" she asked.

"No, Anna . . . well, actually I don't know. I haven't been home for several moons." Link sighed heavily. "Anyway, these are my friends. We need your help." His petition brought silence from Anna as she examined the group with hands on her hips and a scowl on her face. Taking in everything with shrewd eyes, she looked back at Link and nodded. The dogs sniffed around and apparently came to the same conclusion as their owner.

Link let out the breath he had been holding and turned toward the party. "The big one here is Kaltog, this is Serek, Kristina and the little one is Rew. The dragon asleep on that big hairy horse is Breezerunner. He has a broken wing. Kristina is holding Jessabelle, who is a kendrite. She was injured last night. We can't get her to wake up. Do you think you can help us?" Link said in a hurry and sighed after he got it all out.

Anna walked over to Kristina and took Jessabelle gently into her arms. She looked up at the company and welcomed them officially in the banderg manner by saying, "My name is Annalibijopahuntresshisheart. You can call me Anna. Welcome to my home." She turned and led the way to her cabin.

Even though Rew's experience with little cabins in the woods was, at the most limited, he was surprised to find the interior bright, airy and colorful. Anna's cabin reflected her personality with a warm and cozy elegance. The draperies, which hung freshly cleaned and pressed were of a soft pink lace. Fresh cut flowers in colorful vases adorned every corner and stood on the large black stone fireplace mantle. The furnishings were simple wooden items that appeared to have been very recently polished, making the light colored wood glow. Pink cushions that matched the draperies made the hard wood furniture look comfortable and inviting. Rew stifled a yawn as he watched Anna place Jessabelle upon the kitchen table. She examined the eagle gently, probing and touching the bird, looking into her eyes and mouth, and putting her ear to the eagle's chest to listen.

Kristina, Rew and Link watched Anna's ministrations closely, concern over Jessabelle's well-being utmost on their minds. Kaltog and Serek were outside unpacking the mount and tending to the still sleeping Breezerunner.

Anna addressed the group as Serek strode into the kitchen just in time to receive her diagnosis. She said, "It appears that your kendrite friend has a concussion. There are some herbs I could try to treat her with, but I don't know how successful they will be. Time is the best cure for her condition . . . time and rest. I will make up a comfortable bed for her and then go out and hunt down the herb I need. I'm sure you would all like to get some rest and probably some breakfast, eh?"

Kristina smiled warmly, her heart growing a tender spot already for the banderg huntress. "Thank you for all your help, Anna," she said. "I know I for one am very hungry. There is another matter we need to take care of first, however. The baby dragon, Breezerunner, has a broken wing. We administered first aid on the trail and he is asleep now, thanks to Rew, but I am afraid when he wakes up he will be in considerable pain and probably very hungry. Perhaps you could take a look at him and see if there is anything you can do to help."

Anna's expression became animated as she exclaimed, "Oh yes. The dragon. I almost forgot about him. I do hope he will behave himself. A hungry dragon so close to my goldens! Good heavens! And in pain?"

Serek spoke in defense of Breezerunner, "He is really very gentle. I am sure he won't be a problem."

Anna's eyes were wide as she said, "Young man, hungry dragons are always a problem. I have my animals to think about . . . livestock, hunting dogs . . . my beautiful golden retrievers."

Anna seemed so disturbed, if she had a beard, Rew was sure she would be pulling on it. Serek started to reply, "Breezerunner would never . . ."

Rew laughed, "Certainly not! He's just a baby."

Anna shook her head and said, "Very well. I will take a look at him, give him something for the pain and get him something to eat from my stores. But, if he even looks at my goldens sideways . . . I'll . . . I'll pull his teeth out. You folks make yourselves comfortable. I'll be back to cook you breakfast." Anna began to walk out the front door. Serek turned to go with her.

Link stopped her before she stepped out onto the wooden porch. "If you don't mind, I would love to cook breakfast. I haven't been in a real kitchen for longer than I'd like to remember. What do you say?" he asked.

"My home is your home. Enjoy." Anna nodded to Serek they left together. Rew heard Kaltog greet them from the front porch in his deep voice.

While Link went off to explore the kitchen with intense delight, Kristina and Rew went to find some place to wash up. They found a hand operated pump in the back of the house that fed into a large basin of water. Kristina drew a rag from her pack and quickly stripped off her clothes. With a complete lack of modesty, she began scrubbing dirt and dried blood from her skin until it grew pink from the effort. She handed Rew the rag when she was done and he scrubbed off all of the road dirt too. When they both had finished, Kristina washed out her clothes and hung them out to dry on the nearby clothesline. She dressed

THE LEGACY

in a clean riding outfit and brushed her wet hair out thoroughly. She offered the brush to Rew, who declined it, preferring to just give his curls a good brisk shake.

Wonderful aromas tantalized Rew's senses when he and Kristina entered the cabin, feeling immeasurably refreshed from their cold bath. Rew's stomach growled hollowly making him anxious to fill the void. Link was busy in the kitchen and was whistling a cheerful tune when they entered. Kristina offered her assistance, but Link refused her, clearly not wanting anyone edging in on his domain. Link offered them hot cups of tog, a banderg's version of coffee, and shooed them back into the living room, where they made themselves comfortable on the sofa.

By the time Anna and Serek had returned from checking on Breezerunner, breakfast was ready. Anna showed them to a large picnic table behind the house where they were joined by Kaltog, who sat on the ground. Link and Anna served them steaming cups of tog, ice cold milk, banana cinnamon muffins with sweet butter, black deer meat that was cooked with spices Rew could not identify but was tender enough to melt in his mouth, some type of spinach dish with bacon pieces that Rew was surprised to find very tasty, and potatoes with cream and bits of ham. Everybody ate more than their fill and Rew ate more than everybody's fill twice. Link finished his breakfast, patting his distended belly with a look of profound satisfaction. Rew felt delightfully satisfied as well.

They all helped clear the dishes and clean up the kitchen at a leisurely pace. After checking on Jessabelle, who was still sleeping quietly, most of the company settled down in the living room to relax. Link and Anna sat on the porch with Kaltog and enjoyed the freshness of the air. The door was open and a breeze brushed lazily against the lace curtains, carrying a floral and pine scent that reminded Rew of home. *This is very pleasant . . . pleasant indeed.* Rew closed his eyes and savored the feeling.

He opened his eyes again, waking from an almost dozing state when he heard Link clear his throat. "What can you tell me of my family, Anna? Have you seen them? Are they well?" Link sat forward in his seat on the porch in anticipation of some news from home.

Anna's face clouded for a moment before she answered, "I saw Berry and Fibi at the market place the last time I was in town making a delivery of some smoked wild boar to the local merchants and taverns. Berry looked beautiful as usual and Fibi as sweet as ever. Your wife didn't mention that you were absent, but she did look a bit stressed. Now I know why. What business do you have gallivanting all over Risen when Skyview is under attack by sinister forces?"

Link jumped to his feet, grabbed at his beard with his left hand and for the hilt of his absent dagger with his right. "Skyview is under attack!?"

Anna looked sternly at Link as she said, "Stop pulling on your beard or your chin will be as bald as a boulder before Fibi's old enough to take a mate. A beardless father of the bride would be disgraceful. Now, don't panic. I'm sure our warriors can do without you, Link. The enemy's invasion force is having little success at the moment. They have tried to force their way into Skyview by using a battering ram against the northern gate. They might as well have tried to move the entire mountain." Anna chuckled loudly and was soon joined by Link as he quit sulking.

Anna went on, "The fiery arrows they launched from their bows succeeded in burning the gate, destroying it eventually. Although it is defended, it is a shame that it was destroyed. The milkwood both the northern and southern gates were carved from centuries ago came from the forest that used to line the shore where Castle Xandia now stands. That forest was leveled many generations ago and milkwood is now extinct. Considering the masterful craftsmanship put into the making of the gate, it is irreplaceable. Such a shame."

"Our people have been raiding the Saber's camp at night ever since the troops arrived. I think they are beginning to enjoy it a little too much, thinking it is some kind of game. They do things like steal food, take tent stakes out so that when a stiff wind comes up all the tents fall down, empty water containers so the Sabers have to refill them over and over again, untether the horses so they have to be rounded up again; just general nuisance kind of things."

Anna grinned as she thought of a story. "One of the warriors went out and captured some fire ants, snuck into the general's tent at night and released them into his bed. The general woke up screaming from the pain of the tiny little bites, and ran out of his tent, buck naked, covered with angry red ants, flailing his arms and yelling for water. The night watchman hurried to get some water to pour over his distressed general's body, but found each and every container in camp empty. Finally he found some water in the horse's trough, but upon lifting the heavy metal container, the soldier lost his footing, dumped the water onto the ground and proceeded to fall face first into the resulting muck. The general, still being eaten alive by the ants, did the best thing he could have done by flopping down in the muck and rolling around in it until he was covered from head to toe in horse slop. I wish I could have seen it . . . could you imagine . . . a grown man . . . " Anna trailed off into a fit of laughter.

Rew enjoyed Anna's story, but his eyelids were growing increasingly heavy. He jumped off from the comfortable couch, excused himself from his friends, and grabbed his sleeping blanket from his pack. Walking out the door, he joined Kaltog and a snoring Breezerunner on the porch, curled up in the farthest corner and let his eyes finally rest. The late morning sun was warm against his skin and Breezerunner's rhythmic snoring was hypnotic. Feeling exhaustion overcome him, Rew's last thought before falling asleep was for his friend. *Please let Jessabelle be okay* . . .

. . . Rew felt elated as he flew through the sky watching with delight the beautiful wisp with the long curly hair as she dove and spiraled around him, enticing him to join her in play. He turned his head as he heard an eagle screech in greeting, and he smiled happily as he watched Jessabelle glide smoothly toward him . . .

Chapter 15

A CLASH WITH FATE

August 9. I came awake with a jerk and removed my fingertips carefully from the surface of the water. The good feelings that lingered from Rew's dream soon faded and I found myself feeling anxious, although I couldn't pinpoint the cause. Slowly I stretched my cramped muscles before standing up and testing my equilibrium. As if in a state of drunkenness, I exited the room and descended the stairs to my bedroom on the second floor. One of the few luxuries in the tower was the spacious washroom that adjoined my room and the master suite where Shareen had slept. When I entered the washroom, Nina was preparing a hot bath, complete with fragrant bubbles. She looked up at me and smiled in greeting. "Hello dear, your bath is almost ready. There are fresh towels on the stand." She stood up and patted my hand. "I have a tray prepared for you in the kitchen. I will bring it up. Do get some rest after you eat, Gabriel." The motherly tone she took with me grated on my nerves slightly.

Shrugging off the irritation, I smiled and tried my best to be pleasant. "Thank you, Nina. You are very thoughtful," I said. I knew she was missing Shareen and was filling that void somehow by smothering me with attention. I was grateful for the hot bath and all I wanted to do was sink into it, close my eyes and go to sleep. Nina left me alone, and I did slip into the hot steamy water, but I did not, or could not, go to sleep. The nagging feeling I had been having ever since leaving Rew's mind was pressing down heavily upon me and I agonized over its cause. The water in the bath began to turn tepid and I still hadn't a clue as to what was causing my distress, so I dried off, slipped on a soft clean robe and went to my room to eat. The tray that Nina had prepared for me looked delicious, but I could only nibble, finding my appetite waning as my frustration over my unease escalated.

I wrote in my diary and then attempted to sleep, but only tossed and turned, changing the position of my pillow numerous times before throwing it from the bed completely. As I got out of bed to retrieve the pillow, I realized the cause of my distress. Looking down at the last entry I had made in my diary, the date grabbed my attention. Of course! August 9th was the anniversary of my wedding to John. I couldn't believe I had forgotten. It was a very special occasion for us; we always found some new and romantic way to reaffirm our love together. This year was our ninth year and we were spending it apart. My heart ached for John, the void so empty that I thought it would swallow me whole. If only I could be with him tonight, I thought. God! It hurt so much.

I slipped on my robe and slippers and headed back up the stairs to the sixth floor. It was very dark and I had to feel my way down the hallway to the door that stood always closed. Apparently, it was still quite early in the evening and Nina had not yet gotten around to lighting the large candles that lined the stairway and halls. It didn't matter. I could make my own light. I opened the door and entered the dark room. From my fingers came a small spark when I rubbed them quickly together. I lit only one candle in the room; just enough to be able to see into the sight water and make the connection. My heart pounded hard against my chest with excitement.

Anxiously, I sat down in my customary chair, and felt a twinge of guilt when I looked across the basin to where Shareen had sat, remembering that she had strictly forbidden me to do what I was about to attempt. "Sorry Shareen," I said aloud, "I have to do this."

My anxiety was not allowing me to relax easily, and I had to concentrate hard to get my body to respond to my wishes. When my breathing had slowed sufficiently, I reached out and brought my fingertips down upon the cool wet surface of the sight water in the basin. The rune I drew to activate the sight glowed bright green on the surface. I pictured John's face in my mind and thought of everything that made him familiar to me--his smile, his laugh, the masculine scent of him after a hard day at work, the way his arms felt around me, so sturdy and welcoming, the particular scowl that would crease his face when he paid the monthly bills, the fun loving way that he played with the children, so many things came to mind . . . but nothing happened. The water remained still and the dim surface reflected only my fingertips as they touched the cold wetness. I felt my emotions rise bitterly in my throat and I choked back a sob. Standing up, I withdrew my hand from the sight water and paced the dimly lit room. After some time I was calm enough to try again, but again there was no response. I began to think that maybe it just wasn't possible.

My thin slippers padded on the cold stone floor as I paced the room once more. The thought occurred to me to try my sister, who was caring for the children in my absence. Unrelenting fear gripped my soul. "God, help me," I prayed. I sat once again in my chair before the basin and did my relaxation exercises until I felt ready to begin. The cold of the water when I touched it made a shiver run down the length of my spine.

My sister, Carmen, was much stricter than I with the children, but they loved their aunt just the same. She was my senior by three years and I thought she was very beautiful with dark hair, coppery brown eyes, and full rich lips. She seldom smiled, however, tending to be morose by nature. John used to tell me that was why he thought she had never married, because she was too stern and no man would have her. I knew the real reason she was still single was that she was too shy around men and had only dated on a rare occasion. My hope was that someday she would find someone as wonderful as John to love her.

Carmen's lovely face was shown through the water to me. She was busy doing something with her hands . . . cooking dinner. Humming a melancholy tune, she turned toward the kitchen table where the children sat quietly sipping on milk from small the plastic cups that I had purchased at Woolworths last fall. My children, a boy and a girl were young still, nine and seven, respectively. Marguerite and Peter sat at the table with their plates empty, awaiting their meals patiently. My babies! . . .

 . . . "Are you children hungry?" Carmen asked without really expecting an answer. She winced and brought her hands up to her head, suddenly feeling quite dizzy. The feeling soon passed, however, and she shook off the queasiness by taking a deep breath. Carmen served the children grilled cheese sandwiches along with grapes and baby carrots. "Eat up kids, and drink all of your milk so you'll grow up big and strong." *I wish Gabriel would come home. The kids really need her now. Where did that sister of mine take off to? Telling her about John won't be easy. They were so close. She'll be destroyed by the news.*

Carmen grabbed her head with both hands and fell to her knees on the ground. *What about John? What about John? What about John?* echoed in her mind over and over again. The pain in her head was tremendous and Carmen became terrified of what was happening to her. Tears streamed down her cheeks and her breath started coming in heavy gulps. *What about John? What about John? What about John?* "Stop it!" she screamed. The children looked frightened, confused by their aunt's sudden strange behavior. Carmen managed to stand up by pulling her body off the floor with the help of the kitchen counter. *I've got to call the doctor and get a baby sitter.* She groaned softly, trying to hold down the contents of her stomach. *I feel awful.* Carmen reached the wall where the phone hung and picked up the receiver. Shaking uncontrollably, she leafed through the little address book in search of her doctor's phone number. *What's happened to John? Carmen, what's happened to John?* Carmen dropped the receiver and it clattered to the floor as she recognized her sister's presence. *He's dead!* Carmen managed to convey before she passed out on the cold kitchen floor . . .

. . . *He's dead!* I heard the words faintly before everything went black, the contact broken at the other end. Reality became as solid as a cloud. I pulled my fingers from the water and wiped them idly on my robe. "John's dead?" I said aloud in a monotone of shock, not believing my own words. The room seemed to spin and I had to fight to keep from vomiting. *John's dead. No. John's dead. No. John's dead. No!* A scream escaped my lips and traveled throughout the thick stone interior of the tower. I heard footsteps on the stairs and knew that Nina had heard my scream and would be there soon. Dread enveloped me. I didn't

want to move, I didn't want to feel anything, I didn't want to live
. . . not without John.

The door opened and Nina walked in, carrying a brightly lit
lantern. "I heard a sound. Are you all right, dear?"

"No. He's dead. No," I said dully. I was in shock.

She approached me, laid a hand on my shoulder and asked,
"Who's dead, dear?"

"John."

"Gabriel, tell me what's wrong. Who is John?" Nina knelt
down next to my chair and looked into my face with deep concern.

"My husband, John . . . !" I was starting to feel. I didn't
want to feel.

"Oh, dear. I'm so sorry, child. Come with me, Gabriel. I'll
take you to your room." She grabbed hold of my hand and pulled
me up out of the chair. I went along easily.

When we reached my bedroom door, I pulled away from Nina's grasp and said, "I have to go home. My babies are alone and
they need me. I have to go home now." I looked around me in
confusion, not knowing what to do next. The only thing driving
me was the knowledge that I had to return home immediately.

"B.F., I need you!" I cried mentally.

His response was instant, "Gabriel, what distresses you so?"

"Oh, B.F., it's terrible." Tears rolled down my cheeks as the
dragon's compassion filled my heart. "I don't want to feel . . . it
hurts too much. Help me!" I cried.

"Hang on, Gabriel. We're almost there," he said. He began
humming inside my head a complex calming song. A strange
peacefulness filled my heart and mind as I walked down to the
tower's entrance and watched B.F. land on the grassy plain in
front of Ornate. Theo jumped down from the saddle, made his
way quickly toward where I stood in the doorway and enclosed

me in his arms. I hung on to him as my strength gave way and my knees buckled. "John's dead," I whispered and I felt his arms tighten around me. Theo picked me up and carried me to the big leather chair that sat in front of the fireplace. He smelled of dirt, sweat and the sweet muskiness of dragon. He eased me down into the chair, although I was disinclined to let him go. The peacefulness I felt turned to grogginess and my eyelids felt like lead. All of my feelings were muddled. As B.F. continued his song, I rested in a cloud of disembodiment. I struggled against it to no avail. Before I fell into a deep and dreamless sleep, I wondered impassively what B.F. had done to me to make me feel so numb and quietly thanked him for it.

"*You're welcome, my friend. I am so sorry,*" I heard B.F.'s voice whisper. "*Rest easy . . . rest easy. . .* "

Decision to Leave

August 10. I awoke this morning in my own bed with a feeling of disbelief. Remembering last night brought fresh pain abruptly to the surface of my consciousness. Guilt about leaving the situation on Risen unresolved made my actions unsure. My need to be with my children was overwhelming, but I wasn't sure going back home immediately was the right answer. It didn't feel like the right choice. I decided to wait and pack later. First, I needed to talk to Theo and B.F. to try and straighten out my thoughts and get plans clear in my own mind.

After a quick bath, I dressed in a simple gray dress and went downstairs. Theo and Hue sat at the kitchen table eating breakfast and talking quietly. Nina was busy serving the two men and did not see me come into the kitchen. She almost dropped the tray of fresh fruit she was carrying when she turned around and saw me there. Her eyes absorbed my appearance and I saw them mist over before she turned away. I joined the men at the table. Nina brought me a cup of tea and a large plate full of food. The tea was fresh and hot so I sipped on it cautiously, enjoying the strong flavor. Having no appetite, the food on my plate went untouched and I'm sure Nina had to bite her tongue in order not to scold me.

"Theo, I must return home. John . . ." The lump in my throat threatened to choke me. "John is dead and my children need me. Will you take me back to the gate?" I asked.

Theo reached out and touched my hand before appraising me with a serious expression. "I am very sorry about John, Gabriel, and I understand your need to return home. I'm afraid things are reaching a critical stage here, however, and I desperately need your help. In fact, B.F. and I were on our way here already when you called to him last night. Candaz is massing his troops just north of the Skyview Mountains. Something major is at hand. Never before has he assembled his entire army at one location. Always in the past he has kept them dispersed so they could continue to wear down Brightening's defenses on many different fronts. I believe he is getting ready for his final push into the south. If Skyview falls, only defenseless villages lay in his path before he reaches Castle Gentlebreeze. We must stop him now, before he has a chance to conquer Skyview. My troops are on their way north as we speak. I was hoping you would come with me."

I felt torn in two. Although I wished to avoid it, I had a responsibility to help defend Brightening against Candaz. But, my responsibility to my children was much more important. They had to come first. My decision was made.

"*Gabriel, can I give you some advice?*" B.F. asked before I could respond to Theo.

"Yes, B.F. I will listen."

"When you originally came to Risen it was in order to protect your family from Candaz. Your children are safe for now. How long do you think they will be safe from him if you go back now?" he asked.

I thought before answering, not wanting to admit to myself that B.F. might have a point. *"They are protected from him with a spell. I set the spell myself. He can't break through it,"* I said.

"Your husband is dead. You don't know how he died. If you return, Gabriel, Candaz will be able to follow you, and he will get through. This has to be your decision, but, you are my friend and so I will tell you what I know. Your destiny is to finish what you have started here. If you do not fulfill your destiny the repercussions could be devastating not only for Risen, but to all that is and to all that will ever be. This is a personal decision, Gabriel, but also one of global importance. Candaz has served the corruptive forces well in Risen by creating hate and distrust between the races and fear as his armies destroy homes and kill innocent people, men woman and children alike. The decay is fed by the pain he instills and grows stronger every day. Already you can see it creeping into other worlds which were before protected from the corruptive forces' influence. The balance of power is shifting swiftly. If it is not altered now, there is no telling how long we will have left; destined to fight and kill and hate, unable to rejoice purely in the glory of life for the rest of our days. The trend must be reversed now. You have the opportunity to do something about it. I can feel the goodness of your soul and the love you hold in your heart, not only for your children, but for everything that embraces nobility. If you can defeat Candaz, it will help the balance become more equalized. Your children will be safe while you accomplish this goal and then you can return to them freely and without reservation. Do not deny your destiny, Mistress," B.F. said.

I looked into Theo's intense green eyes while I considered B.F.'s words. Frustration over my situation made me want to scream and John's death made me feel like someone had ripped open my abdomen and torn out my insides. Repressing a choking sob that lodged itself in my throat, I reached up and clasped the golden medallion in my hand, feeling the familiar coolness of the metal. I felt so small and insignificant. My fate, I had always believed, was to raise my children and grow old with my husband at my side, eventually to enjoy the freedom of being a grandparent. Why was I being expected to put aside my life and pursue a goal that was far too extraordinary for someone like me to accomplish alone? My heart cried out for relief.

The gold in my hand warmed and I remembered with a rush of emotion that I wasn't alone. Fighting along with me were Rew, Kristina, Serek, Kaltog, Link, Jessabelle, and many, many others. My gaze came to rest on Theo who sat quietly across the table awaiting my decision.

Jessabelle . . .

"Theo!" I choked, standing abruptly and causing the china to rattle noisily on the upset table.

Theo sat upright and regarded me calmly with questioning eyes.

I managed to blurt out, "It's Jessabelle."

Before I knew what was happening Theo was standing before me with his hands roughly clutching my shoulders. "What has happened, Gabriel?" Theo demanded with crisp military authority. When I began to shrink away, he said more gently, "Tell me, please."

"She's been hurt. An enemy soldier knocked her unconscious with the hilt of his sword while she was an eagle. The last time I checked she was still in a coma. That was yesterday. I can go upstairs and check on her again, Theo. It will take a little while." The thought of using the sight again made me cringe, but I was willing do it for him.

Theo's forehead was creased with worry and his jawline moved visibly as he clenched and unclenched his teeth. "Do you know where she is?" he asked expectantly.

"Yes . . . Theo, we can't . . . I can't . . . I have to go home," I said, fighting for the decision I had already made. I was fighting against a destiny that was determined to set its own course. I stubbornly strengthened my resolve to follow my own path.

"Take me to her, now. We must get to Jessabelle. Maybe you can help her," he said. He held my arm lightly and implored me with his eyes that were full of passion and fear.

My resolve crumbled under Theo's intense gaze. I said, "Okay. I will take you to her."

B.F. commented gently in my mind, "*You are doing the right thing, Mistress.*"

Although my position had been swayed slightly, my defenses automatically went up. "*After I see if there is anything I can do for Jessabelle, I still plan on going back home. My children need their mother back, B.F. I will not be diverted from that goal. But, first I'll help Jessabelle.*"

"*Of course, Gabriel.*"

"*I am going home, B.F.*"

"*Of course, Gabriel.*"

The dragon's condescending attitude left me exasperated. Out of the corner of my eye I noticed Nina watching my growing frustration with a grim expression on her face and a reprimand on her lips. Dramatically, I flung my arms in the air, frustrated and fed up with everyone trying to run my life. I turned to see what had become of Theo.

"He went to gather his things." Nina said from behind me as she began clearing the table around where Hue still sat sipping his tea, oblivious to everything as usual.

I headed up the stairs to my bedroom to pack what I thought I would need for traveling, leaving most of my things behind. Climbing to the third floor library, where Shareen and I had spent so much time together, I selected a text on healing, which I stuffed in my bag along with Shareen's spell book. The instruction manual to the Gate sat open on the table exactly as Shareen had left it. Unspent grief played unfriendly games with my emotions. Tears surfaced as I remembered Shareen spending countless hours studying the magnificent manual. I touched it gently, longing to read its secrets, and then closed it with finality, causing a small plume of dust to billow from the ancient pages. With renewed determination to make my own destiny, I turned and left.

Nature's Healing

Theo met me on the grassy plain in front of the tower where B.F. rested patiently. The dragon studied me with his gleaming red eyes and I found my irritation with him vanquished. I scratched aggressively at his eye ridges making him coo softly, while Theo packed our gear into B.F.'s saddle bags. We were mounted and in the air within a half hour of my first mention of Jessabelle. The sun was still low in the eastern sky and mist hung heavily on the plains and over the deep azure waters of Blue Lake as we gained elevation.

B.F. flew swiftly and we were soon past Blue Lake and able to see the Skyview Mountains looming ahead of us. The peaks stood out in bright contrast to the light blue sky. Snow capped the upper elevations even though we were well into summer. As we drew closer, I gave B.F. what directions I could from mental images I had appropriated from Rew's mind. He conveyed confidence to me and I held tightly to Theo's back as we began our descent. A small cabin came into view below us with the chimney exuding a steady stream of gray-white smoke. B.F. landed lightly in front of the cabin, being careful not to disturb the colorful flower gardens that lined the walkway. As usual my stomach protested the landing process and I breathed deeply until my body stabilized.

"*How did you find this place so easily, B.F.?*" I inquired of him as I climbed off his back with Theo's assistance. I know my directions were vague at best.

"*Breezerunner guided me. We've been in communication for some time now. It would seem that we share the same sire.*" B.F. stretched his neck, moving his head back and forth in an almost human display.

"*You are brothers?*" I asked.

"*Only half-brothers. My mother is Jewel. Breezerunner's mother was Zephyr. Our common sire is Skymaster.*"

"Skymaster!" "*Of course.*" I turned around and saw Kristina running toward us.

"Theo!" the princess screamed as she wrapped her arms around her brother's neck. "Thank the Creator you are here. Jessabelle is hurt."

"Yes, I know," he said as he extricated himself from his sister's arms. "How is she doing?"

"She won't wake up. I'm really worried," she said.

A look of anger crossed Theo's face briefly before he concealed it. "I didn't know you cared. After all, she is a kendrite."

Kristina lifted her chin defiantly. "She is my friend, Theo. I have come to . . . appreciate her unique qualities," she said.

He grinned ironically. "You have grown up little sister. I would ask you what you are doing here, but that can wait, for now it is more important that you take us to see Jessabelle."

"Of course. Gabriel," Kristina greeted me before turning and heading toward the cabin where everyone was congregated on the porch.

Kristina introduced Anna to Theo and us both to the rest of the company. We exchanged hurried greetings and then Anna and Kristina escorted us to the kitchen where Jessabelle was laying silently on her small bed. I picked the eagle up and gently examined her before lying her back down. Theo stroked her feathers with his forefinger and then gazed into my face with hope-filled eyes.

I smiled at him and touched his hand before saying, "I will do what I can."

"Rew," I called. When he came into the kitchen, I sent him to fetch the book from my bag. When he returned with it, I flipped through the index until I found what I needed and then spent some time studying the text, while Rew, Kristina, Anna, and Theo watched me anxiously.

I felt confident and hopeful as I looked up again at my friends. "Theo, pick up Jessabelle and bring her outside. I think maybe I can persuade her to wake up," I said.

He picked up Jessabelle's feathered body ever so gently in his strong calloused hands. He cradled her tenderly and spoke words of encouragement as he walked out the front door. I walked past him to a place in the front yard where there was a patch of smooth dirt. Using my finger, I drew an intricate rune in the earth, double checking it with the book to make sure it was accurate. When I was satisfied with my work, I handed the book to Rew for safekeeping and approached Theo, who was holding Jessabelle protectively.

"I promise I'll take care of her. Give her to me," I ordered. He hesitated and then handed the unconscious eagle to me. Kristina came up next to Theo and put her arm around his waist to offer comfort. I turned toward where I had drawn the rune in the sand and put my full concentration into the healing of Jessabelle. Gently, I placed her within the circle of my drawing, positioning her head in just the right spot. I stood up straight and stretched my arms skyward, feeling a gentle breeze through my outstretched fingers and a tingle from the medallion on my chest. The wind gusted briefly and forcefully. I knelt down and touched the edge of the rune with my fingertip, channeling freecurrent energy into the circle, making the drawing glow a bright blue and green. We all watched and waited in anxious anticipation.

Together we witnessed Jessabelle's awakening. She opened her eyes, lifted her head from the ground and finally stood up. Dramatically, she extended her wings to their full seven foot span. The intelligence in her eyes was evident as she looked in our direction and trilled loudly. I held my breath as she began to shape change, not knowing whether she would be able to accomplish it fully after what she had been through. Theo's apprehension was unmistakable as his whole body seemed to go rigid where he stood beside me. I let out my breath when Jessabelle's human form solidified and she smiled in my direction. The only evidence of trauma was a streak of white hair on her right side that ran the entire length of her shiny red mane. She came forward and was immediately engulfed in Theo's arms. There was nobody else in their world as they lost themselves in a kiss. When they finally parted, the rest of the company got hugs all around until Jessabelle again found her way back to her prince.

Watching the two together made me bite my lip in reaction to the deep loneliness I felt inside. A wave of despair touched my soul as I thought of John and the love we had once shared and the life we would share together no more. B.F. saved me from myself once again by saying, *"Most excellent work, Gabriel.*

Shareen has done a wonderful job training you in such a short period of time. I would hate to see it all go to waste. As long as you are still here, maybe you should give the good news to Kaltog about his people being freed. May I say, that was also excellent work."

"Thank you, B.F., I will," I said, ignoring his not-too-subtle prodding. I walked over to where Kaltog was now sitting on the porch, along with Link, Rew and Serek, sat down on the wooden floor and leaned against a support post.

"How does Mistress Shareen fare?" Serek inquired politely.

"I'm afraid she has been killed. It happened at Castle Xandia while she was confronting Candaz. We succeeded in freeing the torgs, but Shareen lost her life in the process. Candaz killed her. However, your people are free, Kaltog." I suppressed the emotion that was threatening to steal my control again. With John dead and Shareen murdered so recently, I was wearing my grief on my sleeve and it threatened to overwhelm me constantly.

Kaltog roared loudly with delight and Rew gave him a big hug before hugging me. "My people are free! This is wonderful news! I am sorry for Mistress Shareen, but I am glad for my people. I will be forever in your debt and hers. How did you do it?" he asked.

"Have you ever heard the story of the Pied Piper? . . . No, I guess you wouldn't have. That's not really an accurate account anyway," I said, smiling up at him recalling all of the friends I had made at Farreach. "I met your father, Rocnor. He and I became fast friends during my stay at Farreach. He is in good health after his captivity and very glad to be back in charge of the torg nation. I spent three days at Farreach and enjoyed your people's hospitality immensely. I was honored when they erected a monument to Shareen's memory in the village square. It touched me deeply."

Link was pulling furiously on his beard as he paced the length of the porch. "Now that Shareen is dead, I suppose our quest is called off."

Rew looked at Link with an expression of astonishment and said, "Why would you think that? Our original goal is still valid."

Link stopped pacing and said, "I was just hoping that maybe I could . . . well . . . go home."

I reached up and grasped the gold medallion between my fingers, wishing I could go home as well. "The quest assigned to you by Shareen is vitally important. Its success is the first step in the process toward healing Risen's wounds. Unless it is accomplished, hate between the races will continue to grow with Candaz's meddling. Trade will never be reestablished and this world will become stagnant, unable to evolve naturally toward a healthy future. I understand your need to return home, Link . . . more than you know. However, you have a job to do just like all the rest of us," I said.

My words to Link stung me like a hard slap in the face. I knew I couldn't follow my heart's desire and return home to my children, not without concluding things on Risen, and that meant ending Candaz's reign once and for all. My determination to make my own destiny still motivated my actions, but my vision of that destiny had changed and so must my actions. Strangely enough, I felt somehow relieved at having finally made the decision to stay and help my friends in their fight. The guilt that assaulted me when I had resolved to leave, no matter what, was lifted from my shoulders, leaving me with new determined strength.

"B.F., I have decided to stay . . . for a little while longer," I told the dragon.

"Yes, I know," he said.

"*How do you know? I thought you didn't eaves drop on people's conscious thoughts.*"

"*I always knew you would stay, Gabriel. You just had to figure it out for yourself,*" he told me.

The rest of the company came out onto the porch chatting happily. Theo had his arm around Jessabelle's waist with a casual familiarity. I felt my heart ache at the site of them and I noticed Kristina glance auspiciously at Serek who returned her look with intensity. The exchange wasn't missed by Theo, who looked to me to confirm his assessment of the situation. I smiled wanly and looked at Rew, knowing he had not missed the exchange either.

Theo cleared his throat and said, "Serek, I hear you have been adopted by a baby dragon. Perhaps you could introduce me to Breezerunner. I would be happy to introduce you to Balls of Fire. Did you know that the two dragons are half-brothers? Perhaps someday I will come to think of you as a brother as well." Theo nudged his sister playfully and laughed without discretion, embarrassing both Kristina and Serek in the process.

"Yes, Theo," I said bitingly. "Why don't you and Serek see to the dragons' needs while the rest of us see to dinner? I'm sure all of us will want to get an early start tomorrow morning."

Link volunteered to cook for us and I offered to help. However, I wasn't about to intrude on Link's territory. Instead, I wanted to have access to Anna's kitchen in order to discretely restock her depleted provisions. I felt it was the least I could do for her generous hospitality. One of her golden retrievers, Sandy, had decided to accompany me wherever I went. She was a sweet dog, who seemed to have an above average intelligence. I don't know why she decided to befriend me, but I was glad for it and enjoyed her warm, soft company while I was there.

That evening we sat down to a wonderful meal and conversed like old friends. After dinner, we enjoyed some cold ale and exchanged stories around a roaring campfire in Anna's back yard. While tears of joy streamed down Kaltog's face, I relayed to them the account of how the torg nation had been freed from slavery by use of the silver harp. Theo brought news about the progress of the war and how new strategies were being tried and tested. We heard two versions concerning the rescue of Breezerunner, one from Link and Kristina, who had successfully distracted the troops and luckily gotten away with their lives, and another from Serek who had actually cut Breezerunner's bonds and set him free. Kaltog and Rew both contributed their accounts of what had happened at Lakeside, where Gerod had kidnapped Kristina and Rew. Anna told us about how her life as a hunter had changed since her husband's death and how the decline in trade had come to affect her. We talked well into the night and had our fill of ale before each of us crawled off to find our own space to spend the night.

I was glad to get away from everyone and finally have some solitary time. But, loneliness has a way of being the harshest when one is alone. As I tried to settle my spirit from the assault of raw emotions, my loved ones faces came to mind and I wept. Rew seemed to sense my need and came to me offering simple companionship and warmth, a heaven-sent comfort. With the wisp cuddled next to me and the dog Sandy curled at my feet, I finally slept and found a welcome escape from the pain that tugged persistently on my heart.

Chapter 16
TRUSTING IN THE TRUTH

The smell of smoke brought Jesse abruptly awake. It was dark, very dark and she couldn't breathe. Choking, she searched for the light on the nightstand next to her bed. At the touch of her finger, the switch flicked on and light flooded the smoke filled room. Jesse jumped out of bed, stuffed the diary in her backpack and yelled to her roommate, "Maryanne! Wake up! Maryanne!" She reached Maryanne's bed and shook the fifteen year old girl frantically. "Wake up!" Maryanne rolled over and started to cough heavily. "Come on." Jesse pulled her off the bed and half carried--half dragged Maryanne out the door. The hallway was clear and smoke billowed out of their room like steam out of a hot shower, setting off smoke alarms overhead. Soon the hall was filled with people running around in nervous excitement. Jesse left Maryanne by herself in the hallway and grabbed the nearest fire extinguisher from off its hanger on the wall. After taking a minute to scan the directions, she reentered the smoky room and doused the carpet and bedding with white powder until the fire was out. It looked to Jesse like her roomy had fallen asleep with a lit cigarette and set the blanket on fire.

When she returned to the hallway, girls were being ushered out of the building through the double doors at the end of the hall by security guards. Joining the crowd of pajama-clad girls, Jesse, still in her jeans and t-shirt with her backpack slung over her shoulder, filed out of the building without receiving even a second glance by the tall security woman who held the door wide open to facilitate the evacuation.

Once outside, Jesse looked around. Her first observation was that the yard was completely fenced in, except for the large driveway gate, which presently stood open allowing fire trucks access to the building. Jesse hadn't planned on escaping, but could not ignore the opportunity being presented to her. She walked calmly, but with purpose, and edged her way between the two fire trucks until she was hidden from the view of people standing around the building watching the scene. Jesse ducked under the truck closest to the gate and crawled to the rear of the vehicle which stuck out just past the open gate. She could see the boots of the firemen as they walked around the truck performing various duties. Waiting patiently until the coast was clear, she came out from under the truck, looked in both directions without spotting anyone and slipped off down the street.

Exultant at having escaped her prison, she walked with a spring in her step as she rounded the corner onto Main Street. Reaching for her cell phone, she remembered that she didn't have it. *I miss my phone.* Instead, she searched for a phone booth and soon found one on the corner of Main and 22nd. The County offices were listed in the white pages and she saw the address of the County Humane Society at 2700 N. 31st Street. A map was not provided in the phone book, but at least she knew which direction to head. She exited the phone booth and headed west along Main Street past 23rd, 24th, 25th and 26th Streets. The town was quiet with the shops already closed for the night. Customers and employees had deserted the area hours before.

Her moccasin clad feet padded almost noiselessly on the cement sidewalk. Alert eyes and ears kept track of every sound and every movement in her vicinity. Jesse instinctively ducked into a dark doorway and held her breath as she spotted a police car using a spot light heading south on 27th Street. The bright light shined down Main Street, sweeping up and down the sidewalks in slow progression. She watched the vehicle turn the corner out of sight and relaxed, drawing air into her lungs once again.

Knowing the policemen had not seen her, Jesse continued down the sidewalk at a brisk pace. Upon reaching 31st Street, she rounded the corner and headed north. The shopping district slowly faded, replaced with office buildings, becoming more modern and spreading further apart as she continued walking. She kept to the shadows as much as she could, keeping off the main sidewalk, taking full advantage of the landscaping lights that illuminated gardens and walkways, casting deep shadows across well-tended lawns.

A squad car raced by with its flashers on, heading in the same direction as Jesse. She flattened herself against the turf, feeling the blades prickle against her skin and almost sneezing at the overwhelming earthy scent of the freshly mowed grass.

Cautiously, she continued. Flashers reflected brightly off from nearby buildings as another squad car passed and Jesse again found herself flat against the ground. Fear was starting to take her control away and she began to run from shadow to shadow, intent only upon reaching her destination undiscovered.

A big marble sign identifying the "County Humane Society" brought Jesse to an abrupt halt. Relief almost made her giddy, until she noticed that a squad car was parked out front, the occupants maintaining a watchful surveillance. She sagged down behind the sign, feeling the tension grab hold of her chest and squeeze until she thought she would not be able to draw another breath. As Jesse leaned back against the cold stone, she reached up and grabbed hold of the gold pendant, feeling the comforting coolness of the metal against the sensitive skin of her fingers. She wished fervently that she could feel her arms around Felcore and to once again maintain the security of having her friend close by.

Trying to gain a semblance of control over her emotions, Jesse closed her eyes for a moment and took deep even breaths. In order to get into the building without detection, find Felcore, and escape, she would need a plan . . . a very good plan and a good measure of luck. Who was she kidding? It was an impossible situation. She had not even been able to break into her car with a coat hanger that time she had locked her keys in it. They would catch her and send her right back to the detention center. It didn't matter. She had to try. Jesse wanted her dog back. *Felcore!* Frustration swelled up again in her throat and she clutched the pendant even tighter, feeling the gold warming between cold fingers.

Jesse jumped as a cold wet nose touched her forearm. Both eyes popped open and she saw that Felcore stood before her, eagerly wagging his tail and begging to be petted. She pulled him down next to her and hugged and scratched the big golden retriever, while tears of joy streamed down her cheeks. With a "snap" she removed the white plastic identification collar used by the humane society and let it fall to the ground. "Oh, Felcore! My boy!" Jesse stroked his silky head lovingly. "How did you . . . ?" The dog sat quietly as Jesse gazed into his shining gold eyes, trying to find in them the mystery behind his sudden appearance. She reached up and again touched the cold metal of the gold pendant that her Grandmother Gabriel had once worn. Felcore's own gold tag hung on his collar along with his rabies tag that she replaced on a yearly basis. "I wonder . . ." A noise made Felcore turn his attention to the street. "Let's go, boy," Jesse said quietly.

Sticking to the shadows, Jesse and Felcore made their way past the police and were out of town before dawn. They kept close to the road, keeping a careful eye on it for any patrols. By midday, Jesse was tired, hungry, and thirsty, but having no better option than to keep going, they walked on.

A late model pickup truck pulled up next to them and the old Native American man inside offered Jesse and Felcore a ride. Although Jesse normally would have refused such an offer, desperation dictated her actions and she accepted the ride without hesitation.

Felcore jumped in the pick-up's bed and settled himself comfortably on a pile of blankets. After taking off her backpack and depositing it onto the floor, Jesse climbed into the passenger seat and said, "Thanks for the ride, mister. You wouldn't happen to have some water for my dog?"

The old man assessed her with intelligent light brown eyes. He had the classic look of a Native American, with darkly tanned skin, aged like wrinkled leather and snow white hair that hung long down his back. A dusty cowboy hat decorated with feathers topped off an ensemble of baggy faded blue jeans and a red and blue flannel shirt. Although dressed casually, rich silver and turquoise jewelry adorned his right ear, neck and hands. His belt buckle was a beautifully handcrafted silver eagle accented skillfully with turquoise pieces. When he spoke his voice sounded lyrical, but dusty with age. "You think of your protector before yourself. That is good." He reached behind the seat of the truck and brought out a gallon of water, which he handed to Jesse, along with a red plastic cup.

She poured some water and held it out the back window for Felcore to drink. He slurped down the contents quickly, spilling half of it in the process. She did a quick rinse, poured another cup for herself and drank down the cool wet liquid. Jesse gave Felcore one more drink before returning the bottle gratefully to the old man. "I really appreciate your help."

"You're running." He stated matter-of-factly.

Jesse didn't know how to reply so she kept silent.

He laughed, making Jesse feel uncomfortable and she inched a little closer to the passenger side door. "No need to be afraid. I won't harm you. Besides, you have a protector and I see you have some magic of your own . . . 'Álíí'" The Navajo word lilted off from his tongue, as he indicated with a crooked finger at the gold pendant Jesse wore around her neck, plainly visible against her white t-shirt.

"Who are you?" Jesse asked, curious how the man could know things about her that she was only beginning to guess.

"My name is Jim McCaw. What is your name?" he asked.

"Jessica Gates. My friends call me Jesse. My dog's name is Felcore." Jesse relaxed a little, but looked behind her to make sure Felcore was faring well.

"You named your protector Felcore from the luck dragon in 'The Never Ending Story'. I like that, Jesse. Cute movie. Where are you headed?" he asked. He kept his eyes steady on the view ahead. His face remained almost expressionless.

"We're going to Las Vegas," Jesse answered automatically and then winced inwardly, regretting having divulged information that maybe she shouldn't have.

"Ah. You and the protector travel to the lightning gate," he said. Again, Jim's statement was without question.

Jesse stared at him in shock and he smiled, with his eyes still watching the road. "How do you know, Mr. McCaw?" she demanded an explanation.

"Ahh. I surprise you with my knowledge of these things. Did you think you were alone in the world, Jesse?" he asked laughing again. "I am a *hataa_ii*. I was told to watch for you and your protector."

Jesse was amazed. She had always thought of the things that had happened with Felcore, the pendant, the writings in her grandmother's diary, to be somehow unreal, fictional. But, her gut feeling told her that all of it was very real and that she was somehow involved. "Who told you to watch for me?" she asked.

Jim looked at his passenger sideways for a moment before returning his attention back to the road and said, "The wind."

Jesse scoffed at his answer, "Really? The wind?"

He laughed and said, "It was a vision given to me. The wind holds power. Understanding is not easy, even for me."

"Explain it to me," Jesse insisted, truly wanting to understand.

Jim said, "Some other time. I will take you as far as Flagstaff. My daughter lives there and we can spend the night with her. But, in the morning I'll have to head back home. Do you have any money?"

Jesse picked up her backpack and checked through the pocket where she kept her money, counting twenty-eight dollars and eighty-six cents. "A little," she answered Jim's question vaguely.

"Well, I'll lend you the money so you can buy a bus ticket into Las Vegas. You can pay me back when you get the chance."

She replied with skepticism tinting her voice, "Thanks. It sounds like you *want* me to go. What interest do you have in this, Mr. McCaw?"

His tone was as serious as the look on his face. "The same as you, Jesse. The same as all of us. Good versus evil. We can make a difference. We should all do what we can, what we are called to do. And please call me Jim."

The rest of the trip was in relative silence. Jim alternately hummed and sang an Indian spiritual song that made Jesse feel somehow impassioned. She slowly drifted off into a fitful sleep . . .

. . . *The sun was high in the sky, but the day was still cool, it being just early spring. The scent of the garden was rich with the aromas of rose and lilac, and the delicate scent of apple blossoms blended in as well. A strange feeling surrounded her, like a separation of body and soul. She was sitting in a wooden lawn chair beside a handsome elderly man who was taking indulgent sips from his cold mug of ale. Five small children played on the lawn with joyous abandon. A golden retriever lay in the corner watching the children attentively while her six small puppies jumped and played along with the children.*

A red-headed boy about the age of five strolled over to where Jesse and the elderly man sat. He was loud with enthusiasm, "Grandma, look at the puppies!"

"Yes, dear," Jesse heard herself saying, "Be gentle and loving with them and they will be your friends. Now go play, William."

"Yes, Grandma." The little boy turned and went back to play with the other children and the fluffy blond puppies.

"Did you ever think life could be this good?" asked the elderly man.

Jesse turned and looked into his shining golden eyes and replied, "No . . . Never." She smiled, feeling the warmth of the sun on her

face and overflowing love in her heart. "No, I never dreamed I could
be this happy."

*She continued to watch the children play with an ambience of
peace and contentment . . .*

. . . The truck took a right turn and Jesse's head banged
against the window. "Ouch!" They were driving through a rich
suburban neighborhood that wound through steep green hills.
Jim slowed the truck and came to a stop in front of a ranch style
home that spoke of elegance and money. A well-trimmed landscaped lawn contrasted well with the red brick house. "Wow,"
Jesse said.

"Nice place, huh? My daughter Susie and her husband live
here. Susie is a doctor of psychology and her husband Tom is an
architect. He is away right now. Come on, Jesse, I'll introduce
you to Susie." Jim got out of the truck and swung the tail gate
down to accommodate Felcore. The big dog jumped down from
the truck and loped happily after Jim. Jesse watched the two of
them walk up the black asphalt driveway that curved gently to
the right before entering the garage. Felcore hesitated, glanced
back and waited for Jesse while Jim kept walking. Jesse got out
of the truck and was joined by an eager Felcore halfway up the
driveway.

Jim waited for them on the porch, opened the door without
knocking and led the way into a spacious living room. Piano
music filled the elegantly decorated room. Soft shades of blue
gray and cream tones were used to give the atmosphere of plush
comfort. Everything was in perfect arrangement upon the two
end tables, the coffee table and the fireplace mantle. A white
grand piano sat in the corner, with the top propped open expos-
ing the piano strings. Upon the stool sat a delicate Native American woman with long black hair braided down the middle of her
back all the way to the waist. She was dressed in a simple yellow

cotton dress. The selection she played Jesse recognized from one of her father's classical albums, but she couldn't remember the name of the composer. The woman hadn't seen them come in, but continued to play until she hit a sour note. She hesitated, consulted her music, and then looked up at them and smiled brightly. "Daddy." She got up and wrapped her arms around Jim before stepping back and scrutinizing Jesse. Felcore insisted that she pet him by pushing his nose into her right hand that hung down at her side. She complied by getting down and scratching his head. She smiled up at me and said, "Hi, I'm Susie.

Jesse couldn't help but smile back. It had been a long time since she had felt so comfortable with anyone other than Felcore. "It's nice to meet you, Susie. I'm Jesse and this is Felcore, my dog. Your dad was good enough to give us a ride. We have a long way to go yet. I guess we should be on our way," she said.

Jim grumbled, "Nonsense. You are staying here."

Susie stood up, rising to her full five foot height. "Please stay here. I would love to hear your story. I'll run you a hot bath and get you a change of clothes. You can stay in the guest room."

Before Jesse could reply, Susie was off. Jim headed in the opposite direction. "Come on, Felcore. I'll get you some food. Hungry boy?" Felcore went off after Jim and left Jesse standing alone in the middle of the elegant blue and cream room clutching her backpack to her chest. She didn't move, but looked around, admiring various pieces of art and beautiful crystal objects. When Susie returned she was standing in the same place feeling dirty and grubby and wanting very much a bath and some clean clothes.

Susie showed Jesse to the guest room, where she had drawn Jesse's bath, filling the tub full of hot water and fragrant bubbles. Jesse soaked until her fingertips could pass for prunes and then dressed in the white sun dress Susie had left for her. She joined her hosts in the kitchen, and after a hearty meal, Jesse, Susie and Jim retired to the living room. Feeling wonderfully refreshed, she stretched out in a chair with Felcore snoring soundly at her feet. She listened half-heartedly as Jim and Susie spoke about family and friends, Jim's ranch, and business dealings. They argued slightly over the tribe's position on certain issues and how they each felt about it personally. They had long ago veered away from the traditional teachings and were somewhat outcasts, but still involved. Jesse was almost asleep when Jim addressed her, "Jesse, how did you learn about the lightning cave?"

She was faced with a dilemma. Should she trust these people with her grandmother's secret? Looking into their faces, she decided to take the chance. "My grandmother, Gabriel, writes about it in her diary. She spent some time in a place called Risen many years ago when my mother was still a little girl. It is an amazing place with many different races and sorcerers, even dragons. I want to see if what my grandmother wrote about was true . . . if the place really does exist. My mother and I stumbled upon a cave when we were out hiking a few years ago that fits Gabriel's description of the lightning cave. That is my destination," she told them.

Jim's eyes sparkled with excitement and asked, "You say your grandmother's name was Gabriel?"

"Yes. Why?" Jesse felt a chill shiver down her spine.

"I know her . . . your grandmother, Gabriel. We met a long time ago. She needed my help, just as you did today," Jim said as he got a whimsical expression on his face and a faraway look in his eyes while he gazed into memories of his past.

Susie sat comfortably next to her father, stroking a calico house cat that was reclined luxuriously in her lap. "That is a coincidence, father. How can you be sure you are speaking of the same woman?" she asked.

"I know for sure, Sue. And this is no coincidence either. We are all tied together. *T'áá 'a_tsogo.* We all share a oneness through God; the sky, the air, the earth, the plants, the animals. Nature wields His force. You can either listen to God's power or ignore it. I choose to listen. Jesse will have to choose also. Your grandmother chose to serve good." Jim got up from the couch, walked over to Jesse's chair and took her hand.

Jesse looked up at the face of a man who had the knowledge of generations and she felt great respect for him and honored that he was willing to share it with her. A twinge of fear rippled through her as she looked into his eyes and recognized his power.

Felcore watched Jim from the floor where the dog lay at Jesse's feet, the retriever's eyes and ears attentive. "You have known pain, Jesse. Let it go now. It is time for you to spread your wings and fly. Do so with a light heart. You have also known goodness and love. Bind those feelings to your soul tightly. Live your life with honor. You have the abilities to amend what is wrong and you will have the opportunity to change the balance. Take care that you swing the balance for good, Jesse."

Jesse smiled up at him, saying sincerely, "Thanks, Jim. I will do my best."

"I know you will," he said.

Susie rose from the couch, the cat still in her arms and said, "Well, I'm off to bed."

Jim turned to her and bent down to place a kiss on the small woman's forehead. "Good night, sweetheart".

Jesse bid her goodnight as well, "Thanks for everything, Susie."

"You're welcome. See you in the morning," she said and headed to her room.

Jim looked down at Jesse before heading off to his own bed and said, "Gabriel is a good person. She has a wealth of energy and has done a lot to change things for the better. I'm glad to have known her granddaughter as well. Good night, Jesse."

"Good night," Jesse said.

She sat up for a little while longer thinking about what Jim had said to her and about everything that had happened that day. She felt things were a lot clearer now, even though the reality of it all felt a little uncomfortable. But, her toe on Felcore's soft coat gave her comfort enough and Jesse had hope that everything would be all right. She mused over Jim having known her grandmother. Susie had called it "coincidence". Jesse wanted to think not. Like Jim, she felt there were other forces in control. She felt sure there was something special inside of herself that remained untapped and Jesse hoped she would find the answer where she was heading.

She got up from the chair and walked to the guest bedroom with Felcore right behind her. Sleep came easy and she did not dream at all.

Jim drove Jesse and Felcore to the Greyhound bus station that morning and bought her a ticket to Las Vegas. They had to convince the clerk that Felcore was a special dog being trained to work with people with disabilities in order to get him on the bus. Jesse regretted leaving Jim. She had grown very fond of him in the short time she had known him. She was more than a little curious, however, how he knew about the lightning cave. As she looked into his warm brown eyes she asked, "Jim, how do you know about the cave?"

"Well, Jesse, the story has been handed down in my family from generation to generation. Long ago a young maiden named Yellow Eyes was not of the people, it is said. She was born of a different world, altogether. She had come through a gate located in the mountains north of the valley we now know as Las Vegas Valley. The gate was inside of a cave marked distinctly with the sign of the lightning bolt, so it is said. Yellow Eyes said to the people, 'The lightning gate can take a warrior to many different worlds if he has courage and bravery.' She shimmered before their eyes and became a glorious golden eagle, soaring up into the sky and coming to land at the feet of the warrior who was to become her husband. The other warriors coveted Yellow Eyes' magic. They went in search of the lightning gate, but were never seen again, it is told. Yellow Eyes remained with the people and gave her husband many beautiful children. The story has been in my family for many generations. The maiden Yellow Eyes was my great great grandmother."

Jim's eyes reflected a hint of gold from the morning sun as Jesse examined them for any deception. Appreciatively, she found only the truth there. She kissed him gently on the cheek before giving her thanks and saying goodbye. Guiding Felcore skillfully through the crowd she boarded the bus with a sleek looking greyhound painted on the side. Felcore settled down in the cramped space under Jesse's seat with an audible groan. She extracted Gabriel's diary from her backpack before stowing the worn out bag in the overhead compartment. She settled down in the comfortable seat, which she knew wouldn't be comfortable for long, and opened the diary to the red ribbon she used as a marker.

Chapter 17

SKYVIEW

August 11. Breakfast this morning began cheerfully, but ended in sadness as we all began to realize that it was the last time we would see each other for a while. We were about to go our separate ways once again. Theo and I were going on dragon back to Skyview to rendezvous with Theo's troops and prepare for war. The company was continuing their journey northeast to the ruined city of New Chance on the eastern coast of Risen. The new member of their company, Breezerunner, was healing fast, even fast for a dragon, whose healing powers were amazing. He was again able to fly but only for short distances at a time. Anna said she was going to head for Skyview in a few days to help with the war effort.

Tears flowed liberally as we said our goodbyes. Theo held Jessabelle with a possessiveness that was understandable. I was impressed with their strong characters. Both of them knew the other was going into a dangerous unknown, but they talked of their future plans to wed and smiled happily at having come back together again. Theo had assured Jessabelle that he could take care of himself when it came to King Shane and his threats. Their joyful celebration of love was heartwarming.

Theo and I were the first to leave and as we mounted B.F.'s back he trumpeted loudly to Breezerunner who was circling in the air above us. Breezerunner trumpeted back and then dove down and landed next to Serek, where he sat proudly. For the first time I heard the small dragon's voice in my head. "*Good luck, Mistress Gabriel.*"

"*Thank you, Breezerunner. Take good care of them for me,*" I said.

"*I will.*"

We took off into the air and I watched as our friends waved goodbye. A warm feeling washed over me as I reflected on the relationships that had been forged. I knew that no matter what happened, I would never forget them. Those good feelings helped to anesthetize the fearsome pain of grief.

I held tight to Theo as we soared over the mountains, steadily gaining altitude until it became difficult to breathe in the thinner atmosphere. Condensation from the wispy clouds clung to my hair and my clothes, eventually drenching me through. The snowcapped mountain peaks below were barely visible through the dense atmosphere, although I could make out the ruggedness of the terrain below. I had been told by Theo that there were no passes through the mountains other than the one that went directly through Skyview, making it a very strategic position. It was no wonder Candaz wished to possess it for himself. If he were to take Skyview, he would have access to all of the southern lands. Apparently neither one of them knew about the narrow pass that Serek had used and that secret would remain safe with me.

The highest peak was directly ahead of us, the summit hidden in the clouds somewhere high above our plane of vision. I was grateful when B.F. began to descend, although my stomach again protested the maneuver. I wondered if I would ever get used to flying dragon back. We landed upon a rocky shelf where Theo unloaded our belongings and we both bid B.F. farewell. It was necessary that we make the rest of the trip on foot since dragon's bane, an extremely offensive weed to dragons, grew lush along the main path into Skyview and B.F. stubbornly (and I mean *stubbornly*) refused to get any closer.

"Do not expect me to go any further. The smell is awful. It is worse than Theo's socks after a day of tournaments. I wouldn't go near the path to Skyview if it was lined with beautiful maidens. Never, ever. Never. Don't ask. I won't go. Not ever."

"Okay, B.F. I think we get it," I responded with obvious sarcasm.

Theo led me down a narrow path that edged along the side of the mountain. The view was miraculous, but I concentrated on my footing, not wishing to take the faster but fatal way down over the edge of the steep cliff. I could see the main path ahead of us as we got closer. Theo pointed out the extremely odorous dragon's bane to me. The weed grew tall along the edge of the main path. Wide leaves of dark green were veined with bright purple and pink, making it beautiful landscaping foliage. Although the scent of the weed was repugnant to dragons, I found it quite pleasant. Oddly, it reminded me of freshly ground coffee beans. By the time we reached the path, I was feeling the strain from the climb in every muscle and had an overwhelming craving for a hot cup of coffee.

"How are you feeling?" Theo asked as he swiped an arm across his brow.

"I'm fine," I rasped, as I reached for the water canister and drank down the tepid liquid sparingly.

We continued down the main path to the north at a vigorous pace. The once well-trodden road was now grown over in areas with grass from its lack of use in recent years. Theo explained, "Skyview used to be a booming center of commerce. Being in the middle of Risen, merchants would stop here on their way north or south, sometimes selling their entire stock here for a tidy profit and then happily heading back home. The gates into Skyview were always kept open in those days, welcoming all who crossed the threshold into banderg territory. That was before Mercin put an end to it all by ruining relations between the races. For many years now the bandergs have kept their gates closed, keeping to themselves and staying safely within the confines of their mountain fortress."

We stopped walking. A massive archway towered before us with a wooden gate, the southern gate, closing Skyview tightly to the outside world within the arches' confines. The gate was elaborately carved with scenes of bandergs engaged industriously in various labors. I could understand why the people of Skyview were distressed over the destruction of the northern gate, which was supposed to have been similar. The gate before me was a marvelous work of art. Words were written atop each door in a language I could not read.

"Greetings weary travelers. Skyview will give you respite. Our home in the mountains is yours. Step through the threshold and be welcome one and all," Theo read the words as if he remembered them fondly from memory. A smile touched his lips as he turned to me.

"It is a beautiful sentiment," I commented a bit derisively. "Now how do we get in?" I was feeling suddenly impatient and edgy and sarcasm was coming easy.

"Good question. Got any ideas?" Theo looked at me expectantly with a foolish grin on his face.

The sour look I returned him was the expression I reserved for silently admonishing my husband when he stepped over the bounds of what I considered decent behavior.

"Just kidding," he said grinning superciliously at me while he removed a large gold medallion from around his neck. A thick gold chain dangled from the heavy disk as Theo turned and approached the closed gate. He examined the carvings for a moment, running his fingers over the rugged surface. Choosing an indentation that matched the characteristics of his medallion, Theo pressed the gold disk against the carving causing the connection to glow with bright blue light. The massive wooden gate began to make a grinding sound before it slowly opened outward.

We walked through the archway and down a long stone corridor that was dark with the torches lining the walls left unlit. Each foot step echoed off from the smooth stone floor with ringing clarity. I tried to lighten my step but was unsuccessful in keeping the noise down. Theo strode boldly forward unconcerned by the echo of his boots as he replaced the medallion around his neck and tucked it under his shirt.

"Where did you get that?" I asked quietly.

"My father gave it to me. He thought it might be useful," he said.

"But how do others, like Anna, get into Skyview? Are there other keys?" I asked.

Theo stopped walking and turned to me with a thoughtful gaze. "I don't know. I believe this is the only key in existence, but the bandergs come and go as they please. There must be another way known only to them."

I said, "I would sure hate to see that key get into the wrong hands." I was thinking what a disaster it would be for the bandergs should Candaz get a hold of it.

"I would die before I let that happen," Theo stated with conviction.

"Let's hope that won't be necessary," I replied.

We heard someone heading toward us from the far end of the corridor. Several bandergs dressed for war in chainmail and helmets, carrying heavy axes and long daggers approached rapidly. The bandergs greeted us with professionalism, bowing and saluting to Theo a bit awkwardly before hastily leading us back the way they had just come. They led us into a grand hall of massive proportions. Natural light flooded the room from slits in the domed ceiling high above us. Potted plants placed at several locations added to the dynamic feel of the room. A fountain graced the middle of the hall, spewing fresh water high into the air from the center of a glittering clear pool spanning thirty feet in diameter. As sun light hit the towering fountain of water, rainbows appeared distributing bright colors in all directions. The stone floor of the hall was made up of sections colored black, red, white and gold.

As we headed toward the opposite side of the hall, bandergs, who were busy with their daily tasks, glanced at us suspiciously as we passed. Curious children were quickly taken by their hands and ushered rapidly out of our way by anxious adults. Their rash reactions surprised me until I realized most of them had probably never seen a human before. We must look pretty strange to them.

We were escorted down a hallway and into a large conference room where we were asked to wait. Theo and I found chairs and succumbed to waiting silently. The thrumming of Theo's fingers on the surface of the table became the sole focus of my senses as my irritation grew.

Following a short noisy ruckus outside the door, several elderly bandergs entered the room. The oldest of them was dressed in a long white tunic with bold blue stripes across the chest. His beard was dark gray and hung long and thick down to the bottom of his torso. The other seven, three females and four males were in similar garb. Two of the bandergs wore trimmed beards and were dressed in silver chain mail and carried polished silver helmets under their arms in military fashion. They nodded to Theo as they entered the room, acknowledging him briefly, and then took seats around the conference table.

When all of the shuffling of chairs and noise had settled down, the banderg in the white tunic with the blue stripes stood and began to speak with a powerful orator's voice. "Prince Theodore, I welcome you to Skyview. Since we last communicated an attack has been initiated against us from the north. As yet, the enemy has been unsuccessful in their attempt to invade Skyview." The chairman's serious expression changed to a grin. "The Sabers have been knocking on our back door, but we refuse to let them in," he said jovially. The room filled with chuckles.

Theo cleared his throat and stood up. He glanced at me briefly. "Chairman Bard, I would like to introduce Mistress Gabriel Thomas. She is the new Master Sorceress of Brightening, taking Shareen's place after her recent death at the hands of Candaz."

"Mistress." The Chairman bowed his head to me, as did the rest of the bandergs seated around the table. I nodded to them uneasily.

Theo continued, "Gabriel, this is Chairman Bard, General Hatch, General Kin, Trent, Jini, Coty, and I'm afraid I haven't

been introduced to the two chairpersons on the end." Theo
looked to Bard.

Bard took Theo's cue and said, "This is Mari, head of our
domestic operations." Theo reached out and shook her hand.
"This is Pasca, Assistant Chef, sitting in for Link, who has been
absent of late." Theo also shook his hand before taking his seat.
Pasca's sharp brown eyes rested on me for a moment before he
returned his attention to Theo.

"Gabriel and I were just with Link last night. He desperately
wants to come home to Skyview and help with the war, but at
the moment he has another duty to perform that is much more
important to the overall cause," Theo said.

General Hatch addressed Theo in a commanding voice,
"And what would that duty be your highness?"

Theo's green eyes sparkled as he turned to face the general.
"I am not at liberty to divulge that information to you or anyone
else at this time, General. What Link's mission is remains classi-
fied in order to insure his safety and the safety of others."

General Hatch unintentionally let a loud "Humpf" escape
his lips as he balked under Theo's scrutiny.

"Gentlemen," Chairman Bard raised his voice insisting on
everyone's attention. "This is inconsequential. It is imperative
that we plan our strategy. The enemy has been camped out on
our door step for days, massing strength as it waits. We can remain safely inside the confines of Skyview for as long as our food
supply holds out. However, I feel this course of inaction would
be foolish. The enemy will be hard pressed to do anything once
the first snows hit and I doubt Candaz is going to sit around and
do nothing while winter in the mountains rapidly approaches. I
assume he is going to make his move soon. I think we should
take the offensive while we still can." General Hatch grumbled
something and Chairman Bard acknowledged him, "General."

Hatch stood up and said, "I agree with the Chairman. Why should we wait to see what the enemy is going to do? I say we attack right now, before they expect it and drive them from our doorstep."

"Gentlemen." Theo remained seated as he pinned every one of them with his eyes. "My entire army is on their way here as we speak. I've just consulted with my dragon, asking that he do a reconnaissance for me. He tells me my troops are moving into position and should be settled in at their designated locations by tomorrow morning. With a coordinated effort, we should be able to drive the enemy back. I suggest we sit tight for another day or so and give my men a chance to rest up and then attack Candaz from both sides, hopefully taking him by surprise."

"It sounds reasonable, your highness," General Kin, a large banderg with an ageless look about him, spoke in a deep gritty voice. "However, I have a feeling we will not have time to wait for your men to rest. My sixth sense tells me that something is going to happen, and soon. I sure wish we knew what to expect from Candaz."

Councilman Bard took the floor, "Well, we do have a sorceress with us now . . . " He looked at me with a gleam in his eye before addressing me directly. "Mistress, are you familiar with the use of sight water?"

I didn't like what he was leading up to and answered reluctantly, "I am."

The door behind me opened and a banderg walked in with a heavily laden tray and began distributing cups and pouring tog from a large steaming pitcher.

Councilman Bard continued on, ignoring the interruption, "I was thinking that perhaps you could use the sight water to make contact with Candaz and find out his plans. We have a basin here at your disposal."

"What you are proposing could be a very dangerous undertaking, sir," I replied, not knowing what would be the result of invading a mind such as Candaz's.

Suddenly, the banderg who had been serving tog stepped deliberately back from the table. The air prickled with power. His shape grew fuzzy as gray mist enveloped his form and the banderg shape within began to twist and turn, shifting spasmodically until the mist lifted and the being materialized as a man . . . Candaz, the sorcerer. Gasps of horror circulated the conference room table as everyone stared.

Candaz curled his lips back in a hideous facsimile of a smile and said, "Yes, a very dangerous undertaking it would be indeed should you decide to try and spy on me using sight. You could not even fathom the degree of pain I could inflict in such an encounter. Fools!" He sneered at the high counselors assembled. "You know nothing of power. I will show you things that will leave you cowering, running for the bowels of Skyview to hide from the reality of my strength."

The counselors recoiled from under the steady glare of the corrupt sorcerer. "Candaz," I said quietly from my seat, gaining his attention. "If the force you wield is as mighty as you claim, why do you find it necessary to spy on us in disguise? I would think you could bring this mountain down around our ears with the snap of your fingers. If you are so powerful, why do you waste everyone's time playing games? Finish it . . . finish it once and for all . . . if you can."

Candaz's face remained impassive with a fixed smile, but his eyes blazed with hatred as he stared at me. Failing to respond to my taunting, he turned to address Theo, "Where is your father, princeling? I see he sends a boy to do man's job while he hides behind the walls of his castle. I hope you are ready to die princeling, but only after you see the death of many others before you.

You could end this all now by conceding victory to me." Candaz lost his smile, his face growing stern and cruel as he bent closer to Theo's face. "Surrender Skyview to me now and you will not have to see all of your family and friends die."

Theo stood up, pushing his chair back abruptly on the stone floor, making the sorcerer unintentionally take a step backward. "Skyview will never be yours. Haven't you learned by now, Candaz, that you are not destined to win this war? We will never surrender to you."

Candaz leered at Theo and spit words foully out of his mouth, "It is you who will not win this war, princeling. You and your shape changer whore will bow to me before you die."

The aura that surrounded Candaz was soot black, reflecting the extent of corruption in his soul. As he eloquently oozed his words of poison, I couldn't help but wonder just how far gone his mind was. Standing up next to Theo, I confronted him. "The prince is right. We will never surrender . . . not to corruption and certainly not to you. Love is a very strong force, stronger than anything you could possibly know. To defeat these people you will have to defeat that force, which will never happen. I pity you. You cannot win. You will never win."

For the first time I thought I saw fear in Candaz's eyes as he considered the reality of my words. "We shall see, Mistress," he hissed. "We shall see." Black smoke engulfed him instantly and when it cleared he was gone.

"Pretty good trick," Theo commented lightly as the rest of the group let out sighs of relief and settled back into their seats.

I stared at the spot that Candaz had recently vacated and shivered.

A Friendly Visit

The Generals, Theo included, started going over the details of the attack and I gracefully took my leave. I wanted to find Berry and Fibi and tell them about Link's mission. It may be top secret information, but in my opinion his family had the right to know. From talking to Link, I knew that he was head chef for the community so I sought out the kitchens, seeking information on where to find his family. After taking several erroneous paths, I finally caught scent of bread baking and followed my nose down numerous hallways and emerged into a kitchen any cook would consider heaven.

The first person I talked to gave me directions to Berry and Fibi's dwelling, which I followed easily. Before not too long I found myself standing at a doorway that was a couple inches shorter than my five foot six inch height. The area was strictly residential with many such doors scattered at various intervals along the stone hallways that ran in an endless maze of twists and turns. There were statues, plants, flower pots and other types of bric-a-brac decorating the outside of each door. Bandergs obviously held their homes in high regard and enjoyed displaying the artistic side of their culture where they resided. The wooden door I stood in front of was painted with colorful flowers and three words that I assumed identified the residence's occupants. The banderg language would be something I would have to study. I knocked with the carved wooden door knocker and stood back to wait, feeling slightly nervous about meeting new people as I always did.

There was no answer and I began to walk away when a couple of banderg woman turned a corner and walked down the hall toward me.

"Are you looking for Berry or Fibi?" The older woman asked civilly. She was dressed in a simple toga-like dress made of a filmy iridescent material that changed from white to soft pastel colors as she moved. Bright brown eyes highlighted her small round face. The cut of her brown hair was severe, straight across at the top of her back and at her eyebrows. She shifted sandal clad feet and readjusted the parcels in her arms as she assessed me cautiously. The younger girl wore a simple blue robe, similar to the one that Link wore, only less ostentatious. Her long dark hair was tied in a single braid that hung down the center of her back. Intelligent brown eyes, exactly like those of the first woman, watched me closely with curiosity.

"Actually I'm looking for both of them," I said.

The older woman looked suddenly suspicious and automatically moved a little further in front of the younger woman protectively. "Who are you?" she asked.

I smiled, trying to remain friendly in the face of the woman's obvious trepidation. "My name is Gabriel. I am a friend of Link's."

The woman's anxiety melted away from her face and her expression changed to one of excitement and curiosity. "You know Link? Do you know where he is?" she asked. She started forward and then stopped short, looking embarrassed. "Oh, I am so sorry. My name is Berry and this is Fibi. What can you tell me about my husband, Gabriel?" She said my name like it was cumbersome on her tongue.

"There is so much to tell. First of all, he is all right . . . " I began.

Fibi interrupted me by nudging her mother gently, "Mother, shouldn't you invite Gabriel in?"

Berry's cheeks reddened with chagrin. She touched Fibi lovingly under the chin before turning a sweet smile on me. "Yes, of course, I apologize again, Gabriel. Please come in. Welcome to our home."

The door opened into a spacious round living area with a smooth stone floor, softened with a plush beige and teal rug that covered the center of the area. Bulky pillows lay on the floor in place of furniture, giving the room an entirely casual atmosphere. Sun filtered down through the ceiling from far above lighting the living area pleasantly. Berry asked me to have a seat. I selected a pile of pillows and sat slowly and experimentally. Until I relaxed, I was not able to fully enjoy the comfort of the living space. Willing my muscles to release their tension, I eased into the luxury of the pillows and began my story. Fibi and Berry sat across from me, leaning forward and listening with rapt anticipation.

I told them everything about Link's quest. Supplying them with my own views, starting from the first day I met him and ending with our departure earlier that very morning. They both sat quietly and listened, their expressions changing subtly from time to time revealing their feelings only slightly. I finished by telling them that Link was now on his way to the east coast to finish his assigned mission.

Berry's face was stern with worry and she wrung her hands over and over again. It reminded me of how Link always pulled on his beard. The gratefulness in her voice leaked through her concern as she said, "Thank you for bringing us this news. You can count on us to keep it a secret. How long do you think Link will be gone? He . . . he will return, won't he?" she asked anxiously.

"I won't give you false hope, Berry, or empty promises. I really do not know what he will be facing. But, I do know the people he is with are good people. They have learned to work together as a team and to care for and protect one another. I believe the chances are very good that they will accomplish this quest and return to their homes safely. How long that will take, I cannot say. I do know this, however . . . what Link does is very important to the banderg nation and Risen as a whole. I am sure you can understand the implications should this quest not succeed. The hate and distrust that has plagued your world for the last few generations would not be terminated, but allowed to fester like a wound not properly cared for," I told her honestly.

Berry looked at Fibi as if glancing into the future. Her eyes misted over as Fibi returned her mother's gaze affectionately. "I understand. I do not want Fibi to live life in fear and distrust as my generation has done and my mother's before me. It may take longer to heal this wound than one generation should Link succeed. But, at least my grandchildren may know peace and perhaps even see the gates to Skyview opened to the outside world once again." Berry smiled, making her small face light up as she patted Fibi's hand that rested daintily upon the folds of her mother's skirt. "Would you join me in a salute, Gabriel?" she asked. Berry stood up, went to the wall and slid open a panel revealing shelves lined with several items, including many books. From the bottom shelf she took down a ruby colored crystal decanter and three miniature ruby red goblets. "We call this liquor Pureacionni. It is saved for very special occasions and this occasion is important to me."

I took the delicate crystal glass Berry handed me and Fibi took the other two. Berry filled my glass first with clear liquid that had a hint of iridescence, like oil in water, and then she filled the two glasses Fibi held out to her before replacing the decanter back on the shelf. After selecting a glass from Fibi, Berry raised her glass and waited. I noticed Fibi stand up, so I did as well. "To Link and his new friends. May their journey be safe and their quest come to a successful conclusion. May they return home unscathed to their loved-ones." Berry drank down the contents of her glass, placed the crystal delicately on the floor and crushed it unmercifully with her foot. Fibi drank her liquor down and did the same destruction with her own foot. Following the tradition as demonstrated before me, I repeated the act, tasting the ethereal almond flavor of the liquor linger on my taste buds as I stepped on the delicate crystal, turning it to dust on the stone floor. Berry said, "Thank you for sharing my salute," before she started cleaning up the shattered crystal with a hand held broom and dust pan.

"It seems like a waste, but my parents believe in tradition," Fibi said.

"Sometimes traditions make little sense to younger generations, but they are worth keeping if only for honoring our elders," I said.

Berry walked up to me and took my hand in her own and said, "I hope that we will have a chance to become friends, Gabriel."

I smiled at her, appreciating the sincerity in her voice. "I would like that very much. Thank you for your hospitality, but I must be going now. Could you possibly tell me where they keep the sight water?" I asked.

"Fibi can take you there. It is in the old part of Skyview, seldom visited. The room where the sight water basin is kept probably hasn't been disturbed for decades. Do be careful, Gabriel." she said.

"I will. Fibi?" I glanced at the young banderg and recognized the trace of fear in her eyes. "If you would like to give me directions, I am sure I can find my way," I told her.

Fibi held her chin higher and her shoulders straighter, feigning bravery and said, "No, I'll take you. Let me grab my lantern in case we need it. I'll be right back."

I thanked Berry again and promised to visit before leaving Skyview. Fibi and I walked for quite some time before leaving the well-tended residential area of Skyview and coming upon the storage warehouses. Huge double doors were painted different colors in order to designate them separately. For instance, building materials red, textiles green, cold storage blue, and dry goods storage was yellow, etc. Walking at a brisk pace, it took us almost a half an hour to pass by all of the warehouse doors. We began to descend into the lower section of Skyview. There was no one around. After a while our feet began to kick up dust as we used halls that hadn't been traversed in some time. Every now and then we would pass a door that hung open betraying a dark and empty interior. "Why was this section of Skyview abandoned?" I asked. Unconsciously, I lowered my voice to almost a whisper in the emptiness.

I noticed that Fibi did the same as she replied, "This section is very old, and although it is built solidly enough, the rooms are much smaller and lack the natural lighting that the new section offers. If we suddenly had a population explosion, I'm sure we could revitalize this area and put it to use, but our population has done nothing but decline for several generations and there is more than enough room for everyone where we now dwell."

As we walked on, rats skittered by us occasionally, squeaking their outrage at being disturbed and making my skin crawl. We finally came to a door marked with a symbol I could read, a rune as opposed to the banderg writings I had been seeing throughout Skyview. It looked out of place on the door we stood in front of and I wondered what sorcerer or sorceress had placed it there. I traced the rune with my finger and opened the door. Fibi came in with me, illuminating the way with her lantern. Cobwebs hung like a delicate veil over the threshold. The basin of sight water sat in the middle of the room untouched by the dust that cloaked the rest of the chamber. There was only one chair, where I sat down and peered into the water, which reflected my own face back at me.

Fibi was watching me closely, her eyes filled with curiosity. Examining her critically, I pondered what I should do with the girl. I was afraid to be left alone, not knowing how long or demanding the session would be or if I could find my way back out, but, I couldn't very well ask her to stay and wait for me either. A lantern lay on the floor below the only shelf in the room. I got up and examined it, finding it to be half full of oil. I made my decision. With a little spark off from my fingertips, I lit the wick and turned to Fibi. "Thank you for guiding me, Fibi. Be careful on your way back home. I'll see you in a couple of days."

"You want me to leave you here, . . . alone?" Fibi exclaimed with surprise and some disappointment.

"Yes. I'll be all right. Oh, could you let Prince Theodore know where I am. I would appreciate it very much." I smiled brightly trying to radiate confidence.

"You want me to talk to the prince?" Fibi's voice showed the excitement she felt by the assignment. "Are you sure you will be okay, Gabriel?" Fibi asked, looking around the room with concern wrinkling her fine features.

"I'm sure." I wasn't, but I said, "See you later, Fibi."

She hesitated a moment before she turned and left me alone in the room. Suppressing the feeling of abandonment, I sat down on the chair and began my relaxation exercises. Visualizing Rew was much easier this time around because I had gotten to know him better during our stay at Anna's cabin. After drawing the rune to activate the water, I pressed my fingertips into the cool wetness and watched for my small friend. When his cheerful face, gold tufted ears and sandy curls appeared, I felt myself ease into his spirit, feel his soul and touch his being. The sun was fall-

ing over the horizon and Rew looked to his left into the darkness
of the forest, wishing he was back at Anna's . . .

Chapter 18

THE EDGE OF DISASTER

. . . The swamp lands stretched off to Rew's right, glowing a soft sickly shade of green in the waning light of dusk. On his left, the thick forest grew darker and darker and more forbidding with each intake of breath. The company had decided to make their way between the two offensive natural barriers on what once had been a trade route running from Skyview to the east coast. The road remained intact although the forest grew thick right to the very edge and the swamp waters crept close to the other. Rew was in flight, but kept close to Kaltog, feeling uneasiness pressing in on him from both sides. They had already lost one member of the company, Kaltog's mount, who had refused to set one hoof on the road. Kaltog had no choice but to leave the mammoth horse behind. Rew's own instincts told him to get out of there . . . and fast! But, he kept going, following Serek, who led the anxious travelers along the ancient path. The swamp smelled of death and decay and Rew wondered if the scent would ever clear from his nostrils again . . . *if we ever get out of this awful place. I feel danger.*

Serek stopped up ahead and waited for the rest of the company to catch up. "It will be dark soon. We have to decide whether to make camp for the night or keep going. Traversing this terrain in the dark could prove to be very dangerous. Of course, camping here for the night could be just as dangerous," he said.

Rew spoke up and gave his opinion right away, "Let's keep going. I don't want to spend any more time here than we need to. Can't you feel it?"

Jessabelle answered him, "Yes. There is something out there." She looked around and scented the air instinctively, turning first toward the forest and then toward the swamp. "Watching and waiting, they are. I can feel the anxiety down to the core of my being, I tell you. Go on, I say . . . go on."

Once everyone in the party had agreed to continue on through the night, Jessabelle volunteered to take the lead. In the form of a wolf, she had excellent night vision and was best suited to take point. Rew flew over Jessabelle's head, looking for any sign of trouble from above. The sun had gone down, but eerily the swamp continued to glow misty green. The light reflected on the edge of the forest, sending shadows of the company members dancing high up on tree trunks as they moved cautiously forward.

Jessabelle loped at an easy gait, confidently traveling in wolf form, her snow white coat drenched in green light. Once in a while she would stop and twitch her nose at some unknown scent in the air and emit a low growl before continuing down the path. Rew noticed the rest of the company perpetually turning their heads to the left and then the right as if expecting an attack from either side at any moment. *I don't like this.* Rew felt extremely uneasy and wanted to obey the voice inside him that shouted, "Run!" Instead, he watched the swamp, which scared him a little less than the forest. When he did turn his head to gaze into the forest all he could see was shadows weaving in and out of the trees. It was quite unsettling.

Continuing the hike and seemingly making no progress at all, the company started to become extremely weary. But, Jessabelle kept them going and they followed her like ants on a trail. Rew began to observe that the luminescence of the swamp didn't appear to be all encompassing. In fact, the eerie glow seemed to follow the company as they walked along the edge of the murky water. Whatever the source, it stayed even with them consistently. Rew flew down to Kaltog's shoulder and told the torg about his findings. Kaltog confirmed Rew's observation with the nod of his head. They watched the phenomenon together for a while before Jessabelle came to a sudden halt.

Her wolf shape melted away and she materialized into human form. Her face showed deep concern as she informed them, "Something follows us."

"Are you talking about the thing in the swamp?" Rew questioned, trying to keep the edge of fear from his voice.

"Yes. Let's keep going. Stay alert!" Jessabelle ordered, letting her eyes rest a moment longer on Serek and Kristina than anyone else.

The two of them had taken up the rear and had been talking quietly together, not paying enough attention to their surroundings so involved were they in each other. Breezerunner cooed softly, contributing in his own way to Jessabelle's reprimand. Serek took the rebuke to heart and pulled the sword from his scabbard, readying it for any split second attack. Kristina followed suit and retrieved the dagger Serek had provided her from her boot sheath, holding it clenched tightly in her fist as she glanced around watchfully. They continued to walk next to each other silently with heightened awareness.

Jessabelle faded back into the form of a wolf and padded out in front of them. Link headed after her followed closely by Kaltog, both of them tense with apprehension. Breezerunner followed on foot, showing the fortitude and strength of his species as he raced to keep up. Kristina and Serek again brought up the rear, with Serek staying right beside Kristina. Rew returned to the sky and watched from above, keeping a close eye on Jessabelle and scanning the swamp nervously.

Rew felt his stomach rumbling loudly. He looked around apprehensively to make sure none of his unseen foes had heard it and pinpointed his position from the noise. *I sure am hungry. We haven't had anything but water since breakfast this morning at Anna's. It seems like so long ago. I wish I was back there now with a belly full of Link's good cooking, curled up on Anna's soft pink cushions listening to friendly conversation.* Rew's stomach growled even louder this time and again he checked for anything that might be listening. As he stared into the forest, Rew saw something move through the trees. A loud crack emanating from deep in the forest made his heart leap into his throat and pound fiercely. He gazed into the depths of the shadows acutely, but nothing happened. *What is it waiting for?*

The first moon was high in the night sky and the second moon was just peaking over the horizon to the east, shining dully like a big white cue ball against the velvet blackness. The company hiked in single file as they headed toward to the horizon, walking a tight rope line between the forest and the swamp. Rew continued to fly, although his wings were growing tired and he felt every stroke with a twinge of pain. He was used to flying fast, and the slow rate of speed it took to accommodate the company was difficult to maintain, especially when all he wanted to do was get away from there as fast as possible. But, he continued grudgingly on, feeling his stomach complain from lack of food and his wings complain from overexertion.

Rew watched the green illumination and thought he could see bubbles surface from time to time, making big rings that spiraled out in all directions. He thought it was strange that the object seemed to keep a regular distance from them as they walked. *Maybe it is a good swamp thing. Maybe Gabriel sent it to light the way and guide us to safety.* As soon as the thought occurred, an overwhelming sensation came over Rew and he knew that was not the case and that they were in serious danger.

Serek called Rew down and told him that Breezerunner would take the sky reconnaissance for a while to give Rew a rest. The dragon couldn't fly long as he was still recovering, but it was good for him to stretch his flight muscles. Rew was very grateful and scratched Breezerunner on the nose and thanked him personally. The wisp took his position on Kaltog's shoulder with the torg's consent and rested his very weary wings. He took some jerky out of his backpack and offered some to Kaltog, who accepted it, and they both chewed on the hard meat while Kaltog continued forward with giant strides. Rew was surprised that Link could keep up with the much bigger torg. He handed a piece of jerky down for Kaltog to give to Link. Link grinned up at him in thanks for only a moment before continuing his scan from side to side, forest to swamp, back and forth.

Loud screeching coming from the forest brought them all to a halt. The horrendous noise assaulted their senses as the screaming intensified into a fever pitch. They gazed searchingly into the thick blackness of the dense foliage. Dark figures could be seen moving through the tree tops at an alarming rate of speed. The small company immediately started walking again, faster and with only one intention . . . to escape. The screeching continued on, following the advancing company, making their fear ten-fold what it had been earlier. Rew forgot all about the hunger in his belly and the aching of his tired muscles. His eyes were wide with fear as he watched the forest raptly and listened with increasing trepidation.

Rew didn't have a weapon, but he sorely wished he did at that moment. Every once in a while he would focus his attention on the swamp to make sure the swamp thing hadn't moved from its usual position, inevitably to return his diligent watch again back to the forest. Another hour passed and the company remained on the path, making unseen progress, as fear worked on tired minds and taunt nerves.

Rew continued his watchful search alternating his attention from the forest to the swamp. The screeching continued at a steady decibel . . . until . . . just as suddenly as it had started, the high pitched noise ceased. A heavy silence fell over the forest, so mute that it hurt the ears. Suddenly, Rew realized he was holding his breath. He stood perfectly still, not moving a muscle, and resumed breathing slowly, quietly. The entire company tensed, clutching ready weapons in sweaty fists as they waited. They watched, looking into the dark forest searching for any sign of movement, hoping they would see none, but wishing they could see something.

A scream sliced cruelly through the silence from behind Rew. He turned to see Kristina struggling frantically to free herself from her assailant, who was dragging the terrified girl quickly toward the swamp. A slimy tentacle, glowing bright yellow and oozing a white foamy secretion, attached itself around Kristina's ankle. The monster's body remained submerged as it continued to haul its prey toward the luminescent water. Kristina thrust her dagger into the ground and held on to the hilt, pulling her body ineffectually against the tentacle. Serek attacked the arm with his sword, slicing through the glowing flesh and leaving big rips in the skin that leaked nasty black blood, but, his efforts did nothing to deter the monster. A tiny cry escaped Kristina's lips as she lost her grip on the dagger. Even as she dug her hands into the dirt, searching for a hand hold, the ground slipped away from underneath her. Serek used all of his strength to hack at the grotesque appendage as it continued to pull Kristina closer and closer to the awaiting dankness.

Rew leapt off from Kaltog's shoulder and ran to Kristina, grabbed hold of her hands, and pulled furiously as she started to scream. Kaltog joined Rew, but neither was able to stop her. Rew had no choice but to let go or be dragged under himself. Kaltog hung on to her for as long as he could, letting out a frustrated roar as her hands slipped from his. Her legs were quickly submerged under the glowing water, then her thighs, followed by her torso and head, abruptly cutting off her screams with an awful gurgle.

Silence once again hung over the company as they stared at the glowing surface of the water. Time seemed to stand still for Rew as he felt his throat tighten. He looked up just in time to get out of the Serek's way as the man took a running leap and dove smoothly into the murky water.

"Squawreeeeech! Squawreeeeech! Squawreeeeech! . . . "

Rew had no time to hope for his friends. Spinning around, he witnessed terrible large winged shadows descending on them from the forest's canopy. There was a horrible crashing and cracking of limbs as trees were ravaged in the onslaught. They swooped down upon the company as they cried out their hair-raising challenge. "Squawreeeeech!" Breezerunner made first contact with one of the creatures, tearing at it with his talons and easily ripping it to shreds. The flock of vicious creatures, numbering well over one hundred, attacked in a suicidal frenzy.

Rew spotted the dagger stuck in the ground where Kristina had planted it. He grabbed it just as one of the creatures descended on him from above. Rew sliced at it, feeling the blade hit bone while blood drenched his hand. The creature fell to the ground and convulsed while the life left its body and its red eyes faded to black. He quickly examined it with morbid interest. The creature had black leather wings with long clawed talons on the ends. The furry body was about two feet long and had a head that was equipped with razor sharp teeth, a monkey-like face and short pointy horns. It also had long arms and legs with long gripping fingers on both appendages. Immediately another of the creatures was upon him. It dug into his arm with sharp talons and Rew screamed in pain. He planted his feet solidly beneath him and fought. The hilt of the dagger made contact with the creature's skull, dropping it to the ground where it lay twitching in the dust.

He glanced across the path from him. In her human form, Jessabelle moved her body with precision, striking with her feet and slicing with knives in both hands. She so enthralled Rew with her speed and agility that he forgot for a moment the danger at hand. He was enraptured by her lethal beauty. The bat monkey creatures fell dead all around her. She was a killing machine.

Rew heard a splash behind him and turned to see an enormous glowing yellow monster emerge from the swamp with Kristina and Serek clinging to it and gasping desperately for air. Serek still had his sword and was hacking at the monster viciously causing dark blood to squirt everywhere, dousing both him and Kristina with its foulness. The creature was no more than a massive blob of flesh with eight long tentacles and a gaping tooth filled hole on what Rew thought might be the bottom of its head.

As he watched the gruesome battle, Rew was hit from behind by one of the winged creatures, knocking him flat against the ground and forcing all the wind from his lungs. He lay flat on his face drawing in painful breaths before rolling over to see the creature flying straight for his face with talons extended. He rolled the other way and the creature missed him by inches. Before it had a chance to recover and swing back into the air, Rew brought the dagger up and disemboweled it with the swiftness of an experienced hunter. Another was upon him right away and he swung the dagger at the creature's neck, decapitating it. He took to the air and sliced in terror at another and another until suddenly the air around him was clear of flapping wings. Gasping for breath, he spun toward the swamp thing.

The monster had Serek around the waist with one of its tentacles and was attempting to squeeze the life out of him. With one long swipe of his sword Serek amputated the tentacle, causing him and the disembodied appendage to fall into the swamp and be lost from sight. Kristina was fighting to get out of the monster's grasp, but was only getting more tightly entwined in its arms. Serek surfaced sputtering and came to Kristina's rescue, cutting at the tentacle that had her around the waist until blood seeped freely from the wound and it finally lost its grip. Kristina fell to the muck with a splash and half crawled, half swam frantically toward shore.

The sun was slowly cresting over the horizon, announcing dawn in its golden brilliance. What remained alive of the winged creatures ceased their attack without delay and fled into the darkness of the forest. The spent warriors turned to their companions who remained still in peril just in time to witness Serek sink his sword deeply into the monster's underside and rip with all of his strength, dealing a death blow to the creature. The monster burst open in a mess of black blood and white foam, its glowing yellow skin fading to gray as it died. A sucking noise was the only tribute to the monster as its enormous body sank slowly into the murk of the swamp.

Kristina reached the edge of the water. Rew and Link helped her onto dry land. She was exhausted, bruised and covered with black slime, but she was otherwise unharmed. Rew looked for Serek in the mess that covered the surface of the swamp. Finally, he caught sight of the battered warrior making his way sluggishly through the sludge toward them. Kaltog took hold of Serek's sword as Rew and Link dragged him from the water. Breezerunner went to him immediately and nudged Serek's neck gently with his snout. Serek threw his arms around the young dragon and dragged himself to his feet with Breezerunner's assistance. He made his way over to Kristina and the two collapsed into each other's arms. She wiped the dirty water off from his face with her hand and kissed him slowly. Serek's face showed clearly his passionate response.

When he finally looked away from her, he grinned at the rest of the company as he observed the dead creatures scattered all around them. "Good creator, what a mess. It looks as though you've had your hands full, too. I thought maybe you all had abandoned me to that swamp thing. Now, I see," Serek said as he winced painfully and put his hand to his ribs.

Jessabelle went to him, touched his arm with gentle hands and said, "A friend we would never abandon. Let's get you and anyone else who is injured fixed up. On the road is where I would rather be. Exhausted we all are, but it would be much better to travel in the light of day."

"I am not spending another night on this trail," Rew declared with conviction, receiving the unanimous agreement from all of his fellow travelers.

Jessabelle played doctor, going from person to person with the medical kit, mending torn flesh and binding injuries. Serek's injuries had been the most serious, a couple of bruised ribs and some nasty cuts, but it could have been much worse. When Jessabelle was finished, they continued eastward down the path, feeling grimy, dirty and tired, but happy to have survived the night and very anxious to put that part of their trip behind them. Rew led the way, feeling unusually energetic after the long hard night. He kept a steady pace, looking back now and then to make sure the company was able to keep up.

By mid-afternoon the swamp came to an end and was left far behind on the trail before the forest ended as well. A low mountain range stood between the company and the ocean. Rolling foothills covered in white birch and dark green aspens sloped gently up toward the mountains. The sun filtered through the leaves in dancing patterns upon their backs as they followed the path. They began climbing in altitude immediately and soon ran across a pleasant meadow with a gurgling creek that ran down from the mountains. They made camp at the edge of the creek on sweet smelling grass and breathed a collective sigh of relief.

Bathing was first on everyone's agenda, so they all stripped down and went swimming in the icy creek together, playing gleefully like children, splashing and dunking one another, until all the grime, dirt and blood was washed away. It felt heavenly to be clean again. Rew lie down in the grass and let the warm sun dry him off. Jessabelle joined him. "You know, Rew, very well you fought last night. My eye I had on you and impressive you were with that dagger. I was wondering. Tell me. Why do you not carry a weapon of your own?" she asked.

Rew watched Serek and Kristina wrestling with Breezerunner in the water and smiled to himself, enjoying the feeling of happiness. "I've never had any reason to. In fact, I have never killed anything before in my life. It was awful, even killing those dreadful creatures. I hope I never have to do it again," he said.

"Another day you may have to fight again, Rew. Used to it you will never be. Apathy can only result if you lose your regard for life. Feeling the pain or the fear is far better than feeling nothing at all." Jessabelle was silent for so long that Rew thought she might have fallen asleep. He gazed over at her, seeing her lying there with the sun shining on her firm white flesh. She was so beautiful. *Theo is a lucky man.*

They cooked over a camp fire the wild turkey Link had trapped for dinner along with some roots and berries they scrounged up around the camp site. It was a delicious feast and Rew had second and third helpings before retiring to his bedroll for the night. Exhaustion claimed him upon lying down and he was soon in a deep and comforting sleep . . .

Chapter 19

HOLLOW VICTORY

August 12 . . . "Gabriel. Gabriel." I awoke with a jolt to my name being whispered in my ear and someone's hand gently shaking my shoulder. My fingers were cold and wet and it took a long moment for me to remember where I was and what I was doing. I must have fallen asleep when Rew did. Memories of the dreams he was having departed along with the sleep, but the feeling of happiness remained with me briefly. I withdrew my hand from the sight water and looked around to see who had awakened me.

Theo towered over me with a frown on his face. He was fully clad in chain mail, leggings, boots, and breast plate and was holding a helmet under his right arm. "Are we at war?" I asked him with amusement as I eyed his incredible garb.

Theo did not return my smile. "We will be at war soon. The army is in position and awaits my command. How are Jessabelle and the others?" he asked. Concern showed on his face even through his princely mask.

"They are well. Can we discuss this later, Theo? I would like to find a place to sleep and I do need to freshen up a bit," I said.

Fibi came forward from where she stood in the doorway, avoiding Theo's eyes with bashfulness. "Why don't you stay with us, Gabriel? I am sure mother would be happy to have you," she offered.

Theo helped me to my feet with strong arms. "That's a wonderful idea. Stay with Fibi. I need to go back out to the field. When you are rested, you can help me out by coordinating things from inside of Skyview. We will be able to communicate through B.F. to keep each side informed on how the battle is progressing. Would you be willing to assist General Hatch and General Kin?" he asked.

"If I can get some sleep. How much time do I have?" I started walking toward the door, stretching my cramped muscles with every step.

"We strike at dawn," Theo reported with an edge of excitement in his voice.

"Very well," I said, not looking forward to the forthcoming fight . . . not at all.

Once we reached Fibi's apartment, I kissed Theo softly on the cheek and wished him luck and safety before he departed. Berry showed me to their guest room, commenting on how it had not been used in some time. The room was simple in design, decorated in soft mauve and gray, the rug and the only wall hanging reminded me of the southwestern United States with a Native American flare. The bed sized cushion on the floor was just a little short for my five foot six inches, but it was comfortable and I was soon fast asleep.

Earthquake!

August 13. I don't know what time it was, but it was still quite dark. I felt I had slept for only an hour when I was awakened by a strange sensation of movement underneath me. The earth seemed to be rocking, growing in intensity with each passing moment until the ground around me felt like liquid. The wall hanging slapped against the wall as if the entire mountain was rocking back and forth. I tried to stand, but was thrown down onto the hard stone floor with enough force to take my breath away. Dust was falling from the ceiling and I was afraid the whole mountain was going to come down around me. Maybe I shouldn't have taunted Candaz to bring down the mountain if he could. Perhaps he could. Struggling to the door on my hands and knees, I managed to make it out into the hallway.

Fibi and Berry came running toward me and helped me to my feet. "We've got to get out of here! The mountain is collapsing!" Berry's panic was quickly spent and she calmly led the way to the front entrance of their home.

We made our way out into the crowded hallway as the ground continued to move. Bandergs were shouting at one another, but moved cooperatively down the hallway. When we arrived in the main hall, the rocking still had not let up. Councilman Bard was directing traffic toward the southern gate, issuing orders to evacuate Skyview as quickly and orderly as possible. The bandergs did as they were told and headed down the corridor quickly. Berry, Fibi and I were joining the line when a loud crack thundered in my ears. I turned and saw the fountain, dominating the center of the hall, split in half. The crack in the stone looked like someone had sliced it precisely down the middle with a sharp knife. My suspicions were confirmed that this was not a natural occurrence. Candaz was to blame for Skyview's earthquake.

Pandemonium broke out, sweeping Fibi and Berry away from me and in the direction that the stampede was headed. Bandergs were being dragged and pushed and stepped on. Water flooded down from the fountain's reservoir, flooding the hall and adding to the chaos. The ground continued to shake violently and I wondered how long Skyview could withstand it.

I felt I had one chance to save Skyview. If freecurrent could start the destruction, freecurrent could end it. I walked to the center of the fountain, where the massive crack defaced the once pristine stone. Kneeling down in the water, I put my hands on the cold hard stone and I began to gather freecurrent energy from around me. My fingers drew tiny runes upon the stone, working at a feverish pace. I felt freecurrent surge through me. The pendant that dangled on my chest burned hot against my skin. Suddenly, the shaking stopped and the crack began to come together until the rock was fused whole once again. The healing of the rock was complete. A pink streak ran through the center where it had been fractured, a scar that would remain forever to mark the day that Skyview had almost fallen.

Battle Stations

When I looked up General Kin was standing before me. "The battle has begun. Candaz's troops have broken through the northern gate. Come. We have work to do," he said, extending his hand to me.

Cold and exhausted, I lifted myself out of the water, took his hand, and followed General Kin down one of two long corridors that headed north. Clenching my teeth against the tremors that shook my body, I tried to keep up. I could smell fresh air blowing down the corridor and soon could hear the shouting of men and the clashing of steel. General Kin led me out the through the gate and into the dark night. We joined General Hatch, who was busy giving instructions to his captain. "Better contact the prince's dragon and get word to him that we have been breached," General Hatch ordered without looking at me as he surveyed the battle field.

I did as he bid me. "B.F.?"

"Yes, Gabriel? Are you all right? I was afraid the earth was going to swallow you whole," he responded with concern.

"I'm fine. Tell Theo that Candaz's troops have breached the northern gate. Fighting is intense. Casualties are occurring on both sides."

"He is bringing his troops up behind Candaz's force. They will be joining the battle shortly," B.F.'s tone was serious.

It was a bloody battle. Weapons like swords, spears and axes inflicted horrible damage to soft flesh. The numbers of the dead and wounded increased as the fight raged on.

The fighting continued on into the dawn of the third day. Theo and I stayed in constant communication through B.F., exchanging information as the battle changed course. I watched the carnage from a safe distance, along with General Hatch, who was dictating strategy to the troops. General Kin was on the battleground along with his men. It was one of the most difficult things I ever had to do, just stand by and watch men being slaughtered. I wanted to put an end to it all, send them all to their rooms without dinner like naughty children. It seemed so pointless.

When I couldn't stomach standing aside any longer, I found the medical tent and lended my help where I could, healing with freecurrent when possible or simply fetching water or holding someone's hand and lending comfort.

It was inevitable the Sabers would to lose in the end. The bandergs were fighting for their home, to protect friends and families and were therefore ferocious opponents. I felt sorry for the men who were losing their lives in order to satisfy Candaz's ambitions. The whole situation was an abomination. I wanted retribution. To put an end to Candaz was becoming my highest ambition.

B.F. was keeping an eye out for Candaz and was to report to me the minute the sorcerer was found. I wished longingly for the confrontation, wanting desperately to end all of this nonsense and spare some lives. The time wore on and still no sign of the sorcerer was reported. Theo declared that the battle was all but won. I wondered what could have happened to Candaz. Why would he abandon his troops in the middle of an important battle? Cowardice? Somehow, I didn't think so. He was up to something.

By the time dusk fell across the land on the third day the battle was over. What was left of Candaz's troops had turned and fled, giving in to defeat. So many lives had been lost. For what?

I went onto the field to help out. Bodies lay in endless heaps of broken flesh. The wounded moved with slow determination through the jumble of misery, trying to keep a grip on survival in the midst of extinction. Blood soaked the ground for as far as the eye could see. While I aided the wounded, I searched for Candaz, hoping to find his lifeless body among the many other that lay mimicking the actions of their final moments. I worked well into the night, but did not find the man I sought. He had somehow escaped. It was necessary that I go after him in order to finish our private war before I could return home. My heart was heavy with grief when Theo met me on the field.

"I have some bad news," Theo proclaimed with passion and anger. He took off his helmet and ran blood stained hands through his sweat matted hair. His green eyes clearly reflected the exhaustion he worked to ignore. Evidence of the fighting clung to his dirty and blood soaked clothing and dulled his once shining armor. I imagined that I probably didn't look much better after days of war, nursing the injured soldiers and sifting through corpses all evening.

"What is it, Theo?" I asked.

"Candaz has escaped," he said.

"You know that for sure?" I asked only to confirm what I already suspected.

"Yes." Theo paused and took my hand in his. For a moment he seemed entranced by our filthy hands as they touched each other. I watched as he turned my hand over in close examination. "There is more," he said without looking up.

"Tell me," I demanded softly, although I was suddenly very frightened to hear his words.

"When the earthquake hit, Candaz was ready and waiting on the other side of Skyview. Trying to escape from being trapped inside the falling mountain, banderg women and children opened the southern gate and ran outside to find safety. Instead of sanctuary they found Candaz there waiting for them. He enchanted them as he did the torg nation, enslaving them and taking their wills away. To the north he escaped, taking almost fifty women and children with him." Theo read the question in my eyes and answered affirmatively, "I am afraid Fibi and Berry were among them."

I was outraged and confused by the sorcerer's actions. "How is this possible? What could possibly be his strategy in kidnapping banderg women and children? Why didn't we know of this earlier? How could he possibly have gotten away with this?" I asked, feeling hysteria threatening to take over what remained of my self-control.

Theo squeezed my hand that he still held in his own. "I couldn't guess his reasons, Gabriel. It doesn't make any sense to me either. I'm sorry. I didn't foresee this. Perhaps the man has lost his mind."

"Perhaps," I had been wondering the same thing for some time. "How long ago did this happen?"

"It occurred while the battle was starting early the first morning," he answered.

"*Why wasn't I told? I might have been able to help. B.F.?*" I demanded an explanation from him and from Theo. "Why wasn't I told?"

"*I did not know, Gabriel. Do you think I would not have told you something this important?*" B.F. responded, sounding indignant and hurt by my question.

"*I'm sorry. Of course you would have told me had you known.*" "I'm sorry, Theo. I didn't mean to sound accusatory." It only took me a moment to decide what to do. "I have to go after them. But, first I have to return to the Tower of Ornate to retrieve the silver harp," I said.

Theo appraised me with concern. "I don't want you to go alone. But, I'm afraid I have many things to take care of here before I can leave."

"I would appreciate your help, but, I would prefer it if you and B.F. headed out after Candaz right away or as soon as you can. There is a chance you might be able to waylay them from getting all the way to Castle Xandia, if indeed that is their destination." I looked at Theo for his consent, which he finally gave with the nod of his head. "I just don't understand his motivation. It baffles me. It's as if he set up this battle as a ruse," she said with a heavy sigh. "I'll summon Skymaster and see if he is available to escort me home before we head to Castle Xandia."

B.F. relayed after a moment, "*Skymaster says he is always willing to do a favor for a beautiful lady. He is on his way right now.*"

"*Thanks B.F.*"

"You're welcome, my friend. I noticed you referred to Ornate as your 'home'. It gives me pleasure that you feel that way," he said.

"Did I say that?" I asked.

"Yes, you did."

"Oh." I left it at that, having no desire at the moment to parry with B.F. over casually dropped phrases or his analysis of the same.

When Theo and I returned to Skyview, the community was in an uproar. Councilman Bard told us that fifty-two of his people were missing and presumed kidnapped by Candaz. They were sending out a contingency of warriors to attempt a rescue. I couldn't convince Bard that the contingency would be in great danger of being kidnapped themselves should they encounter Candaz and his magic. I was determined to arrive at Castle Xandia well before they did to free their people and have the bandergs on their way back home before the contingency of warriors had a chance to arrive. My timing would have to be exceedingly good.

I had just enough time to get cleaned up and change into my riding cloths before I received word from Skymaster that he had arrived and was waiting for me on the shelf on the south side of the southern gate. I found Theo, who was in deep conversation with General Kin, and told him I was leaving and that I would contact B.F. when Skymaster and I were north of the Standing River.

Back to Ornate

Skymaster flew swiftly, understanding my urgency, and the Tower of Ornate finally came into view on the shore of Blue Lake. The sun was just coming up over the horizon, turning the sky brilliant orange and pink, hinting of rain. We landed on the grassy field in front of the Tower and I ran to the entrance, intending to retrieve the silver harp and be on my way again.

"The company has reached the outskirts of New Chance, Gabriel. Breezerunner sends his greetings to you," Skymaster said.

I weighed my options for a moment before deciding I could risk the time it would take to look in on the company. If they were successful in their quest, it could be the turning point for Risen. *"I think I am going to be a little while longer than I thought, Skymaster. Why don't you take this opportunity to find something to eat?"*

"Yes, Gabriel, I think I'll go fishing. Call me when you are ready," Skymaster intoned with a bored yawn.

I left the pack containing my diary and a few other personal things on the floor in the living room. The silver harp sat next to the wall at the top of the staircase. I snatched it and headed to the room with the sight water. After I entered, I placed the harp gently on the floor beside my chair and sat down at the basin. I took a few minutes to catch my breath before starting my relaxation exercises. The rune of activation glowed green as I placed my fingertips on the surface of the water and thought of Rew, rewarded soon thereafter by seeing his face reflected in the water. I easily let myself go and listened for Rew's thoughts. The ocean waves pounded the sandy shore rhythmically, spraying Rew with salty mist . . .

Chapter 20
A SECOND CHANCE

. . . As they walked down the beach, rubble of what had once been lake shore residences could be seen through stands of birch that rustled their tiny leaves gleefully in the ocean breeze, heedless of the ghost town they landscaped. Judging from the size of the building pads that remained relatively intact, the houses had been quite large in their time. The tumbled remains of the city came into view further down the shoreline. Natural erosion from the ocean had caused several buildings to fall into the water, where they sat being eaten away by the waves. Rew was enjoying the feel of the fine textured sand between his toes as they walked along the beach, listening to the waves hammer the shore with a sense of wonder at their power. A flock of seagulls fished off from an ancient pier that miraculously had remained standing. They called to each other in their screeching tongue as they dove gracefully into the water, sometimes coming up with a fish and sometimes coming up without.

Rew thought about what Shareen had told them regarding the Table of Alliance as they made their way carefully through the ruins, heading away from the beach and up into the city. She had said the table was located in the public library building, but had given no indication as to where the building itself might be located in the city of New Chance. At the moment they seemed to be in a residential area, evidenced by pots and pans and other various household items scattered about in the ruins. A library, theoretically, would be located in the center of town, probably next to schools, offices, shops and government buildings. At this point they seemed to be far from the main street.

Rew was slightly familiar with the city of New Chance, having studied its history and the history of its people under the tutelage of his father. After the forefathers of the human race came to Risen in flight from persecution in their old land, they built the city of New Chance on the eastern coast. They became friends with the other races in the land, enjoying free trade and comradery with them all. New Chance prospered as a community, building and growing out and up, starting new industries, and developing as a cultural center. Once well established, the people built ships and sent out teams to explore across the ocean, but the ships were never heard from or seen again. Rumors spread that great sea monsters roamed the waters and had engulfed the ships whole. There were even people in the city of New Chance who claimed to have sighted these monsters cresting periodically above the waves far off shore. After some time, the rumors died off and things went back to normal in New Chance. One day the sky turned black as night and the wind blew hard and fast, throwing mighty waves against the structures that lined the shore. Rain pelted down throughout the city of New Chance and soon even the highest ground was flooded. The people huddled together in the downtown area to ride out the storm. Day passed into night unnoticed, so dark had been the day. Without warning, in the early morning hours a mighty wave swept down upon the city of New Chance, burying everything under ten feet of water. Those few who survived the storm decided to abandon New Chance, not wishing to encounter the wrath of the great sea monsters again. They packed what they could salvage from the mud covered city and headed out to explore Risen and find new places to settle and raise their families. New Chance was left to the ocean and the mythical guardians who inhabited her waters. *I wish I could see a sea monster. That would be really something. I wonder if they look anything like dragons.*

"*I hardly think so.*" Breezerunner responded to Rew's thoughts, insulted for being compared with a sea monster.

"*I didn't mean to insult . . . it is not that dragons are monsters . . . just big . . . and . . . Oh, never mind!*"

"*Apology accepted.*" Swirling red eyes met Rew's gaze when he looked at the big scaly fellow.

"*Dragons certainly are sensitive,*" Rew said as he fluttered up in air in front of Breezerunner's face.

"*Yes, we are,*" Breezerunner agreed and blew Rew gently away. Rew laughed, knowing the dragon could have sent him reeling through the air like a leaf caught on the breeze if he had wanted to. Together they flew a short ways to catch up with the rest of the company.

The powdery dust covering the ruins made the company's footsteps silent as dust plumes billowed mutely from under their feet. The mud that had inundated the city so many years ago had dried, condensing into a fine powder over the decades. New Chance did not have the haunted feeling that some abandoned towns did; it just felt empty, absent of any life whatsoever. Rew started to speak, but the quiet made his voice seem loud and he stopped short. "I think . . . " he looked around feeling uncomfortable as all eyes fell upon him. Rew smiled at them weakly. He started once again, this time in a softer tone, "It might be a good idea if Jessabelle, Breezerunner and I took to the air and tried to locate the library. We could each cover a section of the city and report back here."

"Good idea," Link said as he plopped his pack down on the ground, bringing a cloud of dust up around himself, making him cough and sputter. As the dust settled, Link's beard grew increasingly white, as if he was aging standing there before their eyes. Rew started to laugh and soon everyone else was laughing, releasing pent up tensions at their friend's expense. Link scowled angrily at them for a moment, but soon was laughing too, shaking his beard at Rew and making him sneeze between guffaws.

The areas were designated by Serek. He sent Breezerunner left, Jessabelle right and Rew down the center of town, with instructions to be back before the sun was straight up. Rew flew down low, scanning the ruins below him with sharp eyes. He came upon what appeared to be a park or a town square, perhaps the center of town. A slab for a stage remained intact, but a speaking podium lay tipped on its side and several statues lay in pieces around their marble pedestals. Rew investigated a little further into the park and came upon a pedestal with a thick slab of black marble resting upon it. *That is a strange looking statue.* Rew flew up a couple of feet and landed upon the slab. To his delight it was a map of the city of New Chance carved into the surface of the black marble, the buildings and symbols stood out in white and gold. There was writing on the map, but Rew couldn't read the ancient language. However, he did recognize the symbols.

He examined the map with an expert eye and decided that he stood approximately where the arrow indicated, as he had suspected in the center of town. He quickly found the medical building at the top of the map, closer to residential dwellings. Just to the north of him was the judicial building and the government offices. To his east was a school and just above that was the library. He easily figured out where he had left his friends and laid out the quickest route in his mind from their position to the library. He took one last look, just to be sure of his directions, checked the position of the sun, *just before straight up,* and flew back to where the rest of the company awaited him.

Jessabelle and Breezerunner had already returned when Rew arrived. "I've found it!" Rew flew with lightning speed to individual members of the company, back and forth and around, hugging and kissing when he could get away with it. When he finally settled down he noticed that his friends were not quite as excited by his news as he was. Their heads all hung low and they avoided each other's eyes. Link pulled on his beard with a worried grimace on his face. Kristina twisted her fingers together until her knuckles were white where she stood next to Serek, whose face was devoid of all emotion. Kaltog was drawing little pictures in the dust with his big toe. Jessabelle watched the torg's artistry with avid interest. *They all look so nervous. I guess they are afraid of what will happen when we find the table. They should be happy this quest is just about over.* Rew broke the silence, "Let's eat lunch before we go. I'm hungry."

Jessabelle ceased her fixation and laughed, "Always hungry you are Rew. Bottomless pits you and Link have for stomachs. Which way are we heading?"

Rew frowned, thinking that he wouldn't get any lunch again after all. "It's over that way. Do you see that tall building that is still standing? That is the art gallery and museum. The library is two buildings down from that, just past the school."

Jessabelle smiled warmly at Rew as she hitched her pack up on to her shoulders. "A small park, I saw that would be on our way. Let's stop there for lunch," she said. The smile she gave him melted his heart.

Good. I'm hungry.

Lunch was a simple affair of dried black deer meet and long cakes washed down with tepid water. Rew fantasized about sipping a cold frothy brew and eating Link's tasty cooking. *I wonder if I will ever enjoy Link's cooking again. I'm going to miss him.* He took another bite of long cake, chewing gloomily on the tasteless bread. Kaltog groaned and stood up, stretching his muscular arms well above his head before complaining to no one in particular, "I sure wish we had some of Link's delicacies right now. I am sick of these road rations. A large mug of ale would be a welcome change from water."

Serek stood up and stretched as well. "Well there's no sense in wishing for what we don't have, is there? Let's get going. Rew, lead the way," he said with a scowl on his face.

Cautiously, they walked through the deserted streets. Most of the buildings were flattened, but as they came closer to the center of town, more and more of the ancient buildings remained standing, silently echoing footsteps of the company's passing. Everything was covered in white powdery silt and Rew noticed his normally tanned hands were porcelain white.

Glancing back to make sure the company was still behind him, Rew noticed that Kaltog had been diverted to the back of the group because his large feet kicked up dust in great plumes behind him as he walked. He was, however, getting the worst of everybody else's dust causing him to sneeze violently every now and then. Rew smiled in amusement and turned back just in time to avoid running into a large column that had fallen across the road and now lay in neat three to four foot sections directly in their path. Embarrassed, Rew quickly made his way around one of the sections and continued on his way, pretending he hadn't just nearly smacked face first into the tumbled stone.

They rounded a corner and the gallery and museum building came into view on their right. It was a massive gray stone building with large arched windows that now stood open to the street. A small courtyard graced the front of the building with a dry fountain surrounded by weed infested gardens and broken benches. Rew pictured in his mind the way the tiny area must have been before the flood, water gurgling gently in the fountain as birds sang cheerfully in the trees, the gardens alive with a myriad of colors and lovers whispering sweet words to each other as they sat upon the benches. The fantasy faded and the starkness of the building made Rew feel a twinge of nostalgia for the people who had walked these streets before him.

The next building they passed by on their right was, Rew remembered, the school building. The entire structure was collapsed in on itself, although the playground equipment in the back of the building seemed to be in good shape and even retained some of its original orange and green coloring.

A sign in front of the next building indicated that it was the library, donning the symbol Rew had seen on the map in the center of town. The white marble building was standing in relatively good condition. Huge intricately carved columns stretched from the ground up to the top of the building's roof four stories up. There were eight columns in all and they depicted nature's creatures, each one individually distinct. They were very beautiful and the company took their time examining each column, appreciating the ancient artist's talent.

After pushing open the large double wooden doors, they followed Kaltog into a dark atrium. Rew flew just overhead. He could not see a thing until Link lit a lantern. Tentatively they entered the main library. The huge room was lined with bookshelves, all running parallel to one another in straight evenly spaced rows. Most of the books that had once lined the shelves had long ago crumbled to dust, only a few remained standing stoically in place.

Serek motioned them along, taking the lead and bringing them into a section of the library that was a checkerboard of tables with chairs placed neatly underneath them, four to a table. One reading lantern sat in the center of each table, heavily coated with gray dust. Apparently the flood had not touched the interior of this building, probably protected by the thick marble walls and the heavy entry door. They passed by a few offices and came to a set of stairs leading up. Serek took them up one flight, stopping on the second floor.

The room they entered was a large auditorium that tiered one at a time toward the bottom floor in a circular manner. Link, who held the lantern, walked down the stairs toward the round table that dominated the space. "It's here," Rew uttered under his breath with relief and apprehension.

They all gathered around the white marble table in silence, wondering what they should do next, feeling the tension in the air build. Rew peered intently into the hollow center, trying to catch a glimpse of the magical core. Serek pulled him back and said stiffly, "Let's do this."

Kristina spoke softly, "That's why we are here. Does anyone remember the words?"

Rew began, "I remember . . . "

Serek cut him off abruptly, "Let's get on with it." They all rested their hands on the dusty white surface of the table and waited anxiously.

Rew spoke quietly and without reservation, feeling the excitement build, "Shareen instructed us to approach this task with goodness in our hearts. I know I have come to love and care for all of you during our journey here and I consider the friendships we have established to be precious. I ask all of you now to concentrate on those good feelings while I recite the words."

Serek's face contorted with anger and pain. "Get on with it," he rasped between clenched teeth.

He received looks of concern, but no one outwardly questioned his odd behavior. *I wonder what is wrong with him.*

Rew started the recitation, trying hard to concentrate on the good feelings in his heart and ignore Serek's unfavorable attitude. "Break the chains that bind us all with hate. Swords are drawn in war; blood spilled, souls released, in an endless play for power." Rew paused as he felt Breezerunner tremble violently next to him. "A table in round renders all races equal. The end of intollerance is at hand." Rew could feel the power emanating from the core of the table as he watched closely to see what would happen.

It began to hum with a slight vibration. The air seemed charged with electricity as it would be after a lightning storm. Blue smoke billowed out of the hollow, bright and alive with an electric charge before the sphere-shaped core, about six inches in diameter, levitated through the center of the table and hung in the air a foot above the table's plane. The core was black as night and Rew felt his heart sicken at the sight of it. Kaltog drew back slightly; his eyes were wide with horror. Rew heard intakes of breath from the others. Jessabelle groaned audibly and her face distorted as if in pain. Link was frozen by fear that permeated the air. Tears streamed down Kristina's eyes and she gulped for air. Breezerunner was still shaking violently and Rew could hear a whining sound beginning deep in the dragon's throat. The sphere pulsed with corruption.

Serek gazed at the core with wild eyes before he pulled his sword free of the scabbard. The blade sung in response. He made a howling war cry as he swung the sword down toward the rotten core. The sound of the impact was deafening. Rew heard himself scream as the core shattered in a million pieces and the energy from it swirled ominously around them.

With no warning Serek turned his sword on Link and attacked. The banderg responded quickly, tackling the much bigger man to the ground. The sword was flung from his hand and landed out of his reach with a loud clatter.

Serek and Link struggled upon the floor, but Link was on top and kept all of his weight on Serek's chest. The wild man raged at Link with obscenities Rew had never before heard. Kristina tried to get Serek to calm down, but he did not recognize her or her pleas. Link cried out, "What's wrong with him?"

"He's lost his mind," Kaltog said.

Rew strode quickly over and looked down at the still struggling Serek. He knelt down beside him and pressed his small fingers to Serek's temples and spoke some words of magic that only Rew could understand. Closing his eyes, he reached for Serek's mind using wisp magic. Rew explored through the recesses, bypassing barriers built up by emotional scars and defense mechanisms. Finally he found what he sought. Serek had a tiny speck of corrosion planted in his brain, like a small tumor that had been planted there. He touched the spot and knew Candaz had placed it there some time ago. Rew could feel the corrupt power it contained and took his time as he reached for the powers of nature and requested healing. The harmful tumor was slowly replaced with new vital pink tissue.

Slowly and cautiously, Rew withdrew from Serek's mind and sat looking down into his friend's face as he continued to message Serek's temples. Serek opened his eyes and looked up at Rew with confusion and wide questioning eyes and asked, "What the hell just happened?"

"It was Candaz," he said as he helped Serek to sit up.

The baffled man shook his head, trying to clear it. "The last thing I remember was seeing the table for the first time and then I was lying on the floor with you kneeling over me. What happened?" Serek asked, looking up at the company and letting his gaze rest on Kristina. She came to him in response and kissed him gently on the lips before answering, "You destroyed the core and attacked Link.

"I attacked Link? Why isn't he dead?" Serek said with a slight smile.

"Very funny," Link responded.

Rew said, "In your head I found a spot, a speck of decay, left there by Candaz to compel you to do his bidding when the time had come. It was like a booby trap. You are lucky that little spot of decay didn't rot your brain. If you weren't so hard headed it might have destroyed you. I removed it. You will be all right now, Serek."

"I don't understand how this could have happened! He had no right . . . " he spewed. Serek was upset and angry.

Rew stood up gracefully. "It doesn't matter. It is over now. Shall we try to place the new core? Do you feel strong enough, Serek?"

Serek began to grin. He quickly shook off his anger as he stood up and said, "Sure. Link? Kris?" He took hold of Kristina's waist and gently propelled her to his side, stealing a kiss in the process.

Kaltog swung the leather pack he had been carrying off his shoulder and placed it on the floor. From it he withdrew the new core and placed it in the center of the table where it hovered magically.

Rew spoke the words again and let his feelings flow freely.

As they watched in fascination, the core sizzled before them with freecurrent energy, burning with electric light in a wide array of colors. It illuminated the entire conference room, flooding every corner with its radiance. The freecurrent power was awesome. Rew felt it surge through him, exit through his fingertips and into his friends, making its way around the circle. Every face glowed and Rew felt tears of joy streaking down his cheeks to fall in tiny splashes upon the surface of the table. The core sank back down into the hollow center and the company watched it in wonder as it remained glowing brightly.

Link broke the silence with a bright smile on his face. "We've accomplished what we set out to do. Let's celebrate tonight," he said.

They left the city of New Chance and made camp down on the beach, building a big fire and grilling delicious fish that Kaltog and Serek caught for dinner. They all felt elevated with the weight of the quest off their shoulders and they talked, danced and laughed well into the night. It was decided that instead of heading straight home, they would all go to Skyview to help out where they could.

Rew was looking forward to going to Skyview where he could eat more of Link's cooking and drink as much banderg ale as a wisp could drink. The delay in Skyview gave Rew the opportunity to stay with his friends a little bit longer and he was glad for it. He would miss every one of them when they finally parted company. He hoped with all of his heart that he would remain a part of their lives. The table was once again intact, so it followed logically that things would have to change for the better. If Serek took back Saberville from Candaz and Kristina married him, it would forge a bond between the Brights and the Sabers. Risen would no longer be split in two and the races would be free to come together once again and enjoy free trade and friendship. Rew had high hopes for the future and high hopes for his friends.

When the fire had died down and the plans had all been made, Rew made his way over to where Jessabelle lay on her blanket, staring quietly into the coals. She smiled up at him and took his hand in the warmth of her own. He lay down next to her on the blanket, feeling the heat of her body and enjoying the sweet scent of her skin. Snuggling closer to his companion, Rew let himself drift into a happy and comfortable sleep . . .

Chapter 21

THE ENEMY'S CHAMBERS

Taken Hostage

. . . I felt rough hands around my neck and a painful wrenching as the medallion was torn from my throat. It was replaced with a chain that had a heavy stone hanging from it. Immediately I felt cut off from the freecurrent energy around me. Turning away from the sight water I fought, kicking and punching at my attacker, who avoided me easily by stepping back and confidently laughing. His face was hidden from me in the darkness of the room, but I thought I recognized his laugh from sometime in my past. In a flash, I was heading for the door, avoiding the man as I darted out of the room and down the stairs. Coming around the corner into the dining room I ran into the bodies of Hue and Nina lying on the floor with their necks slit open. Their life blood mingled together in one large puddle around them on the white tile floor. My knees gave way under me and gravity took me down hard as I stared in horror.

"*Skymaster!*" I called desperately, but received no answer. "*Skymaster! B.F.!*"

No answer.

I heard footsteps behind me, but before I could move the man grabbed my arms and tied my hands behind my back. "Why are you doing this? Let me go!" I demanded.

The man's voice was harsh with hate, "I promised you that you would see me again, witch. I always keep my promises." He rolled me over to loosely tie my feet, leaving slack enough to allow me to walk, but not enough to enable me to run. I saw his face. His fat puffy cheeks were overlaid with about a three day old beard and his brown eyes had a yellowish tint. Fetid breath, hot and heavy issued forth from his mouth.

I knew who it was, one of Candaz's men. We had met at Farreach not so long ago. His name was Reid. The question was whether he was under Candaz's orders at the moment or was he working on his own? "What are you planning to do with me?" I asked.

He sneered at me malevolently and said, "Not what I would like to do. Candaz has ordered me to bring you to him unharmed. He has his own plans for you, witch." Reid pulled me up by the arms and I winced in pain. He smiled, taking pleasure in it, and I promised myself that I would not give him the satisfaction again. I was guided out the front door and taken to a horse that was saddled and waiting. He threw me unkindly over the horses back and mounted just behind me.

"You can't expect me to ride like this all the way to Castle Xandia. Please untie my legs so I can sit up right. I will never make it like this. You are supposed to deliver me unharmed," I said. Grudgingly, he got down off the horse, cut my leg bindings and let me sit in front of him. It was extremely uncomfortable sharing a horse with the man. He smelled foul and it was impossible to avoid a close proximity to him. However, I endured the torture stoically, not giving Reid a reason to enjoy my displeasure.

Mentally, I continued to try and contact Skymaster and B.F. while we rode north. The link had somehow been severed, but I kept trying anyhow, determined not to give up hope. I could not use the freecurrent magic. Whatever he had chained around my neck prevented it. Frustration was taking my composure away bit by bit. I was handicapped. Rubbing my thumb and finger together behind my back, I whispered quietly the appropriate words, but was not rewarded with fire. I tried again and again with no success. I could not access the freecurrent or reach the dragons. I was in trouble.

By the time we stopped to make camp for the night, I was completely fed up with being tied up. Reid built a fire and cooked some type of stew for dinner, which he ate himself and offered me none of. For a man who was supposed to deliver me safely to Candaz, he was sure doing everything he could to make me ill. I was given no food or water that night. As I waited for Reid to fall asleep, my will faded and I soon drifted into a restless sleep.

August 15. The next morning Reid and I were back on the trail before sunrise. My head swooned with weakness from lack of food, water and proper sleep. I thought back and realized the last good night's sleep I had enjoyed was back at Anna's cabin. The thought of Anna's cabin brought back pleasant memories and I let my mind day dream about being in the comfort of her home with my friends as company, laughing and crying together, sharing stories and dreams. I wondered how Theo was doing. He should be at Castle Xandia by now. Perhaps he had encountered the kidnapped bandergs while still on the road and had somehow been able to set them free. I prayed for their safety.

I choked back tears that surfaced. My ever present grief was threatening to overwhelm me and I had to work to suppress it. Panic promised to turn my emotions into hysteria. I couldn't let that happen.

Reid finally untied my hands, for which I was thankful. Apparently his plan was to keep me weak enough so that I could not run away. It was working. I could barely stand on my own, let alone go anywhere in my present condition. I tried to remove the heavy chain from around my neck, but it was strong and possibly enchanted and my efforts were futile.

He let me have my bag that he had snatched out of the living room at Ornate. It's too bad he wasn't stupid enough to grab the silver harp as well. At least I have my diary and with my hands untied I have the ability to write about this nightmare. Hopefully we will reach the Running River tomorrow sometime. From there it should be about a two day ride to Castle Xandia. I will be glad to be rid of Reid's offensive company, even though facing Candaz can't be much more pleasant. My physical condition has worsened to the point that I have found myself sleeping on the horse as we ride and leaning on Reid behind me for support. I'm going to not only need a bath, but a flea bath.

August 16. We crossed the Running River today. I was allowed to wash out my riding clothes and bathe in the cool water. It was heavenly while it lasted, even with Reid glaring at me the entire time I washed. I did get to drink some of the river water while I bathed and hopefully my condition will improve before we reach Castle Xandia. Although I know that Reid is in possession of my medallion, I haven't been able to find a way to retrieve it from him. I'll bide my time and wait for the right opportunity to snatch it back.

Return to Xandia

August 23. I have come again to Castle Xandia, this time as a prisoner, arriving in a weakened condition. Candaz was hospitable enough to grant me my own room, which is relatively luxurious, considering my status as a prisoner. It has a large and comfortable bed and a window that looks out over the ocean. Being high up in the castle's tower, however, the window could not provide for my escape. Should I be crazy enough to try such an escape, I would certainly witness my own doom on the rocky cliffs far below. My door is locked from the outside at all times and I am not allowed out of my room for any reason. My meals are brought to me and I have been provided with a wash basin and chamber pot that is changed daily. As yet, I do not know Candaz's purpose in bringing me here. I'm actually surprised he hasn't killed me yet. I spend my time trying to focus and connect with the freecurrent energy, but it continues to elude me. I will never give up.

August 31. Candaz came to me one week ago and revealed his purpose to me. I have spent the last week at the mercy of his demands. He comes to me every night and forces me to have relations with him. He holds no affection for me, but desires an heir with both of our bloodlines. I do not know how much longer I will be able to take it. The thought of dashing my bones against the boulders below is becoming more and more appealing. The only thing that keeps me sane is the thought of my children back home and my need to return to them safely. I pray to God to release me from this prison and the torture that has become my life.

September 30. I fear I am pregnant.

Fibi came to my room today serving my dinner. I tried to talk to her, but she is under some type of spell and nothing I did could break it and get through to her. I hugged her close to me, but she did not return the hug, remaining cold and apart. From my experience with the torgs, I know that deep down inside she is fighting to break through and that she feels and sees and hears everything that goes on around her, but is unable to react. I am hoping that she will continue to serve me so I can see her and give her what comfort I may. It breaks my heart to see her this way, but not to have her with me would be much worse. I pray daily for the bandergs' liberation and mine as well. Why hasn't Theo come for me?

October 16. The weather outside is turning colder with the change of seasons. Storms roll in more regularly from the north bringing dark gray clouds, cold winds and downpours. I am still confined to my room. Boredom has become my life, although I have been allowed to have books to read and have already finished several. Of course, Candaz picks the books strictly for entertainment, nothing with any real content. Unfortunately, most of the literature brought to me is quite dull. I continue to try to access the freecurrent without success. It feels like there is a wall blocking me from the energy, as if there is a spell in place around this room that keeps the freecurrent suppressed. The stone that is chained around my neck is suspicious in nature and could be solely responsible for the absence of freecurrent. I don't know.

I know now for certain that I am pregnant. I was devastated to acknowledge my condition at first, but found out it was a blessing in disguise. When I told Candaz, he immediately stopped his nightly visits to my room. Thank God he will never touch me again.

Fibi continues to serve me my meals and I continue to treat her with love and affection even though she lacks the ability to return it. I wonder where her mother is. I wonder where her father is. Where are my friends?

December 25. It is Christmas day back home and I ache for my children and my home. The baby inside me is growing at a healthy rate and my belly is extending accordingly. The one dress I have with me is getting quite worn out, although I have been mending it regularly. The riding clothes, my only other attire, I can no longer wear due to my size. The next time I see Candaz I will ask him for some material so I can make a new dress. I have been in captivity for over four months and have seen nothing but these same four walls in that length of time. I am beginning to wonder if I will ever be free again. God help me through this.

What has happened to Theo? Why hasn't he come after me? Surely he and the dragons know that I am missing by now. I don't understand what could have happened to them. Why don't they help me? Why doesn't someone help me?

I embroidered a small handkerchief for Fibi and gave it to her as a present today. She accepted the gift from me, lifted it to her face and touched the fabric to her cheek. I watched her intently; surprised that she could manage such an independent reaction. I'm sure I saw a tear come to the corner of her eye. Surprised and hopeful, I hugged her joyously and talked incessantly about things that might cause another reaction in her, but she gave me nothing more and finally left me alone to go about her duties with the hankie clutched tightly in her hand.

January 17. Winter has enveloped Castle Xandia. The snow is deep and the ocean seems grayer and angrier than it was in the fall. As I gaze out my window, the snow falls silently over the water where it ceases to exist as snow once it hits the warmer waves. The baby continues to grow and I am beginning to worry for his safety. I know Candaz has plans for the child and I fear

I will not be able to protect him when the time comes. My fear is tireless.

February 2. I am becoming increasingly despondent. My prison cell offers me little variety and I find myself staring at the same scene day after day out the window. At least the waves of the ocean are alive. Even my daily visits with Fibi grow tedious. I am frustrated over her lack of progress toward freeing herself of the magical chains that bind her. My days seem to all mesh together and I find it hard to keep track of time. I am beginning to wonder if boredom will be the death of me yet.

February 22. Candaz visited me today bringing news that all of my friends believe that I have abandoned them by going back through the gate to my home. I do not know whether to believe him or not, but if it is true my hope for rescue is shattered.

My belly is quite swollen with my pregnancy. Candaz has given no indication of what the future holds, but my imagination expects the worse. I believe that when the child is born, my days will be short lived. As my time grows near I become more depressed. Some days I wish to just have it over with. I wish I knew what to do.

March 18. Winter is hanging on to the country with a tight grip. The wind is howling madly outside my window and I feel a chill down to my bones, even though I am wrapped in a thick woolen blanket. The baby is kicking up a storm, probably reacting to my discomfort. I figure I have about two more months to go . . . and probably two more months to live. *"B.F. where are you? Skymaster???"*

Fibi has been assigned elsewhere and I miss her terribly. She has been my only source of comfort throughout the long winter, and now he has taken her away from me also. I hope she is well wherever she is. Under the circumstances, I can't imagine how. Why has Theo not freed the bandergs? Where is he?

April 4. Xandia is starting to be touched with the first indications of spring, although snow still blankets the ground. Usually spring is a wonderful season for me. I loved to watch the new flowers come up miraculously out of the ground back home, like a fresh beginning every year. The air was always so crisp and clear, with the bitter cold of winter only a distant memory. Both of my children were born in the spring, as this one will be. If only I could see my babies just one more time . . . God! I would give anything to see them again.

May 13. Candaz has been checking in on me daily. I have asked him several times what his plans are for me and for my child, but he has not deemed it necessary to reveal them to me. I hate him from the core of my being.

May 27. It is early in the morning and I have been awakened from a restless sleep by labor contractions. Today will be the day my child is born. I have dreaded this day for several months and now the time has come. What is to become of him? What is to become of me?

A midwife was sent to me around midday to attend the birth. I went into deep labor just before noon and delivered a healthy baby boy approximately four hours later. The baby has been left with me to nurse. I can't help but have mixed feelings considering the child could inevitably be taken away from me at any time. I am deeply afraid . . . afraid to bond with the child . . . afraid to let the child go. I would sooner fling myself from the top of this tower than let my baby go to him. But, I have an obligation to return to my other children. They need their mother too. What am I to do?

Chapter 22

NO LOOKING BACK

The miles passed by and Jesse glanced out the window as they came into view of Hoover Dam. The bus slowed to a crawl as they encountered tourist traffic on the dam itself. Jesse had seen the dam once before when she and her mother had made a camping trip to the area many years ago. She recalled how they had stopped and waited in the long line to take the tour inside the dam. Now Jesse watched with only mild interest, barely seeing the many tourists adorned with various types of camera equipment, making their way toward or away from the long ticket line.

Jesse shifted her body in the seat, trying to relieve the soreness on her bottom. Felcore had slept most of the trip, but now moved restlessly under Jesse's feet. The big golden was obviously just as anxious to get this trip over with as Jesse. Lake Mead sparkled with a pleasant and inviting blue when portions of it could be seen past the hilly desert scenery. She idly gazed out the window as they wound their way down out of the mountains. They drove through Boulder City, a small town overlooking Lake Mead, and then got on the expressway and headed toward Las Vegas.

The skyline of Las Vegas was hazy brown as they descended into the valley. Jesse sat back in her seat and considered her situation once again. From downtown Las Vegas she would have to find transportation to Mt. Charleston. A phone call to her father would be necessary just to let him know she was okay and wouldn't be home any time soon. Jesse dreaded that phone call. If she had her cell phone, she would just get it over with, but without it she had to marinate in her worry. She felt sorry for her father having to deal with all of this and she felt sorry for Jacob too, who couldn't possibly understand why she was doing this to their father. She missed them so much already, but she didn't want to think about that right now. It was important that she keep a clear head and not get caught up in emotions. Jesse felt in her soul that she was doing the right thing by proceeding on to the gate. In fact, she felt a pressing need to get there, almost as if she was being driven by a force she didn't understand.

The bus cruised along the highway, coming fast upon the downtown area. Hotel-Casinos towered above everything else and Jesse recognized some of the more famous names such as Golden Nugget and Union Plaza. They exited off the highway and drove to the bus station. Jesse took her backpack from the overhead compartment and inserted Gabriel's diary, placing the leather bound book with the rest of her stuff. She waited for the other passengers to get off the bus before letting Felcore into the aisle, where he stretched dramatically, arching his back and pointing his nose and tail in opposite directions. They exited into a wall of hot air and headed directly to the station. Jesse joined the line where a clerk was busy selling tickets and answering questions. The line didn't take long to dwindle and Jesse asked the clerk for information about getting transportation to Mt. Charleston. The woman clerk, short and bulky with dark curly hair and a cantankerous disposition informed Jesse that there were no bus lines that went up to Mt. Charleston, but said that the CAT went to the other side of town and suggested that Jesse could walk from there.

Jesse looked up CAT in the phone book and found that it wasn't listed in the white pages, but she did find an ad for CAT (Citizen's Area Transit) in the front pages of the phone book. The recorded message gave her options one through five for specific information and zero for an operator. Jesse pressed zero and talked to a pleasant woman who told her to take route six to the downtown transportation center and then take route eight, which would take her to the west side of town, ending at Smoke Ranch and Rainbow. She hung up and dialed her dad's number and the "O" for operator, instructing her to make the call collect.

Her dad's voice answered, but it was a recording instructing the caller to leave a message. "Dad, it's Jess. I can't explain exactly what's going on, but know that I'll be okay. Please don't worry. I've decided to follow in Grandmother Gabriel's footsteps. Don't come looking for me. You won't find me. Please know that I love you very much. Tell Jacob to be good and that I love him. I'll call you when I get back. I love you." She hung up the phone and stifled a sob.

The CAT bus pulled up outside and Jesse boarded with Felcore, paying the fare of one dollar. The woman driver looked at Felcore disapprovingly, but did nothing to refuse Jesse transportation on her bus. After only a couple of blocks, the driver announced that they were at the downtown transportation center.

The route eight bus took them through Las Vegas. Jesse watched the residential and commercial complexes drift by as the bus cruised smoothly along, making regular stops along its route. The air conditioned bus was cold compared to the outside air and Jesse thought it unusual that she would wish for a jacket when it was one hundred plus degrees outside. When they arrived at Smoke Ranch and Rainbow, Jesse and Felcore got off the bus with only a couple of other passengers. The hot dry air of the desert was blowing in sweltering gusts, scattering dust everywhere. She asked a woman for directions and the woman pointed to the tallest mountain at the edge of the valley to their east. She said she thought Jesse was crazy to walk alone on these roads. Jesse told her that she wasn't alone.

She headed north on Rainbow and came across a shopping center. She stopped there and bought a few things she thought she would need, including a pair of sunglasses and some sunscreen. She asked the cashier if there was somewhere nearby where she could eat cheaply. The cashier said that the Sante Fe was down the road and she could eat at the buffet there for about five dollars.

When Jesse left store, she saw that a man had stopped and was petting Felcore. He greeted her with a friendly smile when she approached. "Hi," he said. "Is this your dog?"

Jesse assessed him quickly and judged him to be a minimal threat. Felcore didn't seem to mind him anyway and her dog was an excellent judge of character. He had dark hair, blue eyes and a nice smile. His attire was simple, khaki shorts, tennis shoes and a t-shirt that had a landscaping company logo up in the corner. Jesse smiled back at him and answered, "Yeah, he's my dog. His name is Felcore."

"I hope you don't mind. I was just waiting for my wife. He's big for a golden retriever. Does he have some mix?" he asked with innocent curiosity.

"No. He's a full-blooded golden. He just eats a lot," Jesse said and laughed.

The man's wife came out and joined them. "Oh, he's a beautiful dog," she said. She knelt down and scratched Felcore behind the ears. The happy dog wagged his tail joyously at all of the attention. The woman was dressed in shorts, t-shirt and tennis shoes like her husband and carried two plastic grocery bags. She had blond hair and sunglasses that hid her eyes. "I'm Pat and this is Dean," she said. "We breed goldens. I can see you take good care of this one. Do you live nearby?"

Jesse over-ruled her suspicious nature by answering the woman's question, "No, Felcore and I are on the road. We are heading up to Mt. Charleston to do some hiking."

"Do you need a lift? We are heading home, but we can take you as far as the Sante Fe," Pat offered as she stood up and took Dean's hand.

Jesse smiled, feeling her suspicious nature relax. She said, "That's where I was going to head to get some dinner. I'd really appreciate a ride."

Pat smiled back at Jesse revealing beautiful straight teeth. "I think we might even have some dog food in the van. Did you say Felcore? Do you mind?"

"I'm sure Felcore wouldn't mind. Thanks. My name is Jesse," she said.

They all got into the white mini-van after feeding Felcore a big bowl of food and water that was refilled three times before his thirst was quenched. Dean and Pat drove her to a large southwestern styled building called the Sante Fe Hotel & Casino and dropped Jesse off at the valet parking. They wished her luck and gave her a business card with their kennel's name printed at the top and their home phone number printed on the bottom with instructions to call if she ever needed anything. Jesse thanked them before she and Felcore got out of the van.

She asked the good looking young valet attendant if she could leave Felcore with him and he said she could, promising to keep an eye on him for her. He even said he would get him a bowl of water. Jesse opened the door and was assaulted by the clamor of change rattling and machines beeping noisily as gamblers tried their luck, staking hard earned money to try and get ahead of the game. The casino was alive with bright lights, flashing slot machines and people playing at various types of gaming.

Jesse walked through the casino until she came across a ramp that led to a restaurant boasting to be the buffet. There was no line and Jesse walked up the ramp and paid the cashier five dollars and some odd cents before waiting to be seated by the hostess whose attire went with the southwestern decor. At the back of the restaurant was a glass wall overlooking an ice-skating rink. She was given a seat where she could watch the ice skaters practicing.

She waited for the waitress to bring her a coke before she went to the buffet line. The deserts on display were tempting, but Jesse knew she didn't need the sugar. She filled her plate with more practical items like vegetables, fruits and some roast turkey. She hadn't realized how hungry she was until she sat down to eat. She went back to the buffet to fill her plate a couple more times before her full belly told her she would have to quit. Satisfied, she went back to the buffet one more time. A small plate of delectable desserts to satisfy her sweet tooth was just the ticket to finish off a wonderful meal. She silently thanked the woman who had recommended this place to her. Felcore was waiting for her outside the casino and she thanked the valet and tipped him a dollar.

It was starting to get dark by the time they reached the highway and began walking north. Cars passed by with little regard for a girl and her dog. She felt a little bit lonely and reached for the comfort of Felcore's furry head with her hand. Night brought cooler temperatures and Jesse was thankful she was not travelling this stretch of ground in the heat of the day. They made good time and after an hour or so reached a sign that said "Mt. Charleston" and pointed to the left. She and Felcore followed the sign and walked along the two lane highway for a long time before the road started to climb as it headed into the mountains.

Cars passed Jesse periodically either going up the mountain or coming back down. She was about ready to make camp for the night, feeling exhaustion wash over her and causing her to reel slightly, when a jeep pulled up beside her. Rock and roll was playing loudly and a boy about Jesse's age leaned over from the driver's seat and turned the stereo down a notch. The blond headed kid who sat in the passenger seat looked Jesse over with bright blue eyes that betrayed arrogance. He smiled and asked, "Can we give you a lift, darlin'?"

Felcore stood rigidly beside Jesse, a low growl rumbling in his throat. She put her hand on his head to quiet him. "No. Thanks, anyway. I'd rather walk," she said.

"Come on. It's a long walk if you're headed to the lodge. Hop in," the boy in the driver's seat said.

"I appreciate the offer, but no," she said. Jesse began walking briskly down the street with Felcore close by her side.

The jeep followed them and Jesse started to become worried that there would be a confrontation. She walked faster as the jeep continued to follow closely. She could hear the boys laughing and joking. When the lights shut off and the jeep's motor was killed, Jesse held her breath and prepared to defend herself. Jim had replaced her knife that the police had taken. She reached for it.

The boys came up next to her on foot. They smelled of beer. Felcore began growling. Jesse cautioned them, "You need to leave me alone and be on your way. I wouldn't want you to get hurt."

"Ha! Not likely. Come on, darlin'. Be friendly," the blond said.

She held her breath and waited.

The blond reached for her, but she grabbed his hand and quickly twisted it behind his back and took out his legs with a sweep of her foot. He went down hard on the pavement.

The other boy, the driver, came at her but was intercepted by flashing teeth as Felcore clamped strong jaws over the boy's wrist. He screamed in pain. The other boy groaned and stood up. He started toward her.

"You don't want to do that. If you behave I'll call him off," she said as she showed him her knife.

"Okay," the boy said.

"Felcore, release him," Jesse ordered.

Felcore complied, but continued growling as he returned to his position at Jesse's side.

She stroked his head as she glared at the boys. "I told you I didn't want a ride. I suggest that you leave, now," she said.

The boy who had been bit grabbed the other's arm. "Let's get out of here. She's not worth it," he said. They ran back to their jeep and peeled out past Jesse, raising dust and gravel in their wake.

Jesse sighed in relief and sheathed her knife back in her boot. Felcore pushed his nose insistently into her hand. She automatically reciprocated giving him affection by scratching behind his ears. The comfort of her new-found confidence made her smile.

They continued walking well into the night without further incident. Jesse found a place off to the side of the road and laid down for a short time before dawn slowly lit the landscape and nudged her awake. She fed Felcore one of the dinner rolls from the buffet and gave him some water while she munched on some dried fruit before hitting the road once again. Jesse figured she would start her search for the cave where she and her mother had begun their hike years before. She remembered they had parked the car at a turn off and there was a riding stable just down the road. Jesse figured they had only a short distance left to go.

Felcore grabbed Jesse's arm gently with his teeth and began pulling her toward the desert. She resisted for a moment and then acquiesced and let her dog guide her. They hiked over rough and rocky terrain in a purposeful direction known only to Felcore.

The desert floor was dotted with a variety of low growing vegetation that Jesse couldn't name. A fragrance, pleasantly aromatic, filled Jesse's nostrils as she and Felcore wound their way through the sporadic foliage. The air was clear and the sky was a bright blue.

After walking well into the day, Jesse thought she recognized some of the landscape. They rounded a hill and Felcore gave a mighty "Rrowf" and stopped walking. Jesse scanned the hill that stood before them. It was covered with low desert brush and Joshua trees. She looked hard for any sign of the cave, but saw nothing, although she knew this had to be the same hill where she and her mother had found it years before.

"Well, Felcore, if it is up there, I don't see it. How about you, boy?"

Felcore barked again and then loped off toward the hill and began to climb. Jesse shrugged her shoulders and followed him up the incline. He stopped in front of a large clump of brush and barked once more. Jesse worked the brush out of the way with her arm, scraping her skin on the rough stems in the process. She felt excitement quicken her blood as she discovered that there was indeed a cave behind the brush. Pushing it far enough out of the way for Felcore to enter, Jesse inched her way through the brush and caught her breath as the coolness of the cave engulfed her body.

She hugged her big dog. "We made it, boy. We're here," she said. Looking up she saw the only source of light coming into the cave issued forth from a large crack deeper inside that was shaped like a lightning bolt. The gate.

Felcore watched with his head resting on his front paws as Jesse built a fire and took out Gabriel's diary from her backpack. She was excited as well as apprehensive. Her life was about to change forever. Quietly, she whispered to God, "be with me, Lord." She watched the constellations rotating slowly on the other side of the gate. She didn't know how long it would take or exactly when she should be ready to go. Resting first was the best thing for her now. She could do that while she kept a watchful vigil. Using her lumpy backpack as a pillow she settled down to read.

Chapter 23

FREEDOM AT A PRICE

May 29. I have named my son Jonathon Theodore Thomas. His eyes are copper brown, just like mine. June 3. A wet nurse came and took Jonathon from me today. She took him with no regard for me, his mother. She stole him out of my arms and fled, locking the door behind her. My hands are raw from pounding and my throat is sore from crying. She should not have taken my son. Candaz will pay for this. I want my baby back!

June 6. I was sitting in the window sill watching the waves crashing on the boulders below, planning my revenge against Candaz, when a bald eagle appeared at my window. I leaned out and called to her, hoping, "Jessabelle?"

The eagle looked at me with intelligent sparkling eyes and trilled twice. She swung around two times and then glided away, with perfect grace and beauty. I knew it had to have been

Jessabelle. Hope soared inside me, lifting me out of the depths of my despair. For the first time in many months I gaze at my appearance in the mirror and am horrified. I have thinned out to look pitiful and ghostly. My once dark and shining hair is dull and has lost its luster. My eyes show wrinkles where there used to be none. Dark circles surround them and they are red from crying. I fixed what I could by brushing out my hair and tying it back off from my face. Anxiously I waited.

June 7. A visitor came to my window today, someone very special to me. I heard a rapping on the glass and turned around to see Rew hovering just outside. I flung the window open with considerable excitement. "Rew, thank God you are here. Quick, come in before someone sees you. Oh, my God! Rew! You are here," I said through my tears.

Rew fluttered in and after giving me an exuberant hug, sat down on the bed. "Gabriel, we've been looking for you for months. It figures that your disappearance was Candaz's doing. Even Theo's sword was unable to locate you. Our reconnaissance has turned up nothing until yesterday when Jessabelle decided to take a closer look at Castle Xandia. Thank the Creator we've finally found you," he said excitedly. I barely heard him, I was crying uncontrollably.

Rew came over to me, taking my hand and gazing into my eyes with sweet compassion. "It has been rough on you, hasn't it? I am so sorry we didn't find you sooner. What has he done to you?"

His blue eyes reflected my shame and my anger. I whispered, "I'm sorry, Rew, I really don't want to talk about it right now." I started to pull away, but Rew held my hand tightly and wouldn't let go.

He smiled amiably and kissed my cheek before saying, "It's okay. You don't have to talk about it now. I have something for you." Rew produced in his hand my gold medallion, gleaming brightly as it rested in his palm.

"Where did you get it?" I asked as I reached out and touched it.

"Theo gave it to me. He ran into a man several months ago in a tavern outside of Vinnia. The man was bragging about how he had stolen a medallion from a witch and he produced it out of his pocket to show off his prize. Theo knew at once that it was yours. He questioned the man relentlessly, but the man led him astray, saying that the owner of the medallion was dead, that he had killed her and dumped the body in Blue Lake. Theo relieved the man of his life and the medallion after his information ran dry. I think he said the man's name was Reid."

"That was the man who kidnapped me. He killed Hue and Nina in cold blood. I'm glad he is dead." The memory brought cold tears to my eyes and the pain of grief throbbed in my heart. Automatically I suppressed the pain, having no knowledge of how to deal with it and no desire to do so at the moment.

"Yes, I know. Theo found their bodies right after your dis-appearance. We looked everywhere for you, Gabriel. Theo has searched all of Risen for you. He even went back to your home on Earth to see if you had returned there. We've been by here many times and never saw a thing. It's very odd. None of our resources gave us a clue that you were here. This room seems to have an enchantment attached to it. It blocks out the freecur-rent magic. You were well hidden from us here." Rew hugged me close and then drew back. "What is this?" he fingered the chain around my neck. "This stone alone would keep you from accessing freecurrent. It absorbs all of the energy from the im-mediate environment including from you. Do you feel weak?" he asked.

"Very," I said, touching the stone.

"I'm not surprised. Let me get this off you," he said. Rew snapped the chain with his fingers like it was made of glass and tossed it quickly out the window. "May I?" he asked as he fastened the gold chain around my neck.

I kissed him lightly on the nose and said, "Thank you, Rew."

Rew smiled brightly. "You're welcome. Now, let's get you out of here," he said as he looked out the window. I followed his gaze and saw two silver dragons gliding in from over the ocean.

"B.F.?"

"*I am here, Gabriel. I am so happy you are safe,*" he said.

"Skymaster?"

"*I am here, also, Gabriel. We have been so worried!. The next time I go fishing, I am going to take you with me,*" he said.

"Oh. Yes, of course."

"Is Theo with you, B.F.?" I asked.

"*Yes, Gabriel, he is on my back. Do you wish me to relay a message to him?*"

My joy at being rescued was dampened by my lust for revenge. I wanted to leave and go back home to my children, but I knew I could not leave things with Candaz unfinished. He had to pay for what he had done to me and I would not leave without my baby. "*Tell him I appreciate the rescue team, but there is something I must do before I leave this place.*"

There was a delay before B.F. answered me, "*He says to stand by . . .*"

"Standby? Seriously!?" I wanted to punch Theodore Wingmaster in the nose.

The two dragons swung by my window, causing a severe draft to sweep the room. The heavy scent of dragon musk tantalized my senses, bringing sudden joy to my heart. I smiled at Rew, who was again sitting upon my bed watching me intently. Theo literally dropped in, landing with graceful ease upon my window sill.

Within seconds we were in each other's arms, hugging, kissing and talking all at the same time. After a couple of minutes he stood back and examined me with a critical eye. "Good Creator, Gabriel. What has that monster done to you? You look dreadful."

"Thank you very much," I retorted with sarcasm. "Where have you been? Why didn't you rescue me from here? Why haven't you freed the bandergs yet?" I asked angrily.

Theo turned away from me and said quietly, "I tried. After searching everywhere, I thought that you were dead. Plans have been in the works to take Castle Xandia back from Candaz and end this war. Father has been quite sick and we were waiting for spring to make our move. The bandergs remain enslaved and we intend to set them free. We didn't want to endanger them in the process. I am sorry. Had I known. What happened here?"

"It is a long story and I wish to be free of this place before the day is done. Would you two like to join me in a little retribution?" I asked.

They both enthusiastically gave positive approval. Rew came to stand by my side. "What is the plan?"

"Rew, how long would it take you to fly to the Tower of Ornate?" I asked him, beginning to form a plan in my head.

He looked speculative for a moment before answering, "It will take probably about a turn, depending on the wind current. Why?"

"I would like you to go there and retrieve an item for me. I left a silver harp in the room on the sixth floor of the tower. Go there, get it, and bring it back here. When you arrive, play it for Candaz's men. If you play the harp with joy and goodness in your heart, it will force the slave masters to release the bandergs in their control. Are you willing to do this for me?"

"Oh, yes! I will leave right now." Rew went to the window sill and jumped into the air. He came back to me and gave me a long kiss on the lips and a tight hug. "I'm so glad we found you, Gabriel," he said and then jumped back out the window.

"Be careful, Rew!" I shouted after him, as he quickly disappeared out of sight.

I turned to Theo and asked, "Are you ready?"

He grinned at me conspiratorially before asking, "What's the plan?"

I lost my nerve for a moment and looked down at my hands, searching for the strength to continue. I felt Theo put his strong arms around me. "Whatever happened, Gabriel, it is over now."

I pulled away from him, suddenly angry again and spat back, "It is not over. It will never be over. Do you know what he did to me, Theo? He took away every ounce of dignity I had. He's kept me locked up in this room for almost a year. He made me pregnant. I had a son . . . and he took him away from me, too. My son . . . "

Theo pulled me close, again taking me in his arms and said, "I am so sorry, Gabriel."

The dam that had been holding my emotions in check suddenly burst wide open and I clung to Theo and cried, spilling out everything, my grief over John, Hue, Nina, Shareen, my baby--obviously Candaz had planned this just to make the most out of hurting me. If he had taken the baby immediately after birth, never having let me see him, it would have been less sadistic. Instead he took Jonathon from me after one week with him, giving me the chance to bond with him, to nurse him and to love him.

I cried it out and then dried my tears. It was time to strike back. I let my anger give me strength. "Theo, first we must find Candaz and take care of him once and for all. Then we'll go find my baby and reclaim him. After that we will set the banderg̵s free," I said.

"There's only one problem," Theo said.

"What's that?"

"How do we get out of this room?" he asked.

"Ah, my dear Watson, observe," I said. Putting my hands upon the walls, I found I could decipher the blocking spell around the room and simply negate it. I was surprised at how strong it was and decided to give my friends some grace for not finding me sooner. After that was accomplished, I expertly drew a rune upon the door, which glowed bright blue and walked through the solid wood. Smiling arrogantly back at Theo, I motioned him through.

As he passed by me into the hall, he looked at me with a puzzled expression on his face. "Watson?" he asked.

"A literary character . . . never mind, Theo. Let's go," I said and started down the hall.

Theo drew his sword and we let the magic it possessed lead the way through the halls of Castle Xandia. I could actually feel the power course through the ancient weapon as the precise etching of the lightning bolt glowed with electric blue fire further and further down the blade with each step we took.

As we drew nearer to our destination and the blade in Theo's hand blazed brightly, butterflies flew wildly in my stomach. Anticipation of finding Candaz left my nerves tight as a bow string. I had to work consciously to keep calm enough to continue walking with Theo down the hall. When we reached the door at the end of the hall I braced myself mentally before putting my hand on the knob. It was locked. As Theo prepared to force his way through it, the door suddenly swung open and a woman appeared dressed casually in a long midnight blue silk gown and slippers. She had dark brown hair cut short and dark blue eyes. Ice cubes clinked against the clear crystal tumbler that she held in her left hand. She took a short sip of her drink before demanding politely, "Yes? What do you want?"

Theo pushed the door open rudely and strode past the startled woman before she had a chance to protest. I followed on Theo's tail as the woman stood there with her mouth agape. "Where is Candaz?" Theo demanded loudly, as he strode the length of the expensively furnished room, his bold burgundy uniform contrasted well with the light blue shades of the room's plush decor.

The woman at the door had regained a semblance of her balance and demanded, "What is the meaning of this? I want you to leave immediately."

I turned to her and was surprised to not see anger in her eyes, but fear. She was one of his victims too. It made me swallow my bitter words and speak to her more gently than I had originally intended, "I'm afraid that would be impossible. We are going to see Candaz, now. Perhaps *you* should leave."

With fascination, I watched her hesitate, glance awkwardly toward the door to my right, set down her drink neatly upon a coaster on the end table and scurry out the front door of the suite. I motioned Theo toward the door on my right. He listened for a moment with his ear up against the wood before bursting it open with his shoulder. Candaz was finishing dressing when we entered, sitting on the bed, pulling on a pair of black leather boots that reached his knees. He gazed up at us with a look of shock which quickly turned to anger, drawing his thick eyebrows together and darkening his face into a mask of brutality. "What are you doing here? How did you . . . " His gaze went from me to Theo and a smile glinted unpleasantly upon his face. "Well, the princeling rescues the maiden in distress from her tower prison. How fitting?" he sneered.

Theo stood unflinching with his hand upon the hilt of his sword. The hatred in his eyes was obvious to me, but his expression remained passively calm. I stood beside him with my fists clenched, not feeling at all calm and not worried about outwardly showing Candaz my hatred. "Where is my son?" I demanded, almost choking on my emotions.

"He is dead, sweetheart," Candaz smirked, satisfying his sick appetite by seeing the pain drench my face.

"You lie! Where is he?" I asked again as I took a step toward him. He stood up from the bed and confronted me, his blackness towering a foot above me.

"You will not see him again. He is dead. I have delayed your execution too long, Gabriel. Such a pity. I could have made it so much faster and less painless for you, but now you will know the true meaning of suffering," he said. He approached me quickly and grabbed hold of my chin, lifting it toward his face and forcing eye contact. A blinding red followed a searing pain that entered through my eyes and went into my brain. I know I screamed but I heard no sound. My only thought was to wish that death would come quickly and end the excruciating pain.

It did end swiftly and I wondered if my wish had been answered and then I felt Candaz's hand slip from my chin as he fell to ground at my feet, a sigh escaping his lips and I knew it was not I that was dead, but him. Theo stood over him and drew his bloodied sword from the sorcerer's side. We both stood and stared at him in wonder, neither saying a word. Candaz stirred and opened his eyes. He wasn't dead after all. "It will not end here," he hissed through clenched teeth. "I will not let you have my son. You will die first." He pulled himself up onto his elbows and somehow made it to his knees, kneeling before us as if in sardonic homage.

He began to chant and draw a rune on the floor. From far below I felt the ground begin to vibrate. The vibrating accelerated until the castle began to sway and moan in protest. "Stop! You'll kill us all!" I shouted as Theo grabbed hold of me and dragged me toward the nearest window. Candaz began to laugh, shrill and hysterical, on and on, as the castle began to spit stones down onto the floor around us. I was struggling to get away from Theo's grasp, but he held me tight and opened the window and stood waiting and watching the sky.

A flash of silver caught my eye and I fought harder to get away. "My baby! Let me go! I might be able to stop this. Let me go!" I shouted.

He held me even tighter than before. "I am sorry, Gabriel. We must leave now. We don't have time. I hope someday you will forgive me." He leapt from the window sill and we landed squarely on B.F.'s back. I heard a crashing noise behind me and I saw the castle begin to crumble, stone by stone and floor by floor. It seemed as if the destruction was being shown on film in slow motion. Dust billowed in great clouds all around us, making B.F.'s shiny silver scales dull gray. Screams could be heard and I gulped down the bile that rose in my throat. We watched the demolition for what seemed like a very long time while B.F. circled above it in the air. When the castle rested flat on the ground I looked down upon the ruins and felt my heart cry out in grief. Theo cradled me in his arms as I sobbed softly. B.F. headed toward a grassy clearing where survivors were gathering and we landed next to Skymaster on the other side of the hill.

A Reunion of Friends

We joined the crowd that had gathered on the grassy slope. People milled about in confusion, wondering what to do next, where to go now that their home was gone. Like an emotional zombie, I worked myself around the crowd, helping Theo administer first aid to the injured. Whispers could be heard that Candaz was dead as we went from person to person. I asked about the bandergs, but nobody could tell me what had become of them, so great was the confusion when the earthquake had struck.

From behind me, I heard someone shout my name and I looked around to find the source. My heart lifted as I saw Rew coming toward me, the silver harp in his hands, and a parade of bandergs following behind him trying to keep up. I ran to meet him and lifted him in my arms in a joyous embrace. Fibi and Berry came toward me, their arms entwined around each other's backs. I put down Rew, who stood by me smiling brightly, and took Fibi and Berry into my arms and hugged them close as well.

Fibi looked into my face, reached up her hand and outlined my cheek gently with her finger. She took the hanky I had made her out of the pocket of her dress and dried my tears with it before drying her own. She spoke softly, "Even though I couldn't express my gratitude to you when I was under Candaz's spell, I felt in my heart everything you did for me. Thank you, Gabriel. Thank you for giving me your love and kindness. You helped me to survive." She smiled up at me and I bent over and kissed her affectionately on the cheek. She glanced at my stomach and seemed puzzled as she asked, "The baby?"

I felt the familiar pain bind my heart, and I looked down at the ground before gaining the strength to look back into Fibi's eyes, "He's dead, Fibi. He was beautiful, but he is gone."

An eagle trilled loudly from up above and all of our eyes turned skyward. Jessabelle glided gently into the crowd and landed next to Theo. The eagle's form faded and in her place stood a woman with shiny red hair. One white streak outlined the right side of her face. She wore a smile that glowed as brightly as her eyes gleamed gold. She glanced at Theo, who took a moment to admire her in silence. Jessabelle came to me and hugged me in her strong arms. The fragrance of her hair reminded me of lilac blossoms and I remembered with embarrassment that I had not had a decent bath in many months. I stepped back from her and she looked into my eyes with keen examination. "Take care of you we will, Gabriel. For you, your friends are here to help share your pain and hopefully lessen your burden. So sorry I am," she said, wiping her own tears away.

"Thank you, Jessabelle. But, I . . . ," I began.

She stepped back and pointed over the hill. "Here they come now," she said.

The woods were beginning to darken with dusk falling over the ocean, making it difficult to see. I squinted in the direction where Jessabelle pointed and just made out their outlines against the dark background. Coming toward us was a large hulk mounted on a massive horse, two people walking side by side, who appeared to be joined at the hip, a short stocky character bouncing as he strolled and a miniature dragon gracing the sky above their heads. I started in their direction, yelling for Fibi and Berry to join me.

We met half way and Kaltog swooped off from his mount and took me in his arms with the gentleness I had come to know as characteristic of the torg people. Kristina and Serek spent a moment with me before going off to find Theo. I wondered how Theo would react to their new relationship. Then paused, remembering that I had been away for over nine months. In that time surely things had changed. Link smiled up at me between hugs and kisses being showered on him by Berry and Fibi. His face glowed with happiness and I found that I had to look away or be overwhelmed by emotions I wasn't ready to face.

Serek immediately took charge of the misplaced people, issuing orders for a temporary camp to be set up along with a hospital for the injured. Apparently many months ago Serek had returned to Castle Gentlebreeze with Kristina. After much begging and pleading on Kristina's part, King Cleo conceded to meet with Serek. It was determined from overwhelming evidence that Serek was indeed Prince Serek Landtamer of Saberville. Kristina and he were married soon thereafter in a double wedding along with Theo and Jessabelle.

Theo and Serek had plans to attack Candaz and take Castle Xandia before the end of spring, but they never got a chance to act upon their plans. Jessabelle showed up at Castle Gentlebreeze with information that I had been spotted at Castle Xandia and my rescue was immediately orchestrated. With Candaz dead, Serek was now free to claim the throne of Saberville as his own, although at this moment the throne of Saberville sat under tons of rubble.

Serek and Kristina made their way through the crowd of misplaced and shaken people spreading calm and hope. They quickly gained the support of the people who had once served Candaz, most of whom had long ago grown tired of his ruthless regime and were hailed that very day as the King and Queen of Saberville.

A makeshift city was set up with tents and supplies shipped in by Theo on dragon back. By the time night had fallen, the area around Castle Xandia was dotted with campfires and tents. People quickly got back to the business of living, cooking dinner and looking after their families. Considering the circumstances, the destruction of property, and lives the day had taken, the camp was fairly cheerful and lively under a full spread of bright and glistening stars.

My friends and I set up camp in a clearing close by, but a bit removed from the rest of the group. Link cooked a delicious meal for us, but my appetite was not healthy and I ate little of it. We discussed the events of the day and told stories of things that had happened in our lives since we had last parted. Besides the marriages between Serek and Kristina and Theo and Jessabelle, Rew had a new wife, whose name was Dolli and they were expecting a baby sometime this coming summer. King Cleo had begun negotiations between the nations of the torgs, bandergs, kendrites and wisps to reestablish trade throughout the region. According to Theo, he was running into plenty of opposition, especially from Jessabelle's father, who was not at all happy about her marriage to Theo. In addition, the king had been battling his health. But, progress, however slow, was progress.

I talked little of my own ordeal and my friends did not press me on the subject. Talking, I knew, would help the healing process to begin, but the wounds were still too raw and my grief was still too fresh and deep.

Couples soon went off to be by themselves and I was left alone before the blazing fire. I curled up in my bedroll and watched the fire dance playfully among the logs. The three nearby dragons began a soft cooing song that soothed my nerves and left me peaceful. I began to drift off to sleep to the deep humming that emanated from their throats. Before I had completely dozed off, however, I thought I heard the sound of a baby crying in the distance. I sat up and listened, wondering if I was swallowed in the world of dreams. The sound of laughter, shrill and sadistic filled the night as the baby continued to cry. It stopped almost as soon as it started and I wondered if I had imagined it after all. Could Jonathon be out there somewhere; alive and in trouble? While I listened to the sounds of the night, trying to hear the cry once more, I cuddling deep down in my blankets and finally fell into a fitful and nightmare-filled sleep.

Candaz's Aftermath

As the mortar and stone rained down around him, Candaz acted fast. Grabbing the first thing he could, a table runner, he tied it around his body to bind the wound in his side. His cloak lay nearby and he threw that on as well. Off from the bedside table he snatched a small crystal bottle and a very old book. Dizziness circled around him and he had to sit down for a second to regain his equilibrium. Gathering his strength, he shuffled over to a small door in the back of the room and opened it. Once it had been a large walk-in closet but he had converted it into a nursery. A bassinet dominated the space. Beside the tiny crib a woman lay on the floor. She was dead; crushed by a chunk of masonry.

Candaz approached the bassinet and peered inside. His child was sleeping quietly, oblivious to the chaos around him. He quickly scooped the baby up in his arms, protected him inside his cloak and ran out the door. As he sped down the hallway, it collapsed immediately behind him. He ran faster, ignoring the pain in his side and the wailing baby. He ran for his life.

Through the throne room and down a set of stairs, at the end of a long hallway and then the chapel was a door that went down to the tunnels that ran under Castle Xandia. The catacombs were where the dead were entombed from the early days when the Landtamer family was in residence. He opened the door and went down the wide staircase into the darkness. Above him the castle was crumbling to dust, but he escaped at the very last minute. His heir was safe.

He used freecurrent to light his way, but he was struggling. The book he carried was heavy and the baby was squirming and screaming. Where the sword had penetrated his side, a searing agony persisted. After making a couple of turns in the tunnels he stopped. He could go no further. Taking deep breaths to calm himself, he cradled the child, swaying with him until the boy also calmed.

Working with one hand, he removed the rocks from the crypt in front of him. In it he placed the book and the little crystal bottle before covering it back up. Quickly he noted the marking on the grave and then continued down the tunnel.

It took him some time to find an exit, but eventually he found a way out. The air was fresh and cool and the night was clear. Looking back up the hill, he could see that Castle Xandia was gone. There were people and tents everywhere in the clearing around the castle. Campfires dotted the landscape and every so often soft laughter could be heard. Candaz made his way to the cover of the woods. The baby began to cry again and he comforted the child. Everything he had worked so hard for was gone. He began to laugh madly. He was still alive. *They* were still alive.

Gabriel

June 10. I stayed with the camp for a couple more days helping Serek and Kristina to organize their people and watching the new construction begin. Both the torgs and bandergs sent a contingency to help out. A fresh start was beginning.

Going home was on my mind the entire time while I delayed my departure but I felt that just being with my friends was helping me to recover some of my strength, to begin the healing process, and to let the pain go, if only just a small portion of it.

Also, in the back of my mind I hoped beyond hope that my baby would be found while I lingered. In my heart I knew he was dead, but accepting that fact wasn't coming easily. The memory of his cry haunted me.

When I was ready to leave, I said tearful goodbyes to everyone before mounting Skymaster. Theo escorted me on B.F. We arrived at the gate by late afternoon and Skymaster and B.F. stood guard over the cave while Theo and I went inside, built a fire and waited.

"Theo, I am so happy for you and Jessabelle. I am curious as to how you got King Shane to agree to the marriage," I said as I watched Theo furrow his brow and then grin slyly.

"Well, it wasn't easy. Father sent a letter to King Shane explaining the circumstances of Jessabelle's disappearance in an attempt to open communications between the Brights and the kendrites. He didn't hear back from King Shane so I decided to go to Colordale myself and speak with Jessabelle's father and ask for her hand in marriage. Jessabelle insisted that she go with me and so together we went before her father and asked his blessing. He only gave in when Jessabelle threatened to completely disown him and to never step foot in Colordale again. What could he do? Prince Jacoby insisted that Shane accept the marriage. Shane was faced with losing his family in order to hang on to his prejudice, or gaining a son-in-law and solidifying peace between Colordale and Brightening. He was backed into a corner and chose the best way out. Jessabelle and I are very happy. I have some news I haven't shared with anybody yet. At this very moment Jessabelle carries the next heir to Brightening," Theo said, smiling broadly and showing his pride.

"Jessabelle is pregnant? Oh, Theo, that is wonderful news," I said, ignoring the pang of pain in my heart. I wanted to be happy for them without feeling sorry for myself.

"I wish you could be here to see our child born, Gabriel. I am going to miss you very much," Theo said, grabbing my hand and rubbing his thumb against the top of it affectionately.

"You know I must go," I said.

"Yes. I do understand. However, Brightening is left without a sorceress and I am left without your friendship," he said. Theo's green eyes showed honest regret.

I didn't know what to say. I reached up and clutched the golden medallion as I had done so many times in my life, finding courage in its presence. It felt very strange leaving Risen and going back home. My life at home was so mundane, easy in a way, full of love and the joy of everyday living. But, on Risen, even though I had lost so much over the past year and a half, I felt more alive as if I belonged here more than there. As much as I wanted to go home and raise my children, I very much regretted having to leave Risen. "I will return, Theo," I said. "After a while. I don't want to cause more stress in my children's lives right now. They just lost their father. But, I will return," I promised.

Theo pulled me to my feet and said, "It is almost time."

B.F. spoke quietly inside my head, *"Take good care of yourself, Gabriel. Remember, that I will always be here for you and that I am your friend."*

"I will miss you, B.F. Thank you for your friendship. I treasure it beyond measure," I said.

Skymaster spoke to me also through our mental link, *"I cherish you, beautiful lady and will miss your warm smile, not to mention your warm behind upon my back. Take care of yourself, Gabriel."*

"You are incorrigible, Skymaster, but I will miss you too," I replied.

Theo pulled a leather pouch from his pack and handed it to me.

"What is this?" I asked feeling the weight of the pouch.

"That is your payment from father for the fulfillment of your contract," he said.

I pulled the strings open on the pouch and poured part of its contents into the palm of my hand. Gems of many colors sparkled in the firelight, red, green, blue, white, pink, purple and a variety of others. The pouch contained a fortune and I was somewhat reluctant to take the treasure. Theo saw my hesitancy, "Take it, Gabriel. You have earned it, plus more. Use it to raise your family."

Theo's eyes glowed bright green, reflecting the flames. I put my arms around his neck and kissed him quickly on the cheek. "Thank you for everything," I said.

We watched the constellations through the gate until the Big Dipper appeared in the sky. I let go of Theo and entered the threshold, turning back only once to gaze at him. "I will be back, Theo. I promise," I said.

I turned around and went through to the other side, hearing behind me, "We'll be waiting, Gabriel. Be well."

Home Sweet Home

I hiked down out of the mountains to the road that night, anxious to be on my way back to my children. A man gave me a ride down the mountain and into Flagstaff. He was a Native American who introduced himself as Jim McCaw. I made small talk with him as we drove down through the mountains in his brand new Ford pick-up. He started asking me questions about where I had been and I found that I couldn't lie to him easily. I ended up telling him my story from start to finish and he listened and asked pertinent questions as if he believed every word I said.

We stopped in Las Vegas and Jim helped me cash in some of my jewels for cash at several different pawn shops downtown. For some reason I found I trusted him completely, as if we were bound somehow to one another and shared a oneness. We discussed this on the way to Flagstaff and I found that he was familiar with freecurrent. We were both warriors fighting on the same side toward the same end. I found it very comforting to talk about my experiences and to have someone believe me.

Jim had business in Flagstaff and could take me no further. I thanked him, tried to pay him for his kindness, which he refused, and then I went to find some other means of transportation.

June 11. I bought a car in Flagstaff and drove the rest of the way home. My feelings were on the surface and my nerves seemed to be frayed raw by the time I reached my house. It was quiet when I pulled into the driveway early in the afternoon. I got out of the car and started toward the front porch, noticing that the barn and the house still needed painting although the gardens had been kept nicely tended and were brilliant with fresh flowers. They reminded me of the gardens in front of Anna's cabin, and with that thought came a pang of homesickness for Risen. Strange, considering I was standing in front of my own home in New Mexico in the United States of America on Earth, the third planet from the sun, and I was feeling homesick for Risen. I shook my head disbelieving my own feelings, but not disregarding my own nature.

Butterflies filled my stomach with a stampede of fluttering as I opened the door, feeling curiously as though I should knock. I walked in and could hear noises coming from the kitchen. Heading that way, I peeked around the corner and saw my sister and the children sitting at the table chatting cheerfully over sandwiches and milk. My heart melted watching them laugh and smile together and I stood there and enjoyed the scene until

Carmen looked up and saw me. Her mouth dropped open with shock and she stayed transfixed for a moment or two before a smile stretched across her face. "Gabriel?" she asked as if she wasn't quite sure if it was me or if she was seeing a ghost.

"Yes, it's me," I said, hearing my voice shaking with emotion.

She stood up and walked over to me while the children watched from their chairs. "Look at you," she said, touching my clothes experimentally. I looked down and realized I still wore the leather riding clothes Kristina had loaned me so long ago. "Where have you been?" Carmen demanded gently, with her voice choking on the words. "John . . . " she began.

"I know. I know that John is dead. There is much to talk about. My tale is for another time, perhaps," I said. I reached out and took her in my arms and we clung to each other for a moment.

I pulled away from my sister and looked at my children who observed us from the safety of their chairs, noticing for the first time how much they had grown. "Peter? Marguerite?" I said.

Peter started slowly out of his chair, unsure as yet of the woman who stood before him. "Mom?"

I held out my arms to him and all his reluctance vanished in a fleeting second and he was in my arms, murmuring, "Mom. I missed you."

Releasing Peter, I walked over to Marguerite and started to take her in my arms also. "Hello baby," I said through my tears.

She stayed at arms-length, looking me in the eyes for confirmation and then smiled sweetly. "Hi, mom," she said and nestled her head against my shoulder. I hugged them both close, until they grew restless of the attention, like children do, and I had to let them go.

May 9, 1995. Eleven years have passed since my last entry in this diary. My children are all grown up and married. Peter

.s a small child of his own, a boy, Jonathon, named after his grandfather. Marguerite has Bill and is busy with her life. I feel confident in leaving them to live their own lives now. God bless them and keep them safe.

I have decided to return to Risen to continue my service as sorceress there. Over the past years I have returned to Risen many times and visited, but I wish to move there permanently. It is my home and I miss it dearly. My need is great to do this and I hope my children can forgive me for disappearing out of their lives. But, they have their own families now and I wish to go on with my life.

This will be my last entry before I leave. My diary I leave locked away for my successor to find. My warning goes with it. Freecurrent is a tool that can be twisted, as it was with Candaz and the corrupt sorcerers who preceded him. The power should only be used for good, never corruption. I leave you my legacy. The choice is yours.

Chapter 24
A NEW BEGINNING

J esse sat before a dying fire in the cave and closed the diary gently, thinking about what her Grandmother had said. She stared at the glowing coals and meditated over Gabriel's final words. Jesse was afraid. She didn't know if she wanted the ability to use freecurrent. "Power corrupts," she thought. However, Gabriel hadn't let the ability corrupt her. Jesse knew she had felt some of the freecurrent energy already. . . the night of the party when Mat harassed her and the night when Felcore was locked within the humane society and she had felt the gold pendant around her throat grow hot as she wished him to her. A part of her wanted to feel that exhilaration again. "Perhaps that is where the danger lies," she said to herself. She sighed, coming no closer to the answer.

She glanced at her watch and saw that it was nearly midnight. Felcore got up from what seemed to be a sound sleep, stretched

.dulgently, and nudged Jesse on the arm with his nose. "What is it, boy?" she asked. He grabbed her arm and pulled.

"I guess it is time," Jesse said to Felcore, patting him for comfort as her stomach began to dance with excitement. Felcore wagged his tail and bounced on his front paws, encouraging her toward the back of the cave. She kicked at the fire, spreading the coals apart so it would go out sooner. After depositing Gabriel's diary into her pack, she swung the weathered pouch to her shoulder and walked determinedly toward the lightning gate.

Felcore stood close by Jesse's side as she watched the constellations change at a precise rate of speed through the Gate's opening. "I hope I can recognize the Condor," she spoke softly to herself. Felcore whimpered softly in response. She waited, watching the sky closely, ready to move into a foreign world and an unknown future. Stars appeared outlining the shape of a Condor, gleaming brightly, twinkling, enticing Jesse to proceed through the gate. She took a step forward, hesitated, put her hand on Felcore's head feeling his soft fur beneath her trembling fingers, took another hesitant step. . . and walked forward through the gate.

THE END

**Look for Book 2 of the
Freecurrent Series "Descendants"**

**And Book 3 the conclusion
of the Freecurrent Series "Dynasty"**

PSIA information can be obtained
www.ICGtesting.com
ted in the USA
W04s1557160316
433LV00016B/475/P

9 780991 475506